CRIED FOR NO ONE

HUBERT CROUCH

Jacket photographs by Joe Dunn of Joe Dunn Arts, New Orleans, Louisiana.

This book is available in e-book version.

ISBN: 1481239473
ISBN 13: 9781481239479

PROLOGUE

Moonlight exposed the lifeless body from the waist down. The feet were petite and bare, toenails painted a bright red. Slender ankles led to tanned, shapely legs, half hidden from view by the simple white dress.

Gloved hands moved timidly forward, gently grasping the ankles. Slowly, the body was inched downward out of the battered coffin. The dress bunched at the waist, revealing white cotton panties. The gloved hands released the ankles, reached forward, readjusted the dress, and then resumed their task.

There were no buttons; the upper portion of the dress ringed with delicate lace. The eyes were closed, and though the makeup was subtle, the face resembled that of a painted porcelain doll. The lips held no smile, yet no frown. They were tightly drawn, seemingly impenetrable.

The gloved hands trembled as they felt their way under the body and gently lifted it from its resting place. Suddenly, bells clanged at a nearby chapel. It was 4:00 a.m. There was no time to waste. The maintenance crew would arrive in a little over an hour. Quickly but carefully, the body was laid in the backseat of the Blazer. The ignition key turned and the engine came to life.

———————————

An hour later, the Reverend Willie Talbot, pastor for thirty years of the Mount Ararat Baptist Church, reluctantly glanced at the alarm clock on the bedside table—5:00. He turned over in bed and was annoyed to see his wife of forty years resting peacefully by his side. It wasn't fair. She had no trouble winding down at night and was usually asleep shortly after her head hit the pillow while he tossed and turned, his mind cluttered with intrusive thoughts and needless worries. And Saturday night was always the worst. Sure, he had planned out the Sunday sermon carefully and rehearsed it over and over, his wife playfully cautioning him that if he uttered it one more time she would file for divorce. But despite the preparation, he just couldn't get a good night's sleep on Saturday night. It didn't matter what he did. And this night was no different.

Reverend Talbot sighed and then sat up in bed. He picked up the wire-rimmed glasses off the bedside table and perched them on his nose, stood up, and shuffled toward the bathroom. Thirty minutes later, he finished the last bite of buttered toast, took a final swig of black coffee, wrote his wife a note, and then headed toward Mount Ararat.

As he slowly drove down Singleton Boulevard, he repeated his sermon, raising his voice at times and lowering it at others. The sermon was flawlessly delivered, concluding just minutes before Reverend Talbot turned his ten-year-old Buick into the gravel parking lot in front of the church.

Mount Ararat Baptist Church was a humble wooden structure, with a small wooden cross for a steeple. The walls needed a new coat of paint. The front yard was bare, grass growing only in small patches. Reverend Talbot stepped out of his car, took two steps toward his church, and abruptly stopped. A large spray-painted black "X" covered the oak doors leading to the sanctuary. The number "666" and the phrases "Satan is my savior" and "House of the Devil" had been spray-painted on either side of the sanctuary doors. For at least five seconds, Reverend Talbot stood frozen in place, unable to comprehend what was in front of him. Then he raced up the church's crumbling concrete steps, pulled a white handkerchief from the breast pocket of his suit jacket, dropped to his knees, and frantically began scrubbing at the words. He began to sob and, against his better judgment, pulled a key from his pocket. With a shaking hand, he inserted the key into the sanctuary lock. But there was no need to turn it—the lock had been smashed. He leaned against the door, and it slowly creaked open. Stepping inside, he peered into the dimness, his eyes following the aisle toward the altar.

A female body in a white dress lay lifeless on the altar, the sanctuary crucifix positioned upside down behind it. For what seemed to be an eternity, Reverend Talbot couldn't move, his eyes glued to the scene in front of him. Then, as he began backing toward the sanctuary entrance, he pulled his cell phone from his coat pocket and dialed 911.

A dispatcher answered.

"This is Reverend Willie Talbot. Devil worshippers have been in my church!"

"What? Would you please repeat that, sir?"

"Devil worshippers at my church! The Mount Ararat Baptist Church, 1901 Singleton! Get the police here, and quick!"

"Are you sure this—"

"Lady, get somebody here quick. My church has been attacked!"

Reverend Talbot hurried back to his car, jumped inside, turned the ignition, and hit the automatic door lock. His eyes darted in all directions and then lingered on the rearview mirror before closing in relief. The Reverend sighed deeply, bowed his head, and softly mumbled a short, desperate prayer.

CHAPTER

1

Alexis Stone frowned at the mirror. She inched closer, carefully examining her makeup, adding some finishing touches of black mascara. Leaning away, she placed the applicator back in its tube and returned her scrutiny to the image in front of her.

She looked all of her twenty-one years, and she was determined to make sure she didn't look a day younger. She squinted as she studied her crystal-blue eyes, now drawn out by eye shadow, as she tried to figure out what still troubled her. It was the lips. They needed to be redder, almost prostitute-red. She slid open the vanity drawer and shuffled through half a dozen lipstick shades before finding the one she wanted. She removed the subtle pink tone with a Kleenex and replaced it with a fire engine hue. She smiled as she painted, remembering all the guys who had compared her full lips to Angelina Jolie's. Task complete, she puckered her lips together in a practiced pout. She reached over to the Bose iPod holder and turned up the volume just as Jim Morrison was bellowing out "L.A.

Woman." This night was going to be different, far different from all the others. She was certain of it.

Alexis rose from the vanity stool, picked up the Victoria's Secret box lying next to her makeup mirror, removed the ribbon tied around the box, and opened the pink and blue tissue paper that held the results of her shopping trip to the mall earlier that day. She brushed the black-and-red-lace bra and thong panties against her face to feel the smoothness and to smell their fresh new scent. The lingerie was as light and delicate as a baby's breath.

She dropped the towel that had been wrapped around her waist and stepped into the panties, adjusting the thong until it rode just above her hips. She put on the bra backward, hooked it together and shimmied it around, moving the hook to the back, placing her arms through the lace straps, and adjusting herself into the sheer cups. She turned toward the full-length mirror hanging on the bathroom door that led to a walk-in closet. Her long black hair, still wet, outlined the chiseled features of her face. Against that mess of hair, her eyes sparkled like blue topaz.

Once again, she grinned as she took in the full effect of the new lingerie. Not that she needed help from clothing to accentuate her body. Her five-foot-three frame was blessed with full, firm breasts, a tiny waist, a flat stomach, and beautifully proportioned hips. Her legs were long and lean, with delicate ankles and petite size 5½ feet. She worked out at least four or five times a week, alternating between aerobics and free weights. The results were obvious. When she put on high heels, which she did frequently, her legs took on a sculpted beauty.

The clock on the vanity read 8:12. She would need to hurry. She still had to dry her hair and get dressed. Talmadge had said he would be there around 8:30 - 8:45 at the latest. But he was always late, the excuses always the same. A senate subcommittee meeting had run over, or some lobbyist had cornered him for a quick drink that had lasted several hours. She shook her head. He was a smooth talker with an explanation for everything.

Alexis continued her dressing ritual. A few minutes after nine she thought she heard the front door to her apartment open and close. She always left a key on the ledge above the door on nights when Talmadge was coming over. The senator was not a patient man. A wait outside her apartment door, no matter how brief, was something to be avoided.

She stepped in front of the full-length mirror for one last inspection. Her eyes darted hurriedly over her reflected image. The cream-colored silk blouse needed adjusting. She opened the collar in front and flipped it up in back to draw more attention to the graceful lines of her neck and collarbone. The skirt was black leather and it was very, very short. She knew when she sat down there would be little left to the imagination. But that was the way she wanted it, especially for this evening. She quickly stepped into the closet and slipped into the black stiletto heels she had picked up at the mall earlier that day. They were perfect. Confident, Alexis made her way gracefully out of her bedroom and toward the bar area, where she found Talmadge Worthman pouring himself a scotch.

He paused, a smile creasing his lips, his eyes tracing and retracing every inch of her body. "You look fantastic!" He placed his glass on the bar and pulled Alexis towards him.

The two embraced hungrily, their lips melting together. Alexis could feel Talmadge's right hand slide between the back of her blouse and skirt, his fingers gently rubbing one of the dimples on her lower back. She playfully pushed him away, gazing into his eyes.

"Take it easy, cowboy. We've got all the time in the world."

She reached up and slid a wineglass from its slot above the bar and removed a bottle of red wine from the wine rack. As she began to cut the foil top from the bottle, Talmadge moved up close to her.

"Here, let me get that for you." He took the bottle from Alexis, uncorked it, and poured her a heavy glass. He picked up his scotch in one hand, the glass of wine in the other, and took the few steps to the living room. He handed Alexis the glass of wine and collapsed on the couch, loosening his tie and kicking off his shoes in the process.

"Did the very important senator have a tough day?" Alexis cooed.

"The usual bullshit. One subcommittee meeting after another. Meetings with lobbyists squeezed in between." Talmadge sighed. "I didn't think I'd ever get away from Horace Garwood. The son of a bitch practically got in the car with me as I was leaving to come over here. He just doesn't know when to shut up."

Alexis rolled her eyes as she sat down next to her lover, the leather skirt shrinking dangerously, exposing most of her bare thighs. Making sure that Talmadge noticed, she used the toe of her right heel to slip out of the other, and then repeated the exercise with her left foot. She prominently displayed her well-manicured feet on the glass coffee table in front of them, the bright red polish perfectly matching the red of her lipstick.

Alexis furrowed her brow. She had forgotten one thing: the music. Still barefooted, she got up from the sofa, went to her bathroom, grabbed her iPod from the holder on her dressing table, and returned to the living room. Alexis nestled next to Talmadge on the couch while scrolling through her iPod's music library.

"I'm thinking soft and sexy. Maybe a little Bon Iver?" She flashed Talmadge an impish grin.

"Never heard of him."

"It's not a him—it's a band, Talmadge. You're starting to show your age. You need to listen to something other than the Eagles, you know."

"I'm not here for music lessons," he chuckled.

Alexis scrolled down the Artist section and made the selection. She got up from the couch, opened the door to the armoire, and placed the iPod in its cradle. "For Emma" began to play, the acoustic guitar and horns blending together, setting the mood. She returned to the couch and asked, feigning interest, "Any important legislation coming down the pike?"

The truth was that Alexis had little knowledge of politics or world events, the only news she got being what she skimmed through on the Internet when navigating to Facebook or YouTube.

At times, she wondered why she was even attracted to Talmadge in the first place. He bore a faint resemblance to a younger Richard Dreyfuss—great smile and great eyes. But his hair was thinning, and he had a noticeable paunch, a constant reminder of their 22-year age difference. He was, after all, just a few years younger than her father. In fact, Talmadge and her father knew each other through annual hunting trips organized by one of their mutual acquaintances, who had made a fortune drilling in the Barnett Shale.

His looks may have had a little to do with Alexis' attraction to him—but very little. She knew there was a confluence of emotions that attracted her: the danger of going out with a married man, and not just any married man but a well-known Texas state senator. And then, circulating somewhere deep inside her, was the recognition that perhaps her little fling with Talmadge was her way of getting back at her father, the great Lackland Stone: self-made millionaire, generous philanthropist, doting father. But only if the world knew what she knew. If only they could peer through the veneer, take just one peek behind the wizard's curtain, the picture would be all too different—not the flattering self-portrait Lackland had painted stroke by stroke for the local townsfolk to admire and adore but rather the picture of a rough-hewn man with a shady past who had hit it big in the oil patch, married well because of it, and then lost his fortune, and his wife's as well, in the high-flying real estate market of Texas in the eighties. A man who, after his fall, had managed through lies to live a masquerade, fooling all in his path and laughing at their naïveté. That was the Lackland Stone she knew, and the one she could never forgive.

"I couldn't give a rat's ass about legislation right now," Talmadge grumbled. "But I can't afford to make any of my constituents mad, not at this point in time anyway."

"You've gotta be kiddin' me. Talmadge, you know the election is a cinch. Those rednecks in East Texas will always vote for you."

"Can't get overconfident. Nope, not taking any chances." Talmadge sipped his scotch, set it on the coffee table, and rubbed his hand up and down Alexis' bare thigh. His voice became more playful. "Enough talk about politics. How was your day, my little coed?"

"Well, I slept through English lit. My Professor is boring as shit! Reciting Chaucer? If I hear any more of that crap, I'm going to throw up."

Alexis playfully undid the top two buttons of Talmadge's shirt, and then unraveled his already-loosened tie, sliding it from beneath his collar and cavalierly discarding it on the floor. "So, I decided to cut my afternoon classes and go shopping." Alexis hesitated, her voice morphing into a seductive, cooing whisper.

She let him kiss her—a long kiss, with his hand sliding down her shirt and caressing her breast. Then, at the very moment his hand began to slide even lower, she pulled away and stared at him, her lips positioned in a well-practiced pout.

"Talmadge," she said, her voice still a whisper, "I need you to be honest with me."

Talmadge leaned back, contemplating his next move. His instincts were usually right on—it's what made him such a powerful politician in Austin—and he sensed Alexis was on a mission. There would be no passionate lovemaking until she got answers, answers she wanted to hear. He was going to have to walk a fine line to get what he wanted from her.

Alexis continued, her voice getting slightly agitated. "We've being seeing each other for seven months now. You've been telling me you love me and that you can't stand your wife. So I want to know—do you want to be with me or not?"

"You know I do, Alexis. You're all I think about."

She paused, and then she made her move. "Talmadge, I want you to tell her about us. I am tired of hiding in the shadows like a criminal." Alexis moved toward him, her fingers fiddling with more buttons on his shirt, her eyes searching his for the truth. "Why don't you just get a divorce?"

Talmadge had sensed this was coming. Alexis wasn't his first. There had been all sorts of young women he had kept on the side. And they all had wanted more. But he had never been with anyone like Alexis. Not even close. He hated thinking about their age difference—and he especially hated to think about it when he went on those hunting trips with her father—but in his eyes, Alexis was no child. She was mature well beyond her years. And, as if to soothe his guilt, she had confided in him on several occasions that she had never been close to her parents. He knew, though, that if his relationship with Alexis were publicly exposed, he would find very little understanding from his friends, especially Alexis' father. Most of all, the political fallout would be devastating. Still, considering everything, he wasn't ready for things to end with Alexis. He needed to stall.

"Alexis, it's just not that easy. You know I'm up for reelection. The press would be all over it."

"What are you telling me, Talmadge?"

"Well . . ." Talmadge hesitated.

"I'm waiting." She stared straight at the opposite wall, her lips drawn tight, her arms folded across her chest.

"Well, I think we should hold off involving Delores and your family, just for a while anyway. Once the election's over—"

Alexis interrupted. "There will always be an election! Do you think I am that stupid? Do you think I want to continue to be your occasional plaything?" Alexis grabbed a pillow and threw it across the room.

"You don't understand, Alexis. You've never been—"

Alexis didn't allow him to finish. She was up and headed to the adjoining kitchen, where her iPhone was lying on the pass-through ledge. "You'd better leave before I call that lard-assed wife of yours."

"Alexis, wait—"

Alexis turned on her phone, her hands shaking, eyes blazing. "Don't try me."

Now a believer, Talmadge jumped up from the couch, grabbed his tie from the floor, clumsily pulled on his tasseled loafers, and headed for the door. As he turned the knob, he pleaded, "If you'll just give me till after . . ."

Alexis looked around for something to throw. Sensing her intention, the senator closed the door quickly and stumbled down the stairs.

After the door shut, Alexis angrily scrolled down her iPod until she found Led Zeppelin's "Whole Lotta Love." She hit play and felt a sense of primal relief as Robert Plant began his raucous intro— "You need coolin', baby, and I'm not foolin.'"

An angry smile creased her lips. Senator Worthman would regret this evening.

She grabbed her wineglass from the coffee table, walked over to the bar, and filled it to the top. She pulled open a drawer and took out a lighter and a pack of cigarettes. Shaking one out and lighting it, she laughed pitifully to herself as she recalled how she had avoided smoking around Talmadge; he didn't like the smell or the taste. What a hypocritical, pompous ass. Alexis felt cheated and used. She was going to find a way to make him pay for making her feel that way. She hated losing at her own game.

She took a drag off her cigarette, followed by a healthy swig of wine. She glanced at her phone. It was a little after ten. She was in no mood to sit around her apartment licking her wounds. She downed the wine, grabbed her purse, her phone, the cigarettes, and her keys, and marched defiantly toward the door.

Senator Worthman steered his Cadillac Escalade past the security gate of Alexis' apartment complex. He pulled the BlackBerry from his coat pocket and speed-dialed Myron Berg, his chief of staff.

"Myron, we've got a problem."

Talmadge could hear the knowing sigh at the other end of the line.

"Things have gotten a little out of hand with a young lady I've been seeing."

"Talmadge, we've been through this before. You promised me the last time you were through with this shit! We just can't afford any fuck-ups this close to the election."

"I know, I know. But this girl, she's different. You should see her. She's incredible."

"I don't have time for this, Talmadge. What's the problem?"

Reluctantly, Talmadge continued. "I just came from her apartment, and we had a little disagreement."

"And?"

"She threatened to call my wife."

"Damn it, Talmadge! The last one cost us $25,000. What do you think it will take this time?"

"She's not after money. Her family's loaded."

"Shit. I'll need some time to come up with a plan."

"I knew I could count on you, Myron. But I don't want to know the details. Just handle it."

"Understood. But swear you won't pull this shit again."

"On my mother's grave."

After giving Myron Alexis' name and address, Talmadge disconnected the call and breathed a sigh of relief. Delores wasn't going to know. Besides, she was in Tennessee visiting her parents.

A smile crossed his face. His wife was out of town. He couldn't waste the opportunity. He would stop off at his favorite restaurant on his way home and have a few drinks and dinner at the bar. And maybe, just maybe, he would get lucky.

CHAPTER

2

Matt Forman was on the couch in his apartment, enjoying a Shiner Bock and the final minutes of a football game, when his cell phone rang. Annoyed, he stretched toward the coffee table in front of him, picked up the phone, and looked at the number on caller id—one of his frat brothers.

"Hey, bro. You watching the game? Yeah, it sucks. You called it—same ol' Cowboys. Until Jerry Jones swallows that big ego of his and quits meddling, they're never going to be worth a shit. You still wanna hit Sixth Street tonight? Cool. See you in about thirty."

Matt clicked off, tossed his phone back on the coffee table, and stretched his arms above his head, turning his torso left and right. An impatient knock interrupted his stretching ritual.

"Door's open," he yelled.

The knocking continued. Matt yelled again as he got up from the couch, "I said, the door's open!" Matt flung open the door and was temporarily stunned to see Alexis Stone, looking like a million bucks, standing in his doorway.

"Hi, Matt. It's been a while."

"You think? Last I remember, we had a date and you didn't show. No call, no text, no email. Come to find out, you had hooked up with somebody else. Now, months later, here you are."

"Okay. I know I was a bitch. But I'm here now, and I need to blow it out in the worst kind of way. So, are you going to forgive me and come out tonight, or are you going to stay mad at me forever?"

Matt couldn't help but stare at her, top to bottom. He caught a glimpse of her black-and-red-lace bra underneath her cream-colored silk blouse. His gaze swept across her tiny black leather skirt and black stilettos. And then those lips, covered in fire engine–red lipstick. He had the feeling that she hadn't dressed up like that just in hopes of running across him. No doubt she had been out on a date earlier that evening that had gone very bad—and she was no doubt looking for some comfort.

Still, he felt the desire rushing back. They had first met at the University of Texas in a public speaking class. Matt, six-two, with six-pack abs left over from his high school football days, greenish-gray eyes with long, curved eyelashes, shoulder-length brown hair, and a cautious smile, was teamed up with Alexis in class for a project. The time they spent together seemed to fly by, whether they were sitting on the banks of Lake Austin waiting for the sun to come up, listening to Bob Dylan while arguing about the meaning of his lyrical masterpieces, or just lounging around.

Matt had been ready to take their relationship to the next level. But he quickly learned Alexis was not ready for commitments of any nature. Rather than get into an extended discussion as to her feelings, however, she did what he never expected her to do. She abruptly cut off all contact. She stood him up on a date and left his emails and voice mails unanswered. Apparently, Alexis figured that was the only way Matt would get the message.

It had taken him several months of hanging out at the fraternity house with the guys before he started dating again. And now, just as he was getting his bearings back, Alexis reappeared, without warning, asking for forgiveness and begging to party.

"So what makes you think I would ever go out with you again? I'm not a fucking idiot."

"Come on, Matt. Look, I'm sorry. I shouldn't have done what I did. I've got some issues."

She looked at Matt with pleading eyes. He just stood there, still shaking his head and saying nothing. Sensing she needed to throw in her cards, Alexis started to turn away from the door and head back to her car.

Matt sighed. "Okay, Alexis, but no forgiveness. Not yet anyway. What you did to me was really shitty."

Alexis gave Matt an award-winning smile. "I hear you. Now grab your keys and follow me to Chuy's. I'll start out by treating you to dinner. I'm starving."

"Why don't we just take my car?"

"Not that I don't trust you, but I'd rather have my car just in case you decide to get back at me and leave me stranded."

"Only you would do something like that," Matt chided.

"See what I mean! Now be nice and follow me."

And just like that, they were back to where they once were, talking Bob Dylan and everything else under the sun as they downed a quick dinner of fajitas and frozen margaritas. Alexis playfully changed the subject whenever Matt asked about what had happened earlier in the evening. She clearly wasn't going there, and Matt decided to let it be. He was unwilling to chance ruining a night that might rekindle a relationship like no other he had ever experienced.

After dinner, they decided to avoid the Sixth Street scene and headed to the Broken Spoke, in South Austin. They toasted each other with tequila shots and danced the two-step, sloshing beers on each other as they strolled unevenly across the dance floor. Several hours later, after stumbling through "I've Got Friends in Low Places," Matt made his move.

"Ready to get out of here?"

"There's a six-pack of Shiner in my fridge with your name on it."

"Sold. Can you drive?"

"As good as you can," Alexis said, slurring her words.

"I'd feel better if we took my car. We can come pick yours up in the morning."

"No way I'm leaving my car here overnight."

"Shit, Alexis. Some things never change. You're still controlling as ever. Okay, I'll follow you to your apartment. You haven't moved since I last saw you, have you?"

"Nope. Same place. Montfort Apartments."

"Is the gate code the same?"

"I can't believe you actually remember it." Alexis smiled and kissed Matt on the lips.

"Come on. Let's get out of here."

Matt didn't need to remember the gate code, as he kept a close distance following Alexis to her apartment. Driving through the gate right behind her, he found a parking spot just two spaces over from where she parked her car.

They staggered up the stairs to the apartment together, Matt thankful they had made it there safely. Pausing in front of the apartment door Alexis dug through her purse for her keys, swaying back and forth unsteadily. Finally finding them, she tried with a wobbly hand to fit the key in the lock. After several seconds, she grinned and handed the keys to Matt, who opened the door on the first try.

Alexis made her way inside, grabbing Matt's shirt and pulling him into the apartment with her. After stepping out of her heels, she took his hand, squeezing it gently, and led him toward the bar.

"You think this is a good idea?" Matt hoped for a yes.

She nodded. "Just one more drink."

Alexis grabbed a Shiner out of the bar fridge for Matt and poured a glass of wine for herself. Stumbling to the living area, she unsteadily placed the drinks on the coffee table and plopped down on the couch. Matt sat down beside her, disregarding the fleeting thoughts cautioning him about getting involved once again.

Alexis put a cigarette to her lips. Matt reached into his pocket, pulled out his Zippo lighter and lit it. Alexis took one deep drag and immediately snuffed the cigarette out in the ashtray. Without saying a word, she put her head down in Matt's lap. She was asleep in a matter of minutes. Matt just looked at her and shook his head.

CHAPTER

3

Jace Forman strolled down the hall toward his office, taking time to greet each employee by name, occasionally inquiring about a family member or a matter of personal interest. He detoured to the break room and poured himself a cup of coffee before stopping briefly at his secretary's desk.

"Morning, Harriett! Could you bring me the general files on Caring Oaks Funeral Home and Cemetery and all the faxes that came in over the weekend?"

Harriett had been Jace's secretary for over fourteen years. Approaching fifty, she was cantankerous and set in her ways but always reliable—and, like all great secretaries, loyal to a fault. She returned Jace's greeting from behind her desk.

"Morning, Jace. The faxes are already in your in-box." With considerable effort, Harriett dislodged herself from her desk chair and began to rummage through the file cabinets behind her.

Jace entered his office, placing his briefcase on the floor next to his leather-backed swivel chair and the coffee mug on his desk. He removed his suit jacket and hung it on the lone coat hanger on the back of his office door, settled in behind his desk, and dialed his son's cell number in Austin. After two rings, his call went to Matt's voice mail.

Jace left a brief message asking Matt to call him back, put the phone in its cradle, and shook his head. Father and son hadn't actually spoken to each other for several weeks. All of Jace's calls had been going to voice mail, with none of them ever returned. He had begun to wonder if his relationship with Matt could be repaired. What in the hell did he have to do to get his son back?

His thoughts were interrupted by a familiar voice.

"Are you busy?' Darrin McKenzie, Jace's paralegal, was standing in the doorway to his office.

Jace swiveled away from the phone on his credenza and smiled. "Not at all, Darrin. Just returning a few calls from last week. Come on in. I've got a new case we need to talk about."

Before Darrin had a chance to respond, Harriett bulled herself through the doorway with an armful of files. "Coming through, Darrin." She plopped the files down on the corner of Jace's desk and sighed as if she had just scaled the Matterhorn. "Anything else, Jace?"

"I think that'll do for now. Thanks, Harriett."

"At your service, Boss." Harriett headed back to her desk, leaving Darrin and Jace alone.

"Harriett's always so cheerful. Lights up any room she blesses with her presence," Darrin offered sarcastically.

"I know, she's definitely an old battle-ax. Sometimes I think about letting her go, but, hell, it would break her heart. This job's her life."

"No need to get all sentimental on me, Jace. I was just making small talk. Hey, I wasn't planning on a long meeting. I just wanted to ask you a quick question about the Hallett case."

Jace pulled open one of the drawers to his desk and retrieved a legal pad, which he casually slid across the desk. He nodded toward the pull-up chair in front. "Actually, we've got more to talk about. Have a seat. This might take a while."

"Door open or closed?"

"Closed, please."

As Darrin turned to close the door, Jace found himself taking in every aspect of her appearance. She was wearing a black cashmere dress that tastefully hugged her curves and fell just above the knee. A colorful scarf hung down almost the full length of the dress, and soft black nylons and black suede high-heels completed the outfit. Her blond wavy hair was pinned up in a French twist, and her subtle makeup highlighted her green eyes. She was just under five-four, weighed about 105 pounds, and easily looked much younger than her 36 years.

Darrin sat down in a chair across from Jace's desk, crossed her legs, and placed the pad in her lap. "So, what's this new case about?"

Jace flipped through several faxes and found the one he was looking for. He scanned it briefly and handed it to Darrin.

"Wallace Arnold, president of Caring Oaks Funeral Home and Cemetery, called me Saturday evening. He was served with the lawsuit I just handed you."

Darrin nodded, not taking her eyes off the document in front of her. Seconds later, she looked at Jace and spoke. "I read about this in the paper a few months ago. It totally gave me the creeps. Who in the world would do something like this? I mean, how perverted is it for some guy to dig up a body?" Darrin shuddered.

"How do you know it was a 'he'? The police have no leads, no suspects, no nothing."

Darrin looked at the lawsuit again. "And so the parents have hired the great Cal Connors, our favorite Fort Worth plaintiff's attorney, to sue Caring Oaks cemetery. What does his ad say?

Something like 'The Lone Wolf—A Breed Apart.' Hard to beat that." Darrin grinned.

"Yeah, Cal's one of a kind, no doubt about it. And, to no one's surprise, he's contending this was all our client's fault. And no doubt this case will get a lot of press. The parents are Olivia and Lackland Stone."

"The Fort Worth socialites? I wonder how they got hooked up with Cal Connors? I mean, he has a reputation for big plaintiff verdicts, but I can't see him exactly running in their circles."

"Neither can I."

"A grave-robbing case? What will plaintiff's lawyers come up with next?"

"Well, let's get down to specifics. We are scheduled for a tour of the cemetery and meetings with the key employees later this week. Before then, we will need to file an appearance in the case. I need you to get that drafted as soon as possible."

"Just the standard general denial?"

"I don't see any ground to transfer the case from Fort Worth, do you?"

"Not on first glance. The body was buried here and that's where the theft occurred. Seems like jurisdiction is pretty solid."

"Harriett pulled all of the files we have on Caring Oaks." Jace nodded toward the mountain of folders Harriett had deposited on his desk corner. "I would like you to go through those and tab anything you think I should read."

"You looking for anything in particular?"

"Annual revenue, average cost of a funeral, burial contracts, mention of any other incidents similar to this one—that type of thing."

Darrin took notes as Jace spoke. "Got it."

"Also, draft an outline of topics to cover in our Caring Oaks interviews and make a note of any additional documents you think we need from our client. And don't forget to bring the firm's camera to the client meeting. We'll definitely want pictures of the crime scene."

Darrin was frantically scribbling down Jace's rapid-fire instructions. She already had a full week of deadlines to work on without this new list of assignments. Her mind was racing, trying to figure out how she would be able to organize everything and get it all done.

As if he could read her mind, Jace continued, "Darrin, I know your plate was full when you walked in here this morning. But I need you on this case. Just send me a list of what else you've got going and I will farm it out to some of our other associates and paralegals."

"That would be great. I've got some discovery due in the Hallett case, a response to a motion for summary judgment that has to be filed on Friday, and—"

"I know, I know. I promise you. I will get all those tasks reassigned this morning. Just email me a list."

Darrin stood, legal pad in hand. "Is there anything else?"

"That's it for now."

She picked up the stack of Caring Oaks files and then walked briskly toward the doorway. She turned toward Jace before exiting. "Open or closed?"

"Closed, thanks." Darrin gently pulled the door shut, leaving Jace to his thoughts.

———————————

Jace had full confidence in Darrin. They had started working together at Hadley and Morgan, an old-line, blue-blooded Fort Worth firm Jace had joined upon graduating from the University of

Texas law school. Several years later, Jace interviewed Darrin for a paralegal position and hired her on the spot.

By then, after slogging his way through the associate ranks, working weekends and late nights, Jace made partner at Hadley and Morgan, but partnership wasn't all he had been told it would be. Jace's compensation received a minor bump—not close to what he'd expected. He was forced to take out a loan to "buy in" to the partnership's receivables and fixed assets, later discovering that the receivables had been on the books for years and had little chance of ever being paid. With a stay-at-home wife, a young son in private school, and a hefty mortgage, Jace found himself living from paycheck to paycheck, making minimum monthly payments on his credit card balances, which continued to grow. Something had to give, so Jace requested an audience with the managing partner, Maurice Morgan. His concerns were addressed with a smile, a pat on the back, and a naked assurance that all partners at Hadley and Morgan had experienced some "financial pain" when they were younger and that things would improve over time. His concerns unresolved, Jace left the meeting and began considering alternatives.

He had received countless overtures from other law firms during his tenure at Hadley and Morgan, but had turned a deaf ear, believing his loyalty would be repaid in spades. What a fool he had been! After his meeting with Maurice, he considered calling the other firms back, to get more details on what they were offering. But in the end he decided he would be trading one bad situation for another. There would still be a bunch of fat cats at the top, slurping all the cream and leaving the curd for young partners like himself. Instead, he decided "big firm" life was not for him. He wanted control over his destiny. And he was willing to take risks to get it. He would start his own law firm. But he would need to be patient and he would need a well-crafted plan.

He continued to put in long hours at Hadley and Morgan and strengthen his bonds with the firm's blue-chip clients. He took those same clients to dinners, Cowboys games, and on ski trips to Crested Butte. He gave them 24-7 accessibility, supplying them with all of his contact numbers and making it clear calling him at home was not an intrusion into his private space. If his clients needed answers to legal questions that were concerning them, he was on call at any hour, day or night.

And his courthouse victories continued to mount, defense verdict after defense verdict. Two years after sitting through his fateful meeting with Maurice, Jace had tried nine cases successfully. Seven had been defense verdicts, one a plaintiff's verdict for less in damages than Jace had offered in settlement, and one a mistrial due to jury misconduct. Asbestos lawsuits, product liability cases, lead paint cases, medical malpractice, whatever came through the door, Jace handled it. There was no better record during that time period for any civil defense lawyer in Tarrant County. And word had gotten out—new clients had come calling. It was time for Jace to make his move.

On a weekend he would never forget, Jace needed a sounding board to help launch his new venture, and Darrin was the perfect choice. Her legal work was superior to most associates', and even some partners. She knew his clients and cases inside and out, and she had a discerning eye for detail. Equally important, Jace knew he could trust Darrin and that nothing they discussed would make its way outside his office.

Together, they made a list of all the clients they felt would follow Jace to the new firm, clients for whom he was the "go-to" guy. They reviewed the firm's annual statements of fee receipts for the past three years and determined what those clients had paid Hadley and Morgan—approximately $2.2 million. They went through the firm's personnel roster and discussed who would be a good fit for the new firm and who wouldn't.

While Jace double-checked the projected fee income for the first year, Darrin added up all of the salaries, including benefits.

She determined what furniture, hardware, software, phones, copiers, and office supplies would be needed, and she estimated their cost. She plugged in an annual leasing fee for offices and, after totaling all the numbers, came up with a rough idea of the first year's expenses. If—and it was a big if, considering all the variables—everything worked out according to her ballpark projections, Jace would net two times his current annual salary the first year, and more in years to come, taking into account improved cash flow and the elimination of start-up costs.

For Jace, it was a no-brainer. He would jump ship and take his chances. And Darrin would come with him.

After making the decision to start a new firm, they went to lunch at Sardine's, a local Italian restaurant, to celebrate over a thin-crust margherita pizza and a bottle of pinot grigio. The Forman Firm had just been born.

The clients' reception regarding his plan was overwhelmingly positive—yes, they were with him. They looked to him, not Hadley and Morgan, for their legal needs. They would gladly sign any letter, acknowledging they wanted their files moved to his new firm.

And the response from the four associates, three paralegals, and three secretaries he approached was equally enthusiastic. They felt underappreciated in their current environment and loved working with Jace. They had complete confidence the new firm would be a success.

The meeting with Maurice Morgan did not go as well. Maurice went on a diatribe. What was Jace thinking? He had a great future with Hadley and Morgan. They were grooming him to become managing partner one day. Maurice even offered him a 20 percent raise. When Jace firmly stated that his mind was made up, Maurice's demeanor and tone changed abruptly. He told Jace his new firm would not last six months and that he would be begging to come back. And Hadley and Morgan wouldn't even think about obliging him, because the firm did not reward disloyalty.

Maurice reminded Jace that he had a wife and child to think about. And then came the kicker: he told Jace that if he took even one client with him, Hadley and Morgan would sue.

Jace reacted stoically as the managing partner ranted and raved, responding with a simple retort: "I have talked with every client about my plan, and without exception, they have promised their full support. In addition, they have pledged to report Hadley and Morgan to the Texas Bar if there are any steps taken, such as a groundless lawsuit, to prevent them from being represented by the lawyer of their choosing. I have nothing else to say to you, Maurice." With that, Jace turned his back on twelve unhappy years of big-firm bullshit and walked out the door; the following Monday morning, the Forman Firm opened for business. Now, seven years later, the firm had grown to twelve lawyers, eight paralegals, over a dozen administrative personnel—and more clients than it could handle. Jace's gamble had paid off big time.

Jace swiveled his chair and faced his computer. He hit the Google icon and entered "Cal Connors" and "jury verdicts." He bit his lower lip as he scanned page after page of hits reflecting multimillion-dollar verdicts Cal had won over the past several years. Jace leaned back in his chair and smiled. "Bring it on, you pompous prick! Bring it on!"

CHAPTER

4

"Ladies and gentlemen of the jury, I would first like to thank you for your time and patience in this case. You have been here for three weeks. You have listened to testimony from twenty-two witnesses. Hundreds of pages of documents have been introduced as exhibits. And now, you are charged with making one of the most important decisions of your lives." Cal Connors paced back and forth in front of the jury box, his opaque blue eyes locking on the eyes of every juror as he walked past them, signaling to them that no one else in the courtroom mattered.

His swept-back, thick silver hair, in stark contrast to his dark Western-style suit, gave him a sagelike demeanor. He had the attention of every juror and spectator, including the reporters, in the courtroom. There were no murmurs, no chatter, no rustling of paper—utter silence, with each person present hanging on Cal's every word.

"But even though you have seen and heard all this evidence, this case is very simple, very simple indeed. Samson Pharmaceuticals sold a drug—a drug promoted to alleviate depression—that did just the opposite."

Cal paused for effect, lowered his head as if in prayer, and then returned his entrancing stare to the twelve people listening intently from the jury box.

"No, it didn't relieve Willie Anderson's depression. It caused him to methodically go to his bedroom, take out the gun he kept in the bedside table drawer, and, in execution-style fashion, fire bullets into the heads of his three precious children as they lay sound asleep in their beds—sweet, innocent children. And then, moments later, he turned the gun on himself. Four people needlessly dead, and all because of one thing. Wall Street profits."

Like an actor in a Shakespearean tragedy, Cal dramatically turned and pointed at the president of Samson Pharmaceuticals, seated with his army of lawyers at the counsel table on the other side of the courtroom.

"I'm not afraid to call it like it is, ladies and gentlemen. That man over there, and his company"—Cal kept his finger aimed at the dark suits across the way—"deliberately put a drug on the market that almost wiped out an entire family. The only remaining member of a once loving family is my client, Laura Anderson, who sits before you today, alone, with nothing but heartbreaking memories of a family that once was."

Cal's voice had gradually dropped from an indignant shout to a soft whisper.

"A handwritten note left on the bedside table simply stated, 'The world is a terrible place. I had to take our children to the land of promise. Forgive me if I was wrong.'"

"And poor Laura . . ." Cal stopped and turned to his client, who was quietly sobbing into a Kleenex. He allowed several seconds to pass and then returned his attention to the jurors. "And poor

Laura had been visiting her elderly parents in San Antonio. When she arrived at her home hours later, she found a scene too grisly for anyone to bear. Her husband of fifteen years was gone, as were her three children, ages twelve, ten, and eight. Her life had been forever ruined, never to be the same. And why? Because Samson Pharmaceuticals wanted more profits so that their stock would soar and their executives up east could line their already-bulging pockets. Samson Pharmaceuticals knew that, in certain instances, rather than alleviate depression, their product Fosorax would actually intensify a patient's feelings of despair and hopelessness. But, ladies and gentlemen, despite this knowledge, they sold the drug without any warning that such side effects were possible."

"Now, you and I know there is no amount of money that can compensate for losing a loved one. But I am asking you here today to send a message to Samson Pharmaceuticals. Let them know their behavior is unacceptable here in Brownsville, Texas. That big companies cannot come in here and run over the good and honest people of this county. Ladies and gentlemen, I am asking you to compensate poor Laura Anderson not only for the loss of her husband but for the loss of her three innocent children."

Cal stopped talking and focused his eyes on each and every juror. He then walked to a blackboard to the left of the jury box. He took a piece of chalk and wrote the figure "$15,000,000" on the board. Then he wrote "$15,000,000" on the board for a second time. Walking back to the jury box, he continued. "Fifteen million dollars in actual damages and an additional fifteen million dollars in punitive damages to punish Samson Pharmaceuticals for its malicious and wanton behavior. That only begins to compensate Laura Anderson for her loss. But it's a start. It's fair. You know those numbers are fair and I know they are fair. Thank you."

Cal nodded to the jury and sat back down at counsel table, putting his arm around his client in a touching attempt to console her. The defense lawyers, all from Houston, dressed in their dark suits and somber ties, stared at Cal, their faces dark with fury. Throughout the trial, they had presented compelling evidence that the drug was safe, that it had helped many forlorn individuals, and that all test data had been submitted to the Food and Drug Administration, which had unanimously approved Fosorax for sale. In addition, they had presented medical records demonstrating that Willie Anderson had been hospitalized on three separate occasions for unsuccessful suicide attempts before taking Fosorax.

Cal's case was so shaky that they had been convinced the judge would throw out the lawsuit before the trial even began. But to their disbelief, Judge Alberto Garcia had denied all defense motions to dismiss. Now the lawyers knew they were in trouble. The case was in the hands of twelve local residents, and the stakes were monumental. Brownsville was known for large plaintiff recoveries, so there was ample precedent for the $30 million worth of damages that Cal had asked the jury to award. And that was Cal's style: swing for the home run, ask for the moon, and you just might get it.

Cal was indeed the Lone Wolf, a label he wore proudly. He reveled when the corporate defendant brought in an endless stream of dapperly clad journeymen to do battle with him in the courtroom. Routinely, he was the only lawyer at counsel table with the widow, or severely crippled plaintiff. In plain view of the jury, he would, at critical times in the case, reach over and consolingly stroke his client's arm as defense counsel strutted back and forth to the witness stand, examining witnesses and introducing documents into evidence. His occasional whisper or gesture to his client was a distraction that, by design, kept the jurors' minds diverted from adverse testimony or damning documents. Cal loved the underdog image he painstakingly created in the jurors' minds as each trial progressed—Cal Connors, David versus Goliath, representing the downtrodden against greedy corporate America.

He was sly and cunning; he knew when to strike and when to lie back and wait for his prey to make a mistake. The nickname Lone Wolf fit him to perfection.

The case was submitted to the jury later that Friday afternoon. Rather than begin their deliberations, the jurors elected to recess until the following Monday morning at nine. Judge Garcia announced in open court that the jury had recessed for the weekend, and he ended the week's session with the bang of his gavel.

Cal spent the weekend in Fort Worth and flew back to Brownsville Sunday night, again renting the cheapest midsize rental car Avis stocked and checking back into the La Quinta motor hotel where he had stayed for the duration of the trial. Sure, he could have stayed at La Posada, the nicest hotel in Brownsville, and he could have rented a Lincoln Town Car. Considering his personal wealth—north of $100 million—money was no obstacle. But he had a persona to cultivate. His choice of hotel and rental car was for effect. What if one of the jurors saw him drive up in an expensive car or come out of an upscale hotel? The David-like image he was working so hard to maintain in the jurors' minds could evaporate instantly. He would stay in the same type of hotel where the twelve people who would decide the case would stay, eat in the same types of restaurants where they would eat, and drive the same type of car they would drive. He would be one of them, at least until the trial was over and a favorable verdict was in hand. And the expensive hotels and cars—they would be left for his adversaries. The picture he wanted would be painted inside and outside the courtroom.

The courthouse was only three blocks from the La Quinta. He spent that Monday wandering the halls of the building, trying to pick up gossip about what the jurors were doing. Things had gone smoothly for him during the trial, almost too smoothly. But you could never tell what might happen during jury deliberations. He didn't want to take a chance on defense counsel arguing that they had witnessed jury misconduct, that they had overheard the jurors discussing improper topics or evidence that was outside the record. No, he would make sure to observe the courthouse happenings with his own eyes and ears. There would be no mistrial in this case.

Monday passed without event. On Tuesday morning, at 8:15, he got a call at his hotel from the court clerk informing him that the verdict was in. Cal parked in one of the parking spaces directly across from the courthouse, a nondescript edifice that had been constructed back in the fifties. He was wearing his signature bolo tie, the clasp in the shape of the great state of Texas; a $200 black suit he had purchased at J.T.'s Men's Wear in Fort Worth; and a pair of custom-made black ostrich-skin cowboy boots, the scales of justice embroidered in the high center of each and "Lone Wolf" on the sides. Although the boots were custom-made and expensive, they would not undermine his carefully constructed image. South Texans loved their cowboy boots. They would sacrifice elsewhere to be able to afford a custom-made pair. The boots added to Cal's mystique and even enhanced his appeal to the locals. And the finishing touch, a black Stetson hat, was fitted snugly upon his head. The hat went with him everywhere. It felt like a part of him, like an arm or a leg. He had never tried a case without it. It was his good-luck piece.

Cal got out of the car and ambled toward the courthouse. He nodded to everyone as he walked up the steps to the entrance, tipping his hat politely to the ladies. Before entering, he humbly declined the requests of several reporters for a statement; the interviews would come later. He entered the courthouse and made his way toward the courtroom of Judge Alberto Garcia.

Laura Anderson was already seated at counsel table in the courtroom. She was simply dressed, as she had been throughout the trial, wearing a short-sleeved cotton dress printed with small blue and yellow flowers and a thin matching belt that made the dress look like a throwback to the fifties. Her black leather shoes had a small heel. She wore no jewelry except her wedding ring and an inexpensive watch her husband had given her for their first anniversary, a detail Cal had been careful to point out during her direct testimony. Her dark brown hair fell naturally around her face, and she continually pulled it back behind her ears. She had put on eye makeup that morning, which had begun to run with the tears that trailed down her face.

Her appearance had not been left to chance. Before the first day of trial, Cal had gone over what she should wear and what she should not, how she should act in the courtroom and how she should not, and the places she should avoid when the trial recessed for the day—bottom line, he had scripted her wardrobe and every action while the trial was in progress. Much like a successful professional football coach, he had left nothing to chance. Turnovers could lose ball games, and missteps in and out of the courtroom could lose trials. There would be no missteps on his watch. He had worked too hard and spent too much money on this case for his client to blow it by some indiscretion.

Five minutes later, the team of defense lawyers entered the courtroom. Three sat at the defense table, and three sat in the front row immediately behind the railing. They were all dressed in their cookie-cutter attire: dark blue silk suits, Hermès ties, and freshly polished wingtips. Their collars were as starched as their personalities. The president of Samson Pharmaceuticals sat in their midst, clad this morning in similar fashion. Cal looked in his direction, made eye contact, and winked. His adversary turned away in disgust, whispered to one of his lawyers, and then shook his head. Cal suppressed a laugh as he thought of the words to one of his daughter's favorite songs, "Ants Marching." Cal was not a big fan of Dave Matthews, but the words to that song had always amused him. So many people play follow the leader and simply go through the motions day after day, but not Cal. He was an original, the real thing, anything but ordinary.

The courtroom was now packed, standing room only. The media had taken great interest in the trial from the outset. Although a few cases involving Fosorax had been previously tried, all were defense verdicts, and none had involved a death claim. The other lawsuits simply declared that Fosorax worsened depression. Hundreds of claims involving the drug had been filed throughout the country, and all eyes were on this Brownsville courtroom to see who would prevail. A big verdict would start a tidal wave of activity by the plaintiff's bar to bring the many cases waiting in the wings to trial. The effect on the financial stability of Samson Pharmaceuticals could be devastating, if not fatal. The stock price would take a nosedive, with irreparable collateral damage to follow. On the other hand, a defense verdict in a county known to be sympathetic to plaintiffs could be the death knell for other cases. Plaintiff's lawyers would be unwilling to pour the kind of dollars into the pretrial workup that would be necessary, and the claims would either be dismissed or settled for nuisance value. The power of the jury box—and the power of Cal Connors—had seldom been on greater display.

The din in the courtroom was abruptly muffled by the bailiff's shout: "All rise, the Fourteenth Judicial District Court of Cameron County, Brownsville, Texas, is now in session, the Honorable Alberto Garcia presiding." The sound of the packed courtroom standing in unison accompanied Judge Garcia's entrance. Clad in a flowing black robe, Judge Garcia stepped up to the bench. He took his seat and then motioned for those present to do the same. He turned to the bailiff: "Please bring in the jury."

The bailiff disappeared and then reappeared with eight women and four men in tow. At the bailiff's directions, they marched single-file and took the seats they had occupied for the past three weeks. Their eyes avoided counsel at both tables and focused on the judge.

Judge Garcia cleared his throat, took a sip of water and then, in a well-rehearsed, slightly accented voice, spoke. "Ladies and gentlemen of the jury, have you reached a verdict?"

An olive-skinned woman in her late fifties stood and answered, "We have, Your Honor."

The judge continued. "Is it a unanimous verdict?"

Without hesitation, she responded, "Yes, Your Honor."

"Bailiff, please bring me the charge from the jury forewoman." The bailiff speedily complied, and Judge Garcia carefully reviewed the answers on each page. To those assembled, the process seemed to take an eternity. The judge began to read the first question submitted to the jury aloud: "Do you find from a preponderance of the evidence that the defendant, Samson Pharmaceuticals, placed into the stream of commerce a product that was unreasonably dangerous?"

He looked up solemnly from the papers in front of him, briefly pausing for effect. "To that question, the jury answered, 'We do.'"

Laura Anderson began to cry. Cal Connors maintained his stoic demeanor. The president of Samson Pharmaceuticals hung his head. The courtroom chatter resumed. Everyone knew the ball game was over and who had won. It was just a question of how bad the score would be. No one would know until the judge reached the portion of the jury charge that dealt with damages.

Several excruciating minutes later, he did: a total award of $30 million, $15 million in actual damages and $15 million in punitive damages—exactly the amount Cal had asked for. Upon that announcement, bedlam reigned. Five bangs of the gavel later some semblance of order was restored. Judge Garcia thanked the jurors for their unselfish and conscientious service, released them, and then disappeared into his sacrosanct chambers.

Laura's hug seemed unending. Finally, Cal politely disentangled himself from her grasp and managed to mutter, "Well, I thought we had it in the bag, but you never know. You just never know."

His mind had already done the math on his cut of the jury award: 40 percent of $30 million. He knew the jury verdict would not stand up before the conservative Texas Supreme Court, but during the appellate process, he would cut a deal. Samson Pharmaceuticals could not take the two years of bad publicity and uncertainty that an appeal would involve. They would settle—and they would pay him a lot of money. He figured somewhere in the neighborhood of half the award. And his share of that—$7.5 million—wasn't bad pay for a good ol' boy who had grown up the son of a steelworker in the Piney Woods of East Texas.

The scene on the courthouse steps resembled a political rally. An army of reporters and cameramen held the front line, pushing and shoving for the best vantage point. Behind them, a diverse group of courthouse regulars and curious onlookers had assembled, anxiously awaiting the next act of the melodrama. The air was heavy with humidity, the temperature hovering close to the 80-degree mark.

Prior to the trial, the local newspaper had run a Sunday feature entitled "The Lone Wolf: A Dying Breed." The article had traced Cal's life from its humble beginnings to his success in the courtroom, representing the common man and middle-class America in a war against the excesses and wrongdoing of a corporate world gone amok. The feature concluded with a lament about tort reform and its hobbling effect on the ability of the Cal Connors of the world to fight the good cause. A synopsis of each day of the lengthy trial followed, hooking many a reader in much the same way as lurid soap operas beguile their viewers. Many of the townsfolk who had assembled outside the courthouse had waited eagerly for the next installment, marveling at the courtroom antics of their hero and later discussing them over coffee at the local diners.

In fact, before the trial started, Cal had paid several visits to the offices of the *Brownsville Gazette,* speaking with the editor and dropping off treats from a nearby bakery for the editorial staff. So it was no accident that the press coverage had been skewed in Cal's favor. And from years of experience Cal knew that, although instructed to the contrary, unsequestered juries read the city paper and were influenced by its content. He had counted on that. And just like everything else he had orchestrated in this cinematic production, it had paid off big-time.

Cal opened the front door of the courthouse to a cacophony of shouts and applause. His right arm wrapped protectively around his client's shoulders, he allowed the chaos to continue for several minutes, openly savoring the triumph and enjoying the tribute before raising his left hand in a cue for quiet. As the noise abated, he surveyed the crowd, making sure that if he ever tried another case in Cameron County, his underdog image would be indelibly etched on the local psyche, putting him a step ahead of his opponent even before the lawsuit was filed. The momentary hush was short-lived, Cal's distinctly deep and deliberate voice breaking the silence, demanding the attention of all present.

"Today the people of Cameron County have spoken. Not for me. Not for my client. They have spoken for justice and what is right and good and fair in this great country of ours." He paused and gestured toward the American flag flapping briskly in front of the courthouse. Enthusiastic applause ensued and a man in the back hollered, "The Lone Wolf for president!" Shrill whistles of approval filled the air and a few shouted "Amen" to the motion. Cal signaled for order and continued his diatribe.

"My client will not get back her husband or children." His eyes cast their gaze downward in despair. "No amount of money can bring my client's family back. But maybe, just maybe, those who sit in their elegant boardrooms, surrounded by priceless paintings and mahogany-paneled walls, thinking of nothing but profits and more profits, will think again before putting a product on the market that can kill, maim, or harm. And if one life is saved, just one, as a result, then we—you and I—have done something to make America a better place. Thank you, and God bless you. Now, if you'll excuse us, it's been a long trial for me and my client."

Cal knew there would be questions that he would answer, but his feigned move toward departure was for effect. He wanted to be begged and cajoled to stay, much like the rock star who leaves the stage prematurely, seeking that deafening, ego-inflating crowd noise entreating an encore. As Cal and his client moved toward the first of the courthouse steps, they were stopped by a reporter's voice.

"Mr. Connors, what impact do you think today's verdict will have on Samson's stock price?" The questioner, a slightly overweight, tomboyish-looking female clad in a light blue pantsuit and flats, looked around at her fellow reporters, searching for approval while awaiting Cal's reply.

"Haven't given it a thought," Cal said quickly. "I'm sure the wizards of Wall Street will figure it out."

Cal had, in fact, given it a lot of thought. Prior to trial, he had made a presentation to Samson's management and defense team, using the possibility of a precipitous stock drop following an adverse verdict to justify an eight-figure settlement demand. He had even employed a respected economist to do some calculations as to how different-sized verdicts might affect Samson's share price. His arguments had gotten the attention of Samson's chief financial officer, but Samson's president and chief executive officer had rejected the idea of paying Cal and his client any more than the cost of defending the case, labeling Cal's presentation nothing more than corporate extortion disguised as settlement negotiations.

A balding man wearing an ill-fitting suit and scuffed-up black loafers was next in line to ask Cal a question at the impromptu press conference. Nervously adjusting his wire-rim glasses, he began his question, momentarily paused as if he had forgotten it, and then rattled it off like machine-gun fire. There was a murmur of confusion from the crowd. Cal came to the reporter's rescue.

"The gentleman wants to know if Samson will pull Fosorax from the market as a result of this verdict. That's a good question."

The reporter smiled, feeling a sense of vindication. He would remember Cal's forbearance when he began writing his article. "Who knows? I would have thought they would have recalled this dangerous drug before now. But corporate America never ceases to surprise me with its greed and thirst for money."

Cal glanced at his watch and grimaced. "I would like to spend the rest of the day answering your questions, but I've only got time for one more. My plane leaves in a little over an hour."

Literally, this was true. His Learjet and crew were ready to depart at any time and, if Cal was there and ready to leave in an hour, that would be the departure time. But the implication to the audience was that he was flying coach on a commercial airliner, just like any other ordinary Joe.

"Mr. Connors?"

The crowd's attention focused on a female reporter in the back of the crowd. Dressed in a navy-blue suit and mid-height matching heels, Leah Rosen stepped forward, causing the exuberant clamor of the crowd to morph into a curious murmur. Her brown hair was cut in pageboy fashion, accenting her fair complexion and over-sized brown eyes. She was wearing glasses, fashionably designed in a square cut of dark tortoiseshell. She stepped forward in Cal's direction, pausing long enough for their eyes to meet. Cal instinctively sensed confrontation and uncharacteristically blinked before gaining composure and zeroing in on his interrogator.

In an authoritative and knowing tone, Leah asked, "Mr. Connors, if your verdict causes Samson, for financial reasons, to pull Fosorax from the market, will your conscience be bothered by the number of people suffering from depression who can't get help for their debilitating symptoms? Will you lie awake at night and wonder how many suicides could have been prevented if this drug had remained on the market?"

Without hesitation, Cal laughed heartily. "Obviously, young lady, you did not sit through this trial. We proved to the jury's satisfaction—"

"That's not my question," the reporter said, boldly interrupting him. "Based upon what you know about Fosorax, does it bother you—"

Cal didn't let Leah finish her question. "Twelve people from this great county have answered the call of their conscience and spoken, and I'm willing to abide by their decision, as should you and whoever you work for."

Wild applause and catcalls echoed the crowd's assent as Cal turned his glare from Leah back to his admirers. With his client at his side, he worked his way through the throng, dispensing compliments and shaking hands. As he escorted his client to her car, Cal caught a glimpse of Leah out of the corner of his eye. She was standing apart from the others, looking as if she knew something they didn't. Cal dismissed her from his thoughts. He was already thinking about his next case—one closer to home, and one that he knew might get just as much attention as this one.

CHAPTER

5

It was mid-morning, and though she would have typically been at the office working, Cal's daughter, Christine Connors, was at home getting a late start to the day. She had showered and was in her robe, headed to the kitchen to pour herself a cup of coffee. Christine was striking in appearance—five feet six inches tall, with auburn hair stylishly cut, a slender build, and clear blue eyes that demanded attention, just like her dad's. Thirty years old, she had had many suitors and proposals of marriage. But marriage just wasn't for her. She was way too ambitious, with many goals to accomplish before ever committing to one man and the confines of motherhood.

In contrast to her father, Christine had soared through undergraduate school, graduating cum laude from Baylor University. She was accepted at Harvard Law School, where she graduated in the top 10 percent of her class and served as editor in chief of the *Law Review*. Law firms everywhere wanted her. But she had turned down offers from every big firm in the state, as well as several Wall Street shops, in favor of going to work for her dad. She had been apprehensive about making that move. After all, she knew the Lone Wolf as her dad, one who loved her more than anything. But she had no idea as to what he would be like as her employer. Would their relationship change? Might it change for the worse? She didn't know. But she did know one thing: the biggest risks routinely yielded the biggest rewards. She had decided to roll the dice. And what a whirlwind ride it had been ever since!

Connors & Associates, as it was known at the time, had no associates. It was a one-man show. True, Cal had surrounded himself with an extremely competent and loyal support staff comprised of two legal secretaries, four paralegals, and two full-time investigators. But if a case went to trial, Cal, and Cal alone, tried it. So how would he react to sharing some of the spotlight? And, equally important, how would his staff react to his daughter being brought on? Would they resent her, welcome her, or would it be a combination of the two?

Christine had sensed from the outset that she would be saddled with a heavy burden the first year or so, until she proved herself. And she was ready for it. She had excelled at everything she had done in life. She knew what the formula was: hard work and persistence. There were no free lunches. Her dad hadn't gotten any on his way to the top, and she didn't expect any handouts either. She would have to earn her way.

After seven months on the job, Cal walked into her office and said, "How would you like to try your first case?" Christine had just passed the bar a few months before but jumped at the chance. She lost. The jury just didn't believe her client: a faulty accelerator had not caused the crash; her client's texting had. Cal had been there for every minute of the trial. He had offered no advice, just observed. After the verdict was returned, father and daughter did a postmortem over dinner.

"What did I do wrong? Why didn't they believe my client?" Christine asked as she stared at her martini.

"You tried the case perfectly. But there is one thing you could have done differently. Watch more carefully when you voir dire the jury panel. Listen to their responses. Don't be thinking about your next question. Ask follow-ups. I had a strong feeling you were going to lose that case after the jury was seated. Do you remember the male juror who was chosen as foreman?"

"Yeah, I remember him. The short, bald-headed guy. What about him?"

"Well, he was twitching and moving nervously when you were questioning him. I didn't have my laptop with me during voir dire but was able to Google him after the trial got under way. Guess what? His father owns a car dealership in Weatherford. That son of a bitch would have never found a car defective, any car."

"Son of a bitch is right. We should move for a new trial. He was clearly biased."

"Not so fast, young lady. You didn't ask the right questions. We have no grounds. You probably shouldn't have won that case anyway."

"And why not?"

"Because your client was texting right before the accident."

"You believe that?"

"Yep. But the important thing is to learn from this. Voir dire and opening statement are the two most important stages of a trial. Picking the people who get to decide your client's case—what could be more important than that? And then making that strong first impression in opening after they are seated. That's how cases are won. Trust me."

Christine did, and ended up winning her next four cases, the last one resulting in a $2 million verdict against a toy manufacturer. And for the next few years, she successfully tried several cases to verdict. Her professional appearance and razor-sharp mind made her a formidable opponent in almost any venue, and her dad knew it. In fact, she would have been seated with him at counsel table in Brownsville but for Cal's fear that the local population might harbor some undisclosed bias toward female professionals, and he just couldn't take that chance.

After Harvard Law, she had accepted an invitation to live in the guesthouse of her father's Fort Worth mansion, near the Colonial Country Club. With more than 3,500 square feet of living space and lavish furnishings, the guesthouse would have been any young professional's dream. But with her success, Christine pined for more privacy and a place a little more urban. She decided a house wasn't for her; she didn't want the upkeep and it felt too "family." She wanted a secure place that was convenient to happening restaurants and a bustling social scene.

She was drawn to downtown Fort Worth, which of late had become very chic and alluring. She went on the Internet and did a search of all the downtown high-rise units on the market. C'est la Vie, a 24-story high-rise in the heart of the city, caught her eye. Recently constructed by Canadian investors, it had everything she was looking for. It was a stone's throw from bustling Sundance Square, which was flush with eclectic restaurants and unique retailers. Bass Hall, a world-respected opera and concert venue, was within walking distance. The location was absolutely perfect! And the high-rise itself was over-the-top. It offered every possible amenity: full-time security, an Olympic-size swimming pool on the building's roof with breathtaking views of Fort Worth and its surroundings, a state-of-the-art workout facility with personal trainers, a full-service spa, and a 24-hour catering facility.

Christine discovered she could purchase a two-bedroom, two-bath, three-thousand-square-foot unit on the twenty-third floor for $1,250,000. It would take another $250,000 to furnish it per her ultramodern, expensive taste. It was perfect! There was only one problem. She had been out of law school just a few years and didn't have that kind of money, not even close. But she did know how to sweet-talk someone who did. Besides, she wouldn't ask her dad to buy it for her; she would ask him to loan her the money. She was confident that she would make it back, and then some, once her practice became more established. It would only take one big verdict. And Connors & Connors, as it was now called, was overloaded with "big ticket" cases. Her dad couldn't try them all. She would keep her eye out for that special case that fit her talents and had "big verdict" potential. That's how her dad had made it, and she was crafted from the same mold. She figured a dinner with her dad was all it would take, and she was right. Six months after she had found her dream home, she was watching her decorator's minions hang the last pieces of artwork and position the last pieces of furniture. La Maison Christine was complete.

And what a feeling it was, a few years later, to pay that loan back to her dad—with interest, no less. Now, settling into an over-stuffed saucer chair in the corner of her living room, she sipped her coffee before picking up her Kindle to read the daily downloaded version of the *New York Times*. Life was good, very good indeed.

And she had a sense it was about to get better. Cal had asked her to help out on a new case he was handling, *Olivia and Lackland Stone* vs. *Caring Oaks Funeral Home and Cemetery*. She put down her Kindle and picked up her laptop from the side table. She hit the power button, brought up the Google icon, and typed in "Jace Forman." There were 33 hits. She scrolled down to the Forman Firm website and entered, quickly moving the cursor to the tab entitled "Our Attorneys." Upon finding Jace, she clicked on and scanned the background of their adversary in their new case:

Jace Forman was born in Shelbyville, Tennessee, in 1964. He attended preparatory school at the Webb School, in Bell Buckle, Tennessee, graduating in 1982. He received a full academic scholarship to the University of the South at Sewanee, from which he graduated magna cum laude in

1987. Upon graduation from Sewanee, Mr. Forman attended the University of Texas Law School. He graduated from UT Law in 1991 Order of the Coif. He also served as managing editor of the Texas Law Review.

Mr. Forman specializes in complex "bet the company" civil litigation. In his career, he has tried over 150 cases to jury verdict. In addition, he has argued cases before both state and federal courts of appeal as well as the Texas Supreme Court.

Christine closed out the firm's website. Pretty impressive credentials. So what? Her dad had barely scraped by in law school, but that hadn't kept him from successfully wooing just about every jury he had ever picked. There was a difference between book smarts and killer instincts. She would take killer instincts any day.

She scanned several of the other hits on her screen. One in particular caught her attention. It read: "Prominent lawyer's wife dies in head-on crash." Christine entered the site. She had a vague recollection of reading this article some time ago. Jace's wife, Camille, had died in a head-on collision with an eighteen-wheeler on I-45. According to the article, Camille had been speeding on her way to Houston when her BMW hit a slick spot, veered off the road, and crossed the median. She had died upon impact. The driver of the semi had been cleared of any fault. Christine shook her head as she zoomed in on the photograph of Camille Forman. She was a beautiful woman. What a tragedy!

Her cell phone rang. "Jury just came back. Fifteen mil in actuals and fifteen mil in punitives. Pack your bags, baby!" her father bellowed. "The plane is on its way to pick you up."

"Congratulations! I knew you'd kick ass! I'll be at the airport within the hour waiting for you!"

Christine was beside herself. A $30 million verdict. Whew! That was one of their bigger ones. She wondered what her dad would be able to settle it for—maybe a half or, worst case, a third of that amount. In any event, their cut would be a home run. And now for the celebration! Based on past history, she knew there would be plenty of alcohol consumed, and war stories told, over the next several days. She smiled at the prospect, but her mood was slightly tempered by the tremendous amount of work to be done on the Caring Oaks file: pretrial discovery had to be drafted and served, subpoenas issued, depositions taken. The firm's investigators needed to get started on a number of assignments, including background checks on everyone employed by Caring Oaks and compiling every bit of information they could find on Jace Forman and the Forman Firm. And she was in charge of getting it all done.

But first things first. She and her dad had some celebrating to do. Twice divorced, Cal had no family but his daughter. Not only was she the apple of his eye, she was his law partner, go-to confidante, and strategist—and the best company he could find to listen to his blow-by-blow re-creation of his courtroom exploits. Christine shook off her trance and hurried toward the bedroom to pack. She needed to leave in thirty minutes. She had no intention of keeping the Lone Wolf waiting.

CHAPTER

6

"Senator, you've got to calm down. There is no need to panic." Talmadge Worthman turned his back on his chief of staff before walking quickly toward the other side of the office. He gazed out the window as he spoke.

"That's easy for you to say. Hell, a young coed I was seeing is found dead, and then her body is stolen from the grave and used in some sort of satanic ritual. And if that's not bad enough, the whole mess is being dug up again in a lawsuit. Now you're telling me to calm down? You're damn right I'm panicked. You would be too. I told you to take care of the situation—not kill the poor girl and come up with some cockamamie cover-up."

"Come on, Senator. You know I'm not a murderer. I could accuse you of the same damn thing. As far as I know, you were the last one to see her alive. But you don't see me pointing any fingers, do you?"

Talmadge let out a long sigh. "You're right, Myron. I apologize. I didn't mean what I said. I'm just not thinking clearly. Just when I thought the investigation was about to be closed, this lawsuit is going to stir up a hornet's nest. For my own peace of mind, let's go over the facts one more time. You said you got to Alexis' apartment . . ."

"Around ten-thirty or eleven, a little after you called me. I knocked on the door. There was no answer. I knocked again—still no response. I figured she was out so I headed home."

"You sure you never set foot in her apartment?"

"Come on, Senator. You've got to trust me. Hell, you've known me for how many years now? Over twenty? I've never lied to you—at least, not about anything important." Myron forced a grin.

Talmadge pulled out the leather chair from behind his desk and took a seat. He leaned forward, his fingers intertwined, his arms resting on the desk in front of him. "So there was no suggestion of foul play at her apartment?"

"According to my contact at the police department, the death is going to be an open-and-shut case. The medical examiner is going to rule the cause of death an accidental drug overdose."

"What about the grave robbery? Any suspects?" Talmadge was up again, pacing nervously, as he spit out questions in rapid-fire succession.

"The Austin PD has no interest in the grave robbery since it didn't happen in their jurisdiction."

"So what do you think I should do?"

"I think you ought to quit worrying about it. If anything surfaces in the investigation, I'll hear about it. Let's just focus on getting you reelected. What do you say, Senator?"

Talmadge shook his head. "Open-and-shut. You sure about that?"

"I'm sure. Nothing's going to come of this."

"And you'll know if anything changes, right?"

"I've got it covered."

"I don't like it, but I guess there is nothing more I can do at this point other than act like nothing has happened, go on with business as usual."

"Couldn't have said it better myself. Let's just put this unfortunate mishap behind us and move on to more-important things."

Talmadge sighed. "You're right, Myron, as usual. I don't even want to discuss this again—that is, unless something develops in the investigation. From this point forward, I've never known an Alexis Stone. You understand me, don't you, Myron? Our little tryst never even occurred."

"I read you loud and clear. Alexis who?"

The senator smiled in response and then began shuffling through some papers on his desk until he found his calendar. He peered over the reading glasses on the end of his nose. "Let's go over my campaign schedule, shall we?"

"Gladly, Senator, gladly."

CHAPTER

7

Caring Oaks Funeral Home had once been the antebellum mansion of a prosperous entrepreneur specializing in saddlery and other leather goods. It had been purchased and converted in the sixties to a funeral home, its charm preserved, its entrance proudly displaying the designation of a historic landmark. On the bottom floor were the visiting rooms, where relatives and friends could pay their last respects before the deceased was put to rest. In addition, there was the chapel, similar in all respects to a moderately sized church, equipped with pews, stained-glass windows, and a pulpit. Down a somber hallway was a large showroom where Caring Oaks "counselors" made carefully worded sales pitches regarding the features of caskets, casket liners, urns, and various other "sales" items prominently displayed throughout. A flower shop offering fresh and artificial arrangements occupied the adjacent space. The Caring Oaks executives had learned the benefits of one-stop shopping. After all, that was the American way.

The upper floor housed Caring Oaks' administrative offices. Although presented to the public as a small, family-owned business, Caring Oaks was one of the holdings of Jackson Funeral Services, Inc., a publicly traded company on the New York Stock Exchange owning over five hundred funeral homes and cemeteries throughout the United States. Even though it was part of a behemoth corporation, Caring Oaks had its own slate of officers and operated autonomously to a large degree, submitting quarterly financial reports to its parent company. Caring Oaks' president, Wallace Arnold, along with the other corporate officers, occupied the converted bedrooms where the family of the home's original owner once slept.

As Jace and Darrin walked up the graceful winding staircase, its dark wood tastefully accented by an antique Persian runner, they both felt they were taking a step back in time. That impression was reinforced when they reached the landing, now a converted reception area, where a rotund, gray-haired lady sat. As if she were angry for being interrupted by their presence, she ordered them to be seated and immediately picked up the phone. "Mr. Arnold, your nine o'clock appointment is here." After making the announcement, she laid the receiver in its cradle and returned her gaze to the romance novel she had been reading when they arrived.

Moments later, Wallace appeared, a short man with a chalky complexion and thinning hair combed straight back. Dressed in a heavily starched white shirt, a silk tie checkered silver and blue, a midnight-blue suit, and recently shined black Italian loafers, he forced a smile and offered his hand to Jace. "Jace, thank you for coming." His dark eyes squinted as he pumped Jace's hand up and down nervously.

"No problem. You remember Darrin McKenzie, my—"

Wallace gently interrupted. "Legal assistant. Of course, Ms. McKenzie." He politely nodded toward Darrin. "Well, my office is just down the hall. Shall we?" He stepped aside, gesturing for his guests to go ahead of him.

At the end of the hall, Jace and Darrin stopped at the door of what had once been the master bedroom of the home. Wallace motioned his visitors inside. After they were seated, Jace quickly focused on the case confronting them.

"Wallace, I understand you had virtually all of the personal contact with the family regarding funeral arrangements for the decedent?" Jace paused for an answer.

"From start to finish. They seemed very distraught. But who wouldn't be after losing a child?"

"Anything unusual about this particular funeral?"

"I hate to sound callous, but the services blur together after you've been in this business as long as I have. During my twenty-five years here I've handled literally thousands of funeral arrangements. Sometimes it's difficult to remember one from the other. But, since this funeral was recent, I do remember the family and some of the details about the decedent's death."

"Did you just deal with the mother and father, or were there siblings involved?"

"As I recall, the decedent was an only child." Mr. Arnold closed his eyes and tilted his head toward the ceiling, as if this would help his concentration. "Yes, they had only the one daughter. I remember them saying she was all they had."

"Why don't you walk us through your contacts with the family?"

"I assume you know the background?" Wallace's eyes darted from Jace to Darrin and then back again.

"Assume we know nothing."

Wallace sighed. "Okay, from the beginning. Alexis Stone, the decedent, was a student at the University of Texas in Austin. A senior, if my memory serves me correctly. She was a beautiful girl. She died of a stroke or heart attack, I can't remember which, at her apartment near campus. Her parents told me there was no family history to explain her untimely death and that the Austin police were looking into it. Mr. Stone seemed convinced there was foul play involved. But I didn't go into that with him. I try to be consoling to families but keep my distance as well." Wallace paused for a response.

"Did Mr. Stone give you any clues as to the type of foul play he suspected?"

"I didn't ask and he didn't volunteer." Wallace glanced at Darrin as she scribbled notes on a yellow legal pad.

"Anything else memorable about your pre-funeral meeting with the Stones?"

"As I recall, they spent a great deal of time picking out the burial container and casket. As you know, we pride ourselves on having a large selection of caskets and liners to choose from. We have everything from an unlined wooden box to a stainless steel casket with imported tufted silk lining."

"And what did they choose?"

"A concrete burial container with a cherry casket—top of the line all the way."

Darrin interrupted. "I take it the container is something separate from the casket?"

"Well, of course," Wallace answered somewhat condescendingly. "The casket houses the corpse. Then the casket is covered by the container."

He looked at Darrin for a response. Her expression reflected confusion.

"Think of it this way. The container, in this case concrete, is like a butter tray. The casket is placed on the bottom part of the container, which is buried in the ground at about six feet. That's where we get the expression 'six feet under,' although technically the body is not buried that deeply—it's more like three feet. Then the casket is covered by the top of the container, and as an added precaution, the top of the container is secured to the bottom by self-locking latches."

"I had no idea." Satisfied with the explanation and amused by the analogy, a faint smile crossed Darrin's lips as she made more notes on her pad.

Jace resumed his questioning. "It's my understanding you still have both the container and the casket Ms. Stone was buried in?"

"Locked away safe and sound in one of our maintenance facilities. You know that we have three hundred acres here to maintain—pretty demanding job, particularly in the heat of a Texas summer."

"We want to see both the casket and container and take some pictures. But before we do that, we have a few more questions. Do you know of anyone else at Caring Oaks who either met with the Stones or had anything to do with the burial?"

"I was the only one who dealt with them. But I did not embalm the body. I am a licensed embalmer but tired of that work several years ago."

"Who embalmed the body?"

"Lonnie Masterson." Wallace cleared his throat. "He's on vacation this week."

"We will obviously need to talk with him."

"I assumed you would. The police spent a little over an hour with him."

"Tell me what Mr. Masterson does at Caring Oaks on a day-to-day basis."

"He prepares bodies for burial. He replaces the blood with embalming fluid and makes the deceased look as lifelike as possible."

Darrin shifted in her chair as she continued to scribble notes.

Wallace digressed to add a little history on embalming. "This practice dates back to the ancient Egyptians, except they used spices rather than chemicals. I think we are the only modern country that allows embalming. Seems like Americans have more difficulty than others coping with the idea that the old body eventually does turn to dust, so to speak. But that's good for business."

Jace filed that bit of information away. He knew he would be confronted with the moneymaking practices related to the funeral business when he and Cal Connors faced off during trial. "So how long has Mr. Masterson been with Caring Oaks?"

"A little over six months. We've been very happy with his performance. The families have oohed and aahed over his work. He is somewhat of an artist."

"We will need to see his personnel file," Darrin interjected. She added apologetically, "Also, we'll need copies of every piece of paper having anything to do with the funeral arrangements and burial of the Stones' daughter."

Mr. Arnold picked up his phone and punched three numbers. "Ms. Shaw, please copy Mr. Masterson's personnel file and put it in the folder with the copy you made earlier of the Stone file." Pause. "As soon as you can. Thank you." He replaced the receiver.

"Anyone else involved before the actual burial?"

"That's it. Just Lonnie and me."

"I'll probably have some more questions but they can wait until we've taken a look at the casket and . . ." Jace hesitated, searching for the proper term.

"Container. Shall we?" Their host rose from his chair. "It'll be easier to drive than walk. My car is parked just outside."

CHAPTER

8

Caring Oaks' administrative offices were a five-minute drive from the maintenance building. As Wallace's Cadillac followed the winding gravel roads connecting different sections of the cemetery, he pointed out natural landmarks. His visitors could not help but admire the grounds, which were exquisitely manicured, crisscrossed by peaceful streams and adorned with towering oaks and mature pecans. It was little wonder that a burial plot in some of the more exclusive sections of the cemetery cost between $15,000 and $25,000. Jace knew he would have to contend with that fact at trial: Cal Connors arguing that Caring Oaks extorted exorbitant sums from grieving families in their time of bereavement, shaming them into buying the best for their lost loved ones. He knew his opponent didn't care one bit about the Stones or the anguish they might be suffering; what he did care about was his cut of whatever the Stones got from this case, whether it was tried or settled. But regardless of what he thought about Cal's methods or motives,

Jace could not discount the fact that Cal was an actor extraordinaire and would make a compelling argument to the jury. And who could predict what those twelve people might do?

"Well, here we are." Wallace put his car in park and, out of habit, locked the doors after Jace and Darrin got out.

The building was nondescript, a prefab rectangular structure, its front doors secured with a heavy-duty latch and lock. Wallace fished a single key from his pocket and unlocked the swinging doors, which he opened and then motioned Darrin and Jace inside. The interior had a musty smell. Although the lighting was poor, Darrin immediately eyed what appeared to be the casket and container in a corner. She headed in that direction. Jace and Wallace followed.

As they pulled back the clear plastic covering from the casket and container, Jace continued to probe for facts. "Wallace, what do you think happened?"

Flattered by the question, Wallace looked at them both, paused for a moment, and began to recount his version. "Well, based on what the grave site looked like the next day and what we are looking at here, I think whoever did this took a shovel and cleared the loose dirt off the bottom half of the grave. Then, they hit the concrete container. The concrete is two inches thick and reinforced with steel wire. They would have needed a sledgehammer, or a heavy rock, to break through that."

Wallace paused, bent over the concrete container, and touched the end of a protruding wire with his index finger.

"It looks like the wires were cut with clippers of some kind, but then I'm really guessing on that. Last came the wooden casket, which would have been child's play after the container."

"Any tools found around the site?"

"Not a one."

"Any valuables buried with the deceased?"

"Nothing noted in our papers. If valuables are buried with a corpse, it is usually reflected on the inventory sheet. The inventory sheet is in the file waiting for you back at our offices."

"Mind if we take some pictures?"

"Be my guest. The police asked that we leave the container and casket the way they were. They have already looked for fingerprints, taken measurements, and cut samples from the wire."

"They find anything?"

"Nothing that they shared with me."

While Jace and Wallace continued their conversation, Darrin photographed the casket and container from every conceivable angle and then rejoined her boss and host.

"How far is the grave site from here?"

"Within walking distance. Shall we?" Wallace gestured toward the open doors.

A few moments later, the trio was staring down at a headstone depicting an etching of a weeping angel.

Jace continued with his fact-gathering. "So is this where she was?"

"No, this is where she is now. You will notice the marker has no identification on it, just the etching."

"It's beautiful," Darrin commented.

"Yes, it is. I understand the grieving angel or the weeping angel dates back to the 1800s. It was a full-sized sculpture created by a Roman artist to mark his grave and that of his wife's. There are a few replicas of the sculpture throughout the world, including one in the Metairie Cemetery, in New Orleans, Louisiana."

"Why isn't there any other identification on the marker?" Darrin asked.

"That was at the family's request. When she was reburied, the Stones didn't want anybody to know where. They were afraid the demented soul who disinterred their daughter the first time might return for a repeat performance."

"Couldn't this have been some high school prank or gang-related activity?" Darrin wondered aloud.

"It could have been but not likely. It was hard work getting to the body. Teenagers would likely have given up when they hit concrete. Besides, there were a lot of other freshly dug graves closer to the point where the police think this psychopath's vehicle entered the grounds. If teenagers were looking to steal a corpse, they would have had plenty of choices before coming upon Ms. Stone's."

"So do you think it was a satanic cult that needed a young girl for one of its rituals?" Jace asked. "I assume you know her body was found on the altar of a desecrated church."

"Yes, I've read all the newspaper and Internet articles."

Darrin, after gazing around the cemetery and noticing all of the headstones and mausoleums, looked at Wallace and asked, "Have you ever had any graves defiled with satanic markings, or other evidence of satanic rituals at Caring Oaks?"

Mr. Arnold's face flushed, his tone turning defensive. "Well, I suppose every cemetery has experienced some desecration. But at Caring Oaks we have not had any more than the usual, and in fact, our record in that regard is probably better than most."

Persistent, Darrin continued. "Could you be a little more specific?"

Wallace was momentarily silent and then reluctantly offered a response.

"We have had marble statues stolen, especially the older ones. Last year two of them were recovered from a local antique dealer. Seems angels of Italian marble are quite in vogue with the well-to-do."

Wallace hesitated, rubbing his chin contemplatively. "And then, I think it was a little over two years ago, there was an attempt to rob a grave. The dirt had been removed from the entire grave and there were cracks in the burial container. Evidently, the would-be grave robbers were scared off or became frustrated by the difficulty of the task."

Jace interjected a follow-up. "I remember that. The police investigated and suspected some sort of devil worship based on what was left behind."

"Yes, I don't remember all the details but the police told me these things were associated with certain satanic cults. It was a painful experience I have tried my best to forget."

"Can you tell us anything about the decedent in that instance?"

"Not off the top of my head but your office should have a file on the incident."

Darrin silently chided herself for not having picked up on this piece of information when she had gone through the firm's database relating to Caring Oaks' cases. She made a mental note to search all incident information relating to grave desecration and satanism when she returned to her office.

Wallace abruptly changed topics.

"Now, do you want to see the grave that was robbed?"

As he spoke, he irreverently walked across several graves and then stood at a spot less than ten yards from the road.

"Here it is."

Jace and Darrin made their way toward the grave, being more careful not to step on those lying beneath.

"This was where Ms. Stone was initially laid to rest. We have decided not to use this site again, for obvious reasons."

Darrin looked around to survey the surroundings. There were other graves in the vicinity, a few remembered with fresh flowers. A stream, thirsty for water, wound its way alongside the road. A huge native oak, its age uncertain, sheltered the entire area with its overhanging limbs. Darrin snapped several pictures.

"I do remember why the Stones chose this site. Mr. Stone loved this big oak—said it would give his daughter something to lean on."

Wallace looked skyward, admiring the tree's height.

"This is one of the oldest trees in the entire cemetery—hard to miss it. Well, anything else you would like to see?"

Jace responded. "Do you have any pictures of the grave as it was found the morning after the theft?"

"They're part of the file. Prints were made for you this morning."

Jace sensed Wallace was ready to end the meeting and get back to work. "I just have a few more questions, Wallace. What condition was the body in when it was brought back to you for reburial?"

"It was still in good condition. I would assume certain tests were performed by law enforcement, and because Ms. Stone died in Austin, was buried in Fort Worth, and was found in a rural church just outside the Fort Worth city limits, the Austin Police, the Fort Worth Police, and the Tarrant County sheriff's office were are all involved. I haven't been able to get much information from any of them. Hopefully, you will have an easier time."

"I'll draft subpoenas for those records as soon as we get back to the office," Darrin said.

"Please keep me updated every step of the way. Because of the publicity involved in this case, the officers in our parent company are going to want frequent status reports." Wallace signaled the meeting was at an end as he began walking to his car. "Well, if there's nothing else, I need to get back to the office. I have an appointment with a family in about fifteen minutes."

They got in the car and headed back to Caring Oaks' offices. Once there, Jace, Darrin, and Wallace said their obligatory good-byes. "Wallace, it was good to see you again. We will be in touch as the case progresses. In the meantime, if you have any questions, just give me or Darrin a call."

"I appreciate it, and I am sure I will be talking with you soon." Wallace nodded to Darrin as he shook Jace's hand and then trod up the front steps to the building entrance. Jace and Darrin watched him walk away, both wondering what he hadn't told them.

CHAPTER

9

Jace and Darrin drove straight to the office. Jace returned a few urgent phone calls from other clients. Darrin responded to some emails and answered some questions from an associate who had been assigned one of Darrin's files while she worked on the Caring Oaks case. Within an hour, they met again in the main conference room, both silent, staring at the files and documents spread out on the table in front of them. Jace was the first to speak.

"Well, what do you think?"

Characteristically, Darrin thought for a moment before responding. "Why in the world would anyone steal a body? It's so bizarre."

"I agree. But as you and I have discovered over the years, people do some crazy shit. Let's go through the possibilities. What about the devil worship scenario? Did you find the file relating to the prior incident?"

"Apparently, the file was miscoded when it was sent off-site for storage. I had Harriett and the entire staff of the storage facility looking for it, and miraculously they found it! It was delivered a few minutes ago." Darrin flipped through the file. "There are some similarities to the instant case. The deceased was female, a little younger, drowned in a boating accident at Eagle Mountain Lake. The police uncovered, pardon the pun, a pentagram spray-painted on the wall of a mausoleum nearby, several candles at the grave site, and a hooded black robe. Speculation was that someone or something scared off the culprits. The crime was never solved. No suspects as best I can tell. Here's a note with what appears to be the investigating officer's name scribbled on it. I'll give him a call first thing in the morning and see if he remembers anything."

Jace grimaced. "If this recent episode was a repeat performance of the one two years ago, it certainly doesn't help our case. Cal will argue that, since it happened once, we should have taken steps, like having security, to keep it from happening again."

"I'll do some research on satanic cults after I talk with the officer involved. Maybe that will give us some insight."

Jace continued hypothesizing. "Moving on to possibility number two, the culprit could have been an old boyfriend or family member, someone who couldn't stand to lose Alexis, someone who had to see her one last time—to say his 'good-byes.'"

Darrin looked at Jace quizzically and shook her head. "How did you come up with that? I mean, the body was found on an altar in a church that had been desecrated, and there were all kinds of signs that devil worshipping was going on."

"I hear you. But that could have been staging to draw attention away from the actual person that committed the crime. Maybe whoever did it knew about the first incident at Caring Oaks and did a copycat of that to send the police on a wild goose chase."

"That's certainly a possibility."

"And let's not forget possibility number three: necrophilia."

Darrin's eyes grew wide and her eyebrows rose. "I can't even think about that, it makes me sick. Someone getting his kicks doing it with a corpse!"

"I know, I know. It's disgusting, but it is a possibility. It's something we have to consider."

"I'll look into it and let you know what I come up with." Darrin shuddered.

"In the meantime, I'll fly down to Austin and see what I can find out about the circumstances surrounding Alexis' death. Maybe I'll get to see Matt while I'm there."

As Jace finished his sentence, his expression turned somber. Darrin knew the look and what it meant. She had seen it many times—Jace thinking about his wife's death and the traumatic imprint it had left on his son. "Jace, are you okay?"

Jace took the cue. "I just don't get it. I can't seem to get through to him."

"He's been through a lot, Jace. Pretty tough losing your mother so suddenly at such a young age. The scars haven't healed yet. Just give him some time."

"The problem is he blames me. He acts like I killed his mother." Jace rose from his seat and walked to a corner of the conference room. His fixed his stare on a high-rise across the street. "It was an accident, for crying out loud—that's all. I wasn't driving the car ninety miles an hour on a slick interstate. Camille was."

"Didn't you and Matt see a counselor for a while? Maybe—"

"Matt didn't even give it a chance. He refused to go after the second session."

Darrin shook her head. "Man, that is tough. The thing I am having trouble with is why he blames you."

Jace turned around to face Darrin. "Darrin, you and I have been working together for years. I know we never discussed it, but surely you knew my marriage was not the best. With my trial schedule and all the traveling, I was rarely home and . . ." Jace stopped in mid-sentence, wondering whether he should continue.

"Jace, we don't have to talk about this. It's none of my business."

"No, I want to talk about it. I respect and admire you. And I need to tell somebody. It's eating me up inside."

Darrin glanced away, not wanting to cross too far over the line of the employer-employee relationship.

Jace continued. "I want you to know the truth. All of it."

"But what more is there? Camille died in a car accident. How could you have been the cause of it? How could Matt blame you?"

"On the night Camille died, we had been arguing. Neither of us realized Matt was home. He had left earlier to spend the night at a friend's but had come back to pick up something. He heard everything."

"It must have been a pretty heated argument."

"It was." Jace hesitated for a moment and then took his seat at the head of the conference table. He took a deep breath before continuing. "To sum it up, I was a shitty husband."

"Jace, you don't need to get into this—" Darrin, feeling uncomfortable, shifted in her chair.

"No. Just hear me out. You remember Katie Hofstra? The associate that worked for the firm a while back?"

"I remember Katie—very cute and outgoing." Darrin raised her eyebrows and looked at Jace. "There were some rumors floating around about why she suddenly left the firm, but I never pay any attention to firm gossip."

"Well, unfortunately, there was some truth to that rumor. Katie and I were seeing each other." He paused, letting the revelation sink in.

Although shocked, Darrin's expression gave away nothing; Katie must have been at least fifteen years younger than Jace. She had never imagined the two of them together.

"Katie was the associate assigned to the case I had in Pittsburgh."

"I remember."

"And she went with me to try it. It was a three-week trial. We worked together and let off some steam together. You can fill in the blanks."

Darrin said nothing.

"After we got back to Fort Worth, we continued to see each other. Camille sensed something, hired a detective, and had me followed. She confronted me with some photos that I couldn't explain."

Darrin bit her lip.

"There were heated arguments, which I am sure Matt overheard. Camille threatened to file for divorce and take everything I had unless Katie left the firm. Ultimately, I asked Katie to leave, which she did."

"Are you still seeing her?" Darrin's curiosity took over.

"No, she moved back home to Chicago. But the damage had been done. Our marriage wasn't worth a damn before the affair and only got worse afterwards. Camille was paranoid about everything. The night of the accident we were in the kitchen fighting over some crazy accusation she was making. I said something—I don't even remember what it was—that set her off. The next thing I knew she had grabbed her purse and keys and stormed out of the house, mad as hell. A few minutes later, Matt appeared in the kitchen. He just stared at me, shook his head, and left."

"Jace, I'm so sorry."

"No reason for you to be sorry. That's just how it is. There are still nights I can't sleep for being taunted by the 'what ifs.' What if I hadn't said whatever I did that made her so mad? What if I had stopped her from getting into her car that night?" Jace shook his head, his gaze catatonic. "I just hope Matt can forgive me and move past this."

"I'm sure he will, Jace. As I said, it will just take time."

Jace glanced at his watch. "Well, enough of my personal problems. Let's get back to Cal Connors and the Caring Oaks case."

Darrin needed a breather. "I'd like to take a break for a minute. Can I get you anything?"

"No thanks, Darrin, I'm good."

"I'll be right back." Darrin slipped out, returning a few minutes later with a bottled water. As soon as she was seated at the table, Jace continued as if their personal conversation had never happened.

"Anything else grab your attention during our meeting with Mr. Arnold?"

"I found it very interesting that Mr. Stone suspects foul play in his daughter's death. I wonder why?"

"Any parent who loses a child doesn't want it to be just a hopeless mystery. They want some sort of resolution. They don't want to think that their child just passed out and died for no reason at all."

"I suppose you're right. You should probably get into that during his deposition."

"Yes, but I want to do my homework first. I'm sure the Austin police have done a thorough investigation. I am hoping to finesse a peek at their file. Find out what you can on the Austin investigators assigned to the case."

Darrin nodded and then asked, "Do you think Alexis' death and the grave robbery could be related?"

"Certainly a possibility. I'll know more after I get a look at the police files." Jace stroked his chin, a nervous habit dating back to his prep school days.

"Well, as crazy as it sounds, we have a satanic cult, a lovesick boyfriend or family member, and a necrophiliac as possible suspects. Any other candidates?"

"I agree with ol' Wallace. It doesn't seem to me this is the handiwork of a bunch of drunken teenagers. Even if they had thought it might be cool to steal a body, they would have thrown in the towel after they hit the concrete vault."

"I agree—teenage pranksters are out." Darrin paused and then continued. "How about someone who works at Caring Oaks? They'd know how to get into a grave—no problem."

"Mr. Arnold is a weird duck but I don't see him as a suspect. But what about this embalmer? What was his name?"

"Lonnie Masterson. I'll take a close look at his personnel file and schedule an interview with him when he gets back from vacation. That should be pretty interesting. After all, how strange would you have to be to work with dead bodies for a living?"

"Pretty damn strange. But there are a lot of unappealing jobs out there. I mean, I wouldn't want to be a proctologist, would you?"

"Very funny, Jace," Darrin grinned. "By the way, do we know if anything happened to the body while it was missing?"

"Wallace would probably know since Caring Oaks did the reburial."

Darrin shook her head. "Not necessarily. If the body had been sexually molested, how would the funeral home know? Or if the body had been subtly mutilated, maybe it wouldn't have been apparent."

"Good point. Any other thoughts?"

"This is kind of iffy, but maybe someone saw her picture in the paper and developed a fixation on her. Someone she didn't even know, like a stalker."

Jace nodded. "It's possible."

"I'll see if I can get some more information on that." Darrin penned another reminder.

"Darrin, go ahead and draft subpoenas to all the law enforcement agencies involved. I want to be ready to serve those if we need them. Also, see if you can get the sign-in book of those who attended the funeral. Maybe there will be some leads in there. Also, interview the pastor who found the body. Make sure he tells you everything he remembers about that morning and whether his church has been desecrated or broken into before."

Darrin looked at Jace and tilted her head to one side. Jace knew this meant that he had missed something and was wondering what it was.

"This is all intriguing about who may have stolen the body, but aren't we losing sight of the fact that we are defending the funeral home for not having security?"

Jace smiled. "Here's my thinking on that. We have to give the jury someone else to blame. Show them who the real culprit is. If we can't give them a name, we at least need to prove that the perpetrator was someone who was so obsessed with Alexis Stone that he or she would have done whatever was necessary to get her body, regardless of the security precautions. If we can show that the perpetrator had that kind of determination and mind-set, then nothing Caring Oaks could have done would have stopped this from happening. And Cal Connors and his clients walk away with a zero verdict."

"And what if our investigation indicates someone at Caring Oaks is responsible?" Darrin asked.

"Then we're in deep shit."

CHAPTER

10

As Jace and Darrin strategized about the Caring Oaks case, Cal Connors steered his rental car toward the Brownsville South Padre International Airport, his exchange with the young female reporter lingering in his mind. There was something about the tone of her voice that bothered him. It was very confident and defiant. And although her accent seemed Texan, he couldn't be sure. Who was she anyway? What news organization did she work for? And what did she know about his workup of the case?

No doubt she was presenting the other side of the argument—that Fosorax's rewards might outweigh the risks. But Samson's trial counsel had made that argument. She was implying much more, that he, Cal Connors, knew more than he had shared with the judge and jury. But he was an advocate, a hired gun. He didn't have to disclose everything. After all, he was the champion of the common man, the Robin Hood of the twenty-first century. Without him, many an injustice would pass without consequence. Satisfied with his rationalization, Cal pressed the accelerator to the floor and turned on the radio.

As he neared the airport entrance, he looked for signs that would direct him to the private hangars. Within minutes he was pulling up next to his Learjet 60, which he had purchased several years earlier for a very pricey $10 million.

Almost 59 feet long, with a wingspan of 44 feet, it was, in his words, "elegance without equal." After buying it, he had spent over $2 million customizing the interior to suit his taste. The cabin had been gutted and redesigned to include a full-service bar, a 42-inch LCD television, a state-of-the-art Bose stereo system, and a sofa that could be converted into a king-size bed. There were two passenger seats, both of which were equipped with pullout desktops. Cal had personally detailed the remodel. He could work hard, play hard, or simply sleep while heading to his destination of choice. It was, as he affectionately called it, his "baby."

Cal's Learjet was registered under the corporate name BullsEye Enterprises, Inc. The name BullsEye was inspired by his mentor, Bobby Elam, who had kept a dartboard in his office with the bar directory photo of whatever adversary he was facing pinned over the bull's-eye. As Bobby plotted his trial strategy, he would throw dart after dart at the image, exclaiming "son of a bitch" gleefully every time the dart struck center. Bobby had given Cal a job straight out of law school, at a time when no one else would even consider hiring him due to his abysmal law school record and brash personality.

After bringing Cal on, Bobby had given him a stack of files— some divorces, some misdemeanor criminal cases, and some small personal-injury claims. In Bobby's opinion, these were all "dog" cases that would be next to impossible to win. Either the facts were bad or the law was bad—or both. The choice of cases was no accident; it was a test. If Cal could figure out a way to win some of these cases, then, in Bobby's opinion, he had what it took to be a trial lawyer. After all, trial lawyers weren't made in law school, they weren't law review editors, they weren't the "bookworm" type. They were actors, charismatic individuals who could make ice cream out of shit. And they were born that way—true salesmen from the moment they came out of their mother's womb. Sure, they had to learn some tricks along the way, but the basic chemistry was there all along. And before Bobby was willing to share any of his trial "secrets," he wanted to test the chemistry and make sure he wasn't wasting his time.

Cal lost the first three cases he tried—two car wrecks and a marijuana possession. After each loss, he interviewed every juror, making careful notes as to what factors had been instrumental in influencing that juror to decide the case against him. He continued to work up the remaining cases Bobby had given him, refusing to settle any of them. The fourth case to go to trial was a "slip and fall" personal-injury case against a convenience store. The facts were troublesome; there had been signs put up on the wall, advising of the slick floor. The plaintiff had only "soft tissue" injuries from the fall, his only medical treatment from a chiropractor. But somehow, Cal had won the case. The damages awarded were minimal, but it was a win against the odds. And it was a confidence builder. When Cal came back to the office and gave Bobby the news, his mentor knew he had found his successor and promptly gave him twenty more files—better cases, with more money involved.

Three years later Cal had tried more than 25 cases, bringing in over $5 million in fees for the two-man shop. Bobby made him a partner, and the firm's name became Elam and Connors. But the partnership was to be short-lived. Bobby died of a heart attack at 49, leaving all of his files to Cal. Saddened by the loss of his mentor but determined to make him proud, Cal kept the firm name for several years and threw himself into the practice. Within two years, he was a multimillionaire, with all the cases he could handle. He had two investigators and three paralegals on the payroll.

And the verdicts kept getting bigger and bigger. Cal built a mansion on three acres in his hometown of Fort Worth and acquired second homes in Vail and Jackson Hole. He bought a private island in the Keys. Of course, to visit all these properties he needed quick transportation, so he bought a private jet. It seemed Cal's appetite for material things was insatiable.

His tax and financial adviser recommended that he deed all of his "toys" to a corporation. If there were accidents involving the jet or vacation homes, Cal would be insulated from personal liability since the corporation would be the owner. Moreover, there might be some tax advantages to this arrangement. Cal had forced plenty of companies into bankruptcy with the big verdicts he had recovered, and he certainly did not want to replicate their fate. So BullsEye Enterprises was formed.

Cal's frenetic work schedule, and on-the-side womanizing, had cost him his first marriage, to his high school sweetheart, Mary. There had been no time for romantic dinners or getaway weekends. There had been little time for sex and, consequently, Cal had no children from that marriage.

He met his second wife, Bonnie Sullivan, at a casino in Reno. A saucy redhead of Irish descent, with an easily stoked temper and an unbridled sexual appetite, she was Cal's match in every sense of the word. She was as wild about him as he was about her, and they were married within six months. Ten months after that, Cal was a father. Bonnie gave birth to Christine Sullivan Connors, a beautiful baby with the engaging blue eyes of her dad and the striking red hair of her mother.

Fatherhood temporarily changed Cal; he spent less time at the office and gave up the one-night stands and heavy drinking. And he doted on Christine, showering her with gifts and attention. But the good times were fleeting. The law beckoned him back with a vengeance. The late hours resumed, the drinking increased, and the womanizing reared its ugly head. As a consequence, the last two years of his marriage had been turbulent and traumatic, with happiness hard to find. After a weeklong trial in Beaumont, Cal returned home to find Bonnie and his daughter gone.

Cal had pushed the envelope too far and lost the two best things in his life. He briefly considered fighting the divorce, seeking custody of his daughter, and wrangling with Bonnie over the millions he had won during their years of marriage. But he searched deep and decided to take a different road. He realized his marriage was over; there was simply too much damage to repair. But all was not lost. He had a wonderful daughter and a soon-to-be ex-wife who had deserved better and who, he correctly believed, still cared for him. So the decision was made. He would not fight the divorce, he would agree to a generous division of property, and he would try and make amends with Bonnie. Maybe that way his daughter would be spared some of the agony caused by his profligate lifestyle and erratic behavior, and maybe they would grow close over time.

His sacrifice had paid off. Bonnie was now remarried, and Cal was happy for her. His relationship with her had mellowed into a strong friendship. Bonnie, in turn, was struck by Cal's determination to compensate for his shortcomings and, more importantly, his dedication and devotion to their daughter. Although still absorbed by his law practice and still game for an occasional walk on the wild side, nothing took precedence over, or stood between, Cal and his daughter. Christine knew it, and her feelings ran as strong; not only did she love her dad, she wanted to be like him. He was her hero.

"Well, John, how is she flying?" As he spoke to his pilot, Cal walked around outside the jet, admiring the sleekness of her lines.

"As always, like a dream. Purrs like a kitten."

"Could you get my rental car back to Avis?"

"Already arranged."

"And La Villa Escondida?"

"I have alerted the caretaker. It will be ready when you and Christine arrive."

"Perfecto. You are always a step ahead of me." His visual inspection complete, Cal jogged up the stairs to the jet's entrance. He couldn't wait to see Christine and tell her all about the trial.

Cal went straight to the bar and poured himself a Dewar's over ice. He slumped down in one of the leather chairs and closed his eyes. A smile crossed his lips. In a few hours, he and Christine would be on his private island in the Florida Keys.

CHAPTER

11

The main residence at Villa Escondida was modest but tasteful. Sea-foam green in color and modern in design, it was located in the island's center. An outdoor patio and tiki bar adjoined the house. Four primitive trails led to white-sand beaches. Accessible only by water, the island was equipped with a covered docking area that housed Cal's deep-sea fishing boat, another toy acquired from his courtroom spoils. There were no televisions, no telephones, no fax machines, and no Internet. Villa Escondida was a throwback to a simpler time and place. As such, it had become a sanctuary for Cal and Christine after the mental and physical drain of a lengthy trial. It was a great place to unwind, to celebrate, to share war stories, and to strategize about the next conquest.

Christine was already in the open-air dining room sipping on a Bloody Mary when Cal shuffled in. "Hey, Lobo, you're finally up! The sun's shining, the breeze is blowing, and a Bloody Mary is calling your name." Christine lifted her glass in a toast to her dad.

Christine and Cal had arrived on the island a little after seven the previous evening. A dinner of raw oysters, baked lobster, and chocolate mousse had been waiting for them. After two bottles of pinot grigio and an animated replay of Cal's trial in Brownsville, the two had finally retired close to two in the morning. Now it was nine, and at the age of 57, Cal was having a little trouble rallying.

"How about a little breakfast. Mauricia has everything ready to make us some huevos rancheros. How good does that sound?" Christine asked.

"Fabulous! We tied one on pretty good last night, if you ask me. And your ol' man doesn't recover from a hangover as quickly as he used to."

Less than an hour later, he was on his second Bloody Mary, having devoured his breakfast. Cal looked around, admiring his surroundings. The sky was cloudless, there was a light breeze blowing, and the palm trees surrounding the outdoor patio and adjacent swimming pool swayed back and forth in graceful rhythm. The temperature was approaching 75 degrees, with the expected high in the low 80s. It was a picture-perfect day in paradise. "So, young lady, what are your plans today?"

"I think I may take the golf cart down to Playa del Christina, lie around in the hammock for a while, take an occasional dip in that crystal-blue water, maybe even drink an ice-cold Corona—just like in the commercial—and then head back to the casa for a little nap. That is, after I have a fresh seafood salad right here on this patio. It's what I call my perfect day!" Christine's eyes sparkled as she stirred her drink.

"*Absolutamente perfecto.*"

Cal and Christine were both fluent in Spanish. Several years back, Cal had spent a month in San Miguel de Allende, taking a crash course in the language for four hours a day and studying Mexican culture and art in the afternoons. Christine grew up taking Spanish in elementary and high school, and again in college.

Plus she had spent a semester in Spain during her junior year in college.

They didn't learn Spanish just for a hobby. In Texas, the jury pool was often made up of a high percentage of Hispanics, particularly in the Rio Grande Valley. In their voir dires in those venues, both Cal and Christine routinely asked questions of potential Hispanic jurors using a perfectly accented Spanish phrase or two. The bond established by that process would often yield dividends during the deliberations if that person ended up as a juror.

Christine gave her dad an innocent smile to soften her request to talk business. "Before we head that way, let me bring you up to speed on a couple of business matters. I know we aren't supposed to talk shop while we are here, but bear with me for just a few minutes." Christine cast a spell on her dad with the smile she had used so effectively on him over the years, and continued. "First, let's talk about the Caring Oaks case. I think I may have told you that Jace Forman is going to be representing the cemetery."

A grin spread across Cal's face. "Jace Forman! You know, I've only gone up against him once, and as I recall, we got a pretty hefty settlement. But he's as good a defense lawyer as they come in Fort Worth. And he's a scrapper. He doesn't have that holier-than-thou attitude most of them have. We didn't try that case, but I got the feeling he would connect well with a Fort Worth jury."

"Your instincts are right on. I did a verdict search, and it appears Mr. Forman has tried cases in a number of Texas counties and has a pretty good track record. He has won most of his cases. And the few that he lost, well, there were no big damage awards. Based on my research, the jury will like him when he walks into the courtroom, and he will have his lesson up."

"Well, well, well. This case will be a welcome change from the one I just tried. Hell, with those stiff-shirted, pompous asses on the other side, it was like shooting fish in a barrel. I still can't believe Samson didn't have the good sense to get local counsel from the

Valley to tell their story. Not that they would have won, but it might have kept the score a little closer." Cal chuckled. "If I whip Jace Forman's ass, then every other defense lawyer in Fort Worth will be even more afraid to take me on. We'll be raking in the settlement money."

"Oh, one other thing," Christine said. "Judge Reinhold has been assigned to the case."

"Keep playing that song. It's music to my ears. He owes me a favor or two. We couldn't be on a better, or more uneven, playing field." Cal rattled the ice in his glass before taking the final sip.

"Reinhold has already put the case on his rocket docket. I checked the local rules, and the cases on his rocket docket have streamlined discovery, time restrictions on depositions, and a trial setting within six months from the date the case is filed. As for the trial setting, we may have to seek a continuance. I don't know how we can be ready for trial in six months or less."

Another smile creased Cal's lips. "Trust me. We won't need a continuance. We will be ready to rock when this case is called. Ol' Judge Reinhold is settling his debt. He knows it is much harder to get ready from the defense perspective. You and I have already done most of our homework and preparation. Forman just got the petition, so he's playing catch-up. He'll be the one filing for a continuance and sweating bullets until then. No, let's leave the trial setting as is. An early setting will pay big dividends for us."

"Whatever you say."

"I still can't get over this grave robbery stuff. Like something out of a damn movie. We got any clues about who did it?"

"Honestly, Dad, I've been so busy putting out other fires while you were in trial that I haven't had time to do a lot on the case. After all, the office doesn't run itself while you are gone. With all your other cases and mine, there was plenty to do while you were in the Valley, making mincemeat out of those stuffed shirts from up east." Christine followed her response with a daring stare.

"Now, don't get testy. I know you've been busy. But we've got to get moving in light of that trial setting ol' Reinhold has graciously given us. We've got to keep the pressure on Forman and his client. And nothing keeps the pressure on a defense lawyer better than having a trial setting staring him in the face. That's for damn sure. So let's decide what needs to get done and then we can head to the beach."

"Fair enough. I have given that some thought. We have two theories of recovery against Caring Oaks. First, Caring Oaks wasn't that "caring" and didn't do enough to protect the dead from vandals, satanists, sexual perverts, and other unwanted visitors. No security guards to patrol the premises and nothing but a chain-link fence to keep the cemetery grounds safe. This was woefully inadequate and breached Caring Oaks' commitment in their brochure to provide 'perpetual care' to those interred on their grounds. We'll get an industry expert to testify that other cemeteries do more and, had Caring Oaks followed industry practice, this horrendous incident would never have occurred."

"This is good," Cal said, leaning back in his chair. "Any leads on experts?"

"I have searched the database of the American Trial Lawyers Association but haven't come up with a name yet. But that's not surprising. It's not every day you get a grave robbery."

"You got that right," Cal said. "This is the first one I've even heard about."

"I have done Internet searches, and believe it or not, this has happened before."

"What in the world would someone want a dead body for?"

"Satanic rituals, necrophilia, emotional attachment, teenage pranks—shall I go on?" Christine paused to let her reply sink in.

Cal just shook his head. "You got my attention."

Christine took a sip of her Bloody Mary. "Man, that tastes good once the ice has melted just a little—"

"All right, all right. I'm waiting."

Christine grinned. She loved to annoy her dad in a playful way. Now that he was all business, he didn't have time for small talk. "Okay, here's one. In Caracas, Venezuela, some robbers under the cover of night slipped onto the grounds of the Las Pavas cemetery. They used crowbars and sledgehammers to break into the concrete vault and coffin of a recently buried wife and mother and then stole her leg bones and skull."

Cal scowled. "You can't be serious."

"As a heart attack."

"So what did they use the bones for?"

"*Santería*." Christine waited for the follow-up.

"What in the hell is *Santería*?"

"It's some kind of cult that combines Catholicism with African and indigenous spiritualism. Those who buy the bones are called *paleros*. They use them in black-magic rituals. Our equivalent, I guess, would be voodoo. The bones are used to cast spells on unfaithful spouses, business rivals—you get my drift."

Cal ran his fingers through his long, silver mane and moaned. "I just can't believe that in the twenty-first century, people believe that crap."

"Well, they do. And according to the Catholic Church, the practice is growing, particularly in Venezuela, where good ol' Hugo Chávez is patronizing it. Seems he feels the Catholic Church is out to get him so he is trying to subvert it in that region of the world."

"So how does that fit into our case? I mean, just because it occurs in Venezuela doesn't mean it occurs here."

Christine nodded. "True, but there are many reported instances of grave robberies in the good ol' US of A. The reasons for the robberies are rarely discovered. You know why? Desecration of a corpse is only a misdemeanor in most states. Not much incentive for law enforcement to do a lengthy and expensive investigation.

Bottom line, we could have more voodoo and satanism going on here than we know."

"And our argument to the jury would be that this could easily have been prevented. I am sure it takes some time to break through a concrete vault. And I bet it's a little noisy, to say the least. So if Caring Oaks had paid a security guard minimum wage to patrol the grounds at night, this would never have happened."

"Bingo. But there is another explanation for the robbery that is even more bloodcurdling." Christine shivered. "Necrophilia—in layman's terms, sex with a corpse."

Cal didn't respond. He just stared at his daughter with a look of bewilderment.

"There are three types of necrophilia. Necrophilic homicide, or when a person murders someone to obtain a corpse he can have sex with. The second is regular necrophilia. The perpetrator doesn't kill anyone; he or she just has sex with someone who is already dead. And the last is called necrophilic fantasy. It's just what it sounds like—the person doesn't actually have sex with a corpse but merely fantasizes about it. Pretty creepy, huh?"

Again, no response. Just an inquisitive look.

"And get ready for this," Christine declared. "In a recent study of the crime of necrophilia, it was determined that, of the one hundred fifty cases reviewed, more people fit into the second category than the other two. And of those who actually molested a corpse, over half of them worked in a morgue or in the funeral industry."

Cal's reaction morphed from one of revulsion and disgust to one of triumph. "If we can prove that an employee of Caring Oaks sexually molested Alexis Stone's body, there is no limit to what I can get the jury to award."

"I hear you. But you would have to prove that management at Caring Oaks had reason to know that the employee in question might do something like that, that there was something in his or her background that should have been a red flag to Caring Oaks."

Cal rattled the remaining cubes in his glass and then drained the last sip of his drink. "Don't worry about that. If I can prove one of Caring Oaks' employees had sex with the lifeless body of Alexis Stone, it will be no problem getting a jury to make the next leap. Trust me on that." Cal locked eyes with his daughter. "I want you to subpoena the personnel files for every Caring Oaks employee who was working there when this incident occurred. I don't care what their job title was—embalmer, grave digger, janitor, it doesn't matter. If you can get me any evidence—and I mean any evidence—that one of their folks was involved in this, we'll get the biggest jury award in the history of Tarrant County."

Christine nodded. "I'll get on it when we get back."

"And Christine," Cal's eyes narrowed as he spoke. "I don't give a rat's ass whether the employee did or didn't molest the body. I just want enough evidence to get to a jury on the issue. And if I do, we'll have more private islands than the law allows. You have my word on that."

"I don't doubt you for a minute," Christine replied.

Cal pushed his chair back from the wicker table and slung a bright orange beach towel over his shoulder. "Oh, there's one thing I forgot to tell you that happened over in the Valley. After the trial, I fielded some reporters' questions from the courthouse steps, all of them softballs that I knocked out of the park until this young lady spoke up and asked me something about my conscience, whether it bothered me. I got a funny feeling about her. Her questions implied she had some dirt on me."

"Dad, I think you are imagining things. I mean, what dirt could she have? Winning is not illegal, at least not the last time I looked."

"I know, I know. But I didn't like it. Get the skinny on her, would you?"

"I'll give the court clerk a call when we get back to Fort Worth. She probably has all the info I'll need to do some background on little Ms. Reporter. Can you give me a description?"

"Short—maybe five-two or -three—glasses, brown hair, late twenties."

"I'll let you know what I come up with."

A smile crossed the Lone Wolf's lips as he extended his arm to his daughter. "Shall we, my dear?"

CHAPTER 12

After spending three weeks in Brownsville covering the *Anderson* v. *Samson Pharmaceutical*s trial, Leah Rosen was exhausted and ready to get home. Her flight did not land in Austin until almost seven. All that time in Brownsville had taken its toll—patchy sleep, chicken-fried fare, and little exercise. She needed her routine back: a good night's sleep in her own bed, a morning jog along the trail hugging the banks of Lake Austin, and healthy food from a nearby Central Market.

At this time of the evening, the cab ride to her apartment from the airport would take less than a half hour. As customary, she had checked her emails and voice mails upon landing. Her boss, Abe Levine, had called. He wanted a status report on the article she was working on. She had texted him and asked for a meeting. His reply had been a simple "ok."

A graduate of the University of Texas at Austin's school of journalism, Leah had toyed with the idea of going to law school but instead opted to take a job with the monthly publication *Texas Matters*. Headquartered in Austin, *Texas Matters* featured articles about the Lone Star State. Different divisions within the magazine covered the medical, legal, and sports professions. There was also a crime division, which wrote about sensational crimes committed within Texas's borders. Started in the late sixties by disenchanted hippies with an antiestablishment bent, the publication had begun with a cult following in the Austin area but, over time, had moderated its stance and gained widespread circulation throughout the state, catering to conservative and liberal subscribers alike.

Shortly after graduation, Leah had been offered a position in the legal division. The offer had appeal, since she could live in Austin, a city she had grown to love. In addition, the job would give her the opportunity to examine the legal profession up close, warts and all, and make a reasoned decision as to whether a career in law might be for her. Although the pay was not great, she had put away a small sum of money she inherited when her grandmother died. Not enough to live in luxury but enough to help her over any rough patches or emergencies while she figured out what she wanted to do with her life.

She had been working for *Texas Matters* for a little over five years when Abe called her in to his office to tell her she was being assigned to cover a high-profile trial in Brownsville. Prior to the assignment, she did grunt work for some of the more seasoned reporters: checking sources, doing research, and hanging out at the Travis County courthouse, trolling for story leads. The work wasn't bad, but it wasn't challenging either. The thought of covering an out-of-town trial solo set her heart racing.

The day after getting the assignment, she flew to Brownsville and headed to the Cameron County courthouse, where she reviewed the voluminous court files. She educated herself about the facts of the case and the backgrounds of the lawyers, parties, and witnesses.

Leah also did extensive Internet research on the plaintiff's lawyer in the case, Cal Connors. She learned he had a trial record that was unequaled, winning fifteen trials in the past five years alone. Interestingly, twelve of the cases had involved claims against drug manufacturers. His legal theory in all the cases had been identical: the drug companies "manufactured" clinical test data in their submissions to the Food and Drug Administration. Accordingly, the approvals obtained from the FDA were fraudulent. In each of the cases, the juries, incensed by this corporate malfeasance, returned multimillion-dollar verdicts.

Leah noted some striking similarities among these pharmaceutical cases. Without exception, they had been filed in the more impoverished and less educated Texas counties: Cameron, Hidalgo, Jefferson, Orange, Zapata, Matagorda, and Morris. These venues had reputations for big jury awards and had been cited by tort reform groups as examples of a judicial system gone wrong. In all the venues the judges were known to have a pro-plaintiff bent. Most had either been plaintiff's lawyers in private practice, been heavily supported by the local plaintiffs' bar when they ran for election, or both. All the trial judges who had presided over Cal's cases had received generous political contributions from Cal's law firm. This gave Leah pause. But that was a battle for another day. Right now, her focus was on Cal Connors.

Leah was unsure whether Abe would like the fact that her first solo story had morphed from a color feature about a trial in Brownsville to an exposé on Cal Connors involving possible legal fraud in cases throughout the entire state. She could see the story unfold in her mind—Cal Connors, a larger-than-life cowboy puppeteer pulling the strings of everyone on his stage. It had been a bull market for Cal his entire career. Not a single dip. Nothing had gone wrong, victory after victory, millions upon millions. But as her taxi made its way from the Austin airport to her lakeside condo, Leah sensed that things were about to change for the Lone Wolf, and not for the better.

The next morning, after an early morning jog along the path around Lake Austin, Leah arrived at the offices of *Texas Matters* a little before eight. She usually wore pants and a blazer to work, but today she'd opted for a brown skirt, white blouse, and high heels. Her recent job assignment made her feel more important, and she decided to dress the part. She wanted to impress her boss with her intelligence and her appearance. In her opinion, those goals were not mutually exclusive.

She had a small interior office on the seventh floor of Travis Tower, a twelve-story office building on the corner of Congress and Eighth Street. Leah opened the door of her office and found it neat and orderly, just as she had left it. There were no files stacked on the floor or strewn over her desk, only a bundle of mail that had accumulated during her out-of-town assignment. She seated herself behind the desk and pushed the mail to the corner—it would have to wait. Her meeting with Abe was in less than an hour, and she wanted to review some of her notes one last time. She reached for her MacBook Pro and, in seconds, was reading about Dr. Howell Crimm.

Dr. Crimm had a résumé equal in length to the unabridged version of *Moby Dick*—degrees from Yale undergraduate and Harvard Med, with multiple scholastic and extracurricular honors at both

CRIED FOR NO ONE

institutions. And then came the publications he had authored and co-authored, as well as the lectures and speeches he had given. They covered page after page with titles that Leah doubted few physicians could understand. She wondered where the good doctor had found the time to write all these important-sounding articles and deliver all these seemingly significant medical lectures.

Leah scrolled back to the start of Dr. Crimm's curriculum vitae. He had been born in Reading, Massachusetts, about 64 years ago. He had gone to local public schools in Reading until his sophomore year of high school, when he was awarded a full ride to Phillips Exeter Academy, a prestigious prep school in Exeter, New Hampshire. At Exeter, he had lettered in soccer, hockey, and lacrosse while graduating with honors. His impressive record earned him a scholarship to Yale, where he was a member of the exclusive Skull and Bones eating club, captain of the Bulldog varsity lacrosse team, and a Rhodes scholar. His achievements at Yale secured his admission to Harvard Medical School. Upon his graduation from Harvard, Dr. Crimm did his residency in psychiatry at Mount Sinai Hospital, in New York City. After completing his residency, he went into private practice in New York for fifteen years before being offered an endowed chair in psychiatry at Midwestern Medical School in Kansas City.

Leah sighed—sure made her résumé look skimpy. Was this guy some kind of robot? No red-blooded human being could garner all those honors, degrees, and achievements. Had he really authored all those publications? Had he really given all those lectures? Who would check? She had read about several instances of résumé fraud that had gone undetected for years, cases of top-tier corporate executives' lying about their qualifications to secure lucrative positions at publicly traded companies. Was the Dr. Crimm on paper for real, or had he fudged on some of his accomplishments?

Leah closed out of Crimm's résumé and scrolled down to view titles of the Internet articles she had found when she Googled his name. She was searching for one in particular. In her haste, she inadvertently scrolled past it, and then scrolled back. She lightly tapped the touch pad, and the article appeared on the screen. The title in bold letters appeared first: "Prominent Doctor Rebuked by Local Trial Judge." The article was over ten years old and had appeared in the *Minneapolis Messenger*. Leah quickly scanned the substance of the article. Dr. Crimm had given testimony in a trial in Minneapolis involving an electrician who'd claimed he had contracted mesothelioma, a fatal disease brought on, in most instances, from asbestos exposure in the workplace. The plaintiff had sued the manufacturer of asbestos-containing ceiling tiles he claimed to have removed to replace wiring in a number of office buildings in downtown Minneapolis. Dr. Crimm had been allowed to testify that, in his medical opinion, the plaintiff had mesothelioma. The trial judge overruled defense counsel's objection based upon Dr. Crimm's sworn assertion that he was board-certified in occupational medicine and, accordingly, eminently qualified to render opinions of this nature.

Two weeks after the jury returned a substantial verdict for the plaintiff, defense counsel submitted an affidavit of a librarian who attested that she had done a comprehensive search of the board certifications in all fifty states and that there was no board certification in occupational medicine for Howell Crimm in the public records of any of them. Confronted with this discrepancy, Dr. Crimm acknowledged by letter that he had been mistaken and withdrew his testimony. The trial judge, in turn, granted the defendant's motion for a new trial and entered an order forbidding Dr. Crimm to ever testify in his court.

Leah flagged the article and then gazed at the ceiling, wondering why Samson's defense team hadn't found it and cited it in their attempt to exclude Crimm from testifying against their client. It certainly went to his credibility and the reliability of his opinions. Her eyes returned to the screen and she leaned closer, scouring the text for clues. The *Messenger* had misspelled Dr. Crimm's name throughout the article. The print now jumped out at her: the article's repeated references were to Howell Crinn, not Howell Crimm. An Internet search of Crimm would have turned up nothing. So why had her search caught it?

One of her professors in journalism had taught her some search tricks. One of them was to try similar spellings of the name of the person being Googled to make sure all the potentially relevant articles were netted. Out of habit she had typed in several variations of the last name Crimm, one of which substituted *N*'s for *M*'s. She silently applauded her investigative work.

Her concentration was interrupted by a firm knock on the door. She glanced at her watch—nine-fifteen. She was fifteen minutes late for her meeting. Leah rose from her seat and hurried to the door, which was just opening. She nearly bumped into Abe.

"Whoa! I just came to apologize for being late. You've probably been by my office several times this morning. My seven-thirty meeting ran late. Can we meet in five?"

"Absolutely."

Abe closed the door, and Leah exhaled a sigh of relief. He did not like to be kept waiting; she had dodged a bullet. But the extra time had been valuable. She now felt confident in her research and the conclusions she had drawn about Dr. Crimm. She grabbed her laptop and a notepad and headed toward the corner office at the end of the hall.

CHAPTER

13

"So, Leah, am I going to lose you to the legal profession?" Abe smiled and motioned for her to take a seat at the conference table positioned in the corner of his spacious office. With floor to ceiling windows, Abe's office provided views of the buildings that lined Congress Avenue, as well as the panoramic hills to the west. His office was a stark contrast to Leah's, cluttered with files, scribbled-on notepads, and half-empty coffee cups. Although cleaned nightly by the building's maintenance crew, there was no evidence of it. This was due, in large part, to Abe's instructions that he did not want anything in his office moved for any reason. He had the distinct ability to put his fingers on whatever he was looking for in a matter of minutes and did not want his "system" disturbed.

"No chance after what I just went through. That statue depicting justice—you know, the lady with the blindfold on—obviously wasn't sculpted with the Texas judicial system in mind."

Leah settled into one of the conference table chairs and Abe slipped into the chair next to hers.

"Really? That bad, huh? I want to hear all about it."

Abe was more than a little relieved. When he had hired Leah, she had told him she might one day want to go to law school. Abe had appreciated her honesty, which he found to be the exception in the candidates he was interviewing just out of school. Most tried to say exactly what he, as their prospective employer, wanted to hear, even if their responses were borderline untruthful. He hoped Leah would stay with *Texas Matters*. She held real promise as a reporter, and he enjoyed working with her.

"I may need to refer to my notes, but for now I'm just going to go from memory." She moved her laptop and notepad to the side and swiveled her chair to face her boss. "Abe, I was caught totally off guard. The trial was nothing like I thought it would be. Let's see. Where to begin."

Leah took a sip of coffee from the *Texas Matters* cup Abe's secretary had discreetly placed in front of her.

"Before the trial I compiled extensive background information on the attorneys, parties, witnesses, and judge, and reviewed the court files to get an understanding of the facts of the case."

Abe nodded approvingly. "Exactly what I would have done."

"Well, to bottom-line it, I concluded before the trial even began that the fix was in. I decided the story should be an exposé on the plaintiff's attorney, Cal Connors, and not a piece on the trial."

"Whoa! Back up, Leah. I send you off on your first solo assignment to cover a trial and you come back to me with a story on one of the attorneys? I don't know what you learned about this Cal Connors, but you've got to have plenty of ammo before you can make accusations like that." Abe got up from his seat and walked to the corner of his office, gazing at the Austin hills in the distance.

"I drafted an article covering the trial only. I know that was my assignment. But I got so caught up in this Connors character.

Things just didn't pass the smell test right from the beginning, so I did some additional research, followed the leads. I thought you would be pleased I had taken some initiative and gone beyond my assignment. Isn't that what good reporters are supposed to do?"

Abe didn't want to dampen Leah's enthusiasm. After all, it was one of the reasons he had hired her in the first place. "I'm not disappointed, Leah. We just need to proceed with caution when we talk about publishing an exposé. You say 'the fix was in.' What brought you to that conclusion?"

Abe's question was all it took for Leah to recount her discoveries and idea for the story. "It wasn't just one thing. It was an accumulation of lots of information. First off, Cal Connors never loses. He files his cases in impoverished counties with poorly educated populations and judges that routinely lean toward plaintiffs in their rulings."

Abe shook his head. "So what? That's our system here in Texas. Sounds like smart lawyering to me. You use the rules to your benefit. If a lawyer has a right to file in a county that would be more sympathetic to his client, then he would be an idiot, and maybe guilty of malpractice, if he didn't take full advantage. I hope you've got more than that." Abe paced to another corner of the office, gazing out the window in a different direction, his back to Leah.

Unruffled, Leah continued. "Cal Connors—his admirers call him the Lone Wolf—has created this Robin Hood image that really sells in these venues where he practices. Guess who is the biggest financial supporter of the trial judge who presided over the case in Brownsville?" Before waiting for an answer, Leah continued. "You got it. Cal Connors."

Abe sighed. "Again, so what? In Texas, making contributions to judges you practice before is perfectly legal provided it's reported and doesn't exceed certain limits. I mean, I would likely have done the same thing. I would want any edge I could get for my client as long as it was not illegal. And the image thing—hell, I love it.

It's sheer brilliance. Persuading a jury is nothing but a form of marketing, and ol' Cal has created a brand that sells. You can't fault him for that."

Leah refused to back down. "I think the system stinks. You may think buying favorable rulings is okay, but I don't. And the hypocrisy of this man, acting like he is one of the townsfolk! It's a crock. He rented a beat-up car to drive to and from the courthouse and then flew off in his personal Learjet. I mean, come on."

Streaks of pink formed on Leah's neck, and her brown eyes narrowed. Abe sensed it was time to back off a little from the devil's advocate role. A little empathy was in order.

"I hear you. I just guess I have become somewhat jaded over the years. What you have told me pales in comparison to some of the shenanigans that go on right up Congress Avenue. Lobbyists wining and dining legislators to vote their client's way, pork being dished out like nobody's business. As the saying goes, sausage making ain't pretty, but sometimes the taste ain't so bad."

"But the sausage has turned here," snapped Leah. "I can't stomach it, and neither should this magazine." Leah paused, realizing she had overstepped. "I'm sorry, Abe. I'm coming on a little strong, but I still haven't recovered from what I learned the last few weeks."

Abe sat down behind his desk and looked at Leah sympathetically. "You are right to be upset. You are right to be indignant. The judicial system needs a fix. And I love your passion for what is right. But we are just working on an article here, and we cannot write that the fix was in just because plaintiff's counsel played by rules that we don't like."

"I know, I know. But there's more. The plaintiff's expert likely perjured himself."

Abe suddenly bolted forward in his chair. "Wait a minute! How in the world do you know that?"

"I did some Internet searches and discovered that Connors has tried twelve drug cases in the past fifteen years. He won all of them, convincing juries to award millions of dollars in each. All of the verdicts were based on expert reports from Dr. Howell Crimm, a professor of psychiatry at Midwestern Medical School, in Kansas City. Credentialed out the wazoo, degrees from Yale and Harvard. I ordered copies of every expert report from the different courts, and from the ones I have received so far, they are practically identical. Each one accused the pharmaceutical company of falsifying clinical data submitted to the FDA. Interestingly, the only drug that treated mental disorders was the one in the Samson case; the others treated physiological, not psychological, problems."

Abe's interest was now piqued. "I am beginning to see where this is going. What else did you find?"

"Dr. Howell Crimm, the author of the reports, had two research assistants at Midwestern who worked with him on some of the reports."

"Have you been able to speak with any of them?"

"I have. Dr. Coleman, his first name is Seth, was easy to locate. After med school, he moved back to his hometown of Topeka and went into private practice. I placed a call to Dr. Coleman. He was polite but protected when I asked him about his research on the court cases. I believe he worked on two of them. In response to my inquiries about the methodology that had been used, he got defensive. He was adamant that proper protocol had been followed. He then ended the phone call abruptly, saying that he had patients waiting."

"Nothing helpful there." Abe stroked his chin. "Have you had any subsequent contact with Dr. Coleman?"

"No. Quite frankly, I didn't see the point. As I said, he was very defensive on the call, almost defiant—he had done nothing wrong, his methodology would withstand peer-review scrutiny, and the data he had supplied to Dr. Crimm had been accurate. I just didn't feel another phone call would have changed anything. I doubt he would have taken my call anyway."

"Agreed. And Crimm's other assistant?"

"Patel. Dr. Sanjay Patel. He is from Mumbai, India. Came to the States for college and then med school. Speaks perfect English but with a pronounced accent."

"How did you get his contact information?"

"Midwestern keeps a database on its former students. I think the school uses it for fund-raising. They wouldn't give me any information on Dr. Patel without his consent. They offered instead that, if I would send them an email, they would forward it to Dr. Patel, who could choose whether to reply. And I did." Leah paused for a moment and took a sip of her coffee before continuing.

"He responded several days later but not by email. He called me on my cell the evening before the trial started."

"How did the conversation go?"

"Not much differently than the one I had with Dr. Coleman. He was defensive about his research. Denied any improprieties in the data he had compiled for Dr. Crimm. Seemed anxious to end the call."

"I assume you have more? I mean, seems to me all the evidence points to Dr. Crimm being on the up and up."

"There's more." Leah's eyes lit up as she continued. "I didn't hear back from Dr. Patel until the day after the jury returned its verdict. He called me. Sounded very upset. He said he had just finished reading an article in the business section of the *New York Times* about a multimillion-dollar verdict that had been rendered against Samson Pharmaceuticals. He said the article indicated that the verdict had been largely influenced by a report from the well-respected physician Dr. Howell Crimm, to the effect that the results Samson had submitted to the FDA seeking approval of Fosorax had been falsified."

"So? He would have known that when he helped Dr. Crimm with the report, right?" Abe furrowed his brow.

"According to Dr. Patel, that's not what happened at all. He researched the information provided by Samson to the FDA to determine its accuracy. Crimm asked him to go through the data with a fine-tooth comb, particularly the case reports relating to side effects. He did so, spending literally hours wading through the data and scientific findings."

"And?"

"Dr. Patel found a few minor discrepancies but overall concluded the data was accurate. He advised Crimm of that in person and then sent him a detailed email, setting out his conclusions."

"Shit. Pardon the French, but that's a game-changer. Nice work, Leah."

"Abe, I know I am pretty green and this story has gone in a direction neither of us expected. I really need your guidance as to what I should do next. I'm sure you have run across instances like this in your many years in journalism. What would you do?"

"Well, first, you have to interview Dr. Patel. And I don't mean on the phone. I mean face-to-face. Assuming Patel sticks with his story and has corroborating documents or other evidence, you will need to schedule a meeting with Dr. Crimm and give him the opportunity to offer his side of the story." He paused, staring at the ceiling. "Also, a face-to-face with Cal Connors is a must. You have to be thorough and even-handed in your investigation. All affected parties must be given their say and the chance to come forward with support for their story. Bottom line, if this isn't done right, we could face one of the biggest libel suits this magazine has ever seen."

"The problem is, I don't have an address or any other contact info for Dr. Patel. When he called me, the screen on my iPhone read 'Unknown Number.' I even considered not answering, thinking it was some salesperson who had blocked his number from my caller id. I tried to get him to give me his number, but he refused—said he would stay in touch."

"Well, do what you can to locate him. He is the key to this thing. Without his help, your story falls apart. I have no doubt you'll track him down. You are pretty resourceful when it comes to that laptop of yours."

Leah furrowed her brow. "Yeah, I know, but I have no clue whether he is still in the States or has returned to Mumbai. But there may be a way to get his number, even though it doesn't show up on caller id. I know a computer geek who graduated with me from UT. I'll check with him."

"Good idea. And it goes without saying that I want to be kept in the loop on this every step of the way. With a story like this, things could get rough."

Leah nodded. She had been so caught up in her investigation that she hadn't considered all of the angles. An uneasy feeling swept over her.

"I want to give you another contact number for me."

Leah searched through her purse and pulled out her iPhone.

"You ready?"

"Shoot."

Abe recited a number and Leah typed it in on her phone. "It's the number to a cell phone I carry with me for emergencies only. I have it with me at all times, and it's always turned on, even if I'm at the synagogue. You're in an exclusive club. The only other people who have that number are my two children."

"Abe, thanks. But I don't think—"

"Maybe I'm being a little too cautious, but I want you to be able to reach me anytime, day or night. We're in this together."

Leah was touched. "I really appreciate your support."

"My pleasure. And I really appreciate your hard work. You've done a helluva job on this. I'm very impressed, Leah." Abe shot her a smile of approval and then glanced at his watch. "Is there anything else? If not, I've got to get ready for another meeting."

"That's all for now." Leah gathered up her notepad and computer and made her way to the door, pausing before opening it. "And, Abe, thanks for trusting me with this assignment. It's opened up a whole new world for me."

As she gently shut the door, Abe sighed. He just hoped his favorite reporter wasn't in over her head.

CHAPTER
14

Jace had no trouble finding the Austin Police Department. He had gotten to know the city well during his law school years. Working part-time as a "gofer" for one of the downtown law firms, he had made the trip to the police department on countless occasions. A lot of things had changed in the capital since his graduation, but that wasn't one of them. Same drab building, same location.

Jace parked in a lot next to headquarters, paid the attendant for a full day, and hustled up the steps of the building. He took the stairs to the second floor and advised the receptionist he was there to see Officer Jackie McLaughlin. The attendant made a quick call and told him Officer McLaughlin would be with him shortly. Jace didn't have to wait long.

"Mr. Forman, Jackie McLaughlin. It's very nice to meet you."

Jackie was not at all what Jace had expected. An attractive Latina female in her mid-thirties, average height, shoulder-length dark brown hair, brown eyes framed by thick, expressive brows, and an obvious fitness buff.

Jace smiled as he extended his hand. "The pleasure is mine. I appreciate your meeting with me on such short notice."

Jackie returned the smile. "As they say, it's my job." Her tone became more businesslike. "I understand you have a subpoena for me?"

"I do." Jace reached into the inside pocket of his suit jacket and pulled out a folded document and handed it to Jackie. She unfolded it and carefully reviewed it.

After several minutes, Jackie looked up from the document. "It appears you've dotted all the I's and crossed all the T's. Why don't you follow me?" Jackie opened a door off the reception area and walked briskly down the hall. She continued the conversation as she walked. "I've got all of the department's files assembled in one of our conference rooms."

"I'm impressed. I thought I would be waiting for several hours while you and your staff pulled everything together."

"Well, it really helped that your assistant, Ms. McElroy—"

Jace politely interrupted, "McKenzie. Darrin McKenzie."

"Right. Sorry, I'm not good with names. Ms. McKenzie faxed me a copy of the subpoena yesterday. She seemed very efficient and professional. You're lucky. It's hard to get good help these days."

"I'll pass along the compliment."

Jackie stopped and opened the door to a nondescript conference room and motioned Jace inside. There were several files and two boxes in the middle of the conference room table.

"Oh, Mr. Forman, would you like a cup of coffee?"

"Please, call me Jace. And, yes, coffee would be great. Black, please."

Jackie poured two cups of coffee from the pot on the credenza next to the wall. She handed one to Jace and then took a sip from the other.

"I'm still trying to wake up this morning." Jackie took another sip. "How about a little background before you look at our files?" Without waiting for a response, Jackie continued. "As you know, this case was assigned to me. It is fairly typical that, when an unexpected death occurs—like this one, where a young person dies—the Austin PD conducts an investigation along with the medical examiner. The fact that we open an investigation does not mean we believe any criminal activity has occurred. We just want to make sure we have done our homework before any of the evidence is lost."

"I understand."

"So my partner and I went to the apartment of the decedent right after her death was reported, we inspected the premises, took some fingerprints, bagged some of the deceased's possessions—the usual procedure for an investigation of this type. The medical examiner autopsied the body and then submitted his findings. What is in this conference room are the results of our investigation and the ME's autopsy. If you do criminal defense work in Fort Worth, you're probably very familiar with how an investigation is conducted, so what I just told you might be secondhand news."

"Actually, it isn't. I have never handled a criminal case of any type in my years of practice, so this is very helpful."

"You are welcome to review the files on your own. I have another case I can work on while you're doing that. Or I can go through the files with you and explain things as we go. I do have to stay with you—departmental policy. We just can't risk having any evidence taken or altered."

"I totally understand. We follow the same practice at our firm when opposing counsel is reviewing our client's files. And I do think it would save a lot of time if we could go through the files together."

"I agree. Okay, let's get started." Jackie took a seat at the conference table and Jace slid into the chair next to hers. "Before we begin, it might help if you told me what your case is about and why it's so important that you see our department's files." Jackie turned toward Jace, her dark-brown eyes meeting his.

"I assume you are aware that the body of Alexis Stone was stolen the night after it was buried."

"I heard about it. But since that happened in another jurisdiction and had nothing to do with her death, the Austin Police Department did not get involved."

"I'm not sure you are right about there being no connection, but I'll get to that in a moment. Lackland and Olivia Stone, the parents, are suing the cemetery where Alexis was buried. That cemetery is my client."

"They are suing the cemetery? What in the world for?"

"They are alleging the cemetery should have had full-time security to watch over the dead."

"No kidding." Jackie's reply was emphatically sarcastic.

"Ain't our legal system great?"

"Pays our salaries, doesn't it?" Jackie retorted. "So how does the Austin PD fit into the picture?"

"Well, I understand the Travis County ME ruled the death accidental, but the father, Lackland Stone, insists there was foul play. I am assuming that is why your investigation is still open."

"You're right about that. I can't tell you how many calls I've gotten from that guy. They're not as frequent as they were, but he drove me crazy for a while. So what are you looking for?"

"I need to know whether her death was an accident, like the examiner found, or if there was foul play involved."

"And what does that have to do with your case?"

"If it was murder, maybe there is some connection between the murder and the theft—like maybe the murderer and the thief are one and the same. You know, the murderer is trying to cover his tracks."

Jace hesitated for a moment, searching for a reaction.

Jackie's expression revealed nothing.

Jace continued. "Maybe there was something in the casket that linked the murderer to her death. I don't know. You're the expert on crime solving, not me." He smiled.

Jackie made a face and shook her head. "I don't think you are headed in the right direction. The ME's already ruled the death accidental—"

Jace interrupted. "That's why I want to see the files—to see if there is any evidence to suggest otherwise."

"Jace, I handled the investigation. I am a thirteen-year veteran of the force. I have handled more investigations than you can count. There was nothing that we came across—nothing—that even suggested anything other than a young coed overdosing during a night of hard partying. And, believe me, with UT being in our jurisdiction, I have seen my share of student overdoses. It's very sad but more common than you would think."

"I'm not questioning your investigative work. I just think the grave robbery might add another dimension to things. If there is a connection, we might be able to help each other."

"Maybe. Okay, let me tell you what we've got." Jackie nodded toward the table, "Those boxes contain what we bagged from the decedent's apartment. Plus, there are three files—the lab file, the ME's file and our investigation file."

"So tell me about the lab file."

Jackie opened a thin manila folder and quickly flipped though it. "Well, it appears there were no blood samples taken at the scene."

"Why weren't there any samples taken at the scene?"

"Very simple. There wasn't any blood. You know, just because there's a death doesn't mean there's blood." Jackie continued. "And there were no hair samples taken."

"Why not?"

"Well, it appears the ME preliminarily concluded at the scene that Alexis' death was accidental, so the department just didn't do the things that would normally be done in a full-fledged homicide investigation. When there is no blood, no sign of a struggle, no murder weapon—the markers you would associate with a homicide—we do not waste resources and valuable time taking samples and doing other things that will have no value. We have a lot of cases that are confirmed homicides, and that's where we concentrate our resources and attention."

Jace nodded his understanding.

"There were some fingerprints taken. Three of those did not match the decedent's. Which means three different people were in the apartment at some point in time other than the decedent."

"Any indication in the file as to who those three people were?"

"No, but again, that's not unusual. If there was some indication that Alexis had been murdered, the department would have run all the traps to see if they could match the fingerprints and then interview those people. But, as I said, there was no indication of foul play so the investigation was cursory. I mean, we have lots of cases where there is evidence of criminal activity, and believe me, we do what we can to find the perpetrators in those instances. But this just wasn't one of those cases. That's it for the lab file."

Jackie put the manila folder next to the stack on the table and then picked up the next file, another thin manila folder. "The ME's file. Give me a moment." Jackie briefly studied its contents and began, "Let's see. There is a death certificate, an accompanying report from the ME, the results from the autopsy and tox screen, and photos taken during the autopsy." Jackie squinted as she reviewed a two-page report. "From the tox screen it looks like she had a blood alcohol level three times the legal limit, a high level of cocaine, and a depressant called Rohypnol."

"And what does the ME list as the cause of death on the death certificate?"

Jackie flipped back to the death certificate. "Cardiac arrest."

"That seems to conflict with the tox results showing she died of an overdose."

"Not really. When someone overdoses, their heart actually stops beating, so listing cardiac arrest as the cause of death is technically correct."

"Do you think it could have been suicide?"

"That is a possibility but not a certainty. She could have accidentally overdosed."

"Does this rule out murder?"

"Most likely. But not a lesser charge like voluntary manslaughter. Ever heard of roofies or ropies?"

Jace shook his head.

"Sometimes they're referred to as the date-rape drug. The trade name of the drug is Rohypnol. It's manufactured by Roche." Jackie searched Jace's face for recognition.

"Yeah, I've heard of it. Guys slipping something into their dates' drinks to loosen 'em up a little."

"It's doesn't just loosen you up, it actually knocks you out and you wake up not remembering much of what happened."

"And the tox screen indicated Rohypnol was found in Alexis' bloodstream?"

"Correct. We do know that roofies are commonly used on college campuses, particularly in this area. They're smuggled in from Mexico."

"Maybe that's why Lackland Stone has been so insistent on the investigation continuing. He probably has convinced himself that this wasn't an accidental overdose."

"I assume you will get a chance to ask him that in your case." Jackie glanced at her watch. "Look, I've got to get going. I have a meeting with a prosecutor in a few minutes. I can be back around two. That will give us the rest of the afternoon to look at what we bagged from Alexis' apartment and review the notes taken during our interviews. Work for you?"

"Sure. Any place to eat around here?"

"Nothing great. There's a cafeteria in the basement and a greasy spoon two doors down."

"Just what I need—another chicken-fried steak with some hundred-weight gravy. My cholesterol count is already off the charts."

"Sorry, but that's the best I can do." Jackie pushed her chair away from the table and stood. She looked at Jace apologetically. "I hate to do this to you, but I can't leave you alone with the files."

"I understand," Jace replied as he rose from his chair and followed her out of the conference room.

When they got to the reception area, Jackie stopped and extended her hand again. "I look forward to seeing you back here at two." Without waiting for a response, she then disappeared through the door behind the receptionist.

CHAPTER

15

At just after two, Jackie and Jace were back at the conference room table. Jackie motioned toward the two boxes in front of them. "Shall we?"

"Looks like they are labeled by room?"

"Really? You must have gone to Harvard." Jackie smiled as she cut the tape sealing the box marked "living room." She leaned against the table, removed the top of the box, and peered inside. Jace stood right beside her, to make sure he didn't miss anything.

"Each item should be marked by location and then identified with a number. Let's see what we have here."

She reached in the box and pulled out three plastic bags—one containing a crystal wine goblet, one a Shiner longneck bottle, and the last one a short whiskey glass. She held them up, one by one, toward the fluorescent light for inspection and passed them to Jace.

"Well, they're properly marked. Some of the prints I referred to this morning were taken from these. You know how prints are lifted, don't you?" She looked at Jace for a response.

"Generally, but not really. As I previously mentioned, I don't do any criminal defense work, so I haven't had to get into that kind of stuff. I have picked up a few things from some of the crime shows but don't know how accurate they are. Hollywood has been known to take a few liberties."

"You got that right. Well, how about a short tutorial?"

"You're on."

"There are three basic types of fingerprints: plastic, visible, and latent. The prints they found on these glasses were likely latent prints left by natural body secretions, such as sweat. They are lifted from the source by 'dusting.' You've seen them do it on *CSI*."

Jackie looked at Jace, waiting for an acknowledgment.

"Those shows are pretty hard for me to stomach. If you've seen one, you've seen them all. But obviously a lot of people like them. Otherwise they wouldn't be on every day of the week. Let's see, there's *CSI Miami, CSI Las Vegas,* and *CSI New York*. Am I missing any? Oh yeah, and *NCIS*, which is a carbon copy of the others with a naval twist. They're pretty formulaic. The few times I've watched them I've felt like I was playing a game of Clue. Hmm, was it Professor Plum in the study with a knife or Colonel Mustard in the dining room with a rope?"

"Those shows are like Chinese water torture if you are in law enforcement. I mean, what police department has a big enough budget to afford all that technology, assuming all those bells and whistles even existed? I'd rather curl up on the couch with a good book."

"I haven't had time to read in so long. Too many distractions." Jace ran his fingers through his hair, as if to remove some of his troubling thoughts. "But please continue with your class on fingerprints."

"As I was saying," Jackie continued, "visible prints are exactly that. For example, if a crime perpetrator got the victim's blood on his finger and then touched something, it would leave a visible print. And then there's the plastic print. It's actually a lasting impression made on a substance. Remember when you played with Silly Putty, pressing down on comic strips to capture the image? Well, the fingerprint you made when you pressed down would classify as a plastic print. Get my drift?"

"I never played with Silly Putty."

Jackie rolled her eyes, reached in the box, and retrieved another plastic bag, this one containing an ashtray. "There were probably more prints lifted off this. And they would be?"

"Latent prints."

"Excellent!"

Jackie pulled another transparent bag out of the box and held it up to the light, squinting as she looked at it from different angles. "Ah, yes, this is the Zippo lighter we found on the coffee table in the living room. It was right next to the ashtray. It's hard to forget—so unusual, with the number thirteen inscribed on one side and a buxom female on the other."

"Could I take a look?"

"Sure, just don't take it out of the bag."

"I wasn't planning on it."

Jackie handed the bag to Jace, who went through the same exercise Jackie had, holding it up to the lone light in the conference room and inspecting it from every angle. As he looked at the lighter through the plastic, his eyes widened. It couldn't be! Matt's high school girlfriend had given him a Zippo lighter at the beginning of his high school senior year. It had a Vargas Girl on one side and the number thirteen—Matt's football jersey number—engraved on the other. Matt had talked about it frequently, making sure he put it in his locker before every game—called it his good-luck charm.

Jace continued to stare at the lighter, speechless. How could it have ended up in Alexis Stone's apartment? Could it have been someone else's? But then again, what were the odds of that happening? It had to be his son's.

"Anything wrong?"

"Must have been that chicken-fried steak I had for lunch."

There was no doubt the lighter belonged to Matt. But Jackie didn't know that. And Jace didn't intend to tell her. His focus now turned to what other evidence the police might have that could incriminate Matt. If he discovered evidence favorable to his defense in the Caring Oaks case, that would be an added bonus, but that was not his main concern. If his son had had something to do with Alexis' death, he needed to know, sooner rather than later. And for now, any evidence that might incriminate his son needed to remain his secret.

Jace found some comfort in the fact that the lighter was buried in a box currently housed in the police evidence room along with thousands of other boxes of evidence relating to thousands of other cases. Maybe the police would never connect the dots. Jace couldn't count on that, but he could sure hope. Game face on, he placed the evidence bag containing the lighter on the table, his eyes expressing interest but not concern.

"What else is in there?"

In response Jackie extracted a large bag containing a multicolored, Indian-style blanket.

"Why in the world did you bag that?"

"As I recall, it was wrinkled up on the couch. Looked like it may have been used on the night of the girl's death. As I told you at the start, we wanted to make sure we bagged any evidence that might be relevant later. We didn't ask the lab to take any fibers. But, since we have this throw, they can still do that. Then, if a fiber from this throw matches one found on a clothing article of a suspect, that's just one more piece of the puzzle."

"Anything else in there?" Jace looked over Jackie's shoulder into the box.

"I think that's it, except for the inventory of everything that was in the room." She quickly surveyed the list. "Nothing remarkable. Couch, stereo, television—the usual stuff you would find in an apartment living room. Oh, there is one other item in here," Jackie said as she extracted an envelope containing photographs. "We took photographs of all the rooms in the apartment to capture what they looked like when we arrived. You can look over my shoulder."

Jace couldn't get any closer without being in Jackie's lap so he simply reshuffled his feet and tried to get the best view of the photographs that he could.

"Let's see. Well, the throw is strewed haphazardly across the couch. See what I mean?" She pointed to the picture. "Looks like there may have been some hanky-panky on the sofa or someone decided to take a little snooze. And doesn't look like there is anything out of order in the kitchen," Jackie surmised as she shuffled to the next photo. "No dirty dishes—spick and span."

Jace rubbed his palms together absentmindedly. There would be no more unreturned telephone calls. There would be no more messages left. Jace would head to Matt's apartment the minute his meeting with Jackie was over. If Matt wasn't there, he would wait until he returned. There was no time to waste—Matt had some explaining to do. Jace sat down in the chair next to where Jackie was standing and scribbled some unintelligible notes on a yellow pad.

"Shall we go to box number two or do you need a minute to finish up your notes?" Jackie inquired as she tried to make out what Jace had just written.

"I'm ready. Just jotting down a few things I need to follow up on when I get back to the office."

"Not a problem." Jackie cut the tape and began to review the contents of the box marked "Bedroom." "First we have some books. Never heard of this one. *The Ravishing of Beauty*, by Anne . . . I can't pronounce the last name. Let's see."

The books were in large individual plastic pouches, which allowed enough space to review their contents without removing them from the plastic. Jackie began to browse through the pages.

"Why in the world did you take her books?"

"Just a minute." Jackie continued to read. "Oh, I remember now."

She handed it to Jace.

"Read a few pages and you may be able to answer your own question. But to shortcut it, people's personal habits, like the books they read, may reveal important clues about the kind of lifestyle they led. In this instance, the book you're currently look-ing at—and may I add, rather intently—reveals some unusual sexual tastes, like bondage. Sometimes people get carried away with that and the next thing you know we have a homicide on our hands."

Jace looked up from his reading. "But we don't have any evi-dence of that here."

"I know, I know. But this may tell us a lot about the company she kept. And don't forget she was the victim of a grave robbery. There might be some link between perverted sex and the grave rob-bery. Who knows at this point?"

Jace's mind was now spinning out of control. Given the stress Matt had been under with the death of his mother, there was no telling what he could have gotten into. Jace felt the walls closing in on him. He had to get out of there as soon as he could.

Jackie pulled out several more books.

"All Anne Rice novels. Maybe she was into the occult."

"Interesting. The occult. Grave robbery. Desecration of the church where the body was found. Maybe there is a connection." Jace's thoughts temporarily switched from Matt to his case, the original reason he had scheduled the evidence review.

"Anything else in there other than books?" Jace asked as he glanced at his watch.

"Patience, please."

Jackie pursed her lips and gave Jace a pained look that needed no interpretation. She then held up a plastic bag containing a framed photograph. She handed the plastic bag to Jace.

Jace pulled the plastic taut to get a better view of the photograph. It depicted two girls on a beach, sporting string bikinis and holding umbrella drinks. Jace recognized Alexis as one of the girls in the picture.

"Alexis Stone is one of the girls. I don't recognize her friend. Is there any way we can take this photo out of the frame and see if there is any reference on the back?" Jace asked as he handed the photograph back to Jackie.

"Not without putting on gloves. Don't want to contaminate the evidence with additional fingerprints. Criminal defense lawyers love it when that happens."

Jackie pulled a pair of plastic gloves out of her pocket. "I thought we might need these," she said as she pulled them on and removed the photograph from the plastic. With some difficulty she managed to extract the photograph from its frame and, turning it over, read the words on the back side.

"Hmm. This was probably a gift from the girl in the photo to Alexis. The inscription reads 'To my BFF, Love Sloan.' And it has the date—June of last year."

"BFF? What in the world does that mean?" Jace inquired.

"You obviously don't have a daughter, and you obviously aren't familiar with texting."

"Right on both counts."

"BFF is short for 'best friend forever.' It is used all the time in texting."

"Mind if I jot down the BFF's name?"

"Be my guest."

This time, Jace's note was totally legible as he jotted down the name of Alexis' friend.

Jackie placed the photograph back into its frame and plastic bag, then peeled off the gloves and tossed them to the side of the table. Next, she pulled out a plastic bag with several over-the-counter bottles inside.

"These are the medications we found in her bathroom cabinet—Advil, Extra Strength Tylenol, Midol, and Alka-Seltzer. Interestingly, there are no prescription medications of any kind. Makes you wonder where she got the tranquilizers, doesn't it?"

Jackie raised her eyebrows as she gave Jace a sideways glance. She then peered in the box to make sure there was nothing left to discuss. Satisfied, she turned her attention to the manila folder tabbed "Interviews."

"This contains the notes from the interviews we conducted of the cleaning lady and the Stones."

"I would really like copies of those statements and photos. And it would be nice to get copies of the lab results as well. I believe the subpoena covers all of these items."

"Anything else on your wish list?"

"Not that I can think of right now."

"I'll have to talk to legal, let them review the subpoena and make sure you can have copies. I'd make them for you now, but the file is still open."

"I understand. Let me know as soon as possible if there are any problems so I can—"

"I know, take it up with the judge. Look, it seems everything is good to go, but I just need to cover myself."

Jace smiled. "I understand. And thank you for your help. It's been a pleasure meeting you, Jackie. One other thing. Once I get the copies of your files, would you mind if I called you if any questions come up?"

Jackie smiled. "Not at all, provided you agree to let me know if you find anything that might help me finally close this case."

"Done." Jace fished for a card in the side pocket of his briefcase. Locating one, he handed it to Jackie. "My office and cell phone numbers are on there."

Jackie looked at the card and set it on the table next to the files and boxes.

Jace grabbed his briefcase and headed toward the conference room door, pausing momentarily to glance over his shoulder before exiting. "I really do appreciate all your help. Maybe we could do a quick dinner next time I'm in Austin—like I said, I don't know anything about criminal investigations. And that's sort of what I'm doing with this grave robbery stuff. I might be able to use some of your professional expertise."

"That might work," Jackie shot him a promising look. "Have a safe trip back to Fort Worth."

CHAPTER

16

Jace walked in a daze toward the parking lot. He passed his rental car and continued on to the far side of the lot before he realized where he was. Retracing his steps, he mentally chastised himself for losing control and letting his mind race. This was no time to panic. He had to focus, rationally analyze the situation.

He stopped in front of the burgundy Chevrolet Caprice and confirmed it was his rental by pushing the unlock button on the key fob. Sliding behind the wheel, he took a deep breath as he turned the key.

Before putting the car in gear, Jace tried to gather his thoughts. He had a mental picture of Jackie solemnly inspecting the cigarette lighter from every angle, looking for distinguishing characteristics. He pictured the Zippo lighter with the custom engraving on one side and the Vargas Girl on the other. He could clearly see the bold inscription of the number thirteen. It was Matt's lighter, no doubt about it. How in the hell did that lighter get in Alexis Stone's apartment?

Jace pulled his cell phone from his jacket pocket and speed-dialed Matt. After three rings his call went to voice mail. He decided to leave a message: "I know you hate my guts right now. I know you have been avoiding my calls. And I know why. But something has come up and I need to talk to you. Not next week, not tomorrow, but right now. This is damn important and I'm not shitting you. Call me back the minute you get this. I mean it."

Jace stuffed the phone back in his pocket, exited the lot, and headed for Matt's apartment complex just off Red River. Within minutes, his ringtone sounded.

"Matt?"

"Yeah, Dad. What's so important?"

"Where are you right now?"

"At the frat house. Some pledge stuff."

"Tell your frat brothers something has come up. You and I need to meet asap."

"When did you get to Austin?"

"This morning."

"What for?"

"That's not important. What is important is that we meet as soon as possible."

"Well, if it's to talk about why I haven't been calling you back, I'm not up—"

"It's not about that. Believe me, you've made your feelings towards me crystal clear in that regard."

"So why all the secrecy?"

"Not over the phone. Have you eaten yet?"

"It's not even five. Of course I haven't eaten."

Jace ignored his son's sassy tone. "Okay, let's meet at El Arroyo. I'll see you there in fifteen minutes."

Jace ended the call without waiting for confirmation. He made a right turn at the next light and headed toward West Fifth Street.

On his way, he dialed Darrin's number. She answered on the first ring.

"Darrin McKenzie."

"What's going on?" Jace's voice was stern.

"Why so serious?"

"Long story. I'll fill you in when I get back." Maybe he would, maybe he wouldn't. But that was the easy way to move away from the topic. "So anything on the Caring Oaks front?"

"You are not going to believe this, but we received an order from Judge Reinhold setting the case for trial in six months."

"You've got to be shitting me!"

"I wish I was. And it looks like a continuance is out of the question. The last sentence in the order clearly states there will be no continuances."

"I can't believe that asshole would set the case so soon. We can't be ready for trial by then."

"I know! I've got a lot of irons in the fire on this case, but, obviously, time is not on our side."

"Any other developments?"

"Well, I talked to our investigator about using his sources to get Alexis Stone's cell phone records for six months prior to her death. We'll be able to see all the numbers for both incoming and outgoing calls and then cross-reference them to names, assuming the numbers are not unlisted. And . . ." Darrin hesitated for effect, "we just might be able to recover any voice mails. There's a possibility that even after the messages are erased, the phone company stores them on some type of backup. It's kinda like emails people think they have deleted, only to learn they were stored on a server."

"I sure would like to know all the people she talked to the week before she died."

"No kidding. Crime stats indicate that most murderers know their victims. So chances are if Alexis was murdered, a big 'if,' the murderer probably called her within days or hours of her death."

"When will we have that info?"

"Within the next few weeks." Darrin took a breath. "I also talked with the Tarrant County Sheriff's Department to see what they would tell me about finding Alexis' body. Seemed like a Mayberry operation to me, and, as luck would have it, the investigator assigned to the case is Barney Fife. He was clueless. No leads whatsoever."

"He had nothing at all?" Jace asked.

"I did manage to pry out of him the type of tests they did on the body after it was found at the church. Apparently they checked to see whether there was any evidence of molestation."

"And?"

"The tests were inconclusive, whatever that means. They did find one interesting tidbit. A large symbol was drawn in black ink on her stomach."

"What type of symbol?"

"I can't be sure, but from the description he gave me, it sounded like a pentagram—you know, a five-pointed star associated with devil worship."

"Well, that would fit in with where they found the body, wouldn't it?"

"It would. A small rural church desecrated with paint referencing the devil. I would say it's a perfect fit. A little too perfect, if you ask me."

"Does Deputy Fife think a satanic cult stole the body?"

"He doesn't know and I can guarantee you he won't find out. He doesn't have the know-how or inclination. All he kept talking about was how understaffed and busy his department was. He did tell me that the same church had been vandalized several times over the past few months. He thought it was white supremacists until the body of a 'white girl' was found on the altar."

"Have you had a chance to interview the pastor who found her?"

"Bad news there. He said he told the sheriff's deputies every-thing he knows. He declined to be interviewed. So, if we want to talk to him, we will have to subpoena him."

"Let's hold off on that for now. I would rather have him talk to us voluntarily than piss him off by serving him with a subpoena."

"I agree. I've done some other digging and have found out some interesting things about satanic cults. Some guy named Anton Szandor LaVey wrote a book called *The Satanic Bible*. It lays out the philosophies of satanism. At one point in the book, he legitimizes human sacrifice. I purchased a copy of the book for our reference."

Jace could hear Darrin's chair swivel as she turned to retrieve the book.

"Let's see." Darrin flipped to a yellow sticky that marked one of the pages. "And I quote: 'Satan represents all the so-called sins, as they all lead to physical, mental or emotional gratification.' It goes on to say that 'anyone who has wronged you is fit and proper for human sacrifice.'"

Jace pulled into the parking lot at El Arroyo, eased into one of the empty spaces, and killed the engine. "Man, that's awful. Any reports of crimes linked with satanic rituals?"

"I have a printout from the Internet on that topic—runs the gamut, from hanging cats to molesting children. Some weird stuff in there."

"How about grave robbing?"

"It's in there too. As well as murdering former cult members if they decide satanism is a bunch of malarkey and opt to leave the group."

"And how does the pentagram tie in with their worship?"

"The five-pointed star is positioned with two points up to sym-bolize the devil's horns. As a matter of interest, the pentagram was found at the scene of several of the Night Stalker murders out in California. Remember that Ramirez character who was accused of fourteen murders?"

"Vaguely."

"Well, anyway, he raised his hand in the courtroom to reveal a pentagram etched in his palm."

"What would a satanic cult do with a dead body?"

"Can't say. But some cults—actually 'gangs' would be a better word for them—purportedly require sex with a corpse as a rite of passage."

"Are you serious?"

"Dead serious. Pardon the pun," Darrin laughed.

Jace heard the sound of Darrin flipping through more pages.

"I did a little research on necrophilia. You wouldn't believe the stuff some of these sickos have posted on the web."

"What kind of stuff?"

"They talk about how you can do whatever you want to a dead person because she'll never complain. All you need is a little Vaseline and some protection and the pleasure's all yours."

Jace grimaced in disgust. "You're kiddin' me."

"I speak the truth. They even suggest making sure the grave is covered with freshly turned dirt and non-wilting flowers. That way you're assured the body is not decaying—still ripe for passionate lovemaking."

"Do these perverts know their victims?"

"Sometimes they do, sometimes they don't."

"What about their psychological makeup?"

"Loners in many instances. Can't find a living mate so they opt for a dead one. That's one category. Then there are those who have suffered a painful rejection and don't want to experience it again. We can't leave out priests or monks—those whose beliefs require a monogamous lifestyle. And then—you won't want to hear this— embalmers, which doesn't surprise me. I mean, after all, you'd have to be one weird duck to want to do that job."

Jace scoured the parking lot, trying to spot Matt's Blazer.

"There was also a case reported of an obsessed boyfriend who just couldn't let his lover go. So he dug up her body, drove two hundred miles from Nashville to Memphis, his dead girlfriend in the passenger seat, rented a hotel room at the Holiday Inn just across the Mississippi from downtown Memphis, and moved in with her."

"So how did that end?"

"He finally turned himself in, pleaded guilty to molestation of a corpse, and spent several months in a low-security psychiatric prison just outside Nashville. Now he's back out, probably still thinking about that girlfriend."

"You know, Darrin, I got into civil law thinking I would do straight-up business litigation, hoping I'd never have to deal with this kind of madness."

Darrin chuckled. "Well, you're in the middle of it now."

"I sure as hell am," said Jace as he noticed Matt's Blazer pulling into the parking lot. "Well, I gotta run."

"Good luck!" Darrin said, knowing Jace would need it.

CHAPTER

17

Jace got out of his rental car and walked rapidly toward his son. The two exchanged an awkward embrace and then headed inside the restaurant. After being seated and ordering two beers, Jace got right to the point.

"Look, Matt, I know you blame me for your mother's death and there is nothing I can do about that right now. But something has come up that we've got to deal with and we don't have the luxury of time."

Father and son's eyes met. Matt nodded for his dad to continue.

"Tell me about your relationship with Alexis Stone."

Matt's eyes widened. "I don't know what you're talking about."

"Come on, Matt. I'd at least like the courtesy of the truth, especially when I'm trying to help you. Let me prompt your memory. Alexis Stone died in her apartment in Austin. She was buried in a Fort Worth cemetery—Caring Oaks, a client of mine."

Matt was ashen. He said nothing.

"I assume you are aware that her body was stolen from the cemetery?"

Matt stared at an imaginary spot on the table and still said nothing.

Jace continued. "Still no response? Okay, I'll continue. Without getting into the legal issues, the parents of Alexis have sued my clients. But that's not why I'm here. I'm here because I was going through the Austin PD's investigative file on Alexis' death, and your lighter was part of the physical evidence."

Matt was finally shocked into a response. "Holy shit!"

"Holy shit is right. It was in a plastic evidence bag—Vargas Girl on one side and the number thirteen on the other. So I have to ask, did you know Alexis Stone?"

"Yeah." Matt began to slowly turn the Pacifico longneck in front of him. The waiter taking their order momentarily interrupted their discussion. Jace immediately resumed his questioning after the waiter left.

"How well did you know her?"

"I knew her."

"Matt, I'd appreciate a little cooperation. If you can't tell, I'm trying to help you."

"It sounds like you're accusing me."

"Don't be ridiculous, Matt. I'm just trying to find out what happened here and make sure we avoid any problems that may come up on this."

Matt desperately wanted to talk to someone, but he was afraid. "If I talk to you, will it be, like, covered by the attorney privilege?"

Jace shifted in his chair. He wasn't sure of the answer to Matt's question, being unfamiliar with the finer points of criminal law, but he answered anyway. "Anything we talk about is covered by the attorney-client privilege, if that's what you're asking."

Matt's shoulders lowered as he sighed in relief. "Dad, I've been wanting to talk to you about this since it happened, but I was so scared, and the whole thing has just freaked me out. I thought it would go away and then I find out you are defending the case! I knew it was just a matter of time before it came back to me. Can you represent me?"

"Whoa, slow down. Who said anything about you needing representation? Let's just talk about what happened and we can figure out where to go from there."

"I didn't kill her!"

"I'm sure you didn't. Let's just start at the beginning. Tell me all about your relationship with Alexis—when you first met her, when you last saw her, and everything in between."

Matt relayed the facts, with his father interrupting him several times to ask additional questions. When he was finished, Jace let out a sigh of relief. If Matt was telling the truth, Alexis was asleep on the couch when he left her apartment. He had to challenge him, though, to see how strong his story was. "You got to be kiddin' me. A beautiful girl is passed out on the couch next to you and you don't try anything. Come on."

"Well, Dad, maybe I'm not like you. Maybe I know when to keep my dick in my pants."

Jace let it go. "So the two of you didn't have sex?"

"No, we didn't. I swear. She was helpless, for crying out loud. It wouldn't have been right."

"So when did you find out she was dead?"

"The next day. I can't remember exactly."

"So why didn't you call me?"

Matt hesitated. He stared at his food and then looked up at his dad. "I thought about it. I even dialed your cell once, but I just couldn't do it. I just couldn't. Not after what you did to Mom."

Jace had no response. He waited for his son to continue.

"So I mentally retraced my night with Alexis. I went over everything that happened. No one knew I had been out with her that night. We didn't see anyone we knew at Chuy's or the Broken Spoke. There was no security guard at her apartment, just the coded gate. I didn't think I had left anything in her apartment. Now I know I was wrong about that. But I haven't done a damn thing wrong."

"So you decided to keep it to yourself?"

"The police weren't knocking on my door so, yeah, that's what I decided to do."

Jace leaned back in his chair and stared at the ceiling. "Okay, let me tell you what I know."

Matt leaned forward, his eyes fixed on his dad.

"This lawsuit, the one I'm working on, may ignite a renewed interest in how Alexis died."

"I read the coroner determined her death was accidental," Matt said pleadingly.

"He did. That being said, whenever a lawsuit's filed, depositions are taken, files are reviewed, people are interviewed. That's what's happening in this case. Just like what I did today when I made a trip to the Austin PD to look at the investigative files. I thought I might find something that would be helpful to my client's defense. Little did I know I would find that you had gone out with Alexis on the night she died."

Matt looked down and sighed. "So what should I do now?"

Jace responded without hesitation. "Just what you've done so far. Nothing. Don't talk with anyone about this. You haven't, have you?"

Matt shook his head. "Nobody. You don't think I should go to the police—tell 'em what I just told you."

"I wouldn't do that just yet. Look, they will have questions as to why you didn't come forward sooner. They might try to put you on the hot seat. We just don't know. I think for now, you do just what you have been doing—nothing. If the time comes when

I think you need to come forward, we'll hire a buddy of mine who just happens to be the best criminal attorney in the state."

"That sounds like a good plan. Dad, I want your honest opinion on this. No bullshit, okay?"

Jace nodded.

"Am I in trouble? Could I get charged with anything?"

Jace looked his son straight in the eye. "Over my dead body."

Matt swallowed hard. "Thanks, Dad. It means a lot that you're here."

"Always, Matt. Always."

CHAPTER

18

Leah woke before her alarm sounded. She turned the clock toward her and squinted at the dimly lit digits—5:03. Ugh, too early to get up. She rolled over and squeezed the pillow, weighing her only two options. She could toss and turn for another two hours until her alarm sounded, thoughts of Cal Connors, Howell Crimm, and Sanjay Patel circling around in her head, or she could get up and be a zombie for the rest of the day. Undecided, she stumbled out of bed, shuffled to the window, and took a peek at the world outside. The lights along the trail were still on, silhouetting a few early risers making their morning runs. Her decision was made. No more sleep today.

Five minutes into her jog, the chaos and clutter of the previous month began to give way to a welcome feeling of calmness and control. This always happened when she exercised. She had read reports that the brain naturally produced serotonin and dopamine during exercise, and her experience told her it was true. Her life was simply too stressful, particularly now, to skip a regimen she knew would keep everything in balance, both mentally and physically.

As she picked up the pace, she thought about Sanjay Patel. Leah's techie friend from college had loaded software onto her cell phone that would enable her to see unknown numbers. But, she wondered, would Dr. Patel keep his promise and call her? If he didn't call, her story was dead—and Cal Connors would win, again. She just couldn't let that happen.

Her jog took the usual thirty minutes. Once back in her apartment, Leah made a beeline for the iPhone on her bedside table. She had two missed calls and one voice mail. She eyed the two numbers, neither of which she recognized. She lightly tapped on the voicemail icon and held the phone to her ear as the message began. The accent was unmistakable. It was Dr. Patel.

"Ms. Rosen, I know this will be a disappointment to you, but I will not be able to assist you in your investigation any further. For personal reasons I must decline. I trust you understand. Hopefully, you will be able to pursue some other avenue to discover the truth. Sorry to leave this news on a voice mail, but I felt the sooner you knew, the better. I wish you the best in your pursuits."

Leah stared into space. Her worst fears had come true. Yes, he had called, but the pressure had gotten to him. How could he live with the fact that Cal, and his former professor, were basically using the Texas judicial system to steal money? How could he? She scrolled back to the call history. The phone number had a 615 area code. She did a quick Internet search. It was the area code for Nashville, Tennessee. Dr. Patel was still in the States! She repressed the urge to call him. She needed to think this through—carefully. And she needed a sounding board. Abe usually got to the office around 8:00. She looked at her Ironman watch—6:50. She would take a shower and be there when he arrived. Maybe her story wasn't dead after all.

As soon as Leah arrived in the office she headed straight for Abe's office. She knocked on his door and waited impatiently for a response.

"Come in," Abe shouted as he looked up from his computer, coffee cup in hand. Leah entered, causing a subtle smile to crease Abe's lips. "Well, what a pleasant surprise. To what do I owe this honor?"

"Morning, Abe. Sorry to interrupt so early, but I really need your help."

Abe smiled. "No interruption. What can I do for you?"

Leah put her iPhone on speaker and placed it in the middle of Abe's desk. As the message played, neither said a word, their eyes occasionally darting from the phone to each other. When the message finished, Leah spoke. "So, what do you think?"

In routine fashion, Abe rose and made his way to the corner of his office, his gaze fixed on some point across the street, his mind elsewhere. "Well, it's not what we wanted, but it could be a lot worse." Abe turned toward Leah. "The good news is we are better off than we were the last time we met. At least he called." Abe reached for his coffee cup and took a sip.

"I suppose you're right. Plus, I've got Dr. Patel's number." Leah picked up her phone and looked at the call history. "It's a 615 area code, which is the code for Nashville, Tennessee."

"Now we have something to work with. The first pieces of our jigsaw are fitting together. I assume you have not called him back."

"No, I wanted to get your ideas before I did anything."

Leah hoped it didn't appear to Abe that she was trying to flatter him. That wasn't her game at all. She had never been in this type of situation before and needed direction from an old hand.

"First, he likely has caller id on his cell and will know it's you if you call him back. He might not take the call."

Leah nodded. "I thought of that. I'm hoping he feels some obligation to explain his decision to me rather than leave me hanging. I mean, that's the least he should do."

"I hear you. But I wouldn't count on it. I may have imagined it, but I sensed a lot of tension in his voice. I have my doubts as to whether he will answer when you call. He may just let you go to voice mail. But we won't know until you give it a try."

"Let's assume that he does take the call. How should I handle it? What should I say?"

"Be empathetic and nonjudgmental. Tell him you understand his reluctance in getting involved in something like this. Try to get him to talk, open up to you. Find out if he is concerned about his family, his career, or something else. We have no idea at this point. We know very little about him. But we do know one very important thing. That article in the *Times* got to him. He was outraged that Crimm took his data, disregarded it, and then lied to secure a big verdict. That obviously really bothered him or he never would have called you in the first place. You have to resurrect those feelings of indignation—give his conscience a wake-up call, but in a gentle, understanding way."

"I hope I can pull it off."

"I have no doubt about it. Dr. Patel just graduated from Midwestern Med School, right?"

"Your memory is right on."

"Then my bet is he's doing his residency at Vanderbilt."

"That would be my bet as well." Leah glanced at her watch—8:20. "Nashville's in the same time zone as we are. When do you think I should make the call?"

"We have no idea what his schedule is, but I think I would try the lunch hour."

"What if I recorded it? I might get some good stuff during the call. Even if Dr. Patel refuses to continue, it just might be enough to support a story."

"Can't hurt. And it's not illegal. Only one party has to consent to the call to make recording it legal."

"I know we have software on our phones here at the office that will record calls, but I haven't ever used it. I'll see if I can get a quick lesson from your secretary."

"She'll be glad to help. I've recorded countless conversations but always get a little primer from Jan beforehand to make sure I don't screw something up. One other thing. I wouldn't tell Dr. Patel that you are recording the call. If you do, he'll clam up. But after he has disconnected, state on the record that the call was between you and Dr. Sanjay Patel, and the date and time."

"Got it." Leah rose from her seat. "I'm going to write out an outline for the call, make sure I cover everything and don't leave any holes. This could be the only opportunity I get to talk with Dr. Patel—that is, if he takes my call."

"Good idea. And good luck. Give me a report whether you reach him or not."

Leah spent the rest of the morning drafting an outline of questions for her conversation with Sanjay Patel, a conversation that might never occur. After a quick lesson on how to use the software in the office phone system to record a call, Leah hit her speakerphone button, cleared her throat, took a deep breath, and then dialed the decoded number of Dr. Patel. Seconds later a voice came on the line: "The person you have called is not available. You may either hang up or leave a message at the tone." Disappointed, Leah hung up. She would not leave a voice mail. She wanted a conversation, if possible. Voice mails could be misconstrued.

She wondered whether Dr. Patel had been with a patient and unable to take her call or had made the conscious decision to ignore it after seeing *Texas Matters* on caller id. She would try again before she left work. If she got his voice mail again, she would infer that he was intentionally ignoring her call and, with Abe's assistance, develop plan B. She emailed Abe and then picked up another file that had been neglected. She needed a distraction until quitting time.

Before leaving her office at the end of the day, she tried her call again. She set her phone in recording mode, positioned her outline in front of her, and carefully dialed the number. Her heart began to thump as she nervously cleared her throat. After several rings, history repeated itself and the same annoying recording began: "The person you have called . . ." Leah ended the call, grabbed her coat, and headed for the elevator. It was time for a change of scenery. On her way home, she decided plan B should wait. She would try the call early the next morning, at six or so. If she got voice mail again, she would be reasonably sure Dr. Patel was ducking her calls.

Standing at her apartment door, Leah stuck her hand into her purse, feeling for her keys. The ringtone of her cell phone suddenly began chiming, and she got frantic, fumbling desperately through her purse's contents in a frantic search for her iPhone. After finding it, she briefly glanced at the number and then dropped her purse to the hall floor. It was Dr. Patel. Although there would be no recording of what she and Dr. Patel discussed, she hit connect and took a seat on the carpet outside her apartment door, her legs folded under her, her back against the corridor wall.

"Leah Rosen."

"Ms. Rosen, there is no need to act like you don't know who this is. I am aware you have my number. I don't know exactly how you got it, but that is not important." Dr. Patel's tone was abrupt and businesslike.

Leah didn't respond but opted to let him continue.

"I know you got my voice mail. I am sure what I said was upsetting to you. It was upsetting for me to make the decision I did, but I had no choice." Dr. Patel paused. Leah sensed he was looking for some kind of reaction, but she had a fine line to walk. She must be honest to a degree, but she had to avoid hitting some trigger that would end the call.

"I have to admit your voice mail took me by surprise, but after thinking about it, I can understand why you have qualms about getting involved in all of this," she finally replied.

There was now a silence on Dr. Patel's end of the line. Leah hoped she hadn't lost him.

"I am very conflicted about this matter," he said. "Although I don't understand how or why my research was manipulated, I'm in the second year of my practice, and my wife and I are expecting our first child in less than two months. I just don't have the time or desire to get involved."

Leah felt good about the way the conversation was beginning. He was opening up to her; she had not even had to ask any questions. She cautioned herself—*go slow, don't push.* "Dr. Patel, I didn't even know you were married, much less expecting your first child."

"Yes. I met my wife in Mumbai. She came with me to America. She is wonderful. And I can't tell you how excited we both were when we found out she was pregnant. And then I inject myself into this Connors mess. I should have kept my mouth shut, just like Dr. Coleman did."

"How do you know that?"

"Seth contacted me. Told me that you had called him, asking questions about the research he had done for Dr. Crimm. He was really worked up. Called you a few names, Ms. Rosen, names

I cannot repeat. He made it clear to me that he was supporting Dr. Crimm. As far as he knew, every protocol had been strictly followed. He then asked if you had called me. Due to his lengthy rampage, I had considerable forewarning of this question and ample opportunity to consider my response."

"And what did you tell him?"

"I told him I had given you the same response—the data that I had provided to Dr. Crimm were correct and would withstand peer-review scrutiny. At the time of the call I had not heard about the verdict, so I was not aware he had disregarded my findings. Seth seemed satisfied, and a bit relieved. He then volunteered he had talked with Dr. Crimm. He probably wanted to see if Dr. Crimm had any idea as to why a reporter was looking into research he had done several years before."

"And?"

"He said Dr. Crimm was very cordial and seemed puzzled by the fact that a reporter would be snooping around his work. According to Seth, Crimm made it clear that doctors needed to stay together and that the consequences of someone falling out of line would be devastating. He suggested that Seth call me and take my pulse."

"Did Crimm elaborate on what he meant?"

"I didn't ask. I simply assured Seth that everything I had done for Dr. Crimm was above reproach and I had no explanation for why a reporter was asking questions. And that was the end of the call."

"And what happened next?"

"After I received that call, I went back to my routine. Practicing here at Vanderbilt is pretty taxing, as you can imagine."

"I bet."

"And then I read about the verdict and called you. I was so upset that Dr. Crimm would lie. And the size of that verdict blew me away. I even wondered whether he would try to place the blame on me if his report were ever questioned. Instinctively, I picked up the phone and called you."

"You did the right thing."

"That's what I initially thought, but after a few sleepless nights, worrying about the damage Crimm could do to my medical career and the toll my involvement would take on my family, I called you and left the voice mail." Dr. Patel paused and cleared his throat. "Look, it appears my former professor may be nothing more than a sophisticated thief, but with all that my wife and I have going on in our lives, I just cannot get involved. The stakes are too high."

"I understand. If I were in your shoes, I would likely react the same way." She didn't know what she would have done, but this was definitely her cue for an empathetic response.

"Ms. Rosen, I very much appreciate your understanding." There was a softness to Dr. Patel's voice.

"Dr. Patel, there is something I would ask you to consider. Let's suppose I can provide you with an absolute guarantee that your name will never be disclosed to anyone other than my boss at *Texas Matters*. As a reporter's source, your identity would be absolutely confidential."

"Confidential?" Dr. Patel asked.

"There have been a number of cases where judges have been asked to order reporters to disclose their sources, and such requests have been denied," Leah continued. "What if I provided you with copies of those court cases so you would not have to take my word for it but could read the courts' holdings and draw your own conclusions? I might even be able to get the law firm that represents *Texas Matters* to write a legal opinion to that effect. Obviously, it would not be addressed to you but would be a general statement of the law in this area. What do you think?"

"I don't know. That might make a difference. But on the other hand, I would just like to forget the past and focus on the future."

"That's totally understandable. But sometimes that's not the best course. Keep in mind that, unless Connors and Crimm are stopped, this practice is going to continue. Count on it. Other med students are going to be compromised, and other innocent defendants are going to be forced to pay lots of money. It's just not right, and it's not going to go away on its own."

Dr. Patel sighed. "I know, I know. But Dr. Crimm is no doubt going to figure out that one of his students is the source, whether you disclose it or not. And I don't know what he and Connors might do. You have to admit there is a lot at stake here."

"I know. But would you think about it? This is not an instance of some young reporter trying to make a big name for herself. I really believe this whole scheme stinks to high heaven, and I am committed to doing something about it. The only thing I know to do is expose their scam for all the world to see."

"Aren't you worried about your future? And what about your safety? I mean, who knows what Connors and Crimm could end up doing to prevent their dirty laundry from being aired. If all this blows, they could go to jail, couldn't they?"

"You don't see many white-collar criminals prosecuted. But, yes, it is a possibility."

"I want to think about it," Dr. Patel said, and then briefly hesitated. "Don't read anything into this, but I would like to see those cases you mentioned, and if you could get something from a lawyer about this privilege you keep mentioning, that would be even better. But I'm not making any promises."

"I understand. I'll email the cases to you tomorrow. It may take a little longer to get you the legal opinion depending on our lawyers' schedules. What is your email address?"

"I would prefer that you send it to my personal email address. Do you have a pen?"

"I will in just a minute." Leah rummaged through her purse lying beside her on the hallway carpet. "Okay, shoot."

Dr. Patel gave Leah an email address, enunciating each letter and number slowly.

"Got it. And, Doctor, I do know this is very tough for you. I really appreciate that you're at least considering going forward."

"I will say one thing, Ms. Rosen. You are a persistent soul."

"I don't know whether to take that as a compliment or a criticism."

"I look forward to receipt of the cases. But just to be clear, I am not committing to anything at this time."

"Understood."

"Good evening, Ms. Rosen."

"Good night, Dr. Patel."

Leah rested her head against the wall and closed her eyes. Their conversation had gone as well as could be expected. There was now a possibility Dr. Patel would be back on the team, taking her story—temporarily, at least—off life support.

CHAPTER

19

The minute Darrin heard Jace in the office she was at his door. "You seen the paper this morning?"

"Don't tell me."

"Yep, the front page of the Metropolitan section. The headline reads, 'Caring Oaks Accused of Gross Negligence in Bodysnatching.' Underneath the headline is a photo of Cal Connors."

"Just great. I'm sure Wallace Arnold will be calling any minute."

About that time, Harriett showed up at his office door with several phone messages in hand.

"Good morning. Wallace Arnold has—"

Jace finished her sentence. "Been calling all morning. No surprise there. Thanks, Harriett. I'll call him back in a few minutes."

"Oh, and we received a twenty-eight-page fax this morning from Cal Connors. I put it on your chair."

Harriett went back to her desk, leaving Jace and Darrin to read the fax.

"Well, looks like Mr. Connors has been busy. These discovery requests cover everything but Wallace Arnold's underwear. Let's see, Cal wants all documents relating to Caring Oaks' net worth, what it spends annually on security, how much an average funeral costs, all the records on Alexis Stone's burial, the personnel records on all of the Caring Oaks employees involved in either burial—you name it, he wants it."

Darrin shook her head. "We are going to be busy. I'll make a copy of the discovery requests and get started on drafting objections. And I'm still working on getting the entire file from Deputy Fife. I'll either finagle it from him or, if all else fails, use the subpoena I've got in the works. I doubt the file has much in it, but I'd like to get a look at any photographs taken of the body and the lab results that were reportedly inconclusive."

Darrin headed for the door and suddenly stopped and turned back around. "Oh, and don't forget, we have an appointment this afternoon with Lonnie Masterson, the embalmer at Caring Oaks."

"No way to forget an appointment with an embalmer," Jace joked.

A few hours later, Jace and Darrin were sitting in the reception area at Caring Oaks.

"Good afternoon, Mr. Forman." Wallace Arnold extended his hand to Jace and at the same time nodded courteously to Darrin. "Ms. McKenzie, it is always a pleasure."

Dressed in his customary dark suit, striped tie, and heavily starched white shirt, Mr. Arnold appeared a bit more nervous than he had the last time they had met.

"Before you meet with Lonnie, I would like to discuss our little case with you, if I might. A few minutes of your time would really put my mind at ease." Without waiting for a reply, Wallace led the way up the winding staircase and down the hall to his spacious office.

Once inside, he motioned for his guests to sit in the antique French chairs positioned in front of his mahogany desk. "So, how are we going to deal with this Connors fellow? I know you saw the article in today's paper."

"Unfortunately, this is the way he operates. It's not the first time he has tried his case in the papers," Jace said. "Puts a favorable twist on the facts and hopes the unfavorable headlines will bring a quick settlement. As I told you this morning on the phone, we can't put a muzzle on Mr. Connors or the press."

Wallace angrily gestured at the paper lying on his desk. "You mean we just sit back and take it? Articles like this are terrible for business. This morning alone we fielded twenty-three calls from people wondering if their loved ones buried here are safe. A couple of them want to come out to make sure their loved ones are still here. My God, can you imagine what it's like to talk to these people?"

"Wallace, I wish I could tell you there was something we could do to stop it but there isn't. The First Amendment gets in the way."

Wallace ignored Jace's feeble attempt at humor. "So what about the lawsuit? What are we to expect in the next week or so? There is a hotbed of gossip in this place. Some of our employees think that, because of this morning's article, the funeral home is under criminal investigation. I need to nip this in the bud."

Jace responded, "I would suggest circulating a short memorandum to all your staff explaining, in layperson's language, what this is all about. For example, tell them that this is a civil suit in which the Stone family is seeking money from Caring Oaks over the grave robbery, that the allegations are without merit, and that the lawsuit will be vigorously defended."

"I assume you can draft something to that effect and fax it to me," said Wallace. "I don't want to say anything that could be damaging to our case."

"Absolutely, we'll get it to you before the end of the day." Jace nodded in Darrin's direction, indicating she had drawn the black bean. She made a note on the yellow pad in her lap.

"Fortunately for you, it looks like this case is going to be over pretty quickly. We received a notice from the court that this case is on what's called the rocket docket, meaning the trial will be set within six months. You should have received a copy of the notice, which Darrin faxed over earlier today."

"I did. And I'm fine with it. I'd rather get it over with sooner than later. I shudder at the thought of being vilified in the press for months."

Jace knew that Wallace had no idea what was involved in getting this case ready for trial. He silently groaned as he began to explain the legal aspects of the case. "First, let's talk about what Mr. Connors and his clients have to prove. For a jury to find in his favor, Mr. Connors must prove that Caring Oaks was negligent in failing to have security patrolling the cemetery grounds and, but for that negligence, Alexis Stone's body would not have been stolen."

Wallace furrowed his brow. His puzzled look caused Jace to try again. "Let me see if I can do a little better. In the legal context, a person or corporation is negligent if it doesn't do what the reasonable person, or reasonable corporation, would have done under similar circumstances."

"And who is this 'reasonable person'?"

"It is a fictitious person created by the jury based on the evidence. For example, if the jury heard that you had experienced fifty body thefts in the last year and still didn't hire security to try and prevent that type of behavior, they might find you didn't act reasonably under the circumstances. On the other hand, if this had never happened before, then they might find there had been no need for security in the past and you had acted reasonably. You with me so far?"

"So far." Wallace seemed interested.

Jace continued. "The next hurdle they have to get over is the 'but for' test I alluded to a second ago. Cal Connors must prove that, if Caring Oaks had security on the night in question, the body theft would not have occurred."

"Isn't that a given?"

"Not at all. I intend to argue that, because of the size of the cemetery, one guy in a golf cart patrolling the area wouldn't have stopped this crazed individual, or individuals, from carrying out their plan."

"So it's possible for a jury to find someone negligent without holding them responsible?"

Jace nodded. "The third thing Connors has to prove is damages. He has contended that his clients, Alexis' parents, suffered mental anguish as a result of this incident. The jury must be convinced of that. In that regard, Mr. and Mrs. Stone will testify about their emotional distress, and that testimony will likely be buttressed by either a psychiatrist or psychologist who counseled them after the incident and who will say that they endured immense suffering."

"Any limit on what the jury can award?"

"That's a good question. The state legislature recently enacted a law capping the amount of punitive damages a jury can award, but it involves complicated parameters, and there are ways to get around it. Bottom line, damages could be astronomical—if the jury gets mad."

"So what's going to happen between now and trial?"

"The legal term is pretrial discovery. We will be using the court system to find out in advance of trial how strong the plaintiffs' case is and where the weaknesses are, and to build our defense."

"And how will we do that?"

"Through depositions, interrogatories, and document requests. For example, Connors will want to take your deposition and the depositions of everyone who had anything to do with Alexis' burial and reburial."

"Why would he want my deposition? I don't know anything about the grave robbery." Their host's tone was defensive.

"I know. But it's just part of the process—nothing to be concerned about. He'll take your deposition in our offices downtown. I'll be there. A court reporter will be there. Connors will ask you questions under oath and the court reporter will take down your answers verbatim. Later, she will type up the questions and answers in booklet form. You will then carefully review your answers for accuracy, make any changes to ensure they are truthful, and then sign the deposition before a notary. Assuming Connors asks the right questions, and you can rest assured he will, he will then know what you know about the facts surrounding this case."

Wallace nervously adjusted his tie. "I still don't understand why I should have to testify. I mean, it's nothing more than harassment."

Jace shook his head and smiled reassuringly. "I don't make the rules, but I'm sure you'll do just fine." He tried to sound convincing, although he had his doubts. "We'll spend as much time as you need before the deposition to make sure you are comfortable with the process." Jace hesitated briefly. "And one more thing. Connors might have your deposition videotaped."

Wallace's concern intensified. "It won't be played on television, will it?"

"Highly unlikely. Videotaping depositions is pretty routine these days—helps lawyers prepare their cross-examinations for trial. In the many cases I have handled over the years, there have been countless depositions videotaped, and I have yet to see one of them played on the local news."

Jace paused, reading his client's eyes to make sure any concern had been allayed. Satisfied, he continued. "Now, let's go over what we've got coming up in this case. Connors has served us with written discovery seeking certain information. We will serve our own on Mr. Connors in the next few days. But what you have to focus on is gathering the information requested and answering his written questions. Darrin will meet with you in the next day or two to go over the questions and help you put together the information. The answers must be sworn to in front of a notary. As Darrin will reemphasize to you later, it is extremely important to be as complete and truthful in your answers as possible. Although the procedure is not as formal as a deposition, the answers are no less important."

Darrin sifted through her briefcase and handed Wallace a copy of the fax they had received from Cal that morning.

Jace continued. "We will object to some of the requests and questions, but most of them are permissible."

Wallace sighed as he flipped through the document. "This is pretty overwhelming. It's going to be a terrible distraction."

"No doubt, but it's just part of the process."

Wallace, sounding like a man already beaten, said, "Well, Lonnie has been waiting for you in a conference room downstairs. He is a very shy young man and about to come undone at the seams over this. Please take that into account when you question him."

"We'll do everything we can to make it as painless as possible, I assure you."

Wallace rose from behind his desk and led his visitors down the hall to the stairway. Darrin and Jace could hear him muttering under his breath as he marched toward the door at the hallway's end.

CHAPTER

20

As they entered the conference room, Lonnie Masterson jumped up, apparently startled. Dressed in an ill-fitting suit and clashing tie, he had slightly crooked teeth and a nose that had obviously been broken several times. But he was not a bad-looking young man. His eyes were light blue, contrasting with his coal-black hair. When introduced to Jace and Darrin, he simply nodded without speaking, his eyes blinking incessantly as he looked down nervously at his shoes.

"Lonnie, as you and I discussed, Mr. Forman is Caring Oaks' lawyer in the case filed by the Stone family. Ms. McKenzie is his assistant. They want to ask you a few questions about your role in the burial and reburial of Alexis Stone."

Lonnie nodded again, his eyes still fixed on his shoes, glancing up from time to time but only at his boss. He made no attempt to hide his discomfort with the process.

"Maybe I should stay," said Wallace. "As I told you, Lonnie's a little reserved." He gave Lonnie a sympathetic smile.

"May I have a word with you outside?" asked Jace. He stepped out of the conference room and his client followed. "Wallace, Darrin and I have found that witnesses are far more candid if their superiors are not in the room when they are being interviewed. I'm sure this is awkward for Mr. Masterson, but many witnesses are that way at first. They are scared to death. Don't worry. I'll put him at ease in no time. I've interviewed literally thousands of witnesses over the years and feel pretty confident I can earn his trust."

Wallace appeared skeptical. "We'll see. I'll be upstairs if you need me."

"Thanks for your help. Darrin will be in touch tomorrow or the next day. If you have any questions in the meantime, you know how to reach me."

In the conference room, Darrin had engaged Lonnie in light, very limited conversation. Upon returning, Jace took a seat as unobtrusively as possible and tuned in to the conversation.

"So you grew up in eastern Tennessee?"

Long pause. "Appalachia."

"Do your parents still live there?"

Another long pause. "Don't know and don't care."

"How long has it been since you visited them?"

Shorter pause. "Ten years."

"You must be around twenty-five?"

Lonnie looked up for the first time. He ignored Jace and directed his answer to Darrin. "Twenty-four. I ran away when I was fourteen."

"Where did you go?"

"Went to Knoxville. Got taken in by a Baptist preacher and his wife. Raised me as their son. Finished high school there and then went to mortuary school, where I learned to be an embalmer." The witness glanced at Jace and then quickly turned away.

"And where did you go to work after mortuary school?"

"Right there in Knoxville. Fillmore Funeral Home."

"How long did you work there?"

"Couple of years—till I wanted a change of scenery."

Darrin grinned. "And you picked Fort Worth?"

Lonnie managed a grin himself. "I'd always wanted to live out west. I drove west from Knoxville until I found a place that suited me."

"And how long have you worked at Caring Oaks?"

"A little less than a year."

Darrin was on a roll. Jace remained the observer.

"And what are your job responsibilities here?"

"I'm an embalmer."

"I don't know much about the funeral business. Tell me what an embalmer does, start to finish."

"We replace the blood with an embalming fluid. People believe that makes the body last forever, but that's a bunch of you know what." Lonnie hesitated. "Only thing embalming does is increase the cost of a funeral. We make a lot of money on embalming."

Darrin changed course. "Do you remember Alexis Stone's body?"

Up came the guard again. The eyes began to twitch. The stare returned to the top of the conference room table. "Yes."

"Tell me what you remember."

Hesitation. "I'm not under investigation here, am I?"

"Of course not. We are on your side. We represent your employer in a civil case. You're a witness, nothing more. You're not charged with anything."

Lonnie seemed relieved. "I remember Ms. Stone." His eyes stared at an imaginary spot on the wall. "She was very pretty—long dark hair and blue eyes. And very young."

"Anything else stand out in your mind?"

"Other than the autopsy scars, not that I can recall."

"Anything specific about the autopsy scars?"

"No, but Caring Oaks doesn't get many bodies that have been autopsied, that's all."

"And the reburial. Were you involved in that?"

"Yeah, but my involvement was very limited. There was no funeral service, and the body had already been embalmed so I touched up her makeup and hair. That was about it."

"Anything about her body that you remember as different from the first time?"

"It was in pretty fair shape, as I remember."

"Any markings on the body that weren't there the first time?"

Lonnie squinted his eyes shut, searching his recollection. "Oh, yeah, there was a faded starlike symbol on her stomach. Looked like it was drawn by a black marker."

"Anything else you can remember that was different about the body when you saw it the second time?"

"Not that I can remember."

"Have you told us everything you can remember about the body, whether it be the first or second time you saw it?"

"That's everything I can remember."

Darrin reached in her briefcase and pulled out a business card. Before she handed it to Lonnie, she looked over at Jace. "That's all I have, Jace. Do you have any questions?"

"I think you've covered everything for now."

Darrin handed Lonnie her card. "If you think of anything you haven't told us, give me a call—the sooner the better."

Lonnie put her card in his wallet.

Darrin rose from her seat and Jace followed. Turning to Lonnie, she said, "That wasn't so bad, now was it?"

"No, ma'am, not at all."

"We'll be in touch."

CHAPTER

21

"You learn anything on that little lady that popped me those questions down in the Valley?"

Cal plopped down on the sofa in Christine's office and scrolled through emails on his cell phone, feigning indifference.

"Yeah, her name is Leah Rosen. She works for *Texas Matters*. Graduated from UT about seven years ago. No page on Facebook or any other social networking site. I couldn't find any articles that she has authored. My suspicion is she's been doing menial research and penning drafts of articles for others to edit and put their name on. I haven't had time to delve into her personal background."

"Sounds like a lightweight. But I'd like you to do a little follow-up just to make sure. Give her a call. Make up a reason for contacting her. I don't need any distractions as I prepare to kick Forman's ass."

"I'll take care of it. By the way, how'd you like that investigative report we received on Masterson?"

Cal smiled. "Couldn't have been any better if I had written it myself. Have we got his deposition scheduled?"

"The day after the Stones are deposed. Do you want to meet with them before their depositions? Mr. Stone is slated to go first."

"Starting at ten o'clock?"

Christine nodded.

"Have them come in around nine. I shouldn't need more than an hour with them. Hell, they don't have a clue as to who robbed their daughter's grave, and we aren't going to offer them as experts on funeral industry practices. The only thing I need to prep them on is the pain and suffering they have sustained as a result of this horrific crime. That shouldn't be hard to do. Any jury is going to feel incredible sympathy for parents who have been through something like that. What could be worse than to lose your daughter— twice! Changing the subject, have you had any luck on finding an expert?"

"Absolutely. I found a guy who used to be with a competitor of Caring Oaks—Quiet Hills Funeral Home. He has an ax to grind with his old company, and the funeral home industry in general. He's prepared to testify that Caring Oaks should have had an iron fence around the perimeter, not that flimsy chain link, and a visitors entrance manned by a guard 24-7."

"Is that what Quiet Hills has?"

"No, but he's going to testify that he continually advised his superiors that they needed to upgrade their security and they refused. According to my discussion with him, he is going to bash the industry in general. Talk about how all they are concerned with is profits and more profits."

"I like it. Is he believable?"

"He's pretty convincing on the phone, but I haven't had time to meet with him face-to-face. I'll get that scheduled in the next few days."

"You're the best." Cal rose from the sofa and meandered toward the door. He paused before making his exit. "We need to start thinking about how we're going to spend all the money we're going to make on this case. Payday is right around the corner." Cal winked at his daughter and then closed the door behind him.

Later that evening, Cal had just finished dinner and, as was customary, was relaxing in the leather "smoking" chair in his mahogany-paneled study, cigar in one hand and brandy snifter in the other. He picked up the universal remote from the adjacent side table and aimed it at the electronic eye hidden in a cabinet underneath the massive floor-to-ceiling bookcase. A built-in flat screen came to life and gave him his menu of choices. He selected "Albums" and then scrolled down to one of his favorites, Cat Stevens's *Tea for the Tillerman*. He pressed "Select" and listened to the haunting intro of "Where Do the Children Play?" He took a satisfying drag off his Cuban cigar and then chased it with a sip of cognac. Closing his eyes, he entered another world, only to be disturbed moments later by the vibrating cell phone in his pocket. Groggily, he fished for the phone and, after glancing at the number, answered.

"Cal Connors."

"Cal, this is Howell. I'm afraid that reporter has gotten to one of my former students."

Cal sat up in his chair, his eyes wide open. "Now, calm down, Howell. You're getting all worked up over nothing. Didn't you tell me you had talked with the students who had helped you on our projects and that they were on board?"

"No, that's not what I said. I talked with Seth Coleman. He was definitely on board. But I was concerned about calling Sanjay Patel. I left that up to Seth. I told Seth to call him and get back to me if he sensed a problem."

"And?"

"Well, he didn't call back."

"So no problem then, right?"

"I don't know about that. Patel marches to a different drummer. He's very difficult to read. Seth might have misread their conversation and thought everything was okay when it really wasn't."

"Hell, Howell, you're making a mountain out of a damn molehill. There ain't a damn thing to worry about. That Indian ain't gonna blow the whistle. He's got too much at stake. Besides, he never even saw the final report you submitted, did he?"

"No, but maybe that reporter showed it to him."

"Now, you don't know that, do you?"

"No, but you told me you had a bad feeling about her. Isn't that right?"

"That's what I said. But that don't mean she's capable of playing in the big leagues. Shit, she's fresh out of college. I promise you, we've got nothing to worry about. I'll do a little detective work, just for insurance purposes. Would that make you sleep a little better?"

"Sure as hell would. Cal, I know I sound like an old lady worrying like this, but we've got a lot at stake."

"And I intend to make sure we don't lose it—not one penny of it."

CHAPTER

22

After her call with Dr. Patel, Leah decided to do some quick research on reporter's privilege. She did have a vague memory from a journalism class she had taken in college that there was a reporter's privilege, but her memory was uncertain as to what it protected. She did not want to make assurances to Dr. Patel that she could not keep. Nor did she want to appear unknowledgeable about this issue when she met with Abe.

She pressed the power button on her MacBook and tapped on the Dashboard icon. Google came up, and she typed in "reporter's privilege." A number of sources appeared and she chose Wikipedia. Her eyes widened. A quick read of the Wikipedia summary indicated that reporter's privilege was not nearly as strong as she had remembered.

The seminal case on this issue involved a reporter with the *Courier-Journal,* in Louisville, Kentucky. In the course of his investigation about drug use in Kentucky, he had actually witnessed hashish being made and had talked with marijuana users. He had been granted an audience with the hashish manufacturers and the pot smokers on the express condition that their identities would remain confidential. After penning two articles about this subject, one of which featured a photograph of a source's hands actually making hashish, he was subpoenaed to testify at a grand jury investigation into illegal drug use. He refused. The case went through the lower courts, ultimately landing in the U.S. Supreme Court. In a 5–4 decision, with several judges writing their own opinions, the court's majority created the standard: in a criminal case, a reporter must reveal sources if the government can demonstrate a substantial relation between the information sought and a subject of overriding and compelling state interest. She read the line again, and again. She hated legalese. Why did lawyers and judges write in legalese instead of English that could be understood by everyone? Were they really more interested in confusion than clarity?

Still, she sensed her situation was less than ideal. If she wrote an article and revealed the wrongdoing of Connors and Crimm, the state and federal authorities would be all over it, and they would likely be fighting over who could lead the investigation. The feds would probably win out, and the case would end up in a federal court somewhere in Texas. And then there would be a grand jury investigation, and the first subpoena to be issued would go to Ms. Leah Rosen. The government would want the names of all of her sources, as well as what they had told her. But what if she refused to testify? What if she simply defied the court's order?

Leah returned to her computer, scanned other articles, and hit upon a more recent case. Judith Miller had been a reporter for the *New York Times*. She had done work on the leak of a CIA agent's identity, Valerie Plame. When subpoenaed to divulge her sources, Miller had refused, citing the "freedom of the press" clause of the First Amendment. Her lawyers contended that her sources were protected by this clause; otherwise, the gathering and publication of information by the press would be stymied and the public's right to know would be infringed. The trial judge disagreed, and so did the Court of Appeals for the District of Columbia. The U.S. Supreme Court refused to hear the case, implying that the justices agreed with the lower courts' decisions. And what happened to Miller in the meantime? She spent weeks in jail. Not a good result, and certainly not something Leah had any desire to experience.

She needed to give Abe a report on her talk with Dr. Patel, as well as discuss her options in light of her morning's research. One thing was clear in her mind: she was not going to lie to Dr. Patel. She had to level with him and let him know she had been mistaken when she assured him his identity would remain a secret if she ran the story. She had to make sure he realized that within days of the story's publication, the odds were she would be subpoenaed to testify about her sources. She would have two choices, neither of them appealing: give up Dr. Patel's identity or be confined to jail until she did. Bottom line, his name would surface, and he would be subpoenaed to testify before the grand jury. Leah sighed. This was going to be a tough sell. Dr. Patel would likely walk away from this fight. And she really couldn't blame him.

Leah decided to call him from her apartment rather than the office. She didn't want any interruptions. Besides, she assumed Dr. Patel preferred to talk at night for the same reasons. Leah reclined against the couch and picked up her iPhone. She went into her contacts and scrolled to "Sanjay Patel" and tapped lightly. Seconds later, Dr. Patel's voice came on the line.

"Ms. Rosen, I didn't expect to hear from you. I haven't yet received the cases and legal opinion we discussed."

Leah swallowed. "The cases aren't coming. I'm calling instead. The law wasn't as I thought. I was, for lack of a better term, flat wrong."

There was a momentary silence on the other line. "I'm not sure I quite understand." Dr. Patel's English remained perfect but his accent became more pronounced.

Leah explained that if the federal government launched a criminal investigation into the story she wrote, she would probably be forced to reveal her sources.

There was another silence.

"Well, as you can imagine, this changes everything," Dr. Patel said.

"I understand."

"I have a wife, a baby on the way, and a professional career in front of me. For me to proceed could be devastating."

"I can't disagree with you." Leah took a breath and decided to lay all her cards on the table. "There is one other issue you should consider."

"Yes?"

"If you do nothing and there is an investigation later, you might become one of the targets."

"What do you mean? I did what Dr. Crimm asked. I reviewed the data submitted to the FDA by Samson and looked for any discrepancies. I found a few minor ones, nothing alarming. I concluded that FDA approval, based upon the data submitted, was proper. And I put my findings in an email to Dr. Crimm. It's as simple as that."

"I believe everything you say. But if the sky starts to fall on Cal Connors and Dr. Howell Crimm, they're going to be looking for a fall guy and looking hard. At least, that would be my guess."

Total silence on the other end of the line except for some rapid breathing.

"If Connors and Crimm's house of cards ever does collapse, and you've stayed mum all along, then don't you think they are going to try to pin the blame on you?" Leah said.

The silence from Dr. Patel was almost deafening.

"Dr. Patel, are you still there?"

"I'm here."

"I mean, it could be your word against Dr. Crimm's, and he has a pretty strong résumé. No offense, but you don't have the contacts or credentials to stand up against someone like that. And I don't have to tell you how ruthless Cal Connors can be. And with their reputations and fortunes on the line, it makes me shudder to even think about what they might do."

"So what would you do if you were me?" Dr. Patel finally said.

Now Leah had the opening she wanted. "Can you retrieve that email—the one where you detailed your conclusions relative to the data on Fosorax?"

"I am ninety percent sure I typed it on my personal laptop. I may have archived it, but even so, I know it can be retrieved."

"If I were you, I would retrieve that email. It will show the date it was sent and Dr. Crimm as the recipient, correct?"

"Absolutely."

"I would make multiple copies and store them in several safe places. Also, you could fax or email a copy to me."

"But you just told me if you run a story on this and a criminal investigation is launched, you would not be able to protect my identity."

"True. But I promise you I will not run the story without talking with you first. And there's one other important twist to the law. If I am not using you as the source for my story—in other words, if I am able to corroborate this scheme using other information and sources—then I would not have to disclose your name."

"Do you think you might find other sources?"

"There is that possibility. Plus, if I have a copy of the email, it will be more insurance against false accusations from your former professor." Leah had done all she could do.

"I'll think about it, Ms. Rosen, I really will. I know how to reach you."

"Thank you, Doctor." And the call was over.

Leah placed her iPhone on the floor next to her. She had no idea what Dr. Patel would decide. This was all about trust. Dr. Patel would have to trust someone he hardly knew. And she just didn't know if he would take that leap of faith. She even wondered whether she would.

CHAPTER

23

The next morning the phone rang in Leah's office. She stared at it, debating whether to let it go to voice mail. She had too much to think about on the Connors investigation to get sidetracked on another matter. She looked at the caller id: Connors & Connors. She immediately picked up the receiver and answered, "Leah Rosen."

"Ms. Rosen, this is Christine Connors. I know we haven't met. Cal Connors is my father. Is this a good time to talk?"

For a moment, Leah couldn't think of a thing to say. She almost dropped the phone. Then she regained whatever composure she had left and replied, "As good a time as any. You know how hectic a reporter's life can be."

"I have an idea. Probably not too different from what I do as a trial lawyer."

"I can see the similarities. But I'm not complaining. I like being busy."

"As do I. Well, I suspect you are wondering why I'm calling you. Actually, it's pretty routine stuff. After every case our firm tries to verdict, we contact reporters who were in attendance to see if there is any information we can supply to aid them in writing their stories. You know, information on the firm, our backgrounds, other cases we've tried—that type of thing. We're very aware of the significance and circulation of *Texas Matters,* and I was just wondering if you would like to ask me any questions in that regard."

Leah wondered how Christine had gotten her name and contact information—probably that gossipy clerk. She pondered her next move and opted to go for the gold. "As a matter of fact, I do have a lot of questions. I have done quite a bit of research on your father—quite a record he's put together."

"Thank you, Leah. We are proud of his accomplishments in the courtroom."

"And I ran across several articles on your victories. Pretty unbelievable for a trial lawyer out of law school for such a short time." If Leah was good at one thing, it was feeding someone's ego.

"I didn't realize you had been so thorough in your investigation. I am impressed. And thank you."

"That being said, I have never seen your law offices or talked with either of you face-to-face. Slight correction—I did ask your dad some questions in front of the courthouse after his victory. But it was a mob scene, as you can imagine, and I didn't really learn much. I think sit-down interviews with you and your dad in a casual setting could provide some real color to my feature."

"When does *Texas Matters* plan on running the story?"

"Well, I was hoping it might make the next issue."

"My dad is pretty swamped right now, preparing for a big trial . . ."

"And what trial is that?"

"One here in Fort Worth. A grave robbery of all things—really weird. But if you could make it up here tomorrow or Monday I will fit you in our schedules. The closer we get to picking a jury, the more difficult it is for us to schedule anything that does not relate to that trial." Christine chuckled. "We become one-dimensional, to put it mildly."

"Understood. How about ten on Monday? I know Southwest has a number of flights from Austin to Dallas Love."

Christine mumbled something about meetings that could be rescheduled and then came back on the line in a strong voice. "Okay, that works. I'll see you then. If something comes up, please call or email me."

"I don't see that happening, but if it does, I will be in touch. See you Monday at ten at your offices."

"I look forward to it."

Leah hung up the phone and made a beeline down the hall to Abe's office. Uncharacteristically, she barged in without knocking. Fortunately, Abe was alone, his back to the door. He wheeled around in his chair to face his unexpected visitor.

"Knocking might have been nice. It's an honored tradition around here to knock before you enter. You might try it next time."

"I am so sorry. I wasn't thinking."

"It's all right. So what's so earth-shattering that it caused you to forget your manners?"

"Christine Connors just called me. I am meeting with her on Monday in Fort Worth."

Abe leaned forward. "And her explanation for the call?"

"She said she and her dad routinely follow up with reporters who attend their trials and wondered if I had any questions."

"Sounds like you may be walking into a trap. How did she get your contact info anyway?"

"I didn't ask but my guess would be Christine called the court clerk in Brownsville. I had to give her my business card and a copy of my driver's license before she would let me review any of the court files."

"So what do you plan to accomplish in this meeting?"

"Well, I hadn't had a chance to tell you yet, but I spoke with Dr. Patel. I told him his identity would not necessarily be shielded by the reporter's privilege if he was a source for my story and a criminal investigation ensued. That caught him by surprise. He told me he couldn't continue—too much at risk with his career, his family, and all. I empathized with him and told him I could understand his reluctance."

"So, we are back to square one?"

"Abe, you should have more faith in me than that," Leah grinned.

"Okay, impress me."

"I asked him to weigh what might happen if he didn't help me. I told him that if, for some reason, the scheme put together by his former professor and Cal Connors started to unravel, he would likely become the fall guy and his credentials and reputation wouldn't hold up very well against Dr. Crimm's if there was a swearing match between them as to who did what."

Abe smiled and nodded his head in admiration. "I'm impressed. Go on."

"I told him it would be his word against theirs. And then he volunteered he had sent Dr. Crimm an email detailing his research and conclusions relative to his examination of the data Samson submitted to the FDA."

"And does he still have it?"

"He thinks he sent the email from his personal laptop and it is in his archive files."

"That would be simple enough to retrieve."

"I also told him that, if he could retrieve it, he should copy it and store it in a safe place."

"Good advice."

"And then I suggested he send me a copy."

"Ballsy. And his response?"

"He expressed hesitation. Told me in a nice way that he was leery of trusting someone he hardly knew with something so critical. I told him that if I could get other sources to use as the basis for my story, I wouldn't have to divulge his name."

"Excellent."

"So, I am going to call Dr. Patel before I meet with the Connors and see if he has found that email. If he has, I am going to talk him into sending it to me immediately."

"And what do you plan on doing with it once you have it?"

"Read excerpts of it to Mr. Connors when I interview him. I won't reveal the source or give him a copy of it. I just want to see his face when he knows I have a document that could undermine his entire career. See if there is concern in his eyes."

"And if there is?"

"I'll know it's all true—that he and Crimm are perpetrating a monumental legal fraud."

Abe chuckled. "Before you run off and confront Mr. Connors with this 'monumental legal fraud,' you need to first get the evidence from Dr. Patel, if it exists, and then outline some well-reasoned, carefully worded questions to confirm your suspicions that will also shield you and *Texas Matters* from any threat of a libel lawsuit from Mr. Connors. It might even be a good idea if you took one of our seasoned male reporters with you to the meeting."

"Abe, I'm not afraid of Cal Connors."

"Well, you should be. Before you meet with him, get your proof from Dr. Patel and then come see me about your next move."

Leah assured Abe she would. But in the back of her mind she knew she wasn't going to let anyone or anything stop her from being at Connors' office the following Monday morning.

CHAPTER

24

Christine sauntered into her dad's office and perched herself on the corner of his massive desk. "Guess who I just talked with?"

Cal looked up from the stack of mail he was going through. "No idea."

"Ms. Leah Rosen."

Cal leaned back in his chair and took a deep breath. "Well, well. And what did Ms. Rosen have to say?"

"She is flying here on Monday to meet with us face-to-face. I used the old story about how we always get in touch with reporters who have covered our trials to see if they have any follow-up questions."

"And she went for it?"

"She couldn't have been more thrilled."

Cal rose from his chair and strolled toward the window. "You should meet with her first."

"I was thinking I should be the *only* one to meet with her. Conveniently, you'll be defending the depositions of the Stones that day."

"That's convenient, now ain't it. How are you going to handle the interview?"

"I'm not going to give her a thing. But you can rest assured I'll pump her for all the information she has on you, this firm, and the article she's writing on the Samson trial."

"That's my girl."

Christine slid off the desk and headed toward the door.

"And Christine?"

Christine stopped in the doorway and turned toward her dad.

"I want a full report the minute I get back from the depositions."

"You'll have it." Christine closed the door. Cal continued to gaze out the window of his office, an approving smile slowly forming on his lips.

CHAPTER

25

Jace sat at the desk in his wood-paneled study staring at the file Darrin had compiled for him to review before he deposed Mr. and Mrs. Stone. As he flipped through the pages, he realized he was too exhausted from working all weekend to concentrate. He decided to turn in, try to get some sleep, and review the materials in the morning before the depositions began. He stumbled toward the bedroom and collapsed on the bed, fully clothed. Minutes later, he was sound asleep.

A little after four-thirty, the phone rang. In a semiconscious state Jace groped for his phone, which was charging on the bedside table. Finding it, he brought it slowly to his ear, his eyes still closed, his head buried in the pillow. In a raspy, barely audible voice, he mumbled, "Hello."

The voice at the other end of the line was desperate. "Dad, it's me, Matt. Are you there?"

Jace immediately sat up on the side of the bed, the adrenaline beginning to flow. His eyes were now wide open, his voice clear and distinct. "Matt? Where are you?"

There was an awkward pause as Matt cleared his throat. "Dad, I'm in the Austin jail."

Jace hesitated before responding. He could sense his son was very upset. The last thing Matt needed was a serious ass-chewing. Besides, that wasn't Jace's style. "What happened?" His voice was calm, reassuring.

"I got arrested."

"I figured that out. Didn't think you'd be spending the night in jail just for kicks."

"Guess I had a little too much to drink."

"You weren't driving, were you?"

"No."

"Then what did you get arrested for?"

"Got in a little fight in a bar down on Sixth Street. They hauled me and the other guy in."

"And what did they book you for?"

"Public intoxication, disorderly conduct, and . . ." The words stuck.

"What else?"

"Resisting arrest."

"Shit. You didn't hit a cop, did you?"

"I don't think so, but I was pretty drunk at the time."

"So I'm your one phone call."

"Sorry. I know this sucks."

"Listen, I think there's a six-thirty Southwest flight this morning that gets in around seven-fifteen. I'll be on it. See you then."

Jace ended the call and crawled out of bed. The day wasn't starting off as planned.

Jace booked himself on the first flight out. On the way to the airport, it dawned on him that the Stone depositions were scheduled that morning. He had been so preoccupied with his son's arrest that the Stone case had retreated to the recesses of his mind. He called Darrin's voice mail at work and left her a message to cancel the depositions. He thought about calling her at home, but it was too early. He made a mental note to follow up with Darrin the minute he landed to make sure she had received his message.

As usual, Jace presented his boarding pass to the gate attendant within minutes of the plane's doors closing. Once he had found a seat, he laid his head back and closed his eyes, his mind racing with disquieting thoughts. Was Matt all right? What had his night in jail been like? He assumed they took his fingerprints. But he had no idea if or when they would run fingerprints to match any others they had on file—like the fingerprints found in the apartment of Alexis Stone.

Within an hour, the Boeing 737's wheels hit the tarmac of the Austin airport. As the plane taxied to the gate, Jace turned on his cell and dialed Darrin's number at home. She answered on the second ring.

"Darrin, this is Jace."

"I know that." Darrin laughed. "You sound like you're calling from Mars."

"I'm on a plane and just landed in Austin."

"You're what? Did you forget about the Stone depositions? They're scheduled for ten this morning."

"Cancel them. Something came up."

"Are you going to leave me guessing?"

"Matt got arrested."

Darrin let out a muffled gasp. "Arrested! For what?"

"A bar fight. I don't think it's anything real serious. I mean, he didn't shoot anybody or anything like that, but I gotta get him out."

"Well, don't worry about anything here. I'll take care of rescheduling the depositions."

"Thanks. I'll call you after I know more."

Jace then searched his BlackBerry directory for the number for Pat Reynolds. Pat was one of Jace's old law school buddies, who also happened to be one of the best criminal attorneys in the state of Texas. They had kept in touch over the years socially and had also referred cases back and forth. He hated to bother Pat and have him rearrange his whole morning for him. But it was time to get him involved, in case Matt's arrest morphed into a murder investigation of Alexis Stone.

Pat's wife answered the call.

"Carla, this is Jace Forman. Is Pat there?"

"He's in the shower. Can he call you back?"

"Not really. I'm on the tarmac at the Austin airport. Any way you could roust him out?"

"Let me see what I can do."

After a few moments, Pat's voice came on the line. "Yeah, boy, what's goin' on?"

In abbreviated form, Jace explained the situation with Matt, not mentioning anything about the Alexis Stone case. He decided not to discuss it with Pat until he had to.

"I'll pick you up outside the baggage claim in about twenty minutes," Pat said. "And don't worry, we'll have ol' Matt out in no time. Piece of cake. See you shortly."

Jace put his phone back in his briefcase and waited his turn to deplane.

CHAPTER

26

Christine Connors was on her cell phone calling Cal. As she impatiently waited for him to pick up, she glanced at her watch—seven-thirty. By this time of morning her dad would have already scoured the Dallas and Fort Worth papers, searching for stories that might involve potential lawsuits and new legal theories and claims plaintiff's lawyers might pursue against unscrupulous corporations. Hopefully he hadn't hit the shower yet. She was relieved when he answered.

"Hey, Dad."

"Morning, Christine! To what do I owe this pleasure?"

"Our service called me a few minutes ago and said they had an urgent message from the Forman firm. Apparently Mr. Forman had some emergency in Austin and needs to cancel the Stone depositions today."

"Well, well, well. How lucky for us. Call his office back and tell them we are happy to accommodate Mr. Forman's schedule.

Be sure and make it clear that our clients are very busy people and it will be very difficult for them to find another time to give their depositions in the near future."

"Got it."

"And one last thing. Tell them we will not reschedule that embalmer's deposition under any circumstances. What's his name?"

"Lonnie Masterson."

"Yeah, ol' Lonnie. His deposition will go forward as scheduled with or without Mr. Forman. He has other lawyers in his firm. If Forman can't make it, one of his other lawyers can cover."

"Agreed. And remember, Leah Rosen is going to be at our office today."

"Damn, I forgot about that. Thanks for the reminder. What time are you meeting with her?"

"Around ten."

"I'll make sure and make myself scarce. I think I hear Judge Massey's clerk calling to schedule an emergency injunction hearing right about that time."

Christine laughed. "I'll see you at the office when your so-called hearing is over."

Christine ended the call and started getting ready for work. She arrived at the office minutes before Leah pulled up in her rental car.

Leah easily found her destination, as it was a four-story building that had the name Connors & Connors emblazoned on the side in platinum-colored letters. The building was a glass box that had been built in the late eighties. The aqua-colored glass contrasted loudly with the platinum letters, announcing to the world that this was the house that Cal had built. On one side of the firm's name was a large symbol of the state of Texas, and on the other, a replica of the scales of justice. "Exactly as I would have pictured it," Leah thought to herself.

She entered the building and announced her arrival to the receptionist, a woman in her early twenties with bleached-blond teased hair and a V-neck sweater revealing the handiwork of a local doc.

"Can I help you, hon?"

Leah shuddered but tried not to show it. She absolutely abhorred another female calling her "hon" or "sweetie," especially if she was older than the other female. "I'm Leah Rosen, and I have a meeting with Christine Connors and Mr. Connors this morning."

"Yes. Ms. Connors is expecting you. Her office is on the second floor. The elevator is right over there, hon." She pointed to the left.

"Thank you," Leah replied as she took in the flamboyant design of the office, a menagerie of paintings, rugs, and sculpture. Nothing seemed to match but all seemed expensive. Rumor had it Cal had traveled the world, picking out all of the furnishings himself—and it showed.

All of the offices rimmed the building's exterior, giving each inhabitant a view of the reception atrium and the world outside. The walk around the perimeter from the elevator to the office of Christine Connors was short. Still distracted by her surroundings, Leah bumped into Christine just outside her office, an empty coffee cup in hand.

"Oh, so sorry. I was just on my way to get a cup of coffee." Christine recognized Leah from the description her father had given her. "You must be Leah Rosen."

"And you must be Christine Connors." The two shook hands.

"Come on in and have a seat. Would you like anything to drink? Water, coffee, a soft drink?" Christine sat down in the leather chair behind her desk as Leah took a seat across from her.

"No, thanks, I'm fine. I must say your offices are really something. Where did you get all the furnishings? I felt like I was strolling through a museum. You've got quite a collection, very eclectic and unique."

"Very diplomatic of you. Your description didn't include the words 'garish' and 'ostentatious.' Mine would have." Christine smiled warmly at her guest. "I take no credit, or blame, for the office decor. Dad did it all. Flew all over the world, picking out a painting in France, a rug in India, a sculpture in Italy. He had it all shipped to Fort Worth and told a local decorator to find places for everything. Evidently, the decorator was appalled. Told Dad that the pieces didn't go together. Dad said he didn't give a damn and told him to work with what he had bought or Dad would find another decorator who would. The decorator was ready to quit until Dad quoted him the hourly fee he was willing to pay."

Leah and Christine both laughed.

"I must say, the decor of the common areas don't compare to the decor of your office." Leah surveyed her surroundings. "I don't think I have ever seen so many plaques and diplomas. Your accomplishments are very impressive. And I'm curious, the painting over there, is that an original Warhol?"

Christine looked over at the painting and smiled admiringly. "It is indeed. This was the album cover design Andy did for the Velvet Underground—you know, Lou Reed's band back in the sixties. I bought it for two reasons. I love Warhol's art and I love the Velvet Underground's music. Got it from a dealer in New York City. Cost me a pretty penny, but for some reason, it makes me smile every time I look at it. The Sixties—must have been a great time to be young. So much incredible music and fascinating art, and so many people living a carefree existence. Sometimes I wish I wasn't so type A."

Leah wondered, as she eyed the painting, what would possess someone to paint a banana, just a plain old banana.

"You get to New York much?"

"As much as I can. I like the smells, the constant noise and activity—it's really invigorating to me. But you can't drag my father there. He hates the crowds. Claims the people are rude. Dad gets passionate in trials, but he's never rude. If he catches a witness lying, he'll let him have it. But he's never mean just to be mean which, as you know, defines a lot of other lawyers. So, long story short, when I go to the City, I go with friends and the Lone Wolf stays behind."

"So tell me about your relationship with your father. I mean, you don't see many father-daughter law offices."

"My parents divorced when I was young. But they both made the best of it. Dad treated Mom right financially and doted on me. Spoiled me rotten, and I loved him for it. His law practice never got in the way. I was his little princess."

Leah noted a faraway look in Christine's eyes, as if she were reliving the memories.

"When I graduated from Harvard, I had lots of job offers, but I couldn't think of a better person to train under than the Lone Wolf. So here I am."

Leah had taken out a legal pad and was furiously jotting down notes for show. "And so how has that been? Practicing with your dad, I mean. Any regrets?"

"No regrets whatsoever. It's been the ride of a lifetime. Dad gave me a ton of responsibility. I tried my first lawsuit when associates I knew at other firms were still doing research or wading through documents. And the money hasn't been bad. What can I say? I would do it all over again in a heartbeat."

"What would you estimate your net worth to be?"

Christine waved her finger. "Out of bounds. That's one thing we don't talk to anybody about. In fact, we don't talk to each other about our own net worth. Way too personal. But nice try, though." Christine shot Leah an approving grin for effort.

"And do you try many cases together, or do you work your cases up separately?"

"Mostly the latter. Sure, we help each other out from time to time when there are scheduling conflicts. Plus, I manage the workup of some of his cases, and we bounce ideas and strategies off each other but, as far as the actual trials go, we fly solo."

Christine glanced at her Lady Rolex. "It's eleven. What time is your return flight?"

"Not until two-thirty. I had one or two more questions for you and then I thought I could meet with Mr. Connors. I should be able to finish my interview with him by twelve-thirty at the latest, which will give me plenty of time to make my flight."

Christine sighed. "I hate to tell you this, but Dad had an emergency hearing this morning. It's probably going to last all day. I would have notified you, but he didn't get the call from the court until your plane was in the air. Some jackass is trying to get an injunction against his client. You know how it is. Lawyers and reporters can't always control their schedules. I'm sorry."

Leah's eyes narrowed, but her smile remained. So it was a trap. The Lone Wolf had his daughter running interference for him. Cal wanted to know what she knew. He didn't want to be ambushed. Leah stared into the piercing blue eyes across the desk from her and made her decision. She would beat him at his own game.

"I understand. I would have loved getting to talk with him, one-on-one. Maybe some other time. Do you have a few more minutes for me?"

"Absolutely. I do have lunch plans, but I'm all yours till then."

"Great." Leah rummaged through her briefcase and pulled out a manila folder, laying it in her lap. "Picking up where we left off, you told me you and your dad pretty much fly solo on your trials, correct?"

"Pretty much."

"When I was doing my research before the Samson trial, I noticed your dad has successfully targeted pharmaceutical companies over the years, nailing them for big money. Did you have any involvement in any of those trials?"

Christine stiffened. "Wait a minute. My father does not 'target' companies. He represents plaintiffs, oftentimes for free, when they need counsel. Some of those plaintiffs have been hurt by exposure to chemicals, some have been hurt by ingesting certain drugs. I would not call that targeting companies."

"Perhaps I used the wrong terminology. I apologize. Let me rephrase, as you lawyers would say." Leah forced a grin. "Did you have any involvement in the pharmaceutical cases your father has tried?"

"Very, very limited. They were pretty much his babies."

"Do you know Dr. Howell Crimm?"

"I know of him. I have never met the man. I know he has testified as an expert witness in some of Dad's trials."

Leah flipped through her manila folder and pulled out a three-page article she had printed off the Internet. She handed it across the desk to Christine and searched her face for clues as she read it.

After she finished her review, Christine cavalierly slid the article back across the desk. "And your question is?"

"Did you know Dr. Crimm had been reprimanded by a judge for giving false testimony as to his credentials?"

"I read the article a little differently. I don't believe Dr. Crimm admitted he intentionally gave false testimony. His memory was simply mistaken. It happens." Christine eyes showed no concern. She was going to be a tough nut to crack.

Leah returned the article to the manila folder and then pulled out a two-page document. "Are you aware that the judgment recently awarded in the Samson case hinged on Dr. Crimm's opinion that the data Samson submitted to the FDA had been falsified?"

"I don't know the details, but that may be true. Do you have a copy of that document?"

"Sorry, but things were so hectic yesterday afternoon that I forgot to make one." Leah lied.

Christine's eyes narrowed. "I hate to be asked about documents I can't review. Sort of unfair, don't you think?"

"We're not in trial, are we? I thought this was just an informal interview. I would have saved these questions for Mr. Connors, but he is conveniently in court."

"Ms. Rosen, you are wasting my time. There are plenty of flights prior to the one you are scheduled on. I would suggest you catch one of those." Christine rose from her chair and stood behind her desk. "I'd be lying if I said it had been a pleasure, and I don't lie. I do wish you a safe return flight."

Leah placed her legal pad and manila folder back in her briefcase and made her way toward the door. Stopping just short, she turned toward Christine.

"One last thing. That document I just referred to—you know, the one I conveniently didn't have a copy of—it proves that everything Dr. Crimm swore to in the Samson trial was one big lie, a 'fraud on the court,' in legalese. Well, have a nice day, Christine."

Without waiting for a reply, Leah closed the door and hurried down the hall. She was so excited she couldn't wait to tell Abe. She had pulled off one hell of a bluff, acting like she had a smoking gun in her hand when she really didn't—at least, not yet. She had seen real concern in Christine's eyes when she held up that document. And that was exactly the way she wanted it.

CHAPTER

27

Calling Pat had been a good move. Everyone at the station seemed to be on a first-name basis with his law school friend, from the receptionist to the arresting officer. In less than two hours, they had arranged Matt's release and Pat was off to douse another fire.

Jace waited for his son on a wooden bench in the reception area, watching inmates walk by in their prison uniforms, manacled together, shuffling along slowly and awkwardly. With horror, he pictured his son in similar attire and shuddered at the thought. Out of the corner of his eye, he spotted Matt coming through the swinging doors at the end of the hall. Instinctively, he jumped up and rushed toward his son. The two embraced, and this time it was not awkward. After several seconds, Jace pulled away to get a closer look at the damage done the preceding night.

"Nice shiner. Looks like the other guy got the better end of things."

Matt smiled faintly. "Couldn't say. Fortunately or unfortunately, don't remember much about it."

"And, man, you smell like a brewery!"

Matt shrugged and looked down dejectedly at the linoleum floor.

"Let's get you back to your apartment and discuss where we go from here. We'll need to take a cab. Mr. Reynolds picked me up at the airport."

"Who is Mr. Reynolds?"

"An old law school classmate of mine you might have heard me speak of over the years. He's also your new lawyer." Jace reached in his pocket and handed his son Pat's card. "Call him later this week. You'll need to make an appointment to discuss your case—how you're going to plead and what to expect."

Matt looked puzzled. "You're not going to represent me?"

"If I did, you'd be spending time in Leavenworth. I don't know shit about criminal procedure. You got all your belongings?"

Matt nodded.

"I'm sure you're ready to get the hell outta here."

"Past ready."

Father and son walked out of the waiting area and down the stairs. During the cab ride to Matt's apartment, Jace, his voice lowered so the cabdriver could not hear, asked his son to describe everything that had happened between the time he was arrested and the time he was released. Although Matt's memory was a little foggy, he did recall a mug shot being taken, being strip-searched and fingerprinted.

Jace's expression never changed. He decided the last thing Matt needed at this moment was additional worry. Matt certainly didn't need to know that the Austin PD could now match his prints against those taken from Alexis Stone's apartment.

As the cab pulled up in front of Matt's apartment, Jace considered how his remaining time in Austin could best be spent. Clearly, his son was hungover and in no mood to discuss the events of the previous evening in more detail. He sensed Matt just wanted to hit the sack and sleep it off. Fortunately, he was not concerned about Matt's mental or physical condition. There had been some joking between them during the cab ride, and Matt's shiner did not look too bad.

All in all, things were as good as could be expected—except for one thing. He needed to find out what the police would likely do with the prints they had just taken from Matt. What would routine police procedure be? His son could not answer those questions, but Jackie McLaughlin could. Jace had one more stop to make before heading for the airport.

"I ought to kick your ass for pulling a stunt like this," he told Matt. "But I am going to let it slide this time. I suppose spending the night in jail was punishment enough."

"Dad, I'm really sorry. I know I was an idiot. So stupid." Matt shook his head in disgust.

"Well, don't beat yourself up too bad over this. We all make mistakes. Lord knows I've made my share. Just go easy on the booze and try and stay out of trouble."

"Will do, Dad. I promise."

"I need to get back to Fort Worth. Got a bunch of alligators nipping at my ass."

"Thanks again, Dad."

Jace nodded reassuringly and squeezed his son's shoulder. "Take care of yourself. If you need me, I'm a call away."

Matt exited the cab and shut the door. Jace watched as his son slowly made his way up the stairs to his apartment and, after glancing over his shoulder one last time, went inside.

The cabdriver turned around. "Airport?"

"No, the Austin Police Department."

A few minutes later Jace was at the receptionist desk at the APD. "Is Jackie McLaughlin in?"

The receptionist looked at a schedule on her desk. "It looks like she has signed out for the day. Is there anyone else who can help you?"

Jace shook his head. "No. I'll just give her a call."

Jace decided it was probably best she wasn't around. He hadn't really had time to plan out what he was going to say without piquing Jackie's interest into why he wanted answers to the questions he would ask. He didn't really know why he had even considered asking her. Then he remembered her big brown eyes and her confident nature and realized he had subconsciously been looking for an excuse to see her again. Not a good move. He was thinking with the little head and not the big one. Jace quickly turned away from the reception desk and headed toward the stairs.

CHAPTER

28

When Leah got to her rental car, she slid in behind the wheel and immediately called Abe. Jan, his secretary, answered.

"Is Abe in? This is Leah."

"Oh, hi, Leah. He's here but he's in a meeting. Do you want me to put you in his voice mail?"

Leah didn't hesitate. "No, this is pretty important."

"Let me stick my head in," said Jan.

Within seconds, Abe was on the line. "Leah, I've been hoping you didn't go off and do something stupid like meeting with Mr. Connors alone."

"Not exactly. I didn't meet with Mr. Connors, but I just got out of a very interesting interview with his daughter, Christine."

Abe made an audible groan. "I was afraid you were at the point where you'd do anything to get this story. I thought we agreed to meet before you did any interviews with Cal or his daughter."

"Well, I think I agreed to meet with you before I interviewed Cal Connors. So technically, I didn't breach our agreement. But, you're right. I probably am willing to do anything for this story. And you were also right about the meeting being a trap. Christine was running interference for her dad. She gave me some lame excuse as to why he couldn't meet with me."

"I'm thankful for that. You have no idea of the consequences that could have resulted from interviewing Cal Connors unprepared. I want to meet with you as soon as you get back to the office to discuss this matter."

"Done. But, Abe, I did get to size up Christine and lay a bombshell on her in the process."

"I'm not sure I follow you."

"Well, first of all, I asked her a lot of background questions, like I would in a real interview. I'll fill you in on all the details when we meet, but one important fact came out. She and her dad don't try cases together. To quote Christine, they fly solo. I assume Cal doesn't want to share any of the glory, not even with his own flesh and blood."

"Doesn't surprise me."

"And Christine denied any involvement in the pharmaceutical cases where Crimm has testified. In fact, she told me she knew of Dr. Crimm but had never met him. And I believe her. Bottom line, I think it is very likely she is not involved in her dad's fraud and probably doesn't even know about it."

"That's pretty hard to believe. I mean, they work in a fairly small law office, don't they?"

"True, but if the Lone Wolf didn't want his daughter to know something, it's my bet he could keep it from her. He's pretty calculating and obviously very smart. He might even be insulating Christine from any liability in the event the house of cards ever does come tumbling down."

"You've got a point."

"Also, I tried and tried to reach Dr. Patel over the weekend about sending me the email containing his research, the one he sent to Crimm."

"And?"

"I never got him. He may have been avoiding my calls. I don't know. Anyway, I didn't reach him so I never got the email."

"Without that you didn't have much to work with, did you?"

"Well, that's sorta true and sorta not. First, I gave Christine a copy of the Internet article indicating Crimm had been reprimanded by a Kansas judge for giving false testimony about his credentials."

"And how did she respond?"

"Very coolly. She didn't get flustered at all—at least, not on the surface. Who knows what was going on inside? Then I pulled a two-page document from my briefcase and pretended to read from it. I used an old lawyer trick I remembered from watching a Perry Mason episode on late night television back when I was in college—pretending to have some damning information in a document that you read from but don't show to the witness. I just held it up and told Christine that its contents would prove Crimm's testimony in the Samson case was one big lie."

"And Christine's response?"

"She requested a copy of the document and, when I wouldn't give it to her, ended the interview. She momentarily lost her cool. I could tell her mind was racing."

"I suspect an interesting discussion between father and daughter may be in the offing."

"That's what I'm hoping." Leah looked at her watch. "Well, I better get going if I want to make the one o'clock. And, Abe, I'm really sorry I breached your trust. I promise it won't happen again."

"Apology accepted. And one more thing, Leah."

"What's that?"

"Great work."

Leah steered her rental car out of the parking lot, casting one last glance at the Lone Wolf's lair. She knew Cal had been in those offices the whole time. And she had no doubt there was a powwow going on between the two co-conspirators at that very moment. If only she could be a fly on the wall.

CHAPTER

29

"I knew it, I knew it, I knew it. That little bitch." Cal paced back and forth as Christine watched apprehensively. "I knew she was up to no good. I could read it in her eyes when she asked me those loaded questions in front of the courthouse."

"But is any of it true? Did Crimm really testify he was board certified, like that Internet article said? I mean, come on, Dad. You can't be mistaken about whether you are board-certified in something. Either you are or you aren't. I didn't let Ms. Rosen know I was concerned, but I was, and still am."

"Now, Christine, you and I both know that experts have egos bigger than the state of Texas. They like to exaggerate their accomplishments. That doesn't necessarily mean they're dishonest. And you can bet that if Ms. Rosen had uncovered any other dirt on Crimm, she'd have given it to you. Hell, one admonition from a judge during an entire career of testifying—that ain't much, if you ask me. Like a mosquito on an elephant's ass."

The analogy really didn't fit but Christine let it pass. "How about that document she said would prove Crimm's testimony in the Samson case was a lie?"

"She didn't give you a copy, did you? No, siree. And there's good reason for that. It's a bunch of shit. There is no such document. Crimm's testimony in that case was right on. Samson cheated the government and the American people. They were the—" Cal's pace had quickened, his voice vacillating for effect.

Christine interrupted him. "All right, all right. You're not giving a closing argument to a jury. I'm just your daughter, who has had a bit of a shock this morning, that's all."

"Christine, look me in the eyes. There is nothing to any of this—nothing at all. I swear to you."

Christine didn't respond.

"Now, one last thing before we close the book on Ms. Rosen and her pack of lies. You told me she works for *Texas Matters,* right?"

Christine nodded.

"*Texas Matters* is owned by Steve Blumenthal. I know Steve—not well, but I know him. I met him at the Texas Trial Lawyers convention in Austin a few years back. Blumenthal was a featured speaker, and a few of us had drinks with him after his talk." Cal paused, gathering his thoughts. "I also know circulation for *Texas Matters* isn't what it used to be and neither is advertising revenue. Everyone's turning to the Internet. Hard-copy magazines are becoming a thing of the past. And Blumenthal knows the numbers better than anyone."

"So what are you suggesting, Dad?"

"One call from me hinting at a libel suit if he runs a negative article on me, Dr. Crimm, or this firm will scare the ever-livin' shit out of him. He can't afford the legal fees such a suit would cost. He knows I could spend him into the ground. Bottom line, it wouldn't be good business for him to take the risk."

"Are you going to make the call?"

"Do I need to answer that question?" Cal shot his daughter a comforting smile and returned to the chair behind his antique desk.

Christine got up from her seat and slowly made her way to the door. After leaving her dad's office, she leaned against the wall. She had an uneasy feeling. She just wasn't comfortable with her dad's responses. If there really was something to what Leah had said, and those accusations appeared in print, their law firm and the enormous wealth they had amassed would be in serious risk. There would be lawsuits against Connors & Connors by every defendant who had gotten hit with a big judgment based on Crimm's expert opinion. Criminal investigations against her dad and Crimm would likely ensue, and she might even get sucked in. At the least, her career, which she had so carefully cultivated, would be forever tainted.

Christine turned and began to walk briskly toward her office, her brow furrowed and lips pursed. Was Leah just a young reporter trying to make a name for herself by fabricating a story about a well-known trial lawyer? Or did she really have evidence proving her dad was hiding a vast legal fraud?

Christine knew Leah could not be underestimated. It was evident from their brief encounter that she was a determined little bitch. Which meant this situation had to be handled perfectly. There was no room for error. Complacency and overconfidence would definitely not be virtues in circumstances like these.

Christine walked into her office and headed for her computer. It was time for her to do a little detective work of her own.

She slid into the chair behind her desk and logged on. She clicked on the Concordance icon, scrolled down to "Expert Reports," and then typed in "Dr. Howell Crimm." She stared at the computer screen, waiting for her search to be completed. There were 23 hits. She clicked on the first one. A pleading entitled "Affidavit of Howell Crimm" appeared on the screen. She skimmed it, and then clicked on the Print icon. She repeated this process 23 times and then walked quickly to the printer behind her secretary's desk and waited for the documents to finish printing. Fortunately, her secretary was at lunch, so there were no offers of assistance or questions to answer.

After sorting the documents and stapling each, she returned to her office and took a seat at the small conference table in the corner. Fifteen affidavits had been filed in various jurisdictions. There were a few out-of-state filings, but most of them had been offered in Texas courts. She recognized many of the cases, but there were three older ones that predated her start date with the firm.

One of the affidavits had been filed in the Samson Pharmaceuticals case. She read the affidavit closely. In it, Dr. Crimm opined that Samson had slanted the test data on a drug called Fosorax in a fraudulent way, presumably to obtain approval from the Federal Drug Administration. The affidavit was short, with few supporting citations. It did contain Dr. Crimm's lengthy, and impressive, résumé as an exhibit. Christine placed the affidavit on the side of the conference table and turned her attention to the next affidavit in the pile of papers in front of her.

She looked at the case style at the top of the affidavit: *Jennings* v. *Pharnum Pharmaceuticals,* in the 134th District Court of Jefferson County, Texas. She had a good recollection of the case since it had been settled two years earlier for several million dollars. She began a careful read of the affidavit. The language Crimm used was remarkably similar to the language of the affidavit used in the Samson Pharmaceuticals case, only the drug was different—Anxil, a drug frequently prescribed to lower cholesterol. Once again, without footnoted support, Crimm contended that FDA approval for the drug had been procured by the use of skewed test results.

Christine quickly scanned the remaining affidavits. There were some minor differences, but Crimm's conclusions were always the same. She took a deep breath, got up, and walked around her office for a minute, then slid into the chair behind her computer. She exited out of Concordance and then logged out of the system. She then logged back in, using her dad's login and password, both of which he had given to her so she could answer questions or retrieve data when he didn't have computer access. She clicked on the Outlook icon—the firm's email program—and then "Sent Items." In the search window, she typed in "Howell Crimm." Fifty-two emails came up. Christine began reading each, starting with the most recent. The first one she read caused her eyes to widen. It was dated a few days after the jury verdict in the Samson case.

"Howell, we kicked ass again. Hell, the jurors loved it when I blew up your affidavit and held it in front of them—all your statements about a big ol' Yankee company committing fraud. They couldn't wait to get back to the jury room and spank them boys. In any event, thanks! And don't worry about what we had to do. Just remember—the ends justify the means. Ciao, Cal."

Christine read the email again—and then again. She always knew that when it came to a lawsuit, her father played hard, but she had no idea he would resort to this. He had suborned perjury, and he had profited handsomely from it. Actually, she said to herself, she too had profited from what he had done.

She sighed and turned her eyes from the computer screen and looked at the gavel on the corner of her credenza, a gift from Justice Lindsay Lofland, a recently retired Supreme Court justice whom Christine had befriended while writing for the *Harvard Law Review*. Her eyes then focused on the many diplomas and awards framed and hanging on the wall across from her desk: *Law Review,*

Order of the Coif, magna cum laude. She had worked her ass off to get where she was.

Christine knew that if she confronted her dad with what she had learned it would only make him defensive and could possibly harm their relationship forever. She also knew that she couldn't count on the fact that Blumenthal, the *Texas Matters* owner, would kill Leah's article.

But she knew she had to get that article killed. For her sake, she needed to handle this on her own, to come up with a backup plan to make sure Leah Rosen's story never went to print—to make sure Leah *never* published anything having to do with Connors & Connors.

CHAPTER

30

Jace's breakfast meeting at the Waffle House with Lonnie Masterson had been disquieting and unproductive. Lonnie had picked at his food and carefully guarded everything he said to Jace. After breakfast, Jace knew no more about Lonnie than he had before. His private investigator had tried to get Lonnie's personnel file from his previous employer without success. How Lonnie would do as a witness remained a mystery. Jace tried to explain the deposition process to him and prepare him for questions he could expect later that morning, but Lonnie didn't seem to understand anything Jace told him.

Jace could only hope that Lonnie was the exception to the rule, one of those introverted people who made an exceptional witness, listening carefully to every question and never volunteering anything. That's one thing Jace felt he could count on with Lonnie. Information had to be painfully extracted from him. On the other hand, Jace sensed Lonnie could be easily flustered and intimidated and was worried he might be easy prey for the master of interrogation, Cal Connors.

Jace and Lonnie got out of the car and made their way toward the front door of Connors & Connors. Lonnie was slump-shouldered and walked as if in slow motion. As they trudged along, Jace repeated his instructions one last time.

"Lonnie, all you need to do is listen carefully to Mr. Connors' questions, think before answering, and then tell the truth. Don't guess. If you don't know the answer to a question, then the only honest answer is 'I don't know.' Follow those rules and you will be just fine."

Jace put his hand on Lonnie's shoulder and made eye contact. "And, remember, I'll be there the entire time. If you need a break, don't be afraid to ask for one. Any questions?"

There was no reply. Instead, Lonnie leaned away from Jace's grasp and opened the door, his eyes in a zombie-like trance. Jace could feel a stress headache building, the fried hash browns in his stomach starting to rumble.

Jace and his client announced their arrival to the receptionist. "We are here for a deposition with Mr. Connors."

"Yes. Mr. Connors is expecting you. He's in the master conference room on the second floor."

They made their way to the elevator. When they arrived at the conference room, they stopped at the entrance to read the inscription on the brass plate above the door: "The Boneyard." Very clever, Cal, very clever. Jace opened the door, only to be momentarily blinded by the videographer's light. Jace was visibly irritated.

"Could you cut that thing off until we get started? It's a little bright."

Cal rose from his seat and made his way around the table to greet his guests. He was dressed in a white shirt, bolo tie, brown suede jacket, fringed at the pockets and down the arms, blue jeans, and light-colored ostrich-skin boots. Cal took Jace's hand and shook it enthusiastically.

"Good to see you, Jace. It's been a while since we had a case together. Seems like it was the CCT case. Your client was Cross Country Transport. You put up a hell of a good fight. And I always admired your decision to settle that case. Hell, I bet the jury would have given me twice the amount you paid me. Nicely done, Counselor."

Jace's expression never changed, but the videographer and court reporter smiled at Cal's backhanded compliment. "And this must be Mr. Masterson," Cal continued. "Good to meet you, son." Cal took Lonnie's hand from his side, holding it firmly and staring into the boy's eyes for an inordinately long time.

Jace interrupted. "Let's get on with it, Cal."

"Never seen anyone so anxious to enter the lion's den," Cal mockingly chuckled. "Let's get going, then."

After everyone had taken their seats at the granite-topped table, the videographer adjusted the light so it focused right in Lonnie's eyes, causing him to squint and squirm nervously in his chair.

"Could you focus that light a little above his head? No need to hit him right between the eyes." Jace was disgusted with the "interrogation room" atmosphere. The videographer looked at Cal for instructions. Cal nodded, and the cameraman upped the beam.

"Everybody ready?" Cal's eyes made the rounds, lingering longer on the witness.

The videographer replied apologetically. "Mr. Connors, if I could have just one minute. I'm not sure I've got the volume right." He awaited an approving nod. Cal obliged, appearing a little annoyed at the request.

The videographer's words were hurried. "Mr. Masterson, say something into your mike, please, sir. I need a reading."

Lonnie looked down at the peanut-size device that had been clipped to his tie. "What do you want me to say?"

"That's fine. I can hear you just fine. We're ready to roll. Hold it for a moment. We're now on the record at 9:08."

Cal turned toward the court reporter. "Would you swear the witness?"

"Mr. Masterson, please raise your right hand."

The court reporter waited for Lonnie to comply. After administering the oath, she turned back to her stenographic machine, poised to record every word said during the proceedings to follow.

Normally, before asking any questions, Cal would go on the record and casually instruct the witness to tell the truth, to make verbal answers instead of nods so that the court reporter could record his answers, and to ask Cal to restate any questions the witness did not understand. He would also instruct the witness that, even though they were in his conference room, the testimony given was just like being in the courtroom before a judge and jury. This time, however, Cal did away with the usual formalities and went straight for the jugular.

"Mr. Masterson, you are currently employed by Caring Oaks Funeral Home and Cemetery, the defendant in this case, is that correct?"

Lonnie nodded affirmatively.

"Mr. Masterson, you'll have to speak out loud. The court reporter can't take down a nod."

"Yes."

"Where did you work before that?"

"Knoxville." Lonnie's eyes stared down at the granite tabletop.

"Do you remember the name of the company you worked for in Knoxville?"

Lonnie continued to look down. "No, sir, I don't."

"Let me see if I can help you a little. Would it have been Peaceful Meadows Funeral Home?"

Lonnie's eyes remained glued to the table.

"Mr. Masterson, was my question confusing? Let me ask it a different way. Before coming to work at Caring Oaks, the defendant in this case, did you work at Peaceful Meadows Funeral Home in Knoxville, Tennessee?"

"I don't remember."

Jace sensed disaster. Cal clearly had some information that he didn't. How could that be? Why hadn't his investigator been able to get the same information Cal had in front of him? He felt his foot began to bounce, and rivulets of perspiration ran down the insides of his arms. He had to try and stop this. He needed to stall, to buy some time.

"Obviously, the witness is overwhelmed by this hostile, intimidating atmosphere and needs a moment to compose himself. Let's break for five minutes."

"No way. And if you take this witness outside this room and interrupt my questioning, I will ask Judge Reinhold to strike the answer you filed in this case and enter a default judgment against your client."

Jace knew Cal wasn't bluffing, and he also knew there was a strong likelihood that Cal's buddy, Judge Reinhold, would grant such a motion. And, more disturbingly, Cal knew that his ruling would be upheld on appeal. After all, the deposition had just started and the questions had not been tricky or difficult. Jace decided to retreat. He couldn't risk it.

"Are you telling this jury you can't remember who you worked for a little over a year ago?" Cal stared at the witness in mock incredulity.

Jace grimaced. He sensed Cal was laying the foundation for something devastating, and he was helpless to stop it.

Cal opened a thin manila folder and extracted a single piece of paper from inside. He handed it to the court reporter and asked that it be marked as exhibit 1 to the witness's deposition.

The court reporter obliged and handed the exhibit back to Cal, who held it in front of himself for a few seconds, then slid it across the conference table in the direction of Lonnie.

"Would you please read to the jury the handwritten words next to the box 'Reason for termination'?"

The witness stared down at the piece of paper in front of him. After several minutes he looked up at the camera, its beam piercing his forehead. His upper lip began to quiver. His eyes twitched noticeably. He opened his mouth as if trying to speak. The words sticking, he pushed back his chair from the table and, with the camera still rolling, got up and walked quickly out the door. All eyes followed him. An uncomfortable silence filled the room. Jace tried to get up but his legs wouldn't respond. He sat there motionless, confused, with no plan to minimize the damage.

Cal calmly leaned across the table and retrieved exhibit 1. He looked squarely into the camera lens and stated, "Since the witness refuses to read the document, then I will. It is entitled 'Termination Notice.'" He paused for effect, his look indignant. "Under the section entitled 'Reason for termination' it states, and I quote, 'Mr. Masterson is under indictment for molestation of a corpse, a felony under Tennessee law.' And the document is signed by Thomas Cargill, President, Peaceful Meadows Cemetery."

Cal turned to Jace, proffering the exhibit, a confident grin creasing his lips. "Any questions, Counselor?"

CHAPTER
31

"He just got up and left?" Darrin's eyes widened.

Jace nodded. "I couldn't believe it. I have never had anything like that happen before. Never."

"So where did he go?"

"Beats me. I called Wallace Arnold on my way back to the office. He went ballistic. Acted as if it was all my fault."

"How could it have been your fault? We interviewed the guy, we reviewed his personnel file at Caring Oaks, who you would assume had done a thorough background check on him, and you met with him before his deposition to give him a preview of what to expect. We can't help it if he lied to us."

"Don't we have our best investigator, Boyce Ramey, on this? He should have caught the lie. He should have been able to get the same damn documents Cal's did. Boyce is the best in the business. I wonder what happened."

Darrin thought for a moment. "Cal's investigator got there first and greased the palm of the HR director or whoever has custody of Peaceful Meadows employment records. That's what happened. I have no doubt about it. Money talks and Cal's investigator slid that money right under the table. Besides, that record was going to come out sooner or later. And no matter how well you had prepped Lonnie, there was no way to make that document go away. The facts are the facts."

"But you know as well as I do that when things go wrong in a case, clients always blame their lawyers, no matter who's at fault. And things went wrong today—in a big way."

"So where do we go from here?"

"First, we've got to find Lonnie—calm him down, get the facts on what happened back in Tennessee. We need to interview the guy who signed Lonnie's termination notice and check the courthouse files. Maybe the indictment was dropped. Either that or Lonnie was cleared by a jury. It has to be one of the two. Otherwise Lonnie wouldn't be walking around as a free man."

Darrin made notes as Jace paced. "Have you gotten Alexis' phone records yet?"

Darrin retrieved a file from the corner of her desk and handed it to Jace. "Just got them this morning. Here's a list of all the incoming and outgoing calls, cross-referenced with names."

"And what do the records show?" Jace anxiously flipped through the file contents.

"Lots of calls, most of them unimportant to our case. However, there were a significant number of calls to two numbers. Sloan Jenkins, apparently a college friend. And the other to—get this—state senator Talmadge Worthman."

"His name's familiar but . . ."

"I have all the scoop on him. He's a Republican from a rural district out in East Texas and nearing the end of his third term—up for reelection."

214

"Is he married?"

"With children. On the surface, he's a devout family man. Lots of rhetoric about family values, the evils of abortion—you know the type. Bought and paid for by the religious right."

"Why would he be—"

Darrin interrupted, sensing his next question. "Apparently, our good senator has one weakness: UT coeds about half his age."

"He was seeing Alexis Stone?"

"Sure looks that way. He certainly enjoyed talking to her. I've got Boyce turning over rocks. Hopefully we'll learn more in the next day or so."

"Anything else in the records?"

"Yeah, interestingly there is not one call to or from her parents. Weird, huh?"

"I don't know. Think of Matt. He got mad at me, and for a while I might as well not have existed."

"Yeah, but you still called him. I just think it's strange, that's all."

"Speaking from my own experience, when it comes to relationships between parents and their kids, you never know. But I'll have a chance to get into that when I depose the Stones. Meanwhile, I think I need to pay Sloan Jenkins a visit. And while I'm in Austin, I should drop in on the senator."

"You'll probably have a hard time getting an appointment with him."

"You'll figure something out."

Jace smiled and winked at Darrin as he headed out the door toward his office. On his way, he stopped at Harriett's desk and asked her if he had had any calls.

"You've had a few. I emailed you on all of them."

Exasperated, Jace asked, "Any you can remember that seemed important?"

Harriet went into her Sent mailbox and scanned the emails she had forwarded to Jace that day. "Not that I can remember.

Oh, wait a minute. This one might be. A Detective Jackie McLaughlin from the Austin Police Department called at 10:32. She said it was urgent."

Jace shook his head at Harriett's nonchalant attitude and hurried into his office, slamming the door behind him. He nervously dialed Jackie's number and waited for an answer, still standing, pacing back and forth in front of his credenza.

"Jackie McLaughlin."

"Jackie, it's Jace Forman."

Her tone was businesslike. "Mr. Forman, I hate to be the bearer of bad news but our new assistant DA, Reginald Cowan, has taken an interest in the Alexis Stone investigation. In that regard, he wants me to bring your son in for questioning."

Jace was momentarily speechless.

"It seems his prints match some of those found in Alexis' apartment. Now, before you say anything, let me just tell you that I do not like to be lied to. You had a court-issued subpoena to review our department's files, and I think I was more than generous with my time in going over those with you and getting copies to your office. If I find out that you were misleading me in any way to cover up your son's involvement, not only will I have your law license, I'll put you behind bars. Now, let's start over. Is there something you haven't told me?"

"Jackie, I promise you, when we went over the evidence together, I had no clue my son even knew Alexis Stone."

"And now?"

"It's a long story."

"I've got plenty of time"

"Not over the phone. Look, I've got to be in Austin to interview some witnesses on this same case. I'll come in tonight and we can meet face-to-face. I think we can help each other on this. If you let me buy you dinner, I will tell you everything I know, and I guarantee you Matt had no involvement whatsoever." Jace wasn't sure

216

what Matt did or didn't do with Alexis the night of her death, but he felt sure his son was not a killer.

Jackie's tone softened somewhat. "Look, I believe the autopsy report. I don't think anyone killed Alexis. And I am not sure why Mr. Cowan has all of a sudden shown an interest in this file. But I want to get to the bottom of it. I'll meet you for dinner, but given the circumstances, I don't think it's appropriate that you buy. We'll share the tab and you'll give me whatever information you have—no holding back. Those are my conditions."

"Fair enough. I'll call you when I arrive."

"I'll be expecting your call."

After Jackie hung up the phone, she rocked back in her swivel chair, positioning her feet on the desk in front of her. "Who is this Jace Forman?" she wondered. She decided it was time to find out.

CHAPTER

32

Leah turned on her cell phone and scrolled through her emails. It was all pretty routine stuff, nothing of pressing importance. She then noticed she had a voice mail. It was from Dr. Patel. She touched the red button next to his name and his voice came on the line.

"Ms. Rosen, I am sorry I did not return your call sooner. I had clinical rounds all weekend. I have given a lot of thought to what we discussed. Please call me at your convenience."

Leah hit the call button and Dr. Patel picked up on the first ring.

"Ms. Rosen, thank you for returning my call so quickly."

"Actually, I've been in Fort Worth. I went to Cal Connors' law firm to interview him and his daughter. She practices with him."

"I see."

"That's why I was trying so desperately to get in touch with you over the weekend. I wanted to see if you had decided what to do with regard to your email to Dr. Crimm. If possible, I wanted to use it in my meeting with the Connors."

Silence.

"Please understand. I wasn't going to give them a copy or tell him who sent the email. I only wanted to read some of the conclusions, just to let them know my investigation was serious."

"So I assume your interview did not go as well as you had hoped, considering you did not have my email."

"Well, it did not go as planned. I didn't actually get to interview Mr. Connors—just his daughter, Christine. She indicated her father had gotten called to court at the last minute. I didn't buy her excuse, but there was nothing I could do."

"So you got nothing?"

"Actually, I'm pleased with the information I was able to get from Christine."

"Which means you no longer need my email?"

"It is even more important now."

Dr. Patel cleared his throat. "I have given this a lot of thought and discussed it with my wife. She thinks I should give a copy to you, that it provides us with some insurance against any accusations that might come up in the future and, at the same time, might play an important role in righting a very serious wrong. That being said, you must promise that you will not run the story under any circumstance if you have to reveal my identity."

Leah could hardly restrain herself. "You have my word."

"I would like that in writing, just for my protection."

"I understand. I will get something to you when I get back to my office."

"That will be fine."

"And, Dr. Patel, you won't regret this. You have made the right decision."

"I hope so, Ms. Rosen, I hope so."

CHAPTER

33

"Mr. Blumenthal's office." The tone was authoritative and to the point.

"Is he in? This is Cal Connors."

"Will he know what this is in regard to?"

"Just tell him it's a social call. We met at the Texas Trial Lawyers convention in Austin a couple of years ago. He was one of the speakers."

"Just one moment, please, and I'll see if Mr. Blumenthal is available."

Cal waited impatiently on the line while scrolling through the news headlines on his computer.

"Mr. Connors, he has someone in his office. Would you like his voice mail, or would you prefer to give me your number?"

"Voice mail would be fine, thank you, ma'am."

"I'll put you right in."

A recorded message filled the line. "This is Steve Blumenthal. I am either away from my desk or in a meeting. Please leave your contact information and the purpose of your call, and I will call you back as soon as possible. Thank you for calling."

"Steve, this is Cal Connors. I am a trial lawyer in Fort Worth. You and I met at the Texas Trial Lawyers convention a while back. Listen, I have an important matter I would like to discuss with you. It concerns a story dealing with a case I tried down in the Valley. One of your young reporters, I believe her name is Leah Rosen, has been working on it. If you would call me back I would be grateful. I look forward to visiting with you."

Cal left just enough information to ensure he would hear from the owner of *Texas Matters* before the end of the day.

Just as Cal was leaving his message for *Texas Matters,* Leah was opening an email from Dr. Patel. As promised, once he received written verification that his name would not be used or disclosed without his prior consent, Dr. Patel had forwarded the research he had provided to Dr. Crimm. It was fifteen pages in length and, in detailed fashion, analyzed the data Samson Pharmaceuticals had provided to the FDA.

Leah was unable to understand many of the medical terms and statistical analyses, but the conclusion at the end of the report was very clear. Although there were some errors in the data submitted, they were of a harmless nature. Accordingly, the number of side effects reported by the control group did not constitute a valid basis for denying approval of the drug.

Leah compared this conclusion with the one contained in the sworn affidavit provided by Dr. Crimm that Cal had used in his lawsuit against Samson. Clearly, Dr. Crimm had manipulated and misstated the facts. Obviously, the multimillion-dollar verdict in the case was based upon perjured testimony and should be set aside.

Leah was ecstatic. She now had credible support for her story. She was on the verge of exposing the biggest legal fraud in Texas history. The only thing she needed was Dr. Patel's consent to use his report or independent corroboration of what it showed. Leah doubted *Texas Matters* would fund a study to demonstrate the fallacy of Dr. Crimm's conclusions. It would be too time-consuming and costly. Plus, it wouldn't demonstrate Crimm had knowingly twisted the data. But Dr, Patel's email did just that. She had to persuade him to let her use that evidence. It was the only way justice would be done. She needed to talk to Abe and get his ideas on how to make that happen.

CHAPTER

34

Jace arrived at the Austin airport a little after seven o'clock. As his plane taxied to the gate, he wondered if things could get any worse. His key witness in a multimillion-dollar case had cratered, and his son was being brought in for questioning in connection with a possible homicide. He had an uncharacteristic moment of self-pity that he immediately dispelled once the plane came to a stop and the passengers began to deplane. At least Darrin had been able to schedule a meeting for him the following day with Senator Worthman. And in less than an hour, he would be having dinner with an attractive detective who he hoped would end up on his side.

Jace pulled his rental car up to the valet stand at Eddie V's around seven-forty. He took it as a good sign that Jackie had agreed to meet him there for dinner, since it was probably one of the more intimate restaurants in town. After checking in with the maître d', he decided to wait in the piano lounge, a dimly lit room with dark stained-wood panels accented by large mirrors on the wall and a hand-painted mural over the bar.

The lounge was crowded. A jazz band softly played some Coltrane in the corner. There were several empty seats at the bar. Jace slid onto one of the stools and ordered the usual, Jack on the rocks. As he took the first sip, he felt a tap on his shoulder.

"Hello, Mr. Forman."

Jackie was wearing a brown sweater dress, cinched in at the waist with a wide brown leather belt. She had on knee-high boots, brown suede, with slim, two-inch heels. A long silver chain completed her outfit.

Jace stood up and turned, grabbing Jackie's hand in a friendly handshake. "Thank you for agreeing to meet with me. And please, I was hoping we could remain on a first-name basis."

"You are welcome, Jace. And I agree, first names are fine."

"Great. Our table is not quite ready. How about a drink while we wait?"

Jackie slid onto the bar stool next to Jace and placed her purse on the bar. "Hmmm, let's see. A vodka tonic with a twist sounds good. Stoli, if they have it."

Jace motioned to one of the bartenders and placed the order.

"I hate to talk shop right off the bat, but I have been pretty uptight since you told me that new prosecutor wants to interrogate Matt."

"I'm sorry if I scared you with my call, but Cowan is all over the Stone file."

"I don't understand how the file came to his attention in the first place." Jace shook his head.

"I was wondering that myself. Apparently, he requested it." The bartender set Jackie's drink down in front of her and she took a sip. "The talk around the office is he got wind of your lawsuit in Fort Worth, with all the publicity surrounding it. He probably thought the case might be a good stepping-stone for his career.

He's young. He needs a headline or two. The minute the *Austin American-Statesman* hears he's looking into the death of a pretty college coed, he'll be on the front page."

"Shit. Not what I wanted to hear."

Jackie's dark-brown eyes stared inquisitively at Jace. "It's time you came clean with me about your son. I have to know what you know about his involvement. Otherwise, there is nothing I can do to help you. Or him, for that matter."

Jace hesitated. He stared back into Jackie's eyes, not sure what to say.

"Look," Jackie said, surprising herself as she touched his arm. "I told you that I don't believe Alexis was murdered. My job is not just to solve crimes but to make sure innocent people aren't railroaded. And Matt is on the verge of getting run over by that train."

"Jackie, would you mind if I asked you a couple of questions first?"

Suddenly, the maître d' interrupted, advising them their table was ready. Jace and Jackie picked up their drinks and followed him to the back corner of the restaurant. Once seated, their conversation resumed.

"Can we make this conversation off the record?" asked Jace.

Jackie set her drink down and stared at Jace. She didn't want to lie to him, but she had no choice. She had to know what he knew, and he wouldn't be forthcoming if he thought she was going to use it against his son. Depending on the information she gained from Jace, she would likely at least note it in her investigative file.

"Off the record."

Jace took a deep breath and let it out slowly. "I'll hold you to that. So, where should I start?"

"Try the beginning."

Their waiter interrupted. "I see you have your drinks. Would you care to hear about our specials for this evening?"

Jace looked at Jackie. "I don't want to be presumptuous, but how does the eight-ounce filet, medium-rare, side order of the twice-baked potatoes, asparagus, and a bottle of David Bruce pinot noir sound to you?"

Jackie was stunned. "Wow. That was presumptuous." She looked up at the waiter and asked, "Could you give us a few minutes?" He bowed in acknowledgment and left.

While Jackie appreciated Jace's decisiveness, she did not want to allow him to set the tone for the evening. She needed to signal he was not in control. After scanning the menu, she said, "Well, Jace, I have to say, the eight-ounce filet, medium-rare, sounds great. But the twice-baked potatoes are just too much. Besides, they are fattening. The asparagus will be plenty for me. I'll leave the wine selection up to you. I admit I'm no connoisseur."

"Done deal."

The waiter appeared a few seconds later and took their orders. "Would either of you care for a salad?"

Jackie nodded her head and Jace took the cue. "We'll both have the Caesar." Jace added, "And there's no rush on the order."

"Understood, sir." The waiter turned and was gone.

"Well, where were we?" asked Jace.

"The beginning."

Jace related the entire story. Jackie listened attentively, occasionally asking a clarifying question. When Jace finished, he downed the last of his Jack, fiddling nervously with the tumbler. "So that's it. Believe it?"

Jackie was silent for a moment, and then asked, "Jace, I need to know what you think. Do you believe him?"

"I know my son through and through. We've had our difficulties, but he's a good kid. He's certainly not capable of murder."

Jackie nodded and paused a moment to consider everything Jace had said. "I believe you."

"I appreciate that. It's the truth."

"But now comes the hard part. You and Matt have got to prove his presence at Alexis' apartment that night was just what he said it was."

"So where do I go from here? How can I slow the assistant DA down?"

"You've got to take the focus off of Matt. Right now he is the only target in the investigation. You mentioned you plan to talk with some of the witnesses tomorrow, right?"

Jace nodded.

"Well, I think we can help each other there. I assume you have had lots of experience in depositions questioning witnesses, but it's a different animal when you question a person of interest in a criminal investigation. I know the ropes in that arena."

"Don't get me wrong. I would appreciate all the help you can give me. But I don't understand why you want to help me."

"Several reasons. The first is, like I said, I believe you. And while I'm not certain you've gotten the full story from Matt, I was at the scene and I believe it was nothing more than an accidental overdose. Second, and I will deny this if it is ever repeated, I don't like the fact that this assistant DA is using this to further his political career while, in the process, questioning the thoroughness of my investigation. So, do you want my help or not?"

"Absolutely."

"Good. Now, I am a trained investigator, not just a beat cop." She emphasized "am." "I've even taken a few courses at Quantico in psychological profiling, so I can offer you some valuable insight about people's motives, what goes on in the criminal mind, that sort of thing."

The waiter unobtrusively served their salads and, after allowing Jace to approve the David Bruce, poured each a glass of wine.

"Let's start with your witness interviews. Who are you planning on interviewing?"

"I was able to obtain Alexis' cell phone records. There were a significant number of calls between two specific people. The first was Sloan Jenkins, her 'BFF' in the photograph in your evidence files. And the second, who was quite a surprise, was state senator Talmadge Worthman. I'm scheduled to meet with the senator first thing in the morning."

"Wow, you have been busy. Calls with Senator Talmadge Worthman—that's very interesting. We should find out if there was anything going on between them, or if she was just trying to get a job interning or something of that nature. Do you know anyone in the senator's district?"

Jace thought for a moment. "I know some lawyers in that area."

"Good, that's a start. When you get in to see him, tell him his voting record impresses you. Even though you don't live in his district, you strongly believe that the Senate needs men like him with strong family values. You want to help him raise money in his district and, before doing so, want to get his input. You could mention you would be glad to co-sponsor a fund-raiser for his reelection campaign, drop a few names of the important lawyers you know in his district you might be able to persuade to join you. Then, here's the important part. Give him a big fat contribution while you're in his office. Nothing gets a politician's attention like money. The good senator is now your friend for a day. Are you with me so far?"

"Keep going." Jace wanted to hear the whole scenario before passing judgment.

"You thank him for his time, noting how busy he is. Then, as an afterthought you ask for a souvenir—a mug, a pen, anything. But make sure he hands it to you."

Jace looked puzzled.

"I want a fingerprint. Then, if there was something going on between him and Alexis, perhaps we could get a match with one of the prints lifted in Alexis' apartment. If we do, I will make sure the evidence gets to Cowan. Then he's got to look into the senator's behavior. After all, he can't overlook the fact that a married senator was in the apartment of a UT coed who turned up dead. You with me?"

"All the way. And that slows Cowan down and—"

"Takes the focus off Matt," said Jackie, giving Jace a knowing look.

Jace looked at Jackie. "You are one smart lady." He wanted to add "and beautiful," but he held back.

Jackie responded with a smile. "Now, make sure you don't handle the souvenir in the same place Worthman does. Then bring it directly to me at the department. I will make sure the prints get lifted immediately by a friend of mine down in the lab."

"Jackie, I'll never be able to thank you enough."

"Let's just call it even for now. I can show Cowan I'm putting in time on the case without actually having to do all of the legwork. Plus, you never know. I may need a favor from you some day."

"All you have to do is ask."

"Let's just get through this, and then we can talk about payback." Jackie smiled. She picked up her wine and swirled it in the glass before bringing it to her mouth and taking a sip.

A trio of waiters converged on the table, scurrying around, serving their entrées, positioning their sides, and filling their water and wineglasses. "Will there be anything else?"

"Not at the moment. Thank you," Jackie said.

Jace smiled and shook his head. This was one headstrong lady.

An obligatory "Enjoy," and the trio scattered in different directions.

Jackie took a small bite of her steak. "This is delicious. How's yours?"

"Great. I'm always a little reluctant to order a steak. My rule is, if you can cook it as well at home, don't order it when you go out. And I can grill a mean steak. Love it—relaxes me. Sprinkle some soaked mesquite chips on slow-burning charcoal, get that smoke going, and then throw a couple of filets on the Weber and let the smoke settle in. Of course, you gotta be sipping on a drink the whole time the steaks are grilling."

Jackie was beginning to relax. "You love to grill, and I'm not bad in the kitchen. My mama was a helluva cook, and I was always in the kitchen with her. I still use a lot of her recipes."

"That settles it. After we get through this mess, it's dinner at my place."

"But you live in Fort Worth and I'm here in Austin."

Jace smiled. "Details, details."

Jackie nervously cleared her throat. "Okay, back to business. I assume you're going to interview Sloan Jenkins, Alexis' friend?"

"I plan on paying her a visit tomorrow as well."

"Good. She could be a treasure trove of information. Since she and Alexis were obviously best friends, I would be surprised if she couldn't tell you who Alexis was seeing, whether her behavior had changed recently, where she hung out, that type of thing."

"That was my thinking as well," Jace replied as he took a bite of his steak.

"When you question her, my only advice is to be honest. Start slowly with less intimidating questions and then feel your way. Establish a common bond—you have a son at UT. Maybe that will break the ice. You never know what will work."

There was a comfortable pause in the conversation. Jackie broke the silence.

"Veering offtrack a bit, there's something else you might think about doing. It's something I learned in my psychological profiling courses. You might want to consider planting a small video camera next to the grave."

Jace was puzzled. "For what reason?"

"With a crime like body theft, we certainly aren't dealing with your normal criminal. There is a chance that the sicko who did

232

this will come back to her grave for a visit. People like this are just wired differently."

"Certainly worth a try." Jace made a mental note to talk to his investigator and Wallace about placing a camera at the gravesite. "There is one other witness I plan on interviewing tomorrow. The maid who found Alexis the morning she died."

"We interviewed her that morning. She really doesn't know anything. Why do you want to re-interview her?"

"The interview notes in the file were brief. I just want to make sure there isn't anything she may remember that could be helpful in the body theft case."

"Suit yourself. But I think you're wasting your time on that one."

Jace took a chance and put his hand on Jackie's and left it there. "I really appreciate all your help on this."

Jackie withdrew her hand, picked up her wineglass, and took a sip. "Jace, I have to be honest with you . . ."

The waiter appeared at the table, and their conversation momentarily stopped as he cleared their plates and asked, "How about an after-dinner drink or dessert?"

Jace looked at Jackie, signaling he was leaving it up to her.

Jackie looked at the waiter. "A cup of decaf coffee would be great, but I don't care for dessert."

Jace ordered the same. Once the waiter disappeared, Jackie continued. "As I was saying, I have to be honest with you. I did a little investigating on you and your son."

Jace raised his eyebrows. "That doesn't surprise me. But I hope you didn't find out about my evil past," he joked.

The waiter unobtrusively served their coffee. "No. But I do know you lost your wife recently."

Jace stared into his coffee as if it held all the answers. "It's been a tough year. If I can just get through the rest of it and keep Matt from having to go through any more than he has already, I'll be a much happier man."

"Do you want to talk about it? I'm a great listener."

"I know you are, Jackie, but I think I am just about talked out for the night. Let's turn to a more pleasing topic. Let's talk about you." Jace's eyes lit up.

Jackie, somewhat embarrassed, glanced at her watch. It was almost eleven-thirty. "I wish I could, but I didn't realize it was so late. I'm a single mom with a seventeen-year-old daughter who went out tonight and she has to be home by midnight. I like to be there when she gets in. I just don't feel good about her coming home to an empty house late at night."

"I don't blame you."

Jackie picked up her purse and pulled out her wallet. Jace, realizing she was going to try to pay for her half of the dinner, immediately grabbed the leather folder holding the bill from the table.

"Jackie, I know I agreed that we would split the bill, but I absolutely insist on paying."

"Jace, I appreciate that, I really do. But I—"

"No arguments on this."

"I have to tell you. I will only be able to hold off on bringing your son in for questioning for a few days. And there is no telling where this investigation may go."

"I understand. But let's hope we stay on the same side."

Jackie smiled sympathetically. "We can hope, but I can't make any promises."

Jace watched as Jackie left the dining room. He was not only hoping they stayed on the same side but that their relationship would evolve into something more serious.

CHAPTER
35

"Mr. Randazzo, I'm Christine Connors. So good of you to come on such short notice. I recognized you by the description you gave me over the phone."

Christine extended her hand, which Michael Randazzo eagerly took and held tightly as he brought it to his lips. She noticed the fine lines of the custom-tailored suit and shirt he wore, the fit shape of his body, and the subtle smell of his cologne. His tanned, wrinkled face made Christine think he was in his late forties, even though his hair was dark black without a strand of gray.

"Ms. Connors, the pleasure is all mine. I just hope I can be of some service. Mind if I call you Christine?"

"By all means. They have our table ready. Shall we?"

Christine and Michael followed the maître d' to an out-of-the-way table in the back corner of the restaurant. After they had taken their seats, Christine leaned across the white tablecloth and whispered, "Thank you for agreeing to meet me here in Dallas.

This is such a sensitive matter, and I didn't want to take the chance on anyone seeing us in Fort Worth."

Michael smiled. "I totally understand. In this business you can't be too careful." He then looked down at the menu. "So many choices, Christine. Any recommendations?"

"Honestly, I've never eaten here, but it's been written up as the best Italian restaurant in this area. Dallas and Fort Worth are not known for their Italian food."

"I appreciate the gesture. Very thoughtful of you to pick a restaurant you thought I might like." His eyes left the menu and zeroed in on Christine's. "So, tell me what's on your mind."

Before Christine could respond, the waiter appeared, took their order, and then left.

"Her name is Leah Rosen. She works for *Texas Matters,* a monthly rag that features personal-interest stories about Texas and Texans."

"We've got a similar magazine in California. I've had dealings with one of the reporters there."

"Well, I don't like to dance around an issue so I'm going to talk straight with you. I need someone to discourage her from continuing with the story she's currently working on." Christine's eyes searched Michael's for a reaction but got none. His eyes were dark and sharklike, utter vacuums, devoid of feeling.

"So why did you pick me? I'm sure you have investigators at your firm who could handle something like this."

"Two reasons. One, I don't want there to be any connection between whatever happens and my firm. And two, you are the best. It's that simple."

Michael nodded. "I'm flattered. What have you heard about me?"

"I've done my research, I can assure you. You have the reputation of being the go-to guy when a celebrity needs some dirt on an ex or a former business partner or, of most interest to me, needs to put a little fear into a nosy reporter."

"Hey, what's the name of this place again?"

"Nonna's."

"You know what that means, Christine?" Without waiting for a reply, Michael continued. "'Grandmother.' It means 'grandmother.'" His gaze took him to another place. "My grandparents came to this country over a hundred years ago. Settled in New York City like so many Italian immigrants did back then. Opened up a little restaurant and made enough to get by. I didn't know my grandparents as well as I would have liked. They died within a year of each other, just after I turned ten."

Sensing Michael wanted to take a detour from their business discussion, Christine followed his lead. "So what took you to L.A.?"

"A job. And then another job. And then another. The New York winters were getting longer and longer, so I decided to move there—sunshine all year long. L.A.'s been good to me, very good to me." Michael cleared his throat, his expression turning serious. "So tell me more about Ms. Rosen."

There was a pause in the conversation as the waiter served their lunch.

"Like I said, she's working on this article about our firm. One that I don't think will be very flattering."

"And you want me to make sure the story never goes to print?"

"Yes, exactly."

"I believe I can make that happen."

"You seem pretty confident."

"I am."

"So what do you have in mind? I don't want to have her . . ."

"You don't need to worry about that. None of my clients want anything that messy. They just want me to scare the shit out of someone who's looking into something that's none of their fucking business. Is that what we're talking about here?"

Christine picked at the salad she had ordered. "Exactly what we're talking about. So what would that entail?"

"It depends on the situation. Some are tougher than others. One of my most challenging cases involved a reporter. It started out with smashing her windshield and leaving a dead fish on her front seat with a simple note that said 'Stop.'"

"Did she?"

"No, she was a stubborn bitch. You know the type."

"I'm afraid that's what we're dealing with here. So how did you get her to stop?"

"I let myself into her house and went through the desk in her office, rearranged some family photos, things like that—just to let her know someone had been there. And I left the same note."

"And?"

Michael laughed and finished the last bite of his veal. "She called the cops and reported the break-in. They opened an investigation."

"So did you lay off?"

"Couldn't afford to. She was still working on the story. I had to stop it."

"So what'd you do next?"

"I posted a sex ad on Craigslist under her name. I created a fake, untraceable email address for interested men to respond to. We emailed back and forth about the kinky sex acts I—excuse me, she—was into and I gave them her address and phone number. Pretty soon she had men calling her, showing up at all hours of the day and night. It literally drove her over the edge."

"Did she stop writing the story?"

"Not only that. She quit the paper and left town." Michael chuckled. "Boy, did I have a happy client. Son of a bitch even paid me a bonus. I couldn't believe it. He had the reputation of being the tightest bastard in the city."

"What if she hadn't quit writing the story after all that? Did you have some type of backup plan?"

"You bet your ass I did. But a nice girl like you doesn't want to know what it was."

"You're right. I don't."

The waiters cleared the table, and Christine signaled for the check.

"So when do I start?"

"Well, we are trying another tactic first, but I don't believe it's going to work. I'll know soon enough. In the meantime . . ." Christine reached into her purse and pulled out a manila envelope containing $20,000 in cash. "This is the retainer we agreed upon. Regardless of whether we ask you to do anything else, consider it a token of our appreciation."

Michael took the envelope and, without examining its contents, put it in the inside pocket of his suit jacket.

"I hate to be paid for nothing."

"It means a lot to me to know you are ready to go if we need you."

Christine rose from the table and Michael followed her lead out of the restaurant. Before heading to their cars, Christine extended her hand one last time. "It has been my pleasure, Michael."

After kissing her hand and looking up at her, Michael responded, "Your confidence is well placed, Christine. I promise if that call ever comes, you will not be disappointed."

CHAPTER

36

Later that evening, Christine was sitting in her dad's office, heels off, her slender feet resting on the other pull-up chair in front of her dad's massive desk. "You never got a chance to tell me what Forman did when his witness walked out of the deposition."

Cal chuckled, his signature boots resting on his desk, an unlit cigar nestled between his thumb and index finger. "Hell, he looked like someone had hit him with a blivit." Cal paused, shaking his head. "It was all I could do to keep a straight face."

"What's a—"

"Blivit. Slang term but one your grandfather used to use all the time—ten pounds of shit in a five-pound bag. You get the idea."

"I'm afraid I do. So what's our next step?"

"Keep the pressure on, turn the heat way up. We've got ol' Wallace Arnold's deposition right around the corner. I bet he's sweating bullets, just like a whore in church. He doesn't know what we've got for sure, but he knows it can't be good."

Christine smiled. "Won't be pretty. What about settlement? Have you given any thought to that?"

"Does a wild bear—"

"Dad, I do know that one. Can we leave the clichés behind for just a little while?"

"For you, my dear, of course. Absolutely, I've thought about settlement. What do you think this case is worth?"

"Well, we don't have any hard damages we can write on the board for the jury to consider—no medicals, no physical disfigurement, no lost earnings. So we're going to be stuck with pain and suffering damages."

"Don't forget punitives."

"You're right. We are going to get to the jury on punitives, considering the judge we have. And the jury might even get mad enough to award them to us."

"Might? You've got to be kidding. We've got a Caring Oaks employee with a past record for molestation of a corpse—"

"The charges were dropped."

"Doesn't matter. The jury will believe he was guilty. You know, the ol' adage 'Where there's smoke, there's fire.' That's what the jury will think. Couple that with the absence of any meaningful security, and punitives are a slam dunk."

"They might not hold up on appeal."

"So? I just want a big jury award I can bargain with. I'm not going to worry about the appeal right now."

"Hard to gauge what number the jury will put on pain and suffering in a case like this. I've scoured the trial reports in all fifty states looking for jury awards in grave robbery cases and haven't found any. It's just so damn weird."

"And that's what I'm going to tell those twelve people sitting in the box. That they are special. That they are the first jury to have the opportunity to send a message to the funeral industry to clean up their act, quit focusing on profits, and spend some money to update their damn security to adjust to these dangerous times we live in. I've been rehearsing my closing in the shower. It gets better each morning."

"I don't doubt it. You've even got me going. So what do you want in settlement—a couple million?"

"Double that and I might—I just might—take it."

Cal's desk phone rang. The caller was identified as the *Fort Worth Herald*. Cal hit the speakerphone button.

"Mr. Connors? This is Evan Alexander." Evan was Cal's inside connection at the paper who kept him apprised of any hot stories Cal might be interested in.

"Evan, what's up?"

"I thought this was something you might want to know. One of our reporters just got word that Mr. Masterson, the embalmer at Caring Oaks, has hung himself."

Christine gasped. Cal smiled.

"Mr. Connors, are you there?"

"Right here, Evan. Right here."

"You may be getting a call from that reporter. And the local television news stations are on it as well. I'm sure they are going to want an interview."

"Evan, you're a good man. I appreciate the heads-up. I will keep you at the top of the list the next time I have anything news-worthy. Take care." Cal disconnected the call.

Christine stared in disbelief at her father. "Dad, I know this is great for the lawsuit, but aren't you upset over Lonnie Masterson's death?"

"He made his bed, not me. Now run along. I need a little privacy to work on my statement to the press."

Christine slipped on her heels, stood, and straightened her skirt. "Dad, I guess you already know that you can come across as a little cold at times."

"Emotion distorts reason. I've got to keep my head in the game." Cal began to scribble notes on the pad in front of him. "Watch for me on the news tonight."

Cal winked at Christine as she slowly closed the door.

CHAPTER

37

At the hotel, Jace struggled with the electronic key card, inserting it several different ways before the little light on the handle turned green. He pushed the door open and wedged through, briefcase in one hand, travel bag in the other. Curtains drawn, the room was pitch-black except for the red numbers on the alarm clock.

He kicked the door shut and threw his bag and briefcase on the bed. The front desk had given him a phone message from Darrin. It said for him to call her as soon as possible. He fished out his cell phone from his briefcase. There were two voice mail messages and a text, all from Darrin. Jace didn't bother checking the voice mail but immediately called Darrin.

"Hey, I got your messages. What's going on?"

"I have some unbelievably bad news." Pause. "Lonnie Masterson hung himself."

"What? Are you shittin' me?"

"I wish I was. Mr. Arnold found him in his apartment."

"How long ago?"

"Earlier this evening. I've been trying to reach you since I found out."

Jace ignored the irritation in Darrin's voice. "Do the police know?"

"All of Fort Worth knows. It was on the ten o'clock news."

"Shit!"

"And to make matters worse, they interviewed Cal Connors."

"Damn it!" Jace glanced at the clock—11:58. "I had no idea how late it was. Sorry I didn't check my voice mails earlier, but it's been pretty crazy down here."

Darrin concealed her curiosity about what had kept Jace out so late and what had caused the slight slur she noticed in his voice. "Mr. Arnold is pretty upset. I need to fill you in on that."

"Let me see if I can call up the story on my laptop and I'll ring you back in a few minutes."

"No problem. I'm awake now."

Jace hung up the phone and pulled his laptop out of his briefcase. He hit the power button and the screen came to life. "Shit," he mumbled under his breath. He needed the hotel password to access its wireless connection. A call to the front desk, and Jace was into the website of the CBS affiliate for Dallas–Fort Worth. He typed in "Lonnie Masterson" and "suicide" and a link came up. He clicked on it. After a short commercial, the story began.

A young female reporter was standing in front of an apartment complex in Fort Worth talking into a microphone and occasionally nodding toward the complex to her back.

"This was an apparent suicide. The police are still investigating, but we do know from sources that the deceased was a possible suspect in the grave robbery incident that has spawned a lawsuit in Fort Worth. With me now is Cal Connors, the attorney representing the victim's parents."

The camera panned out as the reporter, with outstretched arm, held the microphone in front of the Lone Wolf. Dressed in his signature black Stetson hat and boots, a black cashmere overcoat hiding his bolo tie, Western shirt, and blue jeans, Cal forced a pained expression, shaking his head as he spoke.

"This young man evidently killed himself out of guilt—guilt over what he had done to that young girl's body."

Jace thought he could make out a tear beginning to form in Cal's left eye. Meanwhile, the reporter was playing devil's advocate.

"But Mr. Connors, isn't that a rush to judgment? It's my understanding Mr. Masterson was not indicted for the crime. And I have checked with the Tarrant County Police Department, and they say he was never a suspect."

Cal shot her a knowing grin. "But they don't know what I know. You see, Mr. Masterson was indicted for corpse molestation in Tennessee. That's why he scooted on down here to Texas. And then," Cal paused for effect, "I was getting his testimony in the civil case and he ran out of the deposition. Flat refused to answer my questions. Tell me what you would do if you were a juror and heard that story. If that ain't guilt, then the pope ain't Catholic."

The story ended and Jace closed his laptop and dialed Darrin's number. She answered with a question.

"Did you see it?"

"Unfortunately, yes. Cal just used the media, as he always does, to mow down his opposition. He's already pressuring us into making a settlement just to avoid more bad press."

"Well, I hate to hit you with more bad news but . . ." Darrin hesitated.

"Go ahead. I'm already numb."

"When Mr. Arnold called, he was almost hysterical. Said he had to talk with you as soon as humanly possible. I asked if I could help him with anything, but he just kept saying he needed to talk with you. He was alarmingly distraught. I think you need to call him tonight."

"This late?"

"I have never heard anyone so upset. I don't know what he might do. And after what happened today . . ." Darrin's voice trailed off.

"Do you have his number handy?"

Darrin read him the number.

"What other good news do you have for me?"

"Look, Jace, don't shoot the messenger. I've been trying to reach you all night." Darrin sensed she might have overstepped. "I'll hold down the fort until you get back."

"Thanks, Darrin. I know you will."

Jace ended the call and then dialed the number he had scribbled on the hotel notepad. A disturbed voice answered.

"Wallace, this is Jace."

"I thought you would never call. Have you heard what happened?"

"I'm very sorry. Darrin told me and I just saw the news report."

"He's not even human, that Connors fellow. The whole thing is utterly repulsive. He's just after money, that's all. And he doesn't care who he hurts in the process."

"You're right on target." Jace paused, hoping his client would get to what was really bothering him.

"I can't believe Lonnie did what he did. Awful! And I found him. He was such a nice young man. If only I could have gotten to him sooner."

There was an awkward silence. Jace could sense his client searching for courage.

"Now, am I correct in assuming what I tell you is absolutely privileged? I mean, I have to know that."

"There is a privilege between lawyer and client. If you are seeking legal advice from me, then, yes, there is a privilege."

"Okay, then. This is hard, since I know how people like me are perceived by the public." Pause. "Perverts, fags—you name it, I've heard it all."

Jace anxiously ran his fingers through his hair, waiting for the bomb to drop. He said nothing.

"Well, Lonnie and I were more than business associates. We were lovers."

An image of Cal painting this picture to a jury raced through Jace's mind. He waited for Wallace to conclude his confession.

"Jace, are you still there?"

"Right here. And I hate to seem insensitive, but I have to ask you some pointed questions. Are you up to it?"

"Let's get it over with."

"Did anyone else know about your relationship with Mr. Masterson?"

"Not that I'm aware of."

"I mean, did anyone at the funeral home suspect anything?"

"I'm pretty sure they didn't. We kept everything on a very professional basis at work. Besides, he worked as an embalmer. I hardly ever saw him at work."

"When did your relationship start?"

"Well, I interviewed him. There was clearly chemistry between us then. I hired him and we started seeing each other almost immediately."

"Did you know about his trouble with the law back in Tennessee?"

"Not initially. I didn't check his references since I was so taken with him."

Jace flinched at the response. "You learned later?"

"Yes, he volunteered that information to me. Told me he could understand it if I fired him for not telling me during our interview.

But I couldn't. Besides, he swore to me that the charges weren't true. You know, they were dropped because the authorities didn't have enough evidence."

"That's what we've learned as well. In fact, our investigator could not find any criminal charges ever being filed against Lonnie. Evidently, they were expunged on the motion of his court-appointed attorney since there was no real basis to file them in the first place."

"It's just such a tragedy. And that monster on the other side, he doesn't even seem to care that he caused another human being to kill himself. It's all so senseless."

"Wallace, at this point, we've got to control our emotions and focus on kicking Connors' ass at trial."

"I'm all for that. I'll help you in any way I can."

"First of all, have you told me everything, and I mean everything? It would have been nice to know about your relationship with Lonnie from the beginning. And you definitely should have told me about Lonnie's past. But that's water under the bridge. I've got to know everything to be able to defend this case. Is there any other dirty laundry out there? Anything Cal can use against us? Because I know he'll find it, and I have no doubt he'll use it. You can be sure of that."

"I have told you everything. I would have told you about Lonnie and me but I was afraid, afraid you might not understand, afraid you would judge me."

"Wallace, you know me better than that."

Wallace knew Jace was right and moved on to another topic. "What if we countersued Connors for causing this?" There was a newfound confidence in Wallace's voice.

Jace rolled his eyes. "Not a good idea. What Connors did in the deposition and what he said on television are protected. In layman's language, a lawyer can't be sued for zealously representing his client. And what he said on television is covered by the First Amendment." Jace didn't volunteer that it also might be true.

"I can't believe our judicial system. Connors did everything but attach Lonnie's necktie to the light fixture. Does this have any effect on the Stones' case against Caring Oaks?"

Jace hesitated. He didn't want to get into that over the phone. Besides, Wallace was in no frame of mind to hear more bad news.

"Let me give that some more thought before giving you a definitive answer." Jace hedged, buying time. "I'm down in Austin right now. I'll call you when I get back to Fort Worth."

"When will that be?"

"I'm doing some investigative work on your case and will be back tomorrow or the next day at the latest."

"Call me when you get back to Fort Worth. I would like to meet with you as soon as possible."

"Absolutely."

"What should I do in the meantime?"

"Don't talk with anybody about any of this, particularly reporters. Just refer any inquiries or questions to my office."

"Do you think you'll find out anything helpful in Austin?"

"I hope so. I'll fill you in when we meet."

Jace replaced the receiver and looked to the ceiling for answers. None came. He looked at the clock—12:30. He knew Matt would still be up but decided not to call. He had dealt with enough for one day. He got ready for bed and tried unsuccessfully to sleep. He groped for the remote control and flicked on the television. He knew he was in for one of those long, torturous nights.

CHAPTER

38

Senator Talmadge Worthman was the mouthpiece of the religious right. He stood for everything Jace abhorred. Jace was a social liberal, Talmadge a die-hard conservative. Jace had compassion for individual freedom, Talmadge had contempt for ideological diversity. Talmadge believed abortion, without exception, was an abomination and divorce intolerable in every instance. Jace was pro-choice and found divorce unavoidable in certain instances. To Talmadge, there were no shades of gray in life, only blacks and whites. To Jace, there was nothing but gray. Life was complicated and full of riddles, with no clear set of rules to follow.

Knowing Talmadge's type, Jace prepared himself for the morning's meeting. It was going to be difficult to feign support for the senator, but Jace had to be convincing in his dedication to the cause—at least for one morning.

As he drove down Congress Avenue toward the Capitol, Jace rehearsed his act. "I am fed up with the liberal element in Austin and Washington and am determined to make a difference. Although I am not from your district, I am familiar with your voting record. I agree with you in every respect. How could anyone argue against prayer in the public schools? How could anyone be in favor of killing babies? How could anyone be against capital punishment? After all, doesn't the Old Testament clearly set the rule—'an eye for an eye'? Why in the world should we teach safe sex in our schools when the only right answer is abstinence until marriage? Gay rights, who are we kidding? They can, and should be, trained to go straight." Jace felt his stomach churning as he practiced these tired arguments.

Jace found a parking spot next to the Capitol. As he walked across the manicured grounds, admiring the large oak and pecan trees, he gazed up at the gilded lady, adorning the imposing structure's domed roof. He smiled sarcastically, wondering what her take was on all the chicanery that went on beneath her. He couldn't tell whether she was smiling or frowning, or wearing an expression of indifference. Maybe her look was a combination of all three—or at least could be interpreted that way.

Jace walked up the limestone steps and checked his watch. It was a little after eight o'clock. Darrin had managed to schedule ten minutes of face time with the senator at eight-fifteen. He opened one of the heavy oak doors and searched the walls for a directory. Scrolling down the names, he discovered the senator's office was in an adjacent building. Five minutes later he had announced his arrival and purpose to Talmadge's assistant and taken a seat in the reception area. He didn't have to wait long. In a matter of minutes, the senator, clad in a perfectly tailored, navy blue pinstriped suit, arrived. He addressed the receptionist in that affected voice characteristic of his trade. "Morning, Mrs. Butler. Any messages for me?"

A stern-looking middle-aged woman, half glasses dangling from a chain, leaned forward and whispered something to her boss. In response, Senator Worthman glanced over his shoulder and smiled.

In classic politician style, he strutted toward Jace, extending his hand in the process.

"Mr. Forman, I don't believe we've met. Welcome to the Capitol."

Jace rose. The two men shook hands forcefully, the senator firmly grasping Jace's upper arm in the process. Jace spoke, "I am a big admirer."

Talmadge smiled approvingly. "Come on in my office. I'm glad I could squeeze you in this morning. Unfortunately, I don't have a lot of time due to a subcommittee meeting scheduled at eight-thirty."

"I understand, Senator. I was in Austin on business yesterday and decided to stay over, hoping you could find time for a short visit. I just wanted to stop by and let you know how much I appreciate what you're doing, see if there might be something I could do to help."

Talmadge gave Jace an admiring look as they walked into his office. "I don't guess it would hurt if I was a little late for my meeting." He turned toward his secretary and said, "Call Lefty Wilkerson and tell him I will be about fifteen minutes late. If there's a problem, just buzz me." He looked back at Jace and smiled. "I always make time for my supporters."

The decor was plush: walnut paneling, dark hardwood floors, expensive oils, and three oriental rugs of varying sizes. Numerous photographs and plaques decorated three of the walls. Conspicuously placed on a fourth wall was the Ten Commandments, accented by a gold frame. Jace felt his palms begin to sweat as he seated himself in the antique Chippendale chair directly in front of the senator's hand-carved desk. After waiting for the senator to take his seat, Jace began his diatribe.

"Senator, I know you're busy so I'll get right to the point. I have been an admirer of yours ever since you took office. Without boring you with a lot of detail, I believe our country is analogous to the Roman empire. We are headed for a fall. We are rotting from within. Our moral fiber is gone, or close to it."

Jace's eyes intensely fixed on the senator's, creating a bond between them. "We must reverse course. We must get back to basics, to family values, to the things that made this country and state great. And you have made your mark, standing up for the principles you believe in." Jace knew flattery would get him everywhere with a politician.

"Mr. Forman, I appreciate those kind words but—"

Jace was on a mission. He interrupted. "I'm not trying to flatter you. I'm here to support you. You need money in your reelection campaign. And you need volunteers. I can supply you with both."

Jace dramatically retrieved his checkbook from the inside pocket of his suit jacket. After writing out a check for $5,000, he stood up and handed it to the senator. Jace stymied a grin as he noticed Talmadge's eyes darting immediately to the amount.

"Mr. Forman, thank you for your generous contribution. You can rest assured—"

Jace interrupted again. "You needn't say anything. I know a man of your integrity will see that it is well spent." Jace was in control of the meeting, playing the role of zealot to perfection. "As far as volunteers, here is my business card. Call me if you need anything in Fort Worth. And as far as your district goes, I know quite a few of the local lawyers. We're on the same side of the docket—you know, the defense side—defending corporations, doctors, hospitals, those currently under attack by the greedy plaintiffs' bar."

Jace winked, and the senator acknowledged with a nod. "It would be my pleasure to write them, encouraging them to support you in your bid for reelection—maybe even co-sponsor a fund-raiser."

Talmadge was momentarily speechless. He finally mustered a response. "Anything I can do . . ." His voice trailed off.

"Nothing at all. Just keep up the good work." Jace smiled. His eyes then strayed to a burnt orange coffee mug resting on the senator's desk. Scripted in white was the senator's campaign slogan: "Make your vote WORTH it. Reelect WORTHMAN."

Jace stifled a laugh. "Great mug. Catchy slogan."

"I've got one with your name on it," the senator said as he retrieved an unopened cardboard box from a closet in the corner of his office. Straining, he pried open the flaps and pulled out a coffee mug identical to the one on his desk. He proudly offered the mug to Jace, who carefully received it, making sure his fingers touched a different area than the senator's.

"This is great." Jace feigned enthusiastic admiration. "Do you think I might have another—one for home and one for the office?"

"Absolutely. You need a sack or box?"

Minutes later, Jace was heading across the Capitol lawn, a box containing not one but two fingerprinted mugs snugly positioned under his arm. He got in his rental car and carefully placed the box in the passenger seat. He took out his cell phone and dialed Jackie's office number. Her voice mail picked up.

"Jackie, it's Jace. I've got two presents just for you. And I am headed your way to drop them off."

CHAPTER
39

"Mr. Connors, I received your voice mail and am returning your call. What can I do for you?"

"Well, Mr. Blumenthal, thanks so much for getting back to me. I really enjoyed your speech at the TTLA convention. It was very timely given the downturn in the print market. The Internet sure has done a number on it."

"We've lost a lot of great publishing companies—and even more magazines—these past few years."

"Steve, may I call you Steve? Have you had an opportunity to look into what I mentioned in my voice mail?"

"Very briefly. I'm sure my schedule is a bit like yours—lots of deadlines and late-nighters. But I did make a point to visit with Abe Levine, my editor at *Texas Matters* and Leah Rosen's direct supervisor."

"Now, Ms. Rosen, she's a firebrand—seems intent on doing a good job. But I think she's getting a little off track here."

"In what way, Mr. Connors?"

"Call me Cal. Well, she's making some allegations that don't hold water and, as they say in your line of work, are downright defamatory."

"Abe has the highest regard for her work, and from what he told me, Leah is doing a fine job. And you can rest assured we don't publish anything until every statement is fact-checked and well-documented."

"Is that a fact? Ms. Rosen implied to my law partner that one of our expert witnesses was less than truthful. That witness, Dr. Howell Crimm, is one of the most respected docs in the business. Hell, he's got a résumé as long as your leg. There is no way he would lie for me, or for anyone else, for that matter. Ms. Rosen is barking up the wrong tree."

"Well, you may be right. And the protocol we have in place will flesh out any misstatements of fact before an article is published. *Texas Matters* is not a tabloid. It is a high-quality monthly publication."

Cal's voice became louder, and harsher in tone. "Maybe I'm not making myself clear. If *Texas Matters* runs an article on me or my firm that has one derogatory remark in it—and I mean one—I'll sue the hell out of your magazine and Ms. Rosen personally."

"Is that a threat?"

"No, sir. It's a promise. And I have a war chest plenty deep. By the time I get through with *Texas Matters*, no matter who wins, your annual profits will be decimated. And based on my research, your revenue has been declining. That's a shame, Steve. And it would be more of a shame if the red ink got even redder."

Silence on the other end.

"Well, I just wanted to make sure there was no misunderstanding in terms of my intentions."

"I think you have made yourself clear. Very clear, indeed. Good day, Mr. Connors."

"One more thing, Steve. I was thinking about running a big ad in your magazine. You know, a full pager featuring a photo of me and my daughter and listing all our big verdicts. Have your ad person call me."

A click on the other end caused Cal to chuckle under his breath. He replaced the receiver and scrolled through the address book on his computer. Ol' Howell could use an update to ease his mind. The last thing he needed was for the good doctor to lose his cool and do something stupid.

CHAPTER

40

Sloan Jenkins lived in a three-story apartment complex a little less than two miles from where a lifeless Alexis Stone had been found. As Jace pulled into the parking lot, he double-checked the apartment number on his directions: 33. Tony Dorsett's jersey number in the Cowboys' glory days. How could he forget! He stuffed the note back in his pocket and headed toward the complex.

Apartment 33 was on the third level. Jace knocked on the door and waited several minutes. He could hear the muffled sound of one of his favorite Beatles songs, For No One, coming from inside. He knocked again, this time with more authority. The door cracked open. Jace could see eyes peering through, security chain still latched. The occupant was silent, searching her memory for the identity of her caller.

"Ms. Jenkins?"

No response. The eyes continued to stare. The security chain remained intact.

"My name is Jace Forman. I am an attorney from Fort Worth and am working on a case you've probably read about involving your friend Alexis Stone. Her parents have sued the cemetery where she was buried and I am defending the cemetery."

Jace took a chance. If she was close to Alexis' parents, ball game was over. She probably wouldn't talk to him. But based on the phone records and what his investigator had found out about Alexis' relationship with her parents, Jace felt it was a safe bet her friend had never met them. His move was answered by the sound of the security chain being unlatched. The door opened to a college-age girl, clad in faded blue jeans shredded at the knees and a Grateful Dead T-shirt.

"Come in. Sorry if I seemed rude, but it's kinda weird having some guy in a suit come to your door."

Jace stepped inside, and Sloan closed the door behind him. "I would offer you some coffee, but I don't drink it. How about a Coke?"

Jace didn't drink Cokes but accepted anyway in an attempt to befriend his hostess. As he waited, he surveyed his surroundings— a disaster zone. Full ashtrays, empty beer and soda cans, clothes strewn all about. Sloan read his thoughts.

"I'm not the best of housekeepers." She handed him a Coke, simultaneously smiling and shrugging her shoulders.

Jace looked around for a place to sit. The couch was cluttered with several empty CD cases, a stack of what appeared to be class books, and a black bra.

Sloan blushed. "Whoops, let me get some of that stuff out of your way." She quickly retrieved the bra and slid the CD cases and books to one side of the couch. "Voilà. All yours. Make yourself at home."

She took a few steps toward the bedroom and slung the bra through an open door. As she turned and walked back toward the living area, Jace took in her appearance. Her blond, almost white, hair was cut short and close to her head. She was flat-chested, her figure straight up and down, with no curves at all. Her right eyebrow was pierced, sporting a small gold ring, which drew Jace's attention from her ice-blue eyes.

Jace took a seat on the couch in the spot Sloan had cleared. After throwing some magazines on the floor, Sloan curled up in the easy chair across the room, sitting cross-legged, her bare feet petite, toenails painted a dark blue. Her eyes rested on Jace. "Now, what's this about Alexis' parents suing somebody?"

Jace leaned forward as he spoke. "Well, it's a little complicated. First of all, it's not a criminal case. I don't do that type of work." Jace wanted to put her at ease. He could tell from her relieved expression his ploy had worked. "It's a civil case. The parents have sued the cemetery for negligence, which they contend allowed Alexis' body to be stolen."

Sloan's expression was still one of confusion. "Sorry, I really don't understand."

"Let's see if I can explain it a little better." Jace paused a minute, searching for words, and then continued. "You know Alexis' body was stolen from a cemetery operated by my client." It was more of a statement than a question.

Sloan nodded. "I knew her body was stolen from a cemetery. I didn't know who owned it."

"I represent a cemetery in Fort Worth called Caring Oaks. Alexis was buried there after she died. Shortly after her burial, her casket was unearthed and her body stolen. Alexis' parents are suing my client, saying in the lawsuit that the cemetery should have had a security guard patrolling the grounds, which would have prevented the theft."

"Yeah, right. Like a rent-a-guard is going to stop some pervert. So what do the Stones want?"

"Lots of money."

"For what?"

"They claim in their lawsuit that they have suffered severe pain and mental anguish."

Sloan picked up her Coke, took a swig, and then laughed sarcastically. "Yeah, right. Her dad was a dick and treated Alexis like shit. And her mom just turned a blind eye. The family was totally dysfunctional."

"How do you know that?"

"We talked about it all the time. Alexis couldn't stand her father. She and her mom both had a total disrespect for him. So her parents faked everything—happy marriage, fat bank account, successful careers. Alexis went off to a boarding school in seventh grade and the school was only thirty miles away, in Dallas!" Sloan shook her head. "Really weird!"

"I thought Alexis' family had a lot of money."

"That's what everybody thinks because that's the image they paint. A monster of a house, expensive cars, country club memberships—you name it. But that's just a front. I got the real scoop from Alexis. Alexis' mother inherited a boatload of money from her old man, which he made in the freight rail service. She turned over the management of that fortune to her husband, who eventually lost it all in risky real estate and oil deals."

Sloan leaned forward and took a sip of Coke. "At least that's what Alexis said. She told me her mother would read her dad the riot act at least once a week about how stupid he was and that he was a terrible businessman. It drove her nuts."

"Did you ever meet the Stones?"

"Never. I don't believe they ever came to see Alexis here. In fact, I'm sure they didn't."

"If the Stones are so broke, how was it that Alexis was able to afford living in such an upscale apartment?"

"Her grandfather set up a trust for her. Her dad can't get to it."

"What happened to it when Alexis died?"

"I have no idea. It wasn't a topic we ever talked about."

Jace smiled as he realized how "old" he must seem to her. He wondered how good a witness she would be. She would have to be "cleaned up," and the eyebrow ring would have to go, but she had some dynamite information. If the jury believed her, the Stones would come across as a couple of gold diggers trying to rip off his client. But there was always the possibility she might fold under Cal Connors' cross. It would be a risky call but one he could postpone, at least for now.

"Tell me about your relationship with Alexis."

Sloan stretched to the floor for a pack of Marlboro Lights, shook loose a cigarette, and lit it with a purple Bic disposable lighter. She inhaled deeply. As she talked, smoke followed her words. "We were best friends. Met during orientation and were practically inseparable until . . ." Sloan hesitated, a pained expression on her face.

"How about her social life, boyfriends, favorite bars and hangouts?"

After taking a deep drag, Sloan dropped her cigarette in the Coke can and set it on the floor. She gazed up at the ceiling and then looked at Jace, her slender fingers making a temple that partially covered her lips.

"She was seeing some guy for several months before she died. But she was really secretive about it. She never wanted to talk about it."

"Any clue as to who that was?"

"All I know is he was in government. That's all she would ever tell me. Sorta got the feeling he was married."

"Did Alexis have any close girlfriends other than you?"

"Sure, she had other friends, but not close. We were like sisters. She had a key to my apartment and I had one to hers. We went everywhere together. I mean, we both had other friends, but they were just friends, not close in the way Alexis and I were."

"Of course, I understand. Any more you can tell me about this guy she may have been seeing?"

Sloan sighed. "Not really. I do know it changed her—the relationship, that is. I mean, she acted different."

"In what way?"

"She seemed very unhappy. Relationships are supposed to make you happy, aren't they? Well, this one clearly didn't."

"How do you know?"

Sloan looked at her guest, cocking her head to the side. "What does it matter?"

"If Alexis and this guy had some weird relationship, it might help us figure out who dug up her body."

Satisfied with the explanation, Sloan continued. "Well, she was really moody. Didn't want to hang with me much. It was strange." Sloan stared at her visitor, her thoughts somewhere else.

Jace sensed discomfort and decided to change course. "This is going to sound pretty crazy, but was Alexis into anything like devil worship, cults, that type of thing?"

Sloan raised her shoulders and shook her head. "If she was, she didn't talk to me about it."

Sloan glanced at her watch. "Sorry, but I'm out of time. History starts in fifteen minutes." Sloan stood. She stretched, her T-shirt rising slightly, revealing a diamond stud adorning her navel. "I wish I could have been of more help."

"I understand. I should've called first." Jace rose from the couch, changing topics. "By the way, I have a son who's at UT, Matt Forman. Ever run into him?"

"Doesn't ring a bell. But UT is a big place. I'll keep an eye out for him."

"Just don't tell me what he's up to. You know, ignorance is bliss." Jace's haphazard attempt at humor was met with a contrived laugh.

"Thanks for your time. And if you think of anything else, give me a call." He offered her a business card, which she took, glanced at, and then buried in her pocket. She smiled faintly as she closed the door behind him.

CHAPTER

41

Thirty minutes later, Jace coasted to a stop in front of a small, white wood-frame house just west of the old Austin airport. The pockmarked street was lined with similar houses on both sides, a few in better condition than others but all in need of paint and repairs of some form.

In the front yard rusted bikes lay on their sides, their wheels entangled. A broken sidewalk led to the porch, weeds climbing out from under cracks. A wooden bench swing hung from the porch ceiling, several boards missing, its paint mostly gone. Flowering plants in brightly colored pots dressed the porch railing. The front door was half-open, a screen with gaping holes providing the only barrier to the outside. Suddenly, two small children pushed open the door and chased each other outside, giggling and yelling. Their speech was rapid-fire, the words running together, blurred by laughter. They excitedly mounted the rusted bikes and veered down the sidewalk, glancing over their shoulders at the strange car parked next to the curb.

Jace didn't have to knock. A Hispanic woman, jet-black hair pulled tight against her head in a bun, stared at him through the screen.

"Señora Gonzalez?"

The woman nodded, her dark eyes wide and inquisitive.

"*Soy Jace Forman. Es importante que hablamos.*"

Señora Gonzalez stood motionless, without speaking.

"*Soy abogado y tengo algunas preguntas sobre Alexis Stone.*"

Her eyes flashed recognition. She held open the screen door and nodded to Jace. He stepped inside.

Señora Gonzalez appeared to be in her late thirties. A shade over five feet, she wore a heavy black robe that rested on the wooden floor. She smiled timidly at her guest.

"*¿Prefiere usted hablar en inglés o español?*"

"*Inglés es* okay. I try understand."

His hostess walked through a small den that opened into a kitchen separating the living space from two bedrooms and a bath. As she walked, her bare feet peeked from under the robe's skirt, exposing bright pink toenails badly in need of a fresh coat of polish. "You like something to drink?"

"No, thank you. I'm fine." As he answered, Jace looked around the room. The den was tidy and sparsely furnished with an iridescent sofa, wearing the stains of age, and a relatively new television, tuned to a *telenovela*.

Maria Gonzalez quietly reentered the room with a mug of coffee, steam rising from the top. She sat on the edge of the couch, her back straight, as she set her coffee cup on the table and looked expectantly at Jace. "Please, seet down."

Jace obliged and then spoke, slowly and softly. "I'm a lawyer and I represent a cemetery out of Fort Worth."

Maria eyed Jace intently as he spoke.

"The cemetery where Alexis Stone was buried." Jace waited for recognition. His hostess nodded, signaling him to continue.

"You may have read about this in the newspaper—*el periódico.* Well, anyway, Alexis' body was stolen from the cemetery."

A look of horror came over Maria's face, her hand quickly making the sign of the cross and then covering her mouth, muffling a gasp. Momentarily regaining composure, she spoke in a soft voice, reverting to Spanish. "*Que locura, es algo diabólico.*" Her eyes pleaded for more information.

"*Sí, es una cosa horrible.* The police, they are still looking for the person who did this."

"I not know Señorita Stone *muy bien.* I tell police all I know."

"Let me just ask a few questions. Is that okay?"

Maria nodded uncertainly.

Jace uncrossed his legs and leaned forward, looking at her for answers. "What can you remember about Alexis?"

"*Un poco.* I no see her much. I clean once a week. Sundays from eleven to two. Most time I come, she not there. She leave money for me on table."

"How long did you clean for her before she died?"

"Two months, *nada más.*"

"Ever see her with any men—boyfriends, *novios?*"

Maria shook her head.

"How about *amigas?*"

"*Solamente* one time. White hair, very short." Maria held her hand close against her head, visually depicting her description.

Sloan Jenkins, no doubt. Jace continued to dig. "Anyone else you can remember?"

"No."

"What do you remember about the morning when you found Alexis?"

"I tell police everything."

"Well, please, let's go through it again from the time you got there until the police arrived. Try to think back."

His hostess closed her eyes tightly as her brow furrowed.

"It was nice day. I go to apartment a little before eleven. I knock on door and no answer, so I unlock and go inside."

"You had a key?"

"*Sí. La señorita* give me."

"Okay, what happened next?"

"I call for *la señorita*. No answer. I walk to bedroom to start clean and see her in bed but not look right. I wait and watch—she not breathing. I scared. Call 911."

"How long did it take the police to get there?"

"*Rápido.*"

"Do you remember anything after that?"

"They ask me questions. I come home. I not talk to nobody about this until today."

Jace took a business card from his pocket and handed it to his hostess. "*Muchas gracias, Señora Gonzalez.* Thank you for talking with me. If you think of anything else, please call me."

"*De nada. Buena suerte, Señor.*"

Jace walked toward the door and outside. Before he got to his car, he turned and smiled at Maria, who was standing on the porch, watching the two children playing in the yard.

"Your little boys?"

"*Sí,* both of them."

"*Preciosos.*"

Her response, a proud smile.

Jace slid behind the wheel. The clock on the dash read one-fifteen. He hadn't eaten yet. Maybe he could catch Matt for some nachos and a beer. He needed to let him know he might be getting a call from Reginald Cowan and advise him on what to do if he did. Putting the car in gear, Jace headed back toward the UT campus.

CHAPTER

42

"What do you mean you're postponing the story? I've put a lot of blood, sweat, and tears into this. I have Dr Patel's research memorandum, which I'm this close to getting him to agree to let me use. We can't back off this now." Leah paced rapidly around Abe's office, gesturing frantically with her hands, her voice approaching fever pitch.

"Leah, calm down. I know you're disappointed."

"Disappointed? Disappointed?" Leah was leaning over Abe's desk, her face inches from his. "You just don't get it, do you? This is one of the biggest frauds in Texas judicial history, and our owner has decided to, in your words, 'postpone' the story. Did Mr. Blumenthal provide you with an explanation?" Leah walked away from Abe's desk and moved to a corner of the office, her back to her boss.

"He is not a man of many words, but he was very clear in his decision. And I didn't push him."

"And why not? Afraid you'd lose your job?"

"I have more respect for my bosses than you obviously do."

"I'm sorry, Abe. You deserve better from me, much better. I apologize, I really do. But I just don't understand this. We owe it to the public and the Texas judicial system to publish this story. I would like an audience with Mr. Blumenthal. Maybe after he hears what I have learned he'll change his mind."

"I don't think that would be a good idea. He doesn't change course very often. And based on the tone of our conversation, it was my sense he was not in the mood for argument. That's why I didn't push it."

Leah seated herself in the chair in front of Abe's desk, her eyes pleading with his. "Isn't there something we can do?"

"I've been in this business a long time. If I knew of something, I would have already tried it. I think Steve is wrong about this, but he's the boss. He pays our salaries. And Leah, let's be honest. We can guess what Steve is thinking. He can't afford to fight a massive libel lawsuit that Cal Connors would no doubt file against us." Abe's words were tinged with bitter resignation.

"Aren't ethics part of this magazine anymore?" Leah asked. When Abe said nothing, she started to rise from her chair. "Abe, I know you're much further along in your career and that making a change would be difficult for you. But it wouldn't be for me. I'm single, no kids to support. I'm going to find a way to get this story out."

"You're not thinking about resigning?"

"I seriously am."

"Be careful. Snap judgments can ruin lives. You need to think about this—consider all the angles. Steve would not have made the decision he did unless there was a good reason. And he's only saying he wants to postpone the article. So there's still a chance we'll run it."

"Oh, come on, you and I both know he's caving in to pressure, and I just don't think that I can continue to work for a magazine that does something like that. I have no doubt that Connors is somehow behind this decision, and he shouldn't be allowed to get away with it. I can't just throw out the article and walk away. There is too much riding on it. Connors' fraud will continue. It's just not right. I may have no choice but to resign."

"I understand how you feel right now, but I must caution you to step back and think about this. You're making a big decision. At least sleep on it. That's all I ask."

Leah sighed deeply and tried to calm herself. "I don't know, Abe. I just don't get it. I mean, what's reporting all about if stories about the rich and powerful get quashed for financial reasons? That is not what a free press is all about. You and I both know this is a damn good piece of investigative reporting. This dirty laundry needs to be aired. The people need to know what's going on. That's the only way to stop the Cal Connors of the world. I respect you, Abe. You taught me the ropes and I will never forget that. But—" Leah stopped in mid-sentence and looked intently into Abe's eyes. "What would you do if you were in my shoes?"

"Truthfully," Abe said, "I don't blame you for wanting to jump ship. But you are going to find throughout your career, and life for that matter, that things like this happen. My advice to you now is to calm down, think about your future, decide what direction you want to take in life, and make a decision taking your emotions out of it. I know you're upset and mad right now. Take the day off, go for a jog, clear your mind, and sleep on it. If you still come to the conclusion you want to leave, then I'll know that your decision was made thoughtfully and will accept your resignation. I just don't want you to do something rash that you'll regret."

"You're right. I'll think about it and let you know in the morning. And Abe, no matter what decision I make, I'll always be grateful for your guidance and friendship."

"If you want to talk it through with somebody, you have my number."

"Thanks, Abe." Leah headed for the door, confused and angry. There was no way she was going to let this story die.

CHAPTER
43

Hut's had been an Austin tradition since 1939. Resembling a converted gas station from the outside, it was painted white, with red and blue awnings adorning the entrance and windows. An old-fashioned neon sign jutted out from a pole, advertising to the world that Hut's was open for business.

The interior decor hadn't changed in years. A mounted Longhorn head resembling Bevo, the UT mascot, hung from one of the walls, college pennants fell from the ceiling, and photos of famous stars who had frequented the joint were haphazardly positioned throughout. Jace and his son took the first two-top they came to. "What sounds good to you?"

"I'm going with a Dagburger and a Shiner Bock on draft. I don't know any place that serves colder beer than Hut's. Love those frosted fish bowl mugs."

"I remember, I remember. I almost became a fixture here when I was in law school. I don't think anything about this place has changed, including the menu."

After placing their orders, Jace broke the news that a new prosecutor had been assigned to Alexis' case and that he wanted to interview Matt.

"I can't believe this. I didn't do a damn thing and now I'm the target of a murder investigation."

"Matt, there's nothing we can do to stop him. If we try to avoid Cowan and put off a meeting, it'll only make him more suspicious."

"But, Dad—"

"Matt, the facts are the facts. Your fingerprints were found in her apartment. You were with her on the night of her death. It's fair that you get questioned. Just remember, it's all very preliminary. Once the assistant district attorney meets with you and hears your version of what happened, that'll probably be the end of it."

"Yeah, right. I've heard horror stories about people convicted of crimes they didn't commit. Look at that Shephard guy. He actually did time. It was years before he got out of the slammer. And when he finally did, he was so screwed up, his life was shit."

"But look on the bright side. They based a television series and a movie on his story." Jace grinned, trying to alter the mood.

"He never saw them either. He was pushing up daisies at the time. As I recall, he died shortly after his release from prison."

"All right, all right. We're getting a little ahead of ourselves, aren't we? You haven't been charged with any crime. You're going to be asked a few questions—that's it. They don't have any evidence to charge you with anything."

"What if I don't answer any questions? What if I take the Fifth? I mean, I see that done all the time, whether the person is guilty or innocent."

Jace was suddenly worried that Matt had not been forthcoming with all he knew. He wondered why Matt would not want to answer questions. "We'll leave that up to your attorney, Pat Reynolds."

"Dad, I'd feel a lot better if you were representing me."

Jace shook his head emphatically. "You know I don't do criminal work, and that's Pat's specialty. He's one of the best criminal defense lawyers in the state. Besides, I am too emotionally invested in this. It would be a huge mistake for me to represent you. Trust me on this one."

Matt seemed to agree, the logic of the argument breaking through to him. "I guess you're right. You will keep in touch with him, won't you?"

"You know I will. In fact, I talked with Pat on my way over here. We talked briefly about the public intoxication charge he's handling for you. He thinks he can get that dismissed if you agree to do forty hours of public service."

"With everything else going on, I had almost forgotten about that. Do I need to call him?"

"Yes. You can talk to him about that as well as the interview with the assistant DA. How does your schedule look on Monday?

"I have classes all morning but my afternoon is free."

"I'll set something up for three o'clock."

"You're going to be there, aren't you?"

"I wish I could. I'll talk to Pat about it, but I'm afraid my presence might waive the attorney-client privilege. Since I'm technically not your lawyer on this, anything you told Pat while I was present might be fair game for the prosecutor."

"What about the things I've told you so far?"

"They're most likely protected. I think Pat can make the argument that up until now I've been acting as your lawyer. We're fine on that point—nothing for you to worry about." Jace hesitated. "But even if our conversations weren't privileged, it wouldn't matter. Hell, the police probably know most of what we discussed, if not all of it. And if they don't, well, we'll cross that bridge when we have to."

"Are you sure this is just routine?" Matt's eyes expressed doubt.

"Absolutely. Don't worry. It will be fine." Jace lied authoritatively. His cell phone began buzzing, and he pulled it from his pocket, eyeing the number. He nodded to his son, "I have to take this. Jackie, what's going on?"

"Are you sitting down?"

"Don't do this to me. I don't think I can stomach any more suspense."

"Well, I got the mugs to the lab right after you dropped them off, and my buddy over there ran a few quick tests. And guess what? It's just what we wanted. Perfect match with Senator Worthman."

"Yes!" Jace bellowed, making his son look around the room in an apologetic fashion. "So we finally got a break. Cowan's going to have no alternative but to check out the senator."

"That would be customary procedure."

"The timing couldn't be better. As we speak, I am getting ready to drink a Shiner Bock and have a Dagburger with Matt."

"Hut's?"

"Where else?"

"Well, you two have a good time. You deserve it."

"We will, we will. And Jackie, thanks again for all you've done for us." Jace disconnected and smiled. "That was a friend in the Austin PD." Jace intentionally omitted her name in light of the upcoming interrogation. "They just matched the fingerprints of a well-known senator to those taken from Alexis' apartment."

Matt gasped in disbelief. "A senator? What was a senator doing in Alexis' apartment? Oh, no—now I get it. That's why she quit seeing me. She was going out with some big-shot politico." Matt bit his lip. "My ego's a little bruised, but I guess the good news is I'm in the clear, right?"

"We're not quite there yet. But we can breathe a helluva lot easier." Jace took a sip of his ice-cold Shiner and thought a beer never tasted so good.

CHAPTER

44

"All I asked you to do was keep Jace Forman distracted until the damn case gets tried or settled. How difficult is that?"

Cal rolled his unlit cigar from one side of his mouth to the other, causing his words to slur. He hit the speaker button on his phone and rose from his desk. Walking toward the window with a view of the Trinity, he continued his scolding.

"Reggie, you know you wouldn't have gotten this transfer to Austin but for my connections. And you're next in line to become DA—all because of those connections. It's time to pony up."

"Cal, that's what I'm trying to do. You know that. We've been friends ever since I got that DUI dismissed for you when I was in the Dallas prosecutor's office—kept it under the radar screen, no publicity, no nothing. Please don't forget that.

And as far as this investigation is concerned, I've just hit a little snag."

"And what's that?" Cal continued his stare out the window, but his tone had mellowed.

"We've matched some other prints taken from Ms. Stone's apartment."

"Whose?"

"Senator Talmadge Worthman."

Cal grinned. "Under any other circumstances, I would be fucking delighted. That pompous religious righter, he's done everything in his power to run trial lawyers like me plumb out of business with his tort reform shit." Cal cleared his throat. "But I guess the purpose of your call is to tell me you have no choice but to investigate Worthman, which will take some of the heat off of Forman's kid."

"Yes, I will have to investigate Worthman, but I'm still going to stay focused on the Forman boy. I'm planning on bringing him in for an interview next week."

"It'll still give his ol' man plenty to worry about. That's all I want."

"Well, just remember. I wouldn't have even reopened this investigation but for your insistence. The police didn't find any evidence of foul play. I don't really have a valid basis for even bringing in Forman's son."

"I know, I know. And I'm grateful to you for that. You know I always repay favors, Reggie. Always. Keep me posted."

Cal strolled from the window to the phone on the credenza behind his desk and disconnected the call. A thought popped into his mind. What if Senator Worthman were involved somehow in Alexis Stone's death? Even if he walked the charges, an indictment would destroy his career. And the future of the plaintiffs' bar in the great state of Texas would be all the better for it. After the Stone case was in his rearview mirror, he would turn his attention to Senator Worthman and enjoy every minute making sure word was leaked to his source at the *Herald* about the good senator and his tawdry relationship with a college coed. The public outcry would be a joy to behold, not to mention the divorce that would follow.

Just a few miles from Reginald Cowan's office, Leah Rosen opened the door to her apartment, her future with *Texas Matters* at the forefront of her thoughts. She made a beeline to the bar in her kitchen. She grabbed the bottle of Absolut from the counter and poured two jiggers of vodka in the tumbler she had taken from the cabinet above. She topped it with a splash of tonic and then collapsed on the sofa. She brought the glass to her lips and turned it up, way up.

Closing her eyes, she thought about her meeting with Abe. What had happened to make Steve Blumenthal pull the plug on her article? It had to have been a call from Cal Connors—no doubt about it. But what ammunition did Cal have to make Blumenthal take such a drastic step? Her research had been thorough. She had turned up irrefutable evidence that Dr. Crimm had lied in his report. She had seen reporters cut corners in the interest of sensationalism. But this was not one of those instances. Her story was grounded in fact. She had made sure of that. There was absolutely no legitimate claim Cal could make that the story was false. Besides, since his many court cases had been so newsworthy, he was likely a "public figure" in the eyes of the law, and the standard to sue a publication was even greater: he would have to prove the article was published with knowledge of its falsity or a reckless disregard for the truth. No way he could meet that burden.

So what was it? What was Blumenthal's reason for quashing the story? Had Cal's investigator come up with some dirt on Blumenthal's private life, or some improprieties in his professional career, and was Cal using it to blackmail Blumenthal? Or was it simply that the magazine was having financial problems and could not afford to defend any lawsuit Cal might bring?

Leah had heard *Texas Matters* was considering some staff reductions, but that was only rumor. She downed the rest of her drink. She then went to the bar, fixed herself another, and returned to the couch. What was really going on? Should she resign? And if she did, how would that look on her résumé? What would she do for money? How would she pay the rent?

The biggest question for Leah, though, was whether anyone would print her story after she finished it. Wouldn't Cal just apply the same pressure to any newspaper or magazine that considered airing an unflattering story on him or his firm?

Leah took another sip of her drink. But then again, what if she did nothing? How could she call herself an investigative reporter? How could she live with herself knowing that Cal and Crimm were getting away with stealing millions and millions of dollars? And that was exactly what it was: theft. Theft on a grand scale! It would have been no different if Cal, abetted by Dr. Crimm, had walked into the offices of Samson Pharmaceuticals, taken the president hostage, and extorted millions in ransom. Instead of guns, Cal and Crimm had used a perversion of the legal system.

Leah just couldn't let this go. She got up from the couch and went into the kitchen. She peered into the fridge—nothing but a few beers and an outdated bag of salad. She opened the freezer door—two Lean Cuisines. But that would have to do. She slid a Salisbury steak with a side of macaroni and cheese into the microwave and put six minutes on the timer. She hit start and finished her drink as she waited.

Three bites later, she pushed her dinner aside and poured herself a third vodka tonic. As she stared at her drink, she made up her mind. She would keep working at *Texas Matters* but finish the article in the evenings from her apartment. If she had to follow leads or do investigative work during the day, she would take personal time off from *Texas* Matters. She had a friend who was working for *Newsweek* and another working for the *Wall Street Journal*. She would make contact with them to see if they might be interested in a freelance article on Texas justice. She would roll the dice and hope for seven or eleven. If the dice were true, the article would be published. But, most importantly, she would be able to live with herself. If she rolled craps, all would not be lost. She would still have her job at *Texas Matters*. But she would know she had done the right thing. And in her idealistic mind, that was all that mattered.

CHAPTER
45

"Darrin, glad I caught you! I'm on my way to meet with Mr. Arnold this morning. Anything going on at the office I need to know about?"

"I'm glad you called. I didn't know what time you were going to make it back to town last night, and I didn't want to call and wake you up."

"Thanks, Darrin. I've had so much going on I haven't had time to check in."

"No problem." Darrin knew something was up, as Jace usually checked in with her several times a day when he was out of the office. She figured he would bring her up to speed when he could. But her intuition told her there was something going on in Austin that involved more than Matt or the Caring Oaks case. "There are a few things you need to know before your meeting. Mr. Arnold was served with a subpoena yesterday. Connors wants him to show up next week with all of the company's financial information. Also, the court coordinator called. We are number one on the trial docket next month."

"What? There have to be older cases set. How did we get to be number one?"

"I'm sure Connors could answer that question."

"We need to get a motion for continuance on file. No way we can be ready for trial that soon. Draft one and I'll sign it when I get in. Talk to the court coordinator and try to get her to set it for hearing. Anything else?"

"I saved the best for last. We received a settlement demand from Connors."

"And?"

"Ten million! Can you believe it?"

"That's outrageous! But I'll pass it along to Mr. Arnold this morning. With the settlement demand and the subpoena, it ought to be a interesting meeting."

"I'm glad I won't be there. Good luck with that."

Jace drove through a Starbucks on his way to Caring Oaks. He typically never went for the brand, but he was in a hurry and needed a black coffee in the worst kind of way. As he walked into the Caring Oaks offices Jace glanced at his watch: eight o'clock sharp.

Wallace Arnold was sitting in the reception area waiting for him, his arms crossed and a scowl on his face. He caught Jace arriving out of the corner of his eye and rose from his seat.

As Jace approached, he grimaced at his client's condition. Layered bags of skin formed semicircles under Wallace's bloodshot eyes. Several hardly discernible specks of perspiration dotted his upper lip. His right hand trembled faintly as he extended it to his lawyer.

"I thought you were never going to get here." His tone was one of nervous irritation.

Rather than reminding his client of the time, Jace apologized. "I'm sorry if you've been waiting long." The two men made their way to Wallace's office.

"This case—well, I've never had to go through anything like this."

"I know it's been very trying for you."

"That's the understatement of the year." Wallace pulled a white handkerchief from his pocket and patted his upper lip and forehead.

"Wallace, before we get started, we received a settlement demand from Mr. Connors yesterday evening."

"What's that son of a bitch asking for? I'm sure it's outrageous."

"Ten million."

Wallace's mouth fell open. No words followed.

"Yeah, that was my reaction."

"You don't think he's serious about that number, do you?"

"Oh, he'll take less. I settled another case with him several years back. Right now, his bottom line is probably about a third of that, somewhere in the three-million-dollar range."

"I won't pay it."

"I'm not recommending that you do. But it's my ethical obligation to pass his demand on to you."

"Do you have any good news? What did you learn in Austin?"

Jace felt a pang of guilt; most of his time had been spent trying to clear Matt. He knew he was treading dangerously close to ethical violations by not disclosing his conflict to Wallace. But his number one priority was his son, and he had to stay involved in the case—at least until Matt was cleared of any involvement. "Well, we have a possible lead on a boyfriend. He might have had something to do with Alexis' death and the ensuing grave robbery."

"Who is it?"

"I can't tell you that. If I did, and Connors asked you about it in your deposition, you might have to give him the information. Sure, I'd assert the attorney-client privilege, but Connors would get the judge on the line, and from what I've seen so far, he would bend the rules to give Cal what he wants. We just can't take that chance. And you can't testify to something you don't know about."

"Understood. But can you tell me whether it is good or bad for our case?"

"Good. I just don't know how good yet."

"Well, it's about time something went our way. Now, can we talk about my deposition?"

"Absolutely."

"You'll agree that Connors wants to use this deposition as an opportunity to harass me, correct?"

"That is certainly one of his purposes."

"So he will try to get into my relationship with Lonnie, right?"

"Judging from the way he conducted Lonnie's own deposition, probably right off the bat. One of his tactics is to hit the witness with a very uncomfortable series of questions right from the beginning. Think about what he did to Lonnie, starting off with his dismissal at the funeral home in Knoxville."

Wallace shuddered. "Can't you stop him from doing that? What in the world does my relationship with Lonnie have to do with a grave robbery? Surely he is not permitted to go into topics that are totally irrelevant."

"Well, I could instruct you not to answer any questions about your relationship with Lonnie, but, again, he will just get Judge Reinhold on the line and we will debate the point over the telephone. Connors will argue that you hired a suspected body molester, putting all of those defenseless souls buried at Caring Oaks at risk. And you did so for selfish reasons: you wanted to have sex with a young man."

Wallace cringed. "You didn't have to be so blunt."

"He will be. I'm just trying to get you prepared for what you will hear at your deposition."

"How about all these financial documents he wants? I mean, it will take our accounting department days to pull together that information. And what does the net worth of Caring Oaks have to do with this case?"

"Connors will ask the jury to award punitive damages against the company. Literally, he will ask them to punish Caring Oaks for its reckless conduct. As part of his argument, he will show how much the company is worth and how much it would take to inflict the type of punishment that might cause Caring Oaks to change the way it does business. Although I haven't tried a case against Cal, most plaintiffs' lawyers ask for a percentage of the company's net worth. I suspect that is what Cal will do as well."

"That could be in the millions."

"You got it. That's what makes this case dangerous."

"When do we have to get back to Connors on his settlement proposal?"

"I would suggest you think about it, discuss it with your board, and call me so we can talk about how to respond, if at all. In the interim, I will continue to work on this case full-throttle. I'm headed to the office this morning. If you need me for anything, you can reach me there."

"And I'll be here trying to compile all of these records. I'm sure we will speak again soon."

The two men stood and shook hands. "No need to show me out. I think I can find my way."

"Thank you, Jace."

Jace shut the door behind him as he made his way out of Wallace's office. Twenty minutes later he was gazing out the window of Darrin's office at the street below. It was a little after ten. Cal's victory party was unfolding in his mind. He imagined a big black stretch limo with a uniformed driver parked at the curb. It was a well-known Connors tradition to take his clients via limo to Bob's Chop House, a high-end steakhouse, for a celebratory dinner after a substantial jury verdict or seven-figure settlement. He would make sure his press contacts were tipped off to the time and place. After all, one-column inserts in the metropolitan sections of the Dallas and Fort Worth papers were some of the best advertising available—even better than a strategically placed billboard with Cal's picture on it or the neon sign that marked his offices.

After steak dinners, several bottles of expensive wine, and toasts with the best champagne, Cal would escort his clients to Fort Worth's private airport, where his jet awaited to take them to a resort of their choosing for a two-week "all expenses paid" stay. Cal would then deduct the expenses relative to the dinner and vacation trip from his clients' portion of the settlement proceeds or jury award. Thanks to a talkative ex-bookkeeper, Cal's practices were common knowledge among the legal profession but unknown to his unsophisticated clients. To them, he was a champion of the common man, a defender of the downtrodden. And nobody could convince them to the contrary.

Darrin's voice startled Jace. "Well, where should we start—your phone messages or the mail that's accumulated over the last several days?"

Jace ignored the question. "I was just thinking about Connors and all of his bullshit. You know his clients really believe he does this for altruistic reasons, out of the goodness of his big ol' Texas-size heart. That son of a bitch doesn't care about anything but the almighty dollar. Not one damn thing."

Darrin had heard this speech on numerous occasions. She said nothing, allowing Jace to continue his diatribe.

"We've got to get a break in the Stone case."

"I sense you would prefer to discuss strategy on the Stone case before we start going over the mail and other cases."

"Anything in that stack of mail that can't wait?"

"As long as we can go over it sometime today, I think we will be fine."

"Great. I need to bring you up to date on what went on in Austin and the results of my meeting with Wallace."

Jace sat down in the chair across from Darrin's desk. He had given considerable thought to sharing with Darrin the story of

Matt's involvement with Alexis. With the trial rapidly approaching and a new assistant district attorney breathing down Matt's neck, he couldn't take the chance that Darrin would find out about it from another source. If that happened, the trust they had built over years of working together would be shattered. She had to hear it from him.

Jace relayed to her what he knew. He conveniently left out the fact that his source in the APD was Jackie McLaughlin. When Jace stopped talking, Darrin placed the legal pad and pen she had been holding on the tabletop and crossed her arms. She took a deep breath and looked at Jace.

"Damn, Jace. I knew something was up. I just didn't know how serious it was. I don't know how you have been holding up through all this. Is there anything I can do to help? The police don't really think Matt had anything to do with this, do they?"

"I sure hope not. I've just got to keep the pressure on to confirm whether or not Alexis was murdered and, if she was, make sure I find out who did it."

"I'll work as hard as I can on this end." Darrin bit her lip. "I hate to bring this up, but is there any possibility of a conflict of interest in our handling the Caring Oaks case?"

"You let me worry about that. If I need any research on that issue, I'll let you know. For now, it is important for me to stay involved, conflict or no conflict."

"Understood. In that case, let me bring you up to speed on the latest events. I had Boyce plant the video cameras at both grave sites like you asked. So far, nothing has turned up. Of course, I will let you know the minute something does. Also, he uncovered some interesting information on Sloan Jenkins. It appears Miss Jenkins likes other women. She hangs out at a lesbian bar in Austin called a Woman's Choice."

"Catchy name." Jace smirked. "You think Alexis and Sloan might have been lovers?"

"That would be my guess."

"So how do you explain the fact that she went out with Matt and probably had a fling with the good senator?"

"Alexis Stone wouldn't be the first woman to go both ways. Besides, it appears from her behavior that she loved thrills and doing the unexpected. That's my take."

Jace shook his head. "I'll go back and look at the notes from my interview with Sloan. Another visit with her might be worthwhile. And, while we are on the subject of going both ways, Mr. Arnold admitted to me in strict confidence that he and Lonnie Masterson were . . ."

Jace paused, raising his eyebrows.

Darrin gasped. "Oh, no. You're kidding me! I sensed Mr. Arnold was a little different but . . ."

"And, boy, was it painful for him to tell me. He's going through hell."

"I'm sure you told him how devastating that would be to his case?"

Jace nodded. "I gave him a dress rehearsal of the interrogation he's going to endure during his deposition. Believe me, he got the message."

"I hate to say it, but things are not looking good for our case, Jace. We have Lonnie Masterson, the gay lover of the head guy at Caring Oaks, an accused necrophiliac, obviously disturbed, hiding something—"

"I know, I know. All the signs point to him. But there is no objective evidence that links him."

"I guarantee you Cal Connors has enough right now to convince a jury, and Lonnie's no longer around to explain himself."

"Like I said, we have to get a break somewhere, somehow. How about the satanic angle? Have you come across anything we can use to link Alexis' grave robbery to devil worshippers, other than the site where they found her body after it had been stolen? Do the Tarrant County police have any leads yet?"

"Not really. There were no discernible fingerprints at the scene, and tests on whether the body had been sexually molested came back inconclusive. Right now they have no suspects, no nothing."

"Well, bad facts or not, we have to come up with a trial plan."

"How about a five-minute coffee break first?"

"Sounds good. See you back here in ten."

CHAPTER

46

Senator Worthman's thoughts were abruptly interrupted by his secretary's voice coming from the intercom on his office credenza. "Excuse me, Senator. There are two detectives here to see you."

"I'm sorry, Mrs. Butler. Did you say 'detectives'?"

"Yes, sir. From the Austin PD."

"I've got a subcommittee meeting I'm already late for—"

"Senator, they said it would only take a few minutes. They have some routine questions for you regarding a Miss Alexis Stone."

Talmadge could feel the blood rush to his head. His thoughts were racing. Should he ask to have his lawyer present? That would give him more time, but it also might make him look guilty. And if he admitted to even knowing Alexis Stone, then all hell would break loose. Their questions wouldn't end there. They would ask him about the night she died, whether he had been there. How would he explain that? No, he needed to play for time.

Talmadge rose from his leather chair, grabbed his briefcase, and entered his reception area. He extended his hand to both detectives. "Detectives! Always glad to see members of our law enforcement. I understand you need a few minutes of my time. I'd love to visit with you but, unfortunately, I'm already late for a subcommittee meeting."

"This will only take a few minutes" one of the detective said. "We could walk with you to your meeting, if you don't mind."

"I tell you what. My secretary, Mrs. Butler, knows my schedule inside and out." Talmadge pointed in the direction of his secretary, who was anxiously nodding in agreement. "Why don't you visit with her for a moment and she can get you set up with a time when we can talk?"

The senator hurried to the door, the detectives following. "It has been a pleasure meeting both of you. I look forward to answering your questions when we have more time."

"Sir, can you just tell us what your relationship was, if any, with a Miss Alexis Stone? Can we just get an answer to that one question?"

Talmadge quickly made his way out the door and into the crowded corridor, leaving the detectives speechless in the waiting area.

Mrs. Butler began to flip through the calendar in front of her. "Let's see. I don't see an opening in the senator's calendar until one week from this Friday. How does that sound?"

Talmadge made his way out of the building as fast as he could without running. He got into his Cadillac and started driving aimlessly as he made a call. "Myron, are you where you can talk?"

Myron's voice was a whisper. "Let me step out in the hall." There were some undecipherable words muttered as Myron Berg extricated himself from a meeting.

"So what's going on, Senator?"

"We got problems. I just left two detectives from the Austin PD in my office."

"You what?"

"You heard me. I'm not shitting you. I just left two dicks from the Austin PD in my office."

"What did they want?"

"They started off our chat by asking me if I knew Alexis Stone." Silence.

"You still there?"

"I'm here," Myron replied. "What did you tell them?"

"Nothing. I fabricated a meeting and rushed out the door."

"Good thinking."

"But they're not going away. And I think my abrupt departure made them think I had something to hide."

"Well, that's better than spilling your guts. If your affair with Alexis Stone comes out, you won't be able to win a race for dog-catcher. The liberal element will try to run you out of Texas."

"Thanks for those consoling words. I don't know how I am going to get out of this one. If I hire a lawyer and plead the Fifth, I'm sunk. If I don't and tell them everything, I'm sunk. It's a lose-lose proposition for me."

"Well, at least you've bought us some time. We can meet with Finis Fowler. He's one of the best criminal lawyers in the state. He'll come up with something."

"Go ahead and set it up, but don't tell him anything. Just schedule a meeting in his office. I don't want him coming to my office in the Capitol."

"I don't blame you. I understand you are a little jumpy now, but we're going to get out of this mess. I promise you that."

"I sure hope so."

The call ended and Talmadge took the ramp to I-35 South. He didn't know where he was going but he had to get out of Austin—at least for a while.

CHAPTER

47

J ace had dinner alone at a small neighborhood restaurant near his home. He and Darrin had spent most of the afternoon going through a week's worth of mail, emails, and voice mails. It seemed every client in every case had to have something done— not tomorrow but right now. Associates had been summoned for various assignments that would hopefully contain the fires and keep the clients happy until Jace's current storm blew over. His mind, cluttered with deadlines and demands, yearned for a respite, however short.

Jace ordered another beer. He fished around in the inside pocket of his suit jacket for the notes he had taken during his meeting with Darrin that morning on the Caring Oaks case. He began to skim them, hoping something would jump out at him, something he had previously missed. At the top of the list was Talmadge Worthman. What a hypocritical son of a bitch! But there was no way Jace could prove Talmadge had killed Alexis or, more importantly, robbed her grave—at least, not before trial. This was a dead end for now. But the discovery of Talmadge's relationship with Alexis, and his presence at her apartment on the day of her death, was not without value. At the least, it would divert some of Cowan's attention from Matt. Maybe Cowan would postpone his questioning of Matt in light of this new information. Jace would call Pat in the morning and find out if he had heard anything.

And what about Sloan Jenkins? Sloan claimed she and Alexis had been best friends; they even had keys to each other's apartments. Sloan could enter Alexis' apartment anytime, night or day. And then there was the revelation that she was a lesbian. Darrin had made a good point. Maybe Alexis and Sloan had been secret lovers. That fact alone would place her squarely in the line of suspects.

Or maybe it didn't. Jace took another swig from the icy longneck.

What had Matt said about his time with Alexis on the night of her death? He had left her asleep on the couch. He couldn't lock the door— he had no key. But Alexis' maid, Maria Gonzalez, said the door was locked when she arrived the next morning. Alexis had given her a key.

Jace set his beer down and stared at the wall. Someone had locked the door to Alexis' apartment after Matt had been there! And besides Maria, there was only one other person who had a key, at least as far as Jace knew.

Jace looked at his watch—9:30. He would catch a flight to Austin first thing in the morning. Sloan Jenkins knew more than she was telling.

The next day, on his way to the Avis counter, Jace called Jackie McLaughlin to see if she would meet him for breakfast. He was confident she would have some valuable pointers on how to get the truth from Sloan. And get it in a form that would be usable in court.

"Damn," Jace muttered after getting Jackie's voice mail. "Jackie, this is Jace. I am in Austin and was hoping to catch you this morning. Please give me a call as soon as you get this. I'm on to something. Thanks."

Driving on I-35 South, he decided to see if Wallace Arnold was in. He wanted to find out if his client had made a decision about whether to respond to Cal's settlement demand. His gaze alternated from the road to the phone in his hand as he scrolled down his contact list for Wallace's direct dial. On the third ring, Jace heard his client's voice.

"This is Mr. Arnold."

"Wallace, this is Jace Forman. I'm calling from Austin. Had to make an emergency trip down here."

His client responded excitedly. "What for? Could it break open the case?"

"I'll fill you in later. It's too early to tell, and I don't want to get your hopes up."

There was an awkward pause.

"Jace," Wallace said hesitantly, "I've been thinking about the mess we find ourselves in. Nothing has gone right. Lonnie's dead. Business is the worst it's been in as long as I can remember. I see that Connors monster in my dreams at night. I just don't know if I can hold up through the ordeal of a deposition or trial."

Wallace paused, obviously trying to retake control of his emotions. "This has got to come to an end. It's wrong what the Stones and that scumbag lawyer have done, but I can't afford to fight it anymore, personally or professionally."

Jace said nothing. He had experienced this before—clients settling cases not because they had done something wrong but because they just didn't have the stomach for a drawn-out courtroom fight. Jace felt powerless as Wallace continued.

"I have my notes from our last conversation. You believe the case could be settled for about a third of the ten-million settlement demand, is that correct?"

"I can't guarantee it, but that has been my past experience with Connors."

"Well, you have my authority to agree to a three-million-dollar settlement, but do your best to get the number lower so it will be a little easier for our board to swallow. Hopefully, you'll learn something today that will help you in your negotiations."

"I'll do my best."

"And Jace, I want the case settled before I have to give my deposition. None of the board members know about my . . ." His voice trailed off.

"I understand." The other end of the line went dead. Jace placed his phone on the seat. Almost immediately, there was another ring. It was Jackie.

"Jace, I got your message this morning. What's up?"

"I am on I-35 just a few minutes from downtown. Can you meet me for a cup of coffee? It's important."

"The cafe in the Driskill is a few blocks away from my office. I'll meet you there in ten minutes?"

"Thanks, Jackie." Jace ended the call. He looked forward to seeing Jackie, but his mind was far from a social visit. A few minutes later, he was giving his car key to the Driskill valet. As he walked into the cafe, he saw Jackie already seated and speaking with a waiter. When he got to the table, she stood and offered her hand.

"Good morning, Jace! I didn't expect to see you again so soon. It sounds like you may be on to something. Fill me in."

"I need some help from the best investigator I know."

"To do what?"

"You remember that college friend of Alexis'—"

Jackie interrupted. "Sloan Jenkins. No one got much out of her, including you. The only thing that really sticks out in my mind is her trashing Alexis' parents, am I right?"

"On the money."

The waiter reappeared and poured them each a cup of black coffee.

"Will you be having breakfast?" the waiter asked, his eyes darting between Jace and Jackie.

"Coffee is all for me," Jackie responded.

"Waffle and a side order of bacon," Jace replied.

"Right away, sir."

As soon as the waiter left, Jace and Jackie continued their conversation.

"I have a bit of interesting news to start off your day. It seems Alexis' BFF is gay, or at least swings both ways."

Jackie raised her eyebrows and tilted her head. "Interesting. But that doesn't make her a murderer or grave robber, now does it?"

"Not in a vacuum."

Jackie flashed him an "I hope so" look.

"This is only a theory—strictly speculation."

"Don't worry, nobody's going to sue you for slander."

"I think Alexis and Sloan were lovers and—"

Jackie finished the thought. "Alexis threw Sloan over, just like she did Matt, and the proverbial shit hit the fan."

Jace nodded.

"What evidence do you have of Sloan's sexual orientation?"

"My investigator confirmed she hangs out at a club called a Woman's Choice."

"I know the place. That's a pretty good hint of the games she likes to play. But what evidence do you have that she and Alexis were—I guess the proper term is 'lipstick lesbians'?"

"Nothing but a hunch. But there's more. Sloan told me she had a key to Alexis' apartment. According to Matt, he left Alexis sleeping on the couch the night of her death. He had to leave the door unlocked since he didn't have a key. The cleaning lady said when she got to the apartment the next morning, the door was locked. Sloan had to have used the key Alexis had given her." Jace stopped to take a breath.

"So your theory is Sloan was jilted for this politico, she was eaten up with jealousy, she visited Alexis after your son left, and then something happened. What?" Jackie was playing devil's advocate.

"I don't know whether it was foul play or not, but considering that your lab guy found alcohol, cocaine, and some type of date-rape tranquilizer in Alexis' blood, I want to make sure Matt doesn't take the fall for that. He's a good kid, and maybe I'm just a naive parent, but I know he wouldn't be involved in something like that."

Jackie held her coffee cup with both hands and looked down into it before raising her eyes to meet Jace's. "You know, Jace, either way, I'm going to have to turn any viable evidence over to Cowan. So I hope you are right."

"I am right, Jackie, but I need the evidence, if there is any, that it was Sloan who gave her those drugs. That's where you come in. I need your help. How would you approach her? She got a little short with me at the end of our talk the last time. And I am sure if I show up again she will get defensive pretty quick."

"I'll help you, but you are forewarned on the evidence."

"I understand."

"Okay. First, I'd like for you to wear a body camera when you meet with Sloan."

"You mean you want to me to wear a wire?"

"Not exactly. Wearing a wire is uncomfortable and usually causes the person wearing it to become nervous. I want you comfortable and loose when you interview Ms. Jenkins."

"So what do you have in mind?"

"A body camera is the latest in law enforcement technology. It is tiny, undetectable, and can be attached to your shirt lapel or tie clip. We can pick one up at the station on our way to Ms. Jenkins's apartment. Now, are you ready for a little Interrogation 101?"

"I'm all ears."

CHAPTER

48

An hour and a half later, Jace's rental car was headed toward campus. Jackie followed in an unmarked police car.

As Jace hiked up the concrete steps leading to Sloan's apartment, he sensed his palms getting clammy, beads of perspiration forming under his arms and dotting his forehead. He had a lot on the line here, but he had to know for sure. He stopped midway up the stairs, drying his hands on his pants legs. Before resuming his ascent, he nervously cleared his throat, fastened the top button of his white shirt, and adjusted his tie.

His mind flashed back to Jackie's instructions. Go slow. Put Sloan at ease. Get her talking. Make sure she does not feel accused of anything. Weave the web slowly, strand by strand. The instructions seemed so straightforward and simple, yet Jace knew they would be difficult to follow. Trying to shelve his doubts, he bolted up the remaining stairs and walked confidently down the narrow outside corridor toward apartment number 33. Without hesitation, he knocked on the door, gazing around the complex as he awaited a response.

There was none. He knocked again, this time his eyes fixed on the door. Again, nothing. Frustrated, Jace retreated toward the stairs. As he turned at the first step, his peripheral vision caught Sloan Jenkins's eyes, peering in his direction from the doorway he had just left. He abruptly reversed direction, displacing a dejected expression with an inviting smile. As he walked back toward her apartment, he began the dialogue.

"Ms. Jenkins, I apologize if I woke you." The two were now face-to-face. "I would hope you remember me. We talked once before. I'm Jace Forman, the lawyer who represents—"

Sloan interrupted with a nod, her short hair mashed on one side from a hard night's sleep, eyelids heavy, dark circles underneath.

"What time is it?" She yawned as she spoke, making her words barely intelligible.

Jace glanced at his watch. "A little after ten."

Sloan grimaced. "Shit, I've slept through Psychology again. I'm going to flunk that—" Sloan stopped, rethinking her choice of words, and continued, ". . . class. I can't believe it. I know I set my alarm."

She shook her head, motioning her visitor inside. Sloan's housekeeping had remained consistently nonexistent. Clothes were strewn haphazardly throughout; full ashtrays cluttered every table; half-filled glasses stood in ponds of condensate; countless beer cans, some crumpled and deformed, found homes on the floor, on tables, and next to an overflowing trash can. Jace smiled as he viewed the disaster zone.

"Looks like someone had one helluva party."

Sloan flashed her visitor a mischievous look. "You might say that, although my memory is a little foggy. Grab a seat. That is, if you can find one."

After removing a couple of beer cans lodged between the cushions of an overstuffed easy chair, Jace took a seat. Sloan quickly cleared a spot on the sofa and nestled in the corner, drawing her legs beneath her.

"I guess you're back to talk about that stupid case brought by Alexis' parents?" Her eyes searched for confirmation.

"You got it. The trial date is approaching, and I'm trying to tie up a few loose ends."

Sloan shook her head disgustedly. "Like I told you the last time, Alexis and her dad didn't get along—and that's being polite. She never talked with her mother. From all the things that Alexis told me, they were as dysfunctional as a family can get. That's all I know. End of story."

"I remember all that. And I know this is hard for you, you and Alexis being such close friends. I remember you telling me the two of you were like sisters, even had keys to each other's apartments?" As he spoke, Jace was hoping that the body camera was working properly.

"Absolutely, she was my best friend in the world. We trusted each other with anything and everything."

Jace nodded. "Anybody else she was that close to—close enough to trust with her apartment key?"

Sloan's eyes stared at a blank spot on the wall as she shook her head.

Jace sensed discomfort—time to change course. "Can you give me any more information on this politician she was seeing?"

Sloan hesitated. Trance broken, her eyes fixed on Jace's as she tested her memory.

"I think he was a congressman, a senator maybe. And going back to your previous question, he might have had a key, but that's just a guess."

Jace nodded. "Does the name Talmadge Worthman sound familiar?"

Sloan's eyes opened wide. "Worthman doesn't ring a bell but Talmadge does. Yeah, I'm sure of it. I thought it was such an unusual name."

"Did you ever meet him?"

"Oh, no." Sloan's denial was emphatic. "Alexis was very secretive about their relationship. That was way out of character for her."

Sloan got up from the couch and strolled toward the kitchen. "Want something to drink? I've got a bad case of cottonmouth."

"No, thanks."

Sloan retrieved a Diet Coke from the fridge and resumed her position on the couch. "Didn't meet him, see him, talk to him, nothing. Talmadge was just a name to me, nothing more than that."

"How about the day she died? Did you see her that day, talk to her, anything?"

She looked away, set her soft drink can down on the floor, and rubbed her palms together nervously. Jace waited patiently for a response. After several moments of telling silence, one came.

"I don't—I mean, no, I didn't see her or talk to her that day."

"When was the last time you remember seeing or talking to her?"

Sloan's face flushed. She picked up the soft drink can from the floor and took a long sip, buying time. "At least a week. I was busy and she was busy. What's that got to do with anything?" Her eyes flashed distrust.

"I've got evidence you were in her apartment the night she died." Jace gambled.

"That's ridiculous. I was right here. All night."

"That's partially true. You were here part of the night, but at some point after midnight you went to Alexis' apartment."

Sloan jumped up off the couch, went to the door and opened it, staring at Jace. "Are you crazy? Get out. I don't have time for this shit. I've got to get ready for my afternoon class."

"Your fingerprints were found in Alexis' apartment." Jace spoke with convincing authority but without factual support.

"So? I could have left them there a week before."

"These were fresh. Less than twelve hours old." Another bold assertion. Jace had been a quick study.

"Even if I was there that day, that doesn't prove anything. This whole thing freaked me out. I didn't want to get involved. With the police snooping around, I just got a little scared, that's all." Her tone turned defensive.

"Oh, I'm afraid there's more to it than that. You went there the night she died. The door was open. Alexis was passed out on the couch. You woke her. Challenged her about her relationship with the senator and why she had deserted you."

Sloan yelled, "You're full of shit. You're living in fairyland."

"No one else had a key. And the door was locked when the maid arrived the next morning. Give it up, Sloan. Tell me the truth."

Sloan sneered. "You can kiss my ass. I ought to sue you for slander. Now, get out of here. I've got more important things to do than listen to your bullshit." Sloan stood at the open door waiting for Jace to leave.

Sensing any further attempts to unlock the truth would prove futile, Jace walked toward the door. As he passed through the opening, he stopped and turned toward Sloan, their eyes exchanging fire.

"Sloan, I know the truth."

"You don't know a fucking thing," she snapped.

The door slammed behind him the moment Jace stepped outside.

CHAPTER

49

Sloan nervously shook out a cigarette, pacing frenetically. She had to talk with someone. She had no siblings, and she hadn't spoken with her parents in years. They had instructed her never to contact them after she told them she was gay.

Tears formed in Sloan's eyes, which she quickly smeared with trembling fingers. And then it dawned on her. She would call Margaux. Margaux was straight but knew all about Alexis and Sloan's relationship. The three had traveled together time and again. They were close. Margaux wouldn't tell a soul, and she just might have some good advice.

Sloan picked up her cell phone and dialed her number, continuing to pace as the call connected. Sloan breathed a sigh of relief when she heard Margaux's voice.

"Margaux, I need a friend. Someone I can talk to—freely."

"Have I ever let you down?"

"Never. Now that Alexis is gone, I feel like you're my only friend in the world."

"Sloan, you sound scared. What's going on?"

"I was there."

"What do you mean you were there? You were where?"

"The night Alexis died. I went there that night."

"What in the world for? I thought you had broken up for good."

"I know, but Alexis called me around one a.m. She sounded groggy, pretty fucked up. Told me she and her boyfriend—you know, Mr. Big Time Senator—had had a fight and their relationship was over. She told me she needed someone to talk to and that she couldn't stop thinking about me. Said she wanted to get back together."

"So what did you do?"

"I went over there. I was so excited that she wanted me back. You remember how depressed I had been since she threw me over for that asshole. I wanted things to get back the way they had been."

"And?"

"When I got there, Alexis was totally out of control. I don't know how much coke she had snorted, but she was revved up. She began to undo my blouse almost the minute I walked through the door."

Pause, then a sigh.

"We snorted four or five rails of coke and each popped a roofie. I mean, the music was blaring and we were all over each other. Alexis said she wanted to make love all night. Margaux, you still there?"

"I'm here."

"Well, I went to the bathroom and was gone just a few minutes. When I came out, Alexis was lying on the bed. I got in bed next to her but she wasn't moving. I thought she had just passed out. But when I tried to wake her I couldn't get a response."

Sloan began to sob.

"And then I noticed she wasn't breathing. I was so fucked up I didn't know what to do. I tried to give her CPR, but I wasn't sure I was doing it right. She was just this lifeless form in my arms, not responding to anything."

Sloan's sobbing grew louder.

"Damn, Sloan! Why didn't you call 911?"

"I panicked. And I knew she was gone."

Sloan took a deep drag off her cigarette, her hand shaking, tears coursing down her cheeks.

"Sloan, you need to talk to the police about this. This is serious."

"I can't go to the police! What if they don't believe me? What if they charge me with something?"

"Look, you are in way over your head. I think you need to hire a lawyer and talk to the police. I mean, I don't think we should be having this conversation."

"Margaux. I need your help."

"I can't help you with this one. This is totally out of my league. Like I said, call a lawyer. I'm not touching this."

"But, Margaux—"

Margaux ended the call, leaving Sloan staring at her phone, wondering what do next.

CHAPTER
50

"Senator Worthman, so good to meet you." Finis Fowler extended his hand as his new client rose from the reception room sofa.

"Finis, I appreciate your working me in on such short notice. One of my constituents has a personal legal matter that I would like to discuss with you."

Senator Worthman uttered this loud enough for the reception-ist to hear. He wanted to dispel any thoughts that he was seeing a renowned, and extremely expensive, criminal defense lawyer about a personal matter. Finis, casually dressed in a charcoal gray her-ringbone sports jacket, gray slacks, and no tie, took the cue.

"That's what I understand. Come on back."

Finis led the senator down a long corridor to his corner office. He stopped at the entrance and motioned his client inside.

"Let's sit at the conference table. I don't like having a big desk between me and my clients—creates an undesirable barrier."

Talmadge pulled out one of the chairs and took a seat. Finis followed.

"So, I talked with Myron Berg, but we didn't discuss the reason you wanted to see me."

"First, I want to make sure that everything I say to you is privileged. I haven't paid you a retainer yet. Does that make a difference?"

"Absolutely not. But if it makes you feel any better, why don't you give me a five. I'm working on the cheap today." Finis smiled.

Talmadge pulled out his wallet, extracted a crisp $5 bill, and slid it across the table.

"Now that we have that behind us, tell me what's on your mind."

"Yesterday I received an unexpected visit from two detectives from the Austin Police Department."

"Do you recall their names?"

"To tell you the truth, I don't. I was so shocked by their visit I didn't ask. My secretary should have them, though."

"I know you are a busy man. Mind if I call her and ask?"

"Not at all. But be sure—"

Finis interrupted. "To let her know the detectives were there on a matter related to one of your constituents. I get the drill."

"Thank you."

"Okay. Now let's get to why they were there."

Talmadge hesitated.

"I know this is not easy, but the sooner you tell me about it, the better you'll feel. I promise you. I'm not a psychiatrist—far from it—but I do know that."

"Her name was Alexis Stone."

"Go on."

"I was seeing her."

"If I remember right, you are married."

Talmadge nodded.

"So you were having an affair with Ms. Stone?"

Another nod.

"I am obviously not doing my job very well. I need for you to open up. I feel like I'm taking a hostile witness' deposition. In narrative form, tell me what happened."

Talmadge took a deep breath before beginning. "Ms. Stone and I had been having an affair for several months. She was a senior at UT." He stopped, searching Finis' eyes for a reaction.

"Senator, do you think that shocks me? I've seen a lot worse than that. Hell, I've represented college professors who have gotten involved with their students more times than I can count. They get fired by the university and then come to me, asking me to sue for wrongful termination, get them reinstated. I won't bore you with the details, but an older man having an affair with a much younger woman is not a rarity. Plus, it's not illegal. So why were the detectives harassing you?"

"Because Alexis Stone is dead."

Finis shifted in his chair. "When did she die?"

"Months ago."

"And I guess the more important question is how."

"Based upon the news reports I read, her death was ruled accidental by the coroner."

"If that's the case, why has the Austin PD sent a couple of investigators to meet with you?"

"That's just it. I don't know."

"So when was the last time you saw Ms. Stone?"

"The night she died."

"Did the two of you have sex that night?"

"No, we had an argument. I had promised Alexis I was going to leave my wife. But I just couldn't bring myself to do it with the election coming up. Alexis went ballistic and told me she never wanted to see me again. She practically chased me out of her apartment. Threatened to call my wife."

"Go on."

"I was told the investigation was closed, and now this. The only thing I can think of as to why they are coming around now is her parents filed a lawsuit against the cemetery where Alexis was buried. The most bizarre thing happened after her funeral."

"And what was that?"

"Her body was dug up and stolen from her grave site at the cemetery. It was found the next morning."

Finis gave an affirmative nod. "I've read about the case. Very bizarre. But as strange as it is, I don't think that's why the Austin PD are looking to question you. If my memory serves me right, the theft of the body occurred in Fort Worth, so the Austin PD wouldn't be involved." Finis paused for a moment as if to contemplate reasons why the police would pay Talmadge a visit. He sighed and looked up at the ceiling. "So what did you tell them?"

"Nothing. I told them nothing. I was late for a meeting and asked them to schedule an appointment with my secretary."

"That was fortuitous."

"So what do we do now?"

"I will find out which prosecutor is assigned to the case, give him a call, and fish around for what he or she has."

"Won't the fact that I've hired you be a red flag?"

"I'll downplay it—tell the prosecutor you are very busy with the election coming up and don't have time to deal with this. And remember. Innocent people hire lawyers. In fact, that's the smart thing to do when a couple of detectives come knocking at your door." Finis briefly paused, making direct eye contact with his client. "I have to ask this. Did you have anything to do with Ms. Stone's death?"

The answer was immediate. "Nothing, absolutely nothing. You've got to believe me on this."

"I believe you, Senator. I'll be in touch."

CHAPTER
51

J ace walked down the steps of the apartment complex and tried to recall the make of the unmarked car Jackie was driving. He had been concentrating so heavily on what he was going to say to Sloan on the way over that he hadn't noticed. He walked around the parking lot, glancing inside each car to see if he could spot Jackie behind the wheel. He finally hit pay dirt. Jace noticed Jackie had earphones on. He knocked on the passenger window. She held her hand up, her eyes asking that he wait a minute. A couple of minutes later, the passenger door lock clicked and Jace slid inside.

"Well, I did my best. I just couldn't break her. Guess I wasn't as quick a study as I thought."

Jace noticed a smile taking shape on Jackie's face. "So what are you smiling about? I blew it."

Jackie held up a device that resembled an outdated cell phone. "This little baby is a SecPro Cell Interceptor. It intercepts cell phone conversations and records them. You didn't get a confession, but I did!"

"I can't believe it! Will it exonerate Matt?"

"It sure looks that way. I'll get a report typed up, sign an affidavit, and submit it to Cowan. In the meantime, I'll give him a call and let him know what's going on in the case. I'm sure he will want to call a press conference and capitalize on the publicity. Who knows, I may even get a promotion out of this." Jackie turned in her seat so that she was facing Jace and looked at him sincerely. "And I have you to thank."

Jace smiled and took Jackie's hand. "I think I'm the big winner on this one. You cleared my son's name and you took a chance when you didn't have to."

Jackie shook her head. She didn't bring up the fact that, if the evidence had gone the other way, she wouldn't have hesitated to use it against Matt. "Let's just say we made a good team."

"Whatever you want to call it, I'd really appreciate it if you would allow me to take you out to dinner so we can celebrate."

"Let's get this all buttoned up and I'll let you know."

Jace grinned. "And I promise I won't order for you."

Jackie laughed. "Don't you have a case to try?"

"Unfortunately, I do. I'm going to try to make the next flight back to Dallas–Fort Worth." Jace opened the car door to head to his rental car and then paused. "Jackie, thanks again. I really appreciate it."

"You too, Jace. Let me know how your trial goes. I may just take you up on that dinner."

Jace smiled. "You got it."

———————————

On his way to the airport, Jace got in touch with Matt to tell him the good news.

"Dad, I don't know how to thank you. I was so worried. I mean, I've tried to be strong and all, but every night was hell. I wouldn't wish this shit on my worst enemy."

"I'm just glad it's over and done with. And I hope you learned a lesson. I'm your best ally, your best friend, and your strongest supporter. Don't forget it."

"I understand that now. And I promise I won't forget."

"We still have to get a few things taken care of to close this thing out. My friend at the Austin PD is going to get the tape to Cowan, and she's sure he won't want to interview you."

"I just can't believe this nightmare's finally over." Matt said.

Jace glanced at his watch. "Wish I could stay and celebrate with you, but I've got to get back."

"Once things cool down, you think you might fly down for the weekend? Catch a Horns game?"

"You're on. Love you, Son." Jace clicked off and followed the signs at the airport to the rental car return. He called Darrin and filled her in on the great news and asked her to get Kirk McDougal, one of the associates, involved on a new trial strategy in light of Sloan's confession. A few hours later he was sitting at his conference room table across from Darrin.

"What did Kirk find out? Do we have any chance of appealing Reinhold if he denies our motion to postpone the trial, particularly in light of this new evidence?"

Darrin handed a manila file folder across the table. "Kirk's memo is inside. He's already drafted the appellate papers for your review. We would need to file them right after the hearing on our motion for continuance tomorrow, assuming the judge refuses to reset the case."

Jace thumbed through the folder contents. Reading and talking at the same time, he said, "Well, this seems to give us some hope. Judges have broad power to manage their trial docket, but they can be overturned for an abuse of discretion." Scanning the printout of a case Kirk had downloaded as a result of his research, Jace continued. "In this particular instance, the judge put the parties to trial without sending out the proper notice. We don't have those facts here, but some of the language in the opinion seems helpful."

"So should we file it?"

"Absolutely. We've got to pull out all the stops. And the fact that an appeal has been filed might give me some leverage in my settlement negotiations with Connors."

"I'll have Kirk standing by at the court of appeals until we get a ruling."

"How about the Stone depositions?"

"They're on. I scheduled them to begin right after Connors finishes with Mr. Arnold. Connors' paralegal was a little snippy about it, but I told her if she didn't agree to produce them voluntarily, I would subpoena them at their mansion on the hill. She quickly changed her tune."

"Our investigator get any more scoop on them?"

"Nothing more than I've already told you. I do think their mental anguish claim is a bunch of BS. They certainly weren't attentive parents."

"We'll soon find out. And how about Wallace—have you scheduled a time for me to meet with him prior to his deposition?"

"I've tried. He doesn't even want to talk about it. Gets very emotional every time I get him on the line. Says he'll refuse to testify."

"I'll call him later tonight. Maybe I can calm him down a little."

"Good luck. But I doubt you'll be able to work your magic on Mr. Arnold. He's a complete basket case."

"Have you prepared an affidavit for me to sign about Sloan's confession?"

Darrin handed Jace another folder. Inside were the original and three copies of an affidavit, detailing what Jace had learned earlier that day about Sloan and how it affected the need for a rescheduling of the trial. Jace quickly reviewed the affidavit and signed at the bottom, sliding the file back to Darrin.

"Anything else we need to cover?"

"I believe that's it for now." Darrin's eyes focused in on Jace's. "Now that we know the circumstances surrounding Alexis' death, who do you believe stole her body?"

Jace stared at his assistant and shook his head. "I have no idea."

CHAPTER

52

"All rise, the 133rd District Court is now in session, the Honorable Reuben Reinhold presiding."

On cue the door behind the bench opened and a lanky figure, clad in a clergy-like black robe, ascended the three wooden steps to the elevated throne from which justice was dispensed. Before speaking, Judge Reinhold peered over half-glasses, surveying the temporary inhabitants of his domain. He quickly reviewed some files in front of him, stroking his perfectly coiffed brown mane in the process. Satisfied, his gaze returned to his audience.

"The court has several matters to take up this morning. There are two motions for summary judgment and some discovery matters that need to be heard. I will get to them in due course, but the first motion I would like to consider is the motion for continuance filed by Caring Oaks Funeral Home in the case styled *Lackland and Olivia Stone* v. *Caring Oaks Funeral Home and Cemetery*. That case is set for trial Monday morning at nine, and it's a number one setting. I don't see any need in having the lawyers in that case sit around here until noon listening to other motions being argued when they could be spending their time preparing for trial. Are the parties ready in that case?"

Jace rose from one of the pews in the spectators' gallery, which also served as a waiting area for lawyers on "motion" days. "Movant is ready, Your Honor."

From the other side of the gallery came the theatrical, booming response of Cal Connors. "The Stones are ready, Your Honor."

"Gentlemen, please approach."

Jace, leather satchel in hand, maneuvered his way down the pew, up the aisle, and through the thigh-high swinging door that separated the spectators' gallery from the main courtroom, ultimately stopping at one of the two tables positioned in front of the judge's bench. Cal did likewise.

"Mr. Forman," the judge grimaced and shook his head as he spoke. "I have read your motion and I can say I was not pleased."

Jace could feel his face flush and imagined a smug smile dressing the face of his adversary. Judge Reinhold was now leaning forward, glaring over his half-glasses, zeroing in on Jace. "This is a very important case to the parties, and to the community as a whole. I'm sure every person who has buried a loved one at Caring Oaks is watching this case with bated breath."

Jace bit his tongue. His years of experience had taught him that lashing out at a member of the judiciary, no matter how outrageous his or her conduct, rarely paid dividends. He mentally conditioned himself for the tirade to continue.

"Mr. Connors, have you had any problem preparing your case for trial?"

"No, Your Honor, we are ready to go. In fact, we have spent a great deal of time and money preparing for this very setting. To have to do it all over again at a later date would create a tremendous financial hardship on my clients, not to mention additional emotional damage. Your Honor, we strongly oppose any continuance of this case. Mr. and Mrs. Stone have had to live with this nightmare long enough. They need to close this chapter of their lives so the healing can begin."

The judge cleared his throat. "Gentlemen, I am inclined to—"

Jace interrupted. "It is my motion, Your Honor. May I be heard?"

Judge Reinhold sighed, rolling his eyes. "Yes, Mr. Forman, you may be heard. But please make it brief. Remember, I have read your papers. I am familiar with your arguments."

"Thank you, Your Honor." Jace paused briefly. "I agree that this is an important case. It is important to my client as well as to Mr. Connors', a case that merits careful thought and preparation. The case has only been on file for a little less than six months. Since that time, my office has been working day and night, focusing primarily on the type of person who would have committed an unthinkable crime like this and whether security would have deterred them. Only recently have we discovered some very important information in this regard, as reflected in my affidavit. Stated simply, we need a little more time—a month or so—to see if our efforts will pay off, allowing us the opportunity to give the jury all of the facts pertinent to the questions they will be asked to answer."

Judge Reinhold stroked his hair as he spoke, his expression conveying bewilderment. "Mr. Forman, are you telling this court you are going to dispute the fact that one of your client's own employees committed this despicable act?"

Jace tried unsuccessfully to disguise his contempt. "Yes, Your Honor. We believe there are other plausible explanations for what happened."

"I've heard enough. I'm going to deny your motion. As they say, justice delayed is justice denied. The Stone case will proceed as scheduled. The court will take a fifteen-minute recess before taking up the rest of the docket. Mr. Connors, I would like to see you in my chambers on an unrelated matter." The gawky frame of Judge Reinhold rose and exited the courtroom.

Jace stared straight ahead, motionless. He knew the "unrelated" matter the judge and Cal would discuss behind closed doors was not unrelated at all. The judge would want to know if his ruling had turned the screws tightly enough. There might be some discussion of the upcoming election and the need for funds. No one would ever know except the conversation's participants.

As he made his way toward the judge's chambers, Cal peered over his shoulder, directing a parting shot at Jace. "If you want to talk, you've got my number." He disappeared behind the door marked "Chambers of The Honorable Reuben Reinhold."

Jace stepped outside the courtroom and into the corridor. He pulled his cell phone out of his briefcase and speed-dialed Darrin's direct line.

"Darrin McKenzie."

"Well—"

Darrin interrupted. "Let me guess. Judge Reinhold denied your motion. We're picking a jury at nine Monday morning."

"How'd you figure that out?" Jace replied sarcastically.

"You know what they say about a woman's sixth sense. And how was our friend Mr. Connors?"

"Pompous as ever. Judge Reinhold invited him to a private get-together after our hearing—in chambers."

"That is so unethical. Can't you report him to the judicial ethics commission?"

"Sure—and you know what they would do with my complaint. Besides, he and Connors would swear they had discussed personal matters—not anything related to any of the many cases Connors has in his court, including ours. And I would really be in the shit-house in Reinhold's court from now on out."

"Do you want to file the appeal?"

"I think we have to. We're not ready to go to trial on Monday, not by a long shot. And Connors and Reinhold know it. This was the infamous squeeze play—very well executed, I might add. I would be surprised if the 'in chambers' discussion wasn't part of the act. A signal to me of what's to come if I take the case to trial and don't pay Connors' ransom."

"What are our chances in the court of appeals?"

"I've been thinking about that. I go back and forth. Since it's an interlocutory appeal, seeking an immediate stay of a trial setting, it will only take one of the justices to grant us some temporary relief. If we get Justice Owens or Justice Rollins, our chances aren't bad. Otherwise, we can forget it. Are the papers ready?"

"Kirk and I were up here until midnight last night putting on the final touches. He's ready to hand-deliver them to the court as soon as I give him the go-ahead."

"Call him as soon as you get off the line with me. I would like to get the papers filed before noon. I want to catch one of the justices before they take off for the weekend. It would be nice to get a ruling before the end of the day, if possible."

"Got it. Did you talk with our neurotic client last night?"

"I called his cell several times but it kept going to voice mail."

"What time will you be back in the office?"

"Depends. If I think a meeting with Wallace would help, I'll probably head out to Caring Oaks this morning. Otherwise, I'll be in the office in less than an hour."

"I'll see you when you get here."

Jace disconnected and dialed the number of Caring Oaks. A polite female voice answered. "Caring Oaks Funeral Home and Cemetery. To whom may I direct your call?"

"Mr. Arnold, please."

"Just a moment, please." A momentary pause and the voice returned. "I'm sorry, but Mr. Arnold is unavailable. Is there someone else who can help you?"

"It is very important that I speak with him. I would appreciate your letting him know that Jace Forman is on the line. I'll hold."

Another pause. "I'll connect you now."

"Yes, Jace. I hope you have some good news for me. God knows I could use it."

"I wish I did. Our motion for continuance was denied."

Wallace gasped in frustration. "So why does that not surprise me? Everything else has gone wrong in this case—terribly wrong."

"We are in the process of filing an appeal of Judge Reinhold's decision. We are seeking emergency relief, postponing the trial setting."

"And what are our chances?"

"Hard to say. Depends on which justice or justices consider it. And that, in turn, depends on who's at the courthouse on this beautiful Friday. Good golfing weather reduces our chances of getting the matter considered today."

"Are you serious?"

"I'm afraid so."

"So when would the appeal be considered?"

"Monday morning, while we are picking the jury."

There was exasperation on the other line.

"I can't stand the pressure. You've got to get this case settled. I was up all night. I want this over—not tomorrow, not Monday, but this afternoon."

"We're not in the best negotiating position."

"I don't care. Set up a meeting with Connors. Do the best you can do, but get it settled. The next time I talk with you I want this nightmare to be over."

"Well, that went well," Jace thought sarcastically as the line went dead and he realized his client had just hung up on him. Out of the corner of his eye, he saw the swinging doors to Judge

Reinhold's courtroom open and the two men emerge. Both were laughing as they turned toward the elevator. Jace grimaced as he watched the judge put his hand on his adversary's shoulder as the twosome strolled down the hall.

Thirty minutes later, Jace burst into Darrin's office. "Did Kirk get the appeal filed?"

"He called just a minute ago. Everything is filed. Connors' copy is being delivered by the courier service."

"Did he find out what justices are there today? I know he clerked there after law school and knows the lay of the land pretty well."

"He is still tight with Phyllis, the official court clerk. He got the inside scoop, and, keep your fingers crossed, we just might be in luck. Justice Owens is there. The others said they had meetings outside the office. Phyllis told Kirk those meetings were on the first tee at the Colonial Country Club."

"Well, there's some benefit to having a woman on the court." Jace eyed Darrin, looking for a reaction. She ignored the slight. "Just kidding. I think she is a damn good judge, and if anyone would give us the relief we're asking for, she would."

"Did you get in touch with Mr. Arnold?"

"Yes, and the conversation couldn't have been worse. He was irrational, totally out of control. Instructed me to settle, regardless of the cost. That gives me some concern, since I know the principal reason he wants this case to go away is the embarrassment he'll suffer personally if his sexual orientation is disclosed to the world. Hell, he might even lose his job. And once that comes out at his deposition, Connors will leak it to his cronies at the paper in a New York minute."

"Is there anything you can do?"

"Ethically, my obligation is to represent the company, not Mr. Arnold. We have to get approval from the board of directors of any settlement, so Mr. Arnold will ultimately have to sell it to them. That could get a little sticky. I mean, Wallace isn't going to want me to disclose his relationship with Lonnie Masterson to the board. But that is a major risk factor in this case. When that evidence comes in, Katy bar the door."

"So what else can you do?" Darrin asked.

Jace stared at her and then he stared at the floor. He knew he was trapped. "I don't have any choice. I'm going to call Connors after lunch and set up a meeting. I want to make sure he has had an opportunity to review our appellate papers. Knowing Connors, he has probably got some secretarial mole over at the courthouse. If he discovers Justice Owens is there, that will bother him. He supported her adversary in the last election. He knows if the trial setting is delayed, the value of his case could drop precipitously."

"And till then?"

"I'll go through my mail, return a few phone calls, tend to other business. No need in preparing for trial. Wallace has made it abundantly clear he wants this case settled today. I am pretty confident I can talk him out of that position if the case is put off, but otherwise, there's no way. If we don't win our appeal, we don't have any other card to play."

"What about the depositions scheduled for tomorrow?"

"They won't go forward, but I don't want Connors to know that. Let's just put a hold on any work on the case. I'll let you know if anything changes in that regard."

Jace disappeared behind the door and walked toward his office. On his way he stopped by Harriett's desk, retrieved his phone messages, and asked her to order him a club sandwich from the deli across the street. Collapsing into his leather swivel chair, he thumbed through messages. One in particular caught his eye. Jackie McLaughlin had called at 10:53. Jace glanced at his watch—still time to catch her before the lunch hour. He hurriedly punched in the numbers. On the third ring, she answered.

"Jackie, this is Jace."

Her tone was direct, businesslike. "I've got some unpleasant news for you. I got that tape to Cowan. He said it certainly added another suspect to the list but, in his mind, was inconclusive. And he voiced doubt as to the tape's admissibility. He wanted to know how I got it. When I explained, he came unglued. Said he would talk to the chief and make sure appropriate disciplinary action was taken. He even hinted I might lose my job."

Jace interrupted. "You've got to be—"

"I wish I were. I mean, any other prosecutor would have been jumping for joy at a taped confession in a case. I just can't figure Cowan out. Bottom line, he wants to interview your son on Monday."

Jace couldn't believe what he was hearing. He had enough on his plate and now this. "Jackie, I don't know what to say."

"Jace, I have to ask. Do you think he's got another reason to go after Matt?"

"What reason could that be? I had never even heard of Cowan until this case. He certainly doesn't have a bone to pick with me. I just don't get it. But it is what it is, and I have to deal with it." Jace sighed. "Sorry, but I need to go. I've got to get hold of Pat and my son and let them know what's going on."

"I'm sure Pat already knows. And Jace, I'm really sorry about this."

"Nothing more you could do."

"Well, let me know what happens on Monday."

"In the case from hell or the interrogation of my son?"

"Both. I'll keep my fingers crossed."

"I'm afraid I'll need more than that. I'll call you as soon as I can."

Jace stared at his phone, beside himself. Matt was still on the hook despite the taped confession Jackie had delivered to that asshole Cowan. He got up from his desk and paced back and forth. There was something very wrong with this picture. And when he figured out exactly what it was, he was going to make sure those responsible would have hell to pay.

CHAPTER

53

For dramatic effect, Cal held the settlement meeting with Jace in the same conference room where Lonnie Masterson's videotaped deposition had been taken. As Jace entered the Boneyard, Cal immediately jabbed, "Déjà vu, wouldn't you say? I suspect the memories aren't quite as pleasant for you as for me. Am I right?" Cal gestured for his guest to sit in the same chair as Lonnie had. Jace ignored the directive, taking an adjacent seat.

"Let's cut to the chase," Jace said. "We've got a trial setting on Monday and depositions scheduled tomorrow. As you probably know by now, we have asked the court of appeals to stay the trial so we will have an adequate opportunity to develop our defenses—a little constitutional right called due process."

Cal never stopped smiling, but the tone of his voice completely changed. "Yeah, I've read your appeal. You know you don't stand a snowball's chance in hell of getting it granted. So let's get real."

"Who knows? I do know that our papers will get a close look. Justice Owens is well respected for her fairness, unlike some other members of the judiciary."

"Well, I don't care who hears it. No way it'll be granted."

Jace could sense he had hit a nerve. Cal was concerned about the appeal, no doubt about it. Jace continued. "Despite the appeal and my opinion as to its favorable chances, my client would like to explore settlement. But let's talk realistically—none of this 'pie in the sky' shit you've been throwing out."

Cal said nothing and Jace kept going. Temporarily, at least, he was in control of the meeting.

"Now I've had my legal assistant do a computer search of jury verdicts in Tarrant County over the past three years. She pulled up every case where there has been an award for mental anguish, and the awards range between $20,000 on the low side to $3,000,000 on the high side."

Cal interrupted with a pedantic smirk. "There's a distinguishing factor, and a very important one, I might add. I didn't try any of those cases. Applying the Cal Connors multiple of two, the range goes from $40,000 to $6,000,000."

Jace ignored him and continued. "My client has authorized me to offer you $500,000 to settle all claims brought by your clients. Of course, we would need a full release, a confidentiality agreement, and a dismissal with prejudice."

"Come on, Forman, what have you been smoking? Maybe a primer on the facts I'm going to parade before the jury might be of some help in your own assessment of the case. Let's see, where do I begin? Ah, an indicted body molester is hired by a funeral home either without a sufficient background check or despite it. The funeral home then puts that body molester in the position of preparing bodies for burial, the same job that led to molestation charges in another state. Shortly after Mr. Body Molester is hired, an all-American college coed, whose life was cut abruptly short, is abducted hours after her burial, and, we will contend to the jury, her body is sexually molested during the time it is missing. Am I getting warm?" Cal raised an eyebrow, simultaneously tilting his head.

Jace was silent. He peered into his host's eyes, searching for information that Cal might have that he didn't.

"And to beat it all, this funeral home didn't even have a security guard to protect its clientele's deceased loved ones. Have you taken the time to review what your client charges for an average funeral, as contrasted with what it costs them to bury someone? I have. And one of my witnesses will testify to how outrageous it is. Yet despite all this money your client makes off people, including the Stones, in their time of bereavement, it couldn't pay the meager salary of a security guard so the dead could truly rest in peace. Am I getting any warmer?"

Continued silence.

"And who suffered? Who suffered?" Cal banged the table as he spoke and leaned forward toward his opponent. "The parents, my clients, whose only child, a loving daughter, was the light of their life."

Jace was tempted to blurt out what he had learned from Sloan Jenkins about Alexis' relationship with her parents but thought better of it, allowing his silence to continue.

"Oh, believe me, I've got family pictures, some childhood movies, you name it. The jury will see it all. And you know Reinhold will let it all in, right or wrong. All of it."

Jace had no doubt about that.

Cal continued. "No question about liability—that's a given. Let's talk about actuals. In my view, $3,000,000 is a conservative number. I mean, how much is it worth to have your daughter's body stolen from its resting place, not know where it is, who has it, or what's being done with it and then learn it may have been used in some satanic offering? No dollars can justify that agony.

And when I finish my case, this jury is going to want to make sure its verdict sends a strong enough message to every cemetery in this country so something as horrible as this never happens again."

Jace tried to remain stoic, but the argument was powerful, and this was the abridged, nontheatrical version. It would play much better on the big screen.

"And now let us turn the page to punitive damages. Should your client be punished for hiring a known body molester, punished for not having security, punished for making so much damn money off hardworking folks in their most vulnerable time? I have had my economist do a down-and-dirty on what a funeral home the size of Caring Oaks would net on an annual basis. And it ain't chicken feed, believe me. I am going to ask the jury to send a message to Caring Oaks, as well as the entire funeral industry, that burying people is not just about money. It's about caring, like their name says, caring for the deceased, making sure they're safe, making sure their family members still on this earth can sleep at night. I will write '$5,000,000' on the chalkboard—a year's worth of Caring Oaks' net earnings—and ask the twelve ladies and gentlemen of the jury to award that amount in punitives."

"So that gets you to $8,000,000 maximum, one of the highest verdicts in Tarrant County history. Cal, you're out of the park."

Cal ignored Jace. "You came here to find out what it will take to settle this case. That number is $5,000,000. Not a penny less."

"Aren't you going to pass my offer on to your clients?"

"I don't need to. It would insult them. If you want to get the case settled, that would be the worst thing I could do. Sends them the wrong message—then I wouldn't be able to control them. I would suggest you go back to your office, get Mr. Arnold on the phone, tell him to get serious, and get serious real fast."

Jace rose and headed for the door. "And, Jace, tell Mr. Arnold that if he doesn't settle, his deposition tomorrow will not be a pretty sight."

Jace turned around. "And what do you mean by that?"

"Just tell him. He'll know." Cal gave him a smile that met the definition of malevolence. "And I think you already know what my very first question is going to be right out of the box. Right, Counsel?"

As Jace drove back to his office, Pat Reynolds called from Austin. "Pat, have you heard?" Jace asked.

"Yeah, Cowan called me right after lunch. I don't know what's wrong with the son of a bitch. I've never had any dealings with him before, but the position he's taking in your son's case is totally off the wall."

"It's not a 'case' yet, is it?"

"No, bad choice of words. Anyway, we are meeting Monday afternoon. I will want to sit down with Matt that morning. Should I call him, or would it be better coming from you?"

"He'll be devastated. I think it'll be a little easier on him if it comes from me rather than you. What time do you want him in your office?"

"Our meeting with Cowan is at one. If he could get here by nine, that should give us plenty of time. I can have lunch brought in."

"You got it. By the way, I want to be charged your normal rates on this."

"We go back a long way, Jace. No charge on this one. I'm sure you'd do the same for my son." Pat was right—he would. "I'll call you on Monday after we get back from our meeting. And if anything comes up between now and then, I'll let you know. Talk to you."

Jace clicked off the call and sat in the parking lot of his office, tallying up the costs the lawsuit had brought: a suicide, the near emotional breakdown of a respected funeral director, Jackie's threatened demotion. And then there was Matt, who was still being dragged into some power struggle that was none of his doing. Out of desperation Jace pounded his fists on the dashboard. Was the darkest hour just before the dawn? He sure hoped so.

As customary, Justice Owens returned from lunch a little after one. During the lunch hour, Phyllis had placed the appellate papers hand-delivered that morning in a prominent spot on the top of her orderly desk. The words "Application for Emergency Relief" caught her attention, and she began to carefully review the contents. Occasionally, she made a note on the legal pad she always kept on the right side of her desk. At a little before two, she dialed Phyllis's extension. "Could I see you for a moment?"

Seconds later Phyllis appeared at her door.

"Where is Justice Akers?"

"Well, it's Friday afternoon and the weather's nice . . ."

Justice Owens smiled, rolling her eyes. "Should be on the back nine by now."

"That would be my guess."

"Can you reach him?"

"He carries his cell phone in his golf bag. He has made it abundantly clear to me he does not want me to disturb him unless it's an emergency." Phyllis could not resist the urge to pry. She had to see if her hunch was right. "What is this about?"

Justice Owens smiled knowingly. "Those papers you put so prominently on my desk. I am troubled by what's going on in Judge Reinhold's court. I'm reluctant to intervene in managing a trial judge's docket absent the most egregious circumstances, but I think this might rise to that level. I just want a second opinion before taking any action."

"Would you like for me to get him on the line?"

"No need. Just email me his cell phone number and I'll give him a ring." Justice Owens adjusted her reading glasses and looked down at the file. Interrupting Phyllis's exit, she continued, "And Phyllis, there is one more thing. Would you print out a list of the five largest contributors to Judge Reinhold's campaign during the last election cycle?"

"I'll have it on your desk in fifteen minutes."

"Jace, I told you not to call me until you got the case settled." Irritation inflected the words.

"Wallace, please try to be reasonable. Connors is way out of line. Darrin has researched the jury verdicts for the past five years and no verdict even approached his bottom-line demand."

"I don't care. I cannot go through with that deposition tomorrow. I can't personally endure the humiliation that would most certainly result. Besides, we both know that as soon as that deposition is over, I'm going to lose my job. The board will meet and fire me immediately.

The situation now had "conflict" written all over it in bold type. Wallace's decision was being driven by what was in his best interest, not what was in the best interest of the shareholders. Jace had no choice but to confront the issue.

"We have to be guided by what is best for Caring Oaks. That must be our only consideration in determining the number that would represent a reasonable settlement of this case."

"You know I can terminate your services anytime I want. I hired you and I can fire you."

"I am fully aware of that."

"I want the case settled, and I want it settled before my deposition. Is that clear? You let me handle the details with the board." Wallace's voice was quivering, a combination of anger and fear. The line went dead.

Jace, still holding his phone, looked up and shook his head. If only Justice Owens would delay the trial, he might be able to work through some of these issues. It was four o'clock. The walls were closing in. He dialed Cal's number. They would meet again in one hour.

For the third time that afternoon, Justice Owens dialed the cell number for Justice Frank Akers. After several seconds, an all-too-familiar recorded message came on the line: "The cellular customer you are trying to reach is unavailable. Please try your call again later."

Justice Owens surmised her colleague must still be on the back nine or having a toddy with his cronies in the men's grill. In an uncharacteristic display of emotion, she slammed down the receiver and looked anxiously at the wall clock. She would try again in half an hour. If she couldn't reach him then, she would have to make a difficult decision.

She picked up a computerized report from the corner of her desk and shook her head in disgust as she reviewed the list of Judge Reuben Reinhold's main campaign contributors. Cal Connors topped the list.

CHAPTER

54

"Cal, my client has authorized me to increase our offer threefold. Caring Oaks is willing to pay your clients $1,500,000 in full settlement of their claims. The other conditions remain the same, such as a confidentiality clause, dismissal, et cetera." After delivering the offer, Jace scrutinized Cal's countenance for a reaction.

Cal's expression signaled nothing. His gaze remained on the antique corner cupboard diagonally across the room. After several moments of silence, he spoke.

"Did you tell Mr. Wallace Arnold what my clients' bottom line was?"

"Of course. I also went through my analysis of the case. It's my belief that, even if the jury finds liability against my client, the upper range of damages, including punitives, is $3,000,000. That's based upon the facts as we know them now and a careful historical examination of Tarrant County jury verdicts."

"Well, Counselor, let's talk about the elephant in the room. Did you factor in this little tidbit that Mr. Wallace Arnold, president and chief executive officer of Caring Oaks, was Lonnie Masterson's sexual bedmate?"

Jace's expression registered no emotion. He knew how to play the game and was playing it well. "That's been factored in. But for that irrelevant and highly prejudicial fact, I probably wouldn't be here talking settlement at all. Instead, I would be holed up in my office, gearing up for trial."

Cal's revelation was encouraging. He had played his trump card. He wanted to settle.

"Heard anything from the court of appeals?" Cal leaned forward, resting his elbows on the table, gently tapping his fingertips together in rapid succession.

Jace shook his head. "Nothing yet. I am encouraged by the fact it hasn't been denied already. If Justice Owens thought it was meritless, we would have heard by now."

"I don't read it that way. She probably didn't want to fool with it and headed home." Cal got up and strolled confidently to the window. "After all, it's seventy-five degrees and sunny."

Jace didn't respond. His silence encouraged Cal to continue.

"Four million even, real American dollars. That's my clients' counter." Cal had turned back toward the window, facing away from Jace.

"I'll convey the demand and get back to you later this evening." Jace rose from his chair and headed toward the door.

"And Jace, I need signed settlement documents and money in hand by noon tomorrow."

"Let's see if we can make a deal first. We can cover the fine points later."

"I hope you heard me—the documents and the money by noon tomorrow. Those conditions are part of my offer and are deal-breakers."

Jace closed the door and headed down the hall. Once in his car, Jace speed-dialed his client.

J ustice Owens was still in her office, weighing her next move. She decided she would try to reach Justice Akers one last time. She dialed his cell and waited impatiently, thumping her fingers on her desk. After three rings, he answered.

"This is Justice Akers." Chatter in the background.

"Frank, this is Laura Owens."

"Are you still working? Hell, I called it quits at noon. Too pretty to be thinking about all those dull cases. And you should call it a day too. Nothing's important enough that it can't wait till Monday."

Frank Akers had been on the court for fourteen years. Initially elected as a Democrat, he had switched parties when the political winds in Fort Worth had shifted, running as a Republican. In contrast, this was Laura's first term on the bench. She was a neophyte, only ten years out of law school, uncorrupted and extremely bright. She was feeling her way; Frank was the seasoned veteran. Although she tried to disguise it, he was still intimidating to her.

"We received an appellate filing this afternoon with a motion for emergency relief."

"Could you speak a little louder? This crowd noise is drowning you out."

Owens cleared her throat and turned up the volume. "This afternoon we received a—"

Interruption. "Shot a ninety. Killed the front nine but number sixteen ate my lunch. Will you be here tomorrow? Maybe we could meet up for lunch." Words slightly muffled, hand partially covering the receiver. "I'm sorry. That was Jack Smothers. Couldn't ignore him. Now you were saying?"

"Any way you could step into a more private place? This will only take a minute." Owens was surprised by her boldness.

"Sure, let me duck into the dining room. It's practically empty." Seconds passed. "Now, let's start from the first."

"Okay, we received an appeal, coupled with a motion for emergency relief. I was the only one here so Phyllis directed it to me."

"Let me stop you there. Everybody will be in next week. We'll take up the matter on Wednesday morning at the usual time."

"The issue presented in this appeal will be moot by then. The movant is seeking the stay of a trial set for Monday morning."

Momentary silence. "That does complicate things a bit. Whose court's the case in?"

"Judge Reinhold's."

"And the lawyers?"

"Jace Forman and Cal Connors."

"I know them both. And the grounds for the stay?"

Owens editorialized. "The case has been on file for just under six months and Judge Reinhold has railroaded them to trial. The defendant needs more time to prepare."

"What kind of case is it?"

"Seems a girl's body was stolen from—"

"I know the case," Akers interrupted. "Go on."

"I'm reluctant to grant the stay on my own. That's why I called you."

"You did the right thing. We could create some bad precedent here if we intervene. Every lawyer who is unhappy with a trial court's docket management would be filing papers with us. We would be inundated with additional work, and there would be no more Friday afternoons at the golf course."

"I considered that, but this is clearly an abuse of discretion. Judge Reinhold is banking on the fact we will exercise judicial restraint and is obviously taking full advantage. As a side note, guess who Reinhold's biggest contributor was last election?"

"Oh, hell, you didn't have to ask me. It's got to be Cal Connors. That's what he does with all these judges." Without awaiting confirmation, Akers continued. "Well, let me think about this over the weekend. Serious issues are involved. We don't want to act hastily. Let's meet at nine in my office."

"But they will be picking a jury by then."

"No harm done. We can send an order downstairs halting the trial if that is the decision we reach."

"But what if the case settles over the weekend?"

"Then that's one less case we'll have to worry about. Have a great weekend."

"I'll try." Her voice trailed off as she replaced the receiver. Monday morning might be too late. Caring Oaks might settle for some exorbitant amount over the weekend just because they were being forced to trial prematurely. And the whole thing was being skillfully orchestrated by Judge Reinhold and his biggest campaign contributor.

Owens shook her head in disgust. But she had to wait. Otherwise, she would be violating court decorum. And she couldn't afford to do that—not if she had any desire to serve on the Texas Supreme Court. She began packing her briefcase with files to review over the weekend. She closed the briefcase and then reopened it, putting the *Stone* v. *Caring Oaks* file on top of the stack.

As Owens fought Friday afternoon rush hour traffic on the way to her home, Jace sat at his desk in Fort Worth, deep in thought. He now knew the case could be settled. But he was still concerned about the conflict between his real client, Caring Oaks, and Wallace Arnold. He could not pay a premium just because disclosure of Wallace's sexual preference might cause him embarrassment or, worst case, cost him his job. So, Jace asked himself, what was the case really worth based on the facts he knew at this point in time, coupled with the assumption he was going to trial on Monday morning?

Jace reflected back on his first settlement meeting with Cal. He replayed the arguments Cal had made and his rebuttal. Without being able to provide the jury with the name of the person who had actually abducted the body, he was convinced his client would be found liable. And, as Cal put it, what's it worth for loving parents to suffer knowing their daughter's body was stolen, wondering who stole it, and, worst of all, what was done to it. Yes, a jury could easily return a multimillion-dollar verdict, particularly after it heard Caring Oaks' earnings for the past fiscal year. Jace picked up a pen and scribbled "$3,000,000" on the yellow pad in front of him. That was the number it would take. And he had no choice but to pay it. It was minutes before six. He would call Cal and seal the deal before he left the office. The night would be spent getting the settlement documents drafted and a check cut for $3,000,000, payable jointly to the Stones and the Connors & Connors law firm.

Jace shook his head. He was out of options. He got up from his chair and headed toward Darrin's office.

CHAPTER
55

A little after eleven on Saturday morning, Cal Connors was seated at his conference room table, dressed in blue jeans, an embroidered Mexican shirt, and a Santa Fe necklace of silver and turquoise. He picked up the settlement draft of $3,000,000 that Jace had slid across the table and carefully inspected it. A smile crossed his lips. He looked up at his adversary.

"Well, you know you got a real bargain on this. I had you over a barrel or, put a little more crudely, your balls in a vice. Yes, sir, if you hadn't settled this case, me and my clients would have owned Caring Oaks and Mr. Arnold's penchant for young boys would have been splashed all over the papers."

"Come on, Cal. Cut the crap. I paid what I had to pay. Your clients shouldn't have gotten a dime, and you know it. I didn't tell you this, but I know all about their relationship with their daughter or, should I say, lack thereof. This lawsuit was a farce."

"Good work, Counselor, but the jury would never have heard that. And, as they say, that's all ancient history. You got the settlement documents?"

Jace slid a two-page document across the table entitled "Settlement Agreement and Mutual Release." Uncharacteristically, Jace had spent several hours the previous night carefully drafting each line. Without reading a single word of the document, Cal signed in the space indicated, his generous signature intruding into the text of the agreement.

"You got an order of dismissal?"

Jace slid another document across the table. Cal signed at the bottom and passed it back.

"I assume you'll have your girl make copies for me and my clients before Monday. For your protection and mine I want the judge to approve the settlement on the record in open court. You know, just to make sure no one gets cold feet later."

Jace nodded. "Oh, I'm sure the Honorable Reuben Reinhold will do whatever you tell him to do. I'll see you at the courthouse at nine Monday morning." Jace got up to leave.

Cal rose and extended his hand across the table. "Always a pleasure doing business with you, Jace. And be sure to give ol' Wallace my regards. And tell him his secret is safe with me." Cal winked and raised an eyebrow.

After Jace had exited, Cal picked up the check and stretched it tautly. He brought the piece of paper lovingly to his puckered lips and kissed it gingerly. Aloud he smugly remarked, "Let's see now, forty percent of $3,000,000 is $1,200,000—not a bad day's work." He picked up the phone and called Christine.

"Guess what I have in my hand?"

"I assume it's the settlement check in the Stone case."

"You got that right. Let me take you to dinner tonight to celebrate. And I'd like you to come with me to the prove-up hearing on Monday."

"Yes."

"That's my girl! I'll see you for cocktails at my house around seven."

"I'm looking forward to it!"

CHAPTER
56

On his way home from Cal's office, Jace called Darrin on her cell. "Well, got the Stone settlement documents all signed up."

"That makes me sick. What a racket!"

"We've got the settlement prove-up on Monday morning at nine. I'd like you to go to the hearing with me."

"No problem."

"If I don't talk to you between now and then, I'll meet you at the office around eight Monday morning and we can head over to the courthouse together."

"Sounds good. See you Monday."

A few minutes later, Jace's cell phone rang.

"Sorry to call and interrupt your weekend, Jace."

"Are you kidding? You're never an interruption, Pat. I'm on my way for a little beer and barbecue at Angelos. Just got through settling the Stone case that was set for trial Monday."

"I know how that feels. You're gonna feel even better when I tell you why I'm calling."

"I like the sound of that."

"Cowan called me a few minutes ago. He canceled the interview with Matt. Said he had everything wrapped up and wouldn't need him after all. I didn't ask for any details. Didn't want to say anything that might cause him to change his mind."

"Well, well, well. I held off telling Matt about the interview because I had a hunch that, if my case settled, his interview would be canceled. My bet is that Cal Connors had Reggie Cowan in his back pocket." Jace sighed. "That being said, I can't tell you how relieved I am. You don't know what it's like to have your own son caught up in such a mess."

"I can only imagine. Well, we can all put this one behind us."

"Pat, I really appreciate all you've done to help."

"Anytime, my friend. Just make sure Matt puts in that community service time. We don't want that public intoxication charge on his record."

"Understood. And the next time I'm in Austin, I hope you'll let me buy you dinner."

"I look forward to it."

Jace ended the call and took a big sigh of relief. He reflected on the civil and criminal cases coming to an end—how so often justice is never done, and certainly never blind, how the good guys don't always win, how money talks in the corridors of the courthouse. But what profession is perfect? There are doctors whose treatments are more influenced by the fees they can charge than their patients' welfare. And the Wall Street tycoons—the absolute worst—pompous asses just shuffling around money, adding no value, reaping billions as they bankrupt companies and put the country in financial jeopardy. And the politicians—practicing hypocrisy daily, not a truthful word coming from their lips, only saying what they think is necessary to get elected. So be it! Although his life had been far from perfect, he could at least say he had never cheated a client, never lied in court, never done anything in his practice that he was ashamed of—quite a contrast to his personal life.

After several ice-cold schooners of tap beer and a rib plate at Angelos, Jace drove home and plopped down on the couch. He channel-surfed in a feeble attempt to take his mind off the law, at least for the rest of the day. Just before dozing off to sleep, the phone rang. Reluctantly, he picked up the receiver.

"Jace." It was Darrin. "I'm at the office with our investigator. You need to get down here as soon as possible."

"What's up?"

"I really don't want to explain it over the phone. You've got to see it. I wouldn't bother you unless it was important. How quickly can you get here?"

"Twenty minutes."

"We're in the main conference room."

Jace hastily threw on a clean shirt, dragged a comb through his hair, gargled some mouthwash, and rushed to his car. Before turning the ignition key he took a deep breath, wondering if he was ready for what lay ahead.

CHAPTER

57

"All rise." The bailiff bellowed.

Judge Reuben Reinhold assumed his loft of authority and issued his usual command. "Be seated, gentlemen"—and then deferentially to Darrin and Christine—"and ladies, excuse my oversight." He flashed them a grin, polite yet disingenuous, before perching his signature half-glasses on his nose. He quickly glanced through the file in front of him and then continued.

"For the record we are here in the case styled *Lackland and Olivia Stone* v. *Caring Oaks Funeral Home and Cemetery.*"

As the judge spoke, the court reporter captured every word on the stenographic machine directly in front of her, her fingers moving like those of a skilled pianist.

"Are the plaintiffs here and ready to proceed?"

Cal Connors rose from the counsel table to the judge's diagonal left. "We are, Your Honor. I would like to take this opportunity to introduce my clients to the court." Motioning for them both to rise, he continued. "May I present Lackland and Olivia Stone?"

Mr. Stone was dressed conservatively in a dark gray suit, white shirt, and striped tie. His salt-and-pepper hair, dark eyes, and trim physique gave him a distinguished appearance. After rising, he nodded toward the judge, a solemn look on his face. His wife, blond-streaked hair stylishly cut, her face showing less age than her years, followed her husband's lead, nodding at the judge and smiling meekly.

The judge leaned toward Cal and the Stones, attempting to add some informality to the proceedings.

"It is a pleasure to meet you both. Cal—" The judge abruptly cleared his throat—"I mean, Mr. Connors, has told me a lot about you."

Realizing his mistake, his countenance turned crimson. "What I meant is I feel like I know you both as a result of reading the pleadings filed by your counsel in this case." He forced a laugh. "Please sit down."

Cal, still standing, continued. "And you know my daughter, Christine Connors."

"I have had the pleasure of having her in my court on a number of occasions."

Christine stood briefly and nodded in acknowledgment.

A loud noise from the back of the courtroom interrupted the judge's ritual, causing the assembled spectators to turn their heads for a view of who was causing the commotion. Irritated, the judge addressed his next comment to the perpetrator.

"Would you state your name for the record?"

The culprit, dressed casually in blue jeans and a wrinkled white shirt open at the neck, looked up from his task in "who me" fashion.

"Sir, I am talking to you." The judge's tone was stern.

"Evan Alexander."

"Mr. Alexander, can you tell us why you're here for the court's business today?"

"Your Honor," the voice trembled. "I am with the *Fort Worth Herald*. Mr. Connors called me yesterday and told me there might be something newsworthy going on today. So I'm here."

Jace's eyes narrowed. He could feel the blood rush to his face. So that was the way his opponent intended to get around the confidentiality clause.

The judge's tone softened. "Well, this is a free country, and this courtroom is open to the press—that is, unless we have a sealed proceeding, and today's hearing is not one of those. Mr. Alexander, you are certainly welcome here, but the court and its participants would appreciate it if you could be a little quieter."

Relieved, the reporter nodded enthusiastically and took his seat.

"Now, continuing with the proceeding," his gaze turned to Jace. "Mr. Forman, are you ready to proceed?"

"Yes, sir, I am."

"Is a representative for your client here today?"

"Yes, Your Honor." But he did not introduce Wallace Arnold, who was sitting at the counsel table. Jace was showing the judge the minimum in professional courtesy.

"Well, I understand that this case has been settled and we're here to prove up that settlement. Is that true?"

Cal jumped to his feet. "That's correct, Your Honor."

"Mr. Forman?"

"To answer that question, I need to call one witness to the stand."

A look of surprise on the judge's face, an expression of dismay on Cal's. "Oh, come on," he said, turning straight toward Jace. The judge quickly followed suit.

"Mr. Forman, this is highly unusual," Reinhold said. "You know that at a settlement prove-up hearing such as this one, we simply admit the settlement agreement into the record, the parties and their counsel are asked if they are agreeable to it, the settlement terms are made part of the official record in the case, and the case is dismissed. There is no need for testimony."

Confidently, Jace responded. "I agree that's the typical procedure, but this is not your typical case. The defense calls Lackland Stone to the stand."

Cal had gotten back his voice. "I object. We have a signed settlement agreement here. This is inappropriate."

"It certainly is," affirmed Reinhold. "Explain to me why I should even entertain such an idea."

"As the law states, Your Honor, I am entitled at a prove-up hearing to question the opposing party about the settlement to make sure all parties wish to enter into the agreement. All parties are entitled to know today what they are signing and the basis for signing. I don't want anyone to come back to this court and argue they were coerced or tricked into settling this case."

Reinhold grimaced. "And why do you think you need to ask Mr. Stone if he knows what the settlement is in this case? Wouldn't that be Mr. Connors' job? Really, what are you trying to do?"

"Your Honor, I'm simply exercising my client's rights under the law."

Clearly not sure what to do, the judge turned to Cal, giving him a plaintive look. "Mr. Connors, it's his right to do this. And I guess I don't see any harm in letting him call your client to the stand. We all want an ironclad deal here."

Cal just shrugged and sat back down.

"I'll overrule the objection," said Reinhold.

Christine glanced at her father, her face showing concern. Cal gave her a bewildered expression and then doodled nervously on the yellow legal pad in front of him. Something was up—he was confident of that. Jace was too good of a lawyer to want to interrogate Stone without a reason.

Reinhold nodded politely toward Cal's client. "Mr. Stone, would you please take the stand?"

Lackland sat motionless at counsel table, his dark eyes staring straight ahead. After several seconds, Reinhold repeated the request, this time with less politeness. In response, Lackland slowly leaned toward his attorney, whispering something in his ear, which Cal answered with a shrug. Slowly, the witness rose from his chair and walked across the wooden floor, his posture erect, defiant. Taking his seat in the witness chair, Lackland shot a piercing stare at Jace. After swearing the witness, the judge nodded for Jace to begin his questioning.

"Mr. Stone, you're one of the plaintiffs in the case, is that correct?"

The witness nodded.

Reinhold intervened. "You must answer out loud. The court reporter can't record a nonverbal response."

"Yes." The witness responded indignantly.

"Now, you've sued my client for millions of dollars in this case, contending they negligently allowed your daughter's body to be abducted from her grave, is that right?"

"That's correct."

"Mr. Stone, where were you this past Saturday night?"

"Olivia and I went to a charity function at the Colonial Country Club." Lackland shook his head. "What is the relevance of this anyway, Counselor?" He looked at the judge and shrugged his shoulders.

Cal was on his feet. "I have held my tongue, Your Honor, giving opposing counsel as much latitude as possible. But inquiring into my client's social life is beyond the pale. I'm sure the court's got other business. Let's get on with what we're here to do today and approve the settlement."

The judge peered at Jace over his half-glasses. "I agree with Mr. Connors. What relevance does this line of questioning have?"

"One more question, Your Honor, and I think the relevance will become apparent."

"Continue." The judge sighed, shaking his head.

"At 1:35 Saturday night, excuse me, Sunday morning, did you visit the grave of your daughter?"

Lackland's eyes transformed to slits, his lips tightened, and several beads of perspiration began to form under his prominent nose.

"I don't know what you're talking about. I was with my wife of thirty-two years all night Saturday." His eyes darted to Olivia at counsel table. She stared at her husband, her eyes widening in disbelief.

"I'm a distraught father. I still haven't gotten over this. I live with it day after day," Lackland finally stammered, turning his gaze back to Jace. "What are you suggesting—that I'm not allowed to grieve over the death of my daughter, no matter what time of night it is?"

Lackland then looked at Cal, as if begging him silently to end this interrogation. But like Lackland's wife, Cal was, for a rare moment in his life, utterly speechless. Jace slowly rose from his chair and let the seconds tick away, allowing the pressure inside the courtroom to build and build.

"Why did you really go to your daughter's grave that night?" he asked Lackland. "Was it to tell her something that perhaps your own wife, and your own attorney, do not know?"

It was a masterful performance. Olivia's mouth had dropped open, and Cal kept scribbling on his yellow pad, his head down, as if he couldn't bear to see what was about to happen next.

"You went to your daughter's grave to ask for forgiveness for stealing her body, didn't you, Mr. Stone?" Jace continued. "You stole her body so you could bring this trumped-up lawsuit against my client, force an exorbitant settlement that would net enough money for you to make the interest payments, at the very least, on your massive real estate debt and, for the moment, preserve the integrity of the Stone name."

Lackland was now standing, shouting. "Connors, can't you stop this man? This is slander. I want to sue that son of a bitch." The witness pointed a trembling finger at Jace.

"Sit down, Mr. Stone." As if finally recognizing what his true role was, the judge gave Cal a sympathetic shrug and then turned to Jace. "I assume you have factual support for these serious allegations?"

"Yes, we do, Your Honor. With the court's permission, we would like to set up some equipment. My technical people have got this down to an art. It should only take a few minutes."

Lackland interrupted. "This is preposterous. I have business to attend to. I refuse to sit here while this shyster hurls insult after insult at me and my family. I won't stand for it! He and his client have inflicted enough pain on us already." The witness stood again and began to step down from the stand, glaring at Jace in the process.

"You'll not leave that witness chair until you're excused by me, Mr. Stone. Is that clear? Now take your seat. And don't get up again or I'll hold you in contempt." The judge's voice was loud and firm. Lackland slumped back in his seat. The judge turned his attention back to Jace. "So what will this video depict?"

"Without going into detail, it will demonstrate the falsity of the testimony that Mr. Stone has given this morning to Your Honor—every last bit of it."

Lackland could not restrain himself. "I went to her grave site. I was torn up. I had to say good-bye one last time." The witness began to cry. "There is no crime against that. You haven't lost a daughter, Mr. Forman. You can't imagine the anguish, the sleepless nights, the living hell you go through. And now you are trying to put me through that all over again." Lackland turned his eyes toward his counsel, who now sat rapt with attention. "I want out of this settlement. I want to go to trial. We'll own this fucking funeral home."

The courtroom erupted with whispers and gasps. Judge Reinhold pounded his gavel to restore order. "Quiet. This court is still in session. And Mr. Stone, you will never again use profanity in my courtroom. Otherwise, the bailiff will escort you to the county jail. Is that clear?" The judge cleared his throat. "Are your video folks ready, Mr. Forman?"

"They are, Your Honor."

"You may proceed."

Jace nodded toward the two technicians who had set up the screen and projector. Seconds later, the screen was filled with the eerie scene of a cemetery in the dark of night. Lackland stepped out of his car and walked slowly from the access road, past several headstones, and then stopped at what appeared to be an unmarked grave. A howling wind accompanied his approach. After reaching his destination, he looked to either side and over his shoulder, and then kneeled to the side of the grave. A faint sob could be heard as the reel rolled. And then the words "I'm sorry, I'm so sorry," the sobs becoming louder and more uncontrolled. "But I had to. I had no other choice. I was broke. Your mother and I would have been ruined. We needed the money and this was the only way to get it." Lackland's head lay on his daughter's grave as his sobs continued.

Time seemed to stand still in the courtroom. It was one of those moments that almost never happen: the real, unvarnished truth coming out, irrefutable and undeniable. Jace never took his eyes off Alexis' father. Neither did anyone else in the courtroom. Even Cal, who for the first time in his career had nothing to say, stared at his client, whom he thought he knew.

"That's enough. You don't have to play any more of the tape," Lackland finally said, his voice composed and yet defiant. He raised his head and stared at everyone there. "Yes, I did it. I wasn't thinking right. I was under so much pressure—so much pressure. Do you have any idea what it's like to be on top of the world one day and then in the gutter the next? That's what was happening to me. I had lost everything. This was my chance to, at least, buy some time, to make a comeback. It was the only chance I had." Lackland put his head in his hands. "The only chance I had."

Jace shook his head in disgust. "Your Honor, I have no further questions for this witness."

Judge Reinhold sternly addressed the witness. "You may step down, but do not leave the premises. Your conduct in this case and in my courtroom raises some very serious criminal questions." The judge looked to Cal. "Mr. Connors, I assume you had no knowledge of this."

For a moment, Cal noticed Evan Alexander in the front row of the spectators' benches, head down, writing profusely. He rose, and in a somber voice replied, "None whatsoever, Your Honor." Cal leaned over to consult with Olivia, who whispered something in his ear. Then he turned back to the judge. "And I'd like to put in the record that Mrs. Stone likewise had no knowledge of her husband's actions."

"Mr. Forman, I assume your client has no desire to proceed with the settlement negotiated over the weekend?"

"Your assumption is correct, Your Honor. Not only that, I ask the court to dismiss this case with prejudice and refer this matter to the district attorney's office for investigation. Extortion is a very serious offense in this state, as are perjury and grave desecration."

"Any response, Mr. Connors?"

"None, Your Honor."

"All right then. The court finds this settlement was procured by fraud and is, therefore, null and void. The court further finds that this case should be dismissed with prejudice to its refiling. Mr. Forman, please prepare an appropriate order."

Judge Reinhold audibly sighed and then continued. "Further, the court finds this case was an attempt to use the judicial process to extort money and hereby refers the matter to the district attorney's office for investigation. We are now in recess." With that pronouncement, the judge's gavel came down, and he disappeared behind the door to his chambers.

Wallace Arnold jumped up and threw his arms around Darrin. He then turned and shook Jace's hand with such emotion that Jace thought he had torn a rotator cuff.

Jace then turned to look at Cal, searching for some evidence of remorse. He found none. As Cal stuffed his papers in his briefcase, he stared back at Jace with a "there'll be a next time" smirk on his face. He then walked confidently, his back straight and his head held high, Christine by his side, down the aisle toward the courtroom exit. As they walked, they were greeted by a familiar figure, who emerged from one of the spectator pews.

"Mr. Connors, I'm Leah Rosen. I don't believe we have formally met. I asked you a few questions after your big verdict down in the Valley." Leah then turned to Christine. "Always a pleasure to see you, Christine. Mr. Connors, I have a few questions to ask you. Is now a good time?"

Christine and Cal walked on, ignoring the question.

Leah rushed up and began to walk beside them. "Mr. Connors, I'm writing an article entitled 'The Lone Wolf: Texas Justice Gone Wrong' and would really like your input. I want you to have every opportunity to rebut any of the preliminary conclusions I have reached."

Cal stopped and turned to face Leah, his eyes searing with anger. Jabbing his finger near her face, he replied, "You publish anything about me, or anything I've ever done, and it'll be the mistake of a lifetime. You got that, little lady?"

Cal did not wait for a response but grabbed Christine's elbow and escorted her quickly into the crowded corridor and then out the courthouse door. They hurried down the steps to the floor below and ducked into an unoccupied courtroom.

"Damn. I'm sure glad to get the hell out of there," Cal told his daughter. "You don't think Judge Reinhold suspected I had anything to do with that legal charade, do you?"

Christine just shook her head, her thoughts somewhere else. "No, he could tell you were just as shocked as everyone else in the courtroom. No chance he thought you were in on it."

"Well, personally, I hope that sick bastard goes to prison. Stealing his own daughter's body from the grave. It doesn't get much worse than that. And then the nerve of that little bitch to come up to me and threaten me after I had just suffered the most humiliating defeat of my legal career. What was the name of the article she said she was working on?"

"The name's not important. Besides, that article will never go to print."

"How do you know?"

"A little birdie told me."

The Lone Wolf smiled. "What are you keeping from me?"

"Nothing. It's just my sixth sense." Christine began to rummage through her purse until she found her cell phone. "I'll meet you at the car. I've got to make a quick call on that Dixon case. Think I might have it settled."

"Well, one of us needs to be bringing in some money. I'll pull the car around and pick you up downstairs."

"Thanks, Dad. I'll see you in a minute."

As soon as he was out of earshot, Christine scrolled through her contacts on her iPhone, tapped on a number, and waited for a response. A husky voice answered.

"Michael Randazzo."

"Michael, it's Christine. You're on."

EPILOGUE

The Flying Saucer in Sundance Square was noisy and alive with activity. Stevie Ray Vaughan's unequaled instrumental version of Jimi Hendrix's "Little Wing" filled the room.

"I could do without a case like that for a while. It about killed me. I can only imagine what it did to you." Darrin grinned as she peeled the Carlsberg label from the beer bottle in front of her. Jace motioned the waiter for another Shiner for himself and another Carlsberg for Darrin.

"It took a toll, but the ending was sweet."

"What an idea, miking the grave. Who would have ever thought?"

"Never would have occurred to me. I've got Jackie to thank for that."

Darrin ignored Jace's answer. "So all that satanic stuff was just to throw everyone off the trail."

"Yep, pretty damn sick. I can't believe any father would do something so disgusting. It was bad enough that he dug up her body but then to put it on the altar of a church under an upside-down cross is hard to even think about. His lawyer will probably try to get him off with some kind of insanity defense."

"And even if he doesn't, he probably won't serve any time. Our criminal justice system is so messed up. Seems like as soon as some-one gets put away, he's out on the street again. Did you see the article in the paper a few days ago—"

"Are you kidding? I haven't read the paper in weeks. World War III could have broken out for all I know."

Jace's cell phone began to buzz. He pulled it from his suit pocket and looked at the screen: Jackie. "Hey, I need to take this. Do you mind?"

"No problem. I need to go to the ladies' room anyway."

Jace nodded as he took the call. "Jackie, I hadn't had time to call you. We won! Case over. And my client didn't have to pay a cent."

"You've got to be kidding me. And you were so worried about the case. What happened?"

"It's a long story—much too complicated to discuss over the phone. And you heard about Matt?"

"Yeah, I got the skinny. I just can't believe it. I bet he is on cloud nine."

"And so is his father." Jace saw Darrin heading to the table out of the corner of his eye. As she approached, Jace excused himself and stepped outside the bar. "I can't wait to tell you all about it. How about that dinner in Fort Worth? You do the sides and I'll grill the steaks."

"Sounds pretty tempting. You got any dates in mind?"

"How does next weekend sound?"

"Let me check my calendar. I'll text you later."

"I won't take anything but a yes."

Jackie laughed. "Congrats again on everything."

"I couldn't have done it without you." Jace disconnected the call and returned to the table.

"Who was that?" Darrin asked curiously. "You were mighty secretive." A knowing grin creased her lips.

"It was Jackie. I hadn't had time to call to tell her the good news. And I couldn't hear a damn thing in this place. Too much noise."

Jace quickly changed the subject. "So, you got dinner plans?"

"I thought you'd never ask."

"Let's do something special. How about we jump in the car and head to Dallas. I haven't eaten at that Stephan Pyles' restaurant, have you?"

"No, but I've read about it. It's gotten rave reviews." Darrin cocked her head. "You sure this is a good idea?"

"Couldn't be any surer."

"And your celebration plans, Mr. Big Shot?" she teased, the three beers beginning to take hold.

"I haven't given it much thought—a trip to someplace where I can kick back and do nothing, just veg out. I'm thinking beach. Kauai might be nice. But then you can't beat the crystal-blue water of the Caribbean. Tough call."

"I assume you're not going by yourself."

"Not by choice, anyway."

"And the lucky lady?"

Jace grinned. "Got any ideas?"

THE END

AUTHOR'S NOTE

Although the setting for this novel is Fort Worth, Texas (a wonderful city which I visit frequently and dearly love), it is not intended to portray any real person in that city, or in the state of Texas as a whole. All of the characters, and many of the places, are purely fictional (although I have dined at, and enjoyed, many of the restaurants referenced in the narrative and would unreservedly recommend them to the reader). Any similarity to a real person is coincidental. There is no Cal Connors or Jace Forman. Alexis Stone, as well as her parents, are of my own creation. Samson Pharmaceuticals does not exist, nor do any of the jurists described in the novel. There is no Caring Oaks Cemetery to my knowledge. The case of Harold and Olivia Stone v. Caring Oaks Cemetery was entirely a product of my imagination (although inspired by an actual case I handled years ago).

I have been a trial lawyer in Dallas, Texas for the past thirty-five years and, as such, have witnessed firsthand how judicial contributions can taint the process. Many jurists would agree our current judicial election process in which lawyers are asked to contribute to the campaigns of jurists they practice before is ill-advised, and certainly does not "avoid any appearance of impropriety" – to the contrary. This is not a problem unique to the state of Texas but is found in any state where judges are elected. We must find a better way to select those who are charged with the responsibility for administering justice in a fair and impartial manner.

This is my first novel. It was many years in the writing as I had a law firm to run and cases to try during its composition. Fortunately, I had many excellent resources to draw upon along the way. Thanks to Skip Hollandsworth whose edits and advice were invaluable. Thanks also to Amy Nettle, Clay Small, Richard Crouch, Bradford Bricken, Merrie Clark, Tom Hanson, Cindy McMillin, Tom and Bonnie Ruffin, and my daughter, Adair Webb, for giving the manuscript a careful read and offering their instructive input as to how it could be improved.

And my heartfelt thanks to my wife, Doris, without whose insightful reads, imaginative ideas and enthusiastic encouragement this novel would never have happened.

Hubert Crouch
January, 2013

Author Biography

Hubert Crouch is a graduate of Phillips Andover Academy, Vanderbilt University, and Southern Methodist University School of Law. He is a practicing trial lawyer in Texas, with over thirty-five years of experience in the courtroom. In addition to practicing law, he has taught Free Speech and the First Amendment and Legal Advocacy to undergraduates at Southern Methodist University and was recently awarded the Rotunda Outstanding Professor Award. An avid rock and roll fan, he has played guitar in a Sixties "cover" band for over thirty years. He and his wife split their time between their home in Dallas, Texas and their mountain retreat near Sewanee, Tennessee. You can visit his website at www.hubertcrouch.com.

STAY TUNED FOR THE SEQUEL!

SAY THE WORD

Expected release date 2014

Made in the USA
Middletown, DE
27 May 2015